BY MOONRISE

BY MOONRISE

JACKIE DANA

WATERCOLOR MOON

A WATERCOLOR MOON BOOK

Published by Watercolor Moon, LLC

2900 W. Anderson Lane C-200 #318

Austin, TX 78757 USA

BY MOONRISE

For information visit:

JackieDana.com

ISBN 978-0692557907

First Edition: December 2015

10 9 8 7 6 5 4 3 2 1

For my parents

CHAPTER 1

"I don't want you driving alone."

Kate leaned against the pew in front of her, pretending to pray to a god she didn't even know. The lingering aroma of incense filled the air, and the bells chimed the hour. Her mother had never worshipped in a church like this, but Aunt Teresa said Melanie would have appreciated the ritual. Kate didn't argue the point, figuring one service was as good as another. "I'll be fine," she told her aunt. "I'd like to stay a little while longer."

"Leo told me you'd say something like that." She placed a hand on Kate's shoulder. "Take all the time you want. We'll be waiting in the car outside, and we'll drive over to Alana's house together." With those words her aunt drifted down the aisle, her purple silk jacket billowing behind her as she headed towards the exit.

Kate exhaled, the breath catching in the pockets of her cheeks. Her family had been hovering over her for three days now, fearing she'd fall apart like a dandelion gone to seed. They should have known better. She didn't grow up to be fragile. Her mom had seen to that. They way they acted, it was as if they had never met Melanie or her daughter.

She slipped from her seat and approached the coffin. Grateful it was closed, she placed her hand on the varnished wood. The ring on her middle finger sparkled in the light of the candles, a small cabochon crystal inlaid within a silver band. It had been her mother's favorite ring, and ever since she was a child it felt like magic to her. And now it was hers, along with a lifetime's worth of personal possessions she had never wanted to inherit.

Caring little for proprieties, she leaned over the casket, as if trying to hug her mother one last time. "Mom, why now?" she whispered. "You still had so much you wanted to do." It still was impossible to accept she was gone. A heart attack, they said, just past her 50th birthday. It was even harder to comprehend that this was the last time she would ever be with her.

At that moment, a woman's voice startled her. «Aleira. It is time to go home.»

She opened her eyes and straightened up. Gazing around the chapel, Kate was ready to challenge whoever had dared to disturb her. Her complaint was forestalled when she realized no one else was there.

Suddenly feeling foolish, she returned to her seat and gathered up her possessions and the program that featured her mother's smiling face. If she was late to the wake, they'd be sending out a search party.

***

Grief competed with concentration as she struggled to do her job.

As she typed, she had to hit the delete key over and over to erase typos. It was an open secret that the partners were considering downsizing her team. Knowing that everyone was under scrutiny, she had no choice but to push through her grief to get everything done. Just focus, she urged herself.

When she stopped writing for a moment, gathering her thoughts, the voice from the church returned, like a specter hovering at the edge of her vision, reminding her to go home. Even now, as she read her email, it was as if the speaker was there, whispering over her shoulder. Twice she had turned her head suddenly, as if she'd catch someone behind her, but no one was ever there.

It made no sense. There wasn't really anyone talking to her. She hadn't ever heard voices before, and she was pretty sure she wasn't losing her mind. Then again, her quick internet search on the topic of "hearing voices" was simultaneously unproductive and depressing.

Was it grief, perhaps, or was she being haunted?

She didn't believe in ghosts, so she wrote it off as a product of stress and exhaustion. The weekend was coming up, and she could relax then.

For an hour she was productive, and finished the first half of the marketing campaign proposal. It had to be solid work, the best she had ever written.

The voice in her head didn't seem to agree with her progress. Like a song she couldn't stop thinking about, the voice insisted she pay attention to it rather than to the work in front of her. Shortly before lunch she stopped to check her email, but that just encouraged the voice to repeat its message again.

It was enough that she flung herself back in her chair, clutching at her hair. "Damn it, just stop!" she demanded of the imaginary entity, and then caught herself. Had she said that out loud?

A friendly blonde head peeked over the partition. "You all right?" her colleague Janine asked.

Kate buried her face in her hands in embarrassment.

"I get migraines too. It's probably the fluorescent lights."

"Yeah, probably." Kate rubbed her eyes, contributing to the idea that she had a headache.

In a low voice, Janine continued. "Maybe you tried to come back to work too soon. I know how close you were to your mom. I don't want to be presumptuous, but that's a hard thing to deal with, and you haven't had a lot of time to work through things. Maybe you should just take the rest of the week off?"

"No, I'll be fine," Kate said. "Thanks for checking on me, but I've got a lot to catch up on. I'll be okay."

"Can I at least get you something? Some coffee?"

"Sure, that would be nice," she replied, doubting it would help, and when Janine stepped away, Kate tried to resume her work.

As she closed out her email and returned to her report, she was able to work solidly again for about half an hour, and a full page of coherent text scrolled up the monitor. Then the voice returned, so loudly this time that she couldn't focus at all on the task at hand. «It's time,» she heard a voice whisper over and over. With her elbows on the desk, she curled her hands behind her head, trying to keep from screaming. Then, sucking in an angry breath, she pushed herself away from the computer and marched down the hallway to the restroom, where she splashed cool water on her face.

Gazing at her reflection, she shoved some stray auburn hairs behind her ears and rubbed her eyes. Today they wanted to be green, she thought abstractly to herself, often amused at her chameleon irises that changed depending on her mood. She didn't *look* crazy, which was some consolation. Not much, mind you, but she'd take what she could get.

Be strong, she told herself, as if her mother was here to remind her. *You can get through this.*

Her mother. She leaned against the sink as she pulled her mom's ring from her finger to examine it more closely. Despite her mother wearing it for three decades, it remained a perfect circle with no scuffs or nicks on the surface. She slid it back onto her finger, where it fit perfectly, as if made for her.

"Oh Mom, I wish you were here," she said softly. She needed her support, now of all times. Between the stress of this job and the wreckage of a failed relationship, her mom had been her anchor... and now she was drifting.

"Get over it," she told her reflection. "You have work to do. Make her proud." Of all times in her life, Kate had no room now for self-indulgence or weakness. She couldn't stumble now.

She blinked and abruptly left the restroom.

Walking quickly down the hall, she stopped at the entrance to her cubicle, and knew she wasn't going to get any more work done. Grabbing her bag, she headed to the front counter. "I'm not feeling well," she announced to Thomas, a young hipster with black glasses who by day worked as their receptionist and by night played drums in a seventies retro band. "Will you let Roger know?"

***

«Aleira.» The voice said insistently, as if trying to wake her up. It repeated the word once. «Aleira.»

She had tumbled into bed, having found just enough energy to change into her nightgown, and passed out like she was drunk, sleeping for hours. Then the dreams began.

«Who's there?» She replied in her head as she rolled over and sat up, straining her eyes to see against the darkness. «What do you want?»

She heard a sigh, as if someone stood beside her. A rush of air. Then the voice came again. «It is time.»

"Why are you doing this?" She jumped from her bed and replied aloud, as if someone was in the room with her.

«Step into the light.»

"What light? What do you mean?" She could see nothing. There was no light. In frustration, she repeated once again, "who are you?" A part of her told her that she was still dreaming, but she felt compelled to participate.

There was a rush of wind, a stirring of dust. «Step into the light,» the voice repeated.

Again she asked, "who are you?" She looked around. "Where are you?"

Suddenly there was water everywhere, as if she had been submerged into a deep pool. Before it could frighten her—for she never lacked a breath—it disappeared, and she was dry.

«Step into the light,» the voice commanded for the third time. It was louder than before. Now she felt intense heat, as if a fire burned at her shoulders, but she was not injured by it.

Kate could scarcely breathe now. What was happening now made no sense. If this was a dream, and not her losing her mind, she needed to wake up. But there was no time to figure out how to wake herself, or indeed for any further reflection of the situation. She felt something—or someone—push her from behind. As if she was on the edge of a precipice, she tumbled forward, but did not land on anything. In fact, she continued to fall, but never landed on the ground.

Then there was light—very, very bright light—as if she had fallen into the sun itself. There was nothing else but light everywhere she looked. Even her own body seemed to be made of light.

«It is time.»

Standing before her, in the middle of the intense brightness, was a woman of great beauty and power. She wore a brilliant gown of silver, and her hair was like bright copper. Kate immediately knew that the woman had no true physical form, but at the same time there could be no more imposing figure.

«Come to us. It is time.»

"I can't... I don't know what you mean!"

The woman clenched her fist and Kate's breath was squeezed from her. «You are Aleira. The knowledge is part of you.»

She desperately swam deep into her thoughts, into her most hidden memories, trying to make sense of this. "You have the wrong person. I don't know what you mean!"

Then the woman clenched her other fist, and she swooned. Suddenly impressions danced at the edge of her consciousness. Memories that were not hers, words and images that she could not interpret, came spilling through the cracks in her consciousness. Faces of strangers, hills covered with blue flowers, spiral towers, the crash of waves below her feet.

"Don't do this to me. I don't know what you want from me!"

«Come to us now.» The woman commanded her. «Step into the light. Otherwise all will be lost.»

"That doesn't make sense. I can't do something if I don't know how to do it!"

With those words, the incessant voice finally went silent, and she was finally certain she was awake. And the only thing she could hear was the rumbling of thunder and the dance of raindrops outside.

Climbing back into bed—her heart beating faster than her word processing speed, and apparently just as uncertain—she was trying to figure out the significance of the dream. Nothing made sense. What did it mean? Was she really supposed to do something, and if so, what? She turned to look at her clock. It was 3:00 am.

She then looked down at her right hand. Her mother's ring glowed softly in the darkness. "What the hell?" Sucking in a sharp breath, she froze in place, staring at her hand as if it belonged to someone else. With another deep breath and trembling fingers, she slid the ring off and tossed it to the blanket beside her. Suddenly the room was awash in silvery light, as if a beacon had been focused through the small circle and was spilling out the other side.

"Step into the light," the voice had insisted. What did that mean? What was going on? Was this some elaborate prank? Angry now, she knocked the ring to the floor, but the action made it glow that much brighter.

"Get away from me!" She threw the ring out the window. As it fell, the light poured from the ring, extending outwards for a dozen yards like a big glowing ball. It still glowed brightly as it came to rest in the garden.

She flopped back on her bed and tried to go back to sleep, but the memory of the mysterious woman's command echoed in her head. Burying her head under her pillow did no good, for that just brought up an image of the woman with the shiny copper hair.

"Damn it, why is this happening to me?" She launched herself from the bed and looked out the window. Nothing had changed—the light from the ring was as strong as ever.

Whatever was happening to her, and whatever was causing the light, the guilt of tossing the ring outside gnawed at her. It was her mother's ring, after all. She couldn't leave it outside, for someone to steal.

Disregarding the downpour and lightning crackling overhead, she ran barefoot across the wet garden path. As she entered the sphere of light, a prickly sensation was Kate's only warning something was about to happen; then she saw a bright flash, and then there was nothing at all.

CHAPTER 2

Her limbs ached, but she couldn't figure out where she had been hurt—or how. Kate heard someone else breathing, indicating that she wasn't alone, and then she realized she was being carried in someone's arms.

Was she still alive? All things told, it seemed rather unlikely.

Pain crept into her fingers and toes, and traveled up her limbs, setting her entire body tingling with a stinging, prickly feeling. Well, it wasn't pain, precisely. It was like a foot falling asleep, except in this case every part of her body had gone numb, and now the blood was returning.

The man holding her must have felt her tremble as her limbs regained sensation. "*Bei ta shar rui*," he said, his words unintelligible but gently spoken. He set her down in tall grass, and she discovered she was wrapped within something warm and soft, that had the faintest scent of rosemary—a blanket, perhaps, or a coat. Then he knelt down beside her and put his hands on either side of her face, warming her ice-cold skin, and then stroked her cheeks lightly.

There was no time to register fear, for she was unable to remain conscious for long. When she next opened her eyes the moon was much lower in the sky. She heard men talking, though she could not understand what they said. One held a cup to her lips. The liquid inside had a sour taste but she swallowed it all the same, feeling too ill to fight their efforts, and she soon fell back asleep.

CHAPTER 3

"Are you the one?" A heavy-set man grabbed her arm.

"I'm sorry, I don't understand—" Kate tried to pull free from his grip, and her tongue froze in her mouth. She had no idea who he was, or where she was, other than that they stood in a narrow corridor carpeted with expensive rugs, with wall hangings draped across smooth grey stone walls. A few windows opened to a courtyard, giving her the idea that it was just past dawn, while the hallway was lit by candles perched on tall stands and oil lamps hanging on iron sconces. Having no idea where she was beyond that, it was just her luck that the first person she encountered greeted her with veiled hostility.

The man who had accosted her was wearing a long tunic the color of weak tea over a white shirt laced at the neck and sleeves, with a belt that sagged low on his waist, and thick knitted tights tucked into sturdy leather boots. And he didn't try to mask his impatience. "Bhara, are you the woman who they brought to the gatehouse last night?" He stared at her from under long wiry eyebrows, his brown eyes carefully appraising her appearance. "The guards told us that you were found in the torrapon. Who are you, and what were you were doing there? Surely you know that's forbidden?"

"What do you mean?" she asked. Simultaneously flustered by her situation and disturbed by his tone of voice, Kate replied rudely, "what the hell are you talking about? Who are *you?*"

His eyebrows arched at her questions, but he did not release her arm. In a low voice he stated impatiently, "I am not in the mood for games, Bhara. Tell me what you were doing there or I will turn you over to the Senvosra myself."

She tried to remember, though more for her sake than his. Only a few minutes before, she had awoken alone in a dark room, the air smoky and cold. She hadn't recognized her surroundings—a small room with bare stone walls, with coals glowing dimly in a hearth near the foot of her bed. A neighbor must have found her—but where had they taken her, and who had exchanged her wet nightshirt for a thin slip? The chilly air made her shiver, and she had reached for the blanket. As her eyes had adjusted to the low light, she had spied a long woolen dress draped across a chair. As odd as it was, her shivering dictated action, and seeing nothing better, she slipped the gown over her head, and slid her feet into leather slippers that she also found on the chair. Unable to locate a light switch, she had just stepped from the room when this man had accosted her in the long hallway.

Annoyed by his manners, she pulled herself free from the fat man's grasp. His attitude towards her did nothing to sweeten her own disposition. "I have no idea what you're talking about. Even if I did, why should I tell you anything, when you refuse to tell me who you are?"

He sighed, and made a bitter face. "Bhara, I am Bhagal Abranir, and I serve on the Council Vosidari. Is that sufficient?" Now his eyes glided from her head down to her toes. Without allowing her the time to reply, he continued. "I was told you were ill." He leaned closer to her, until she could smell his sour breath. "You look well enough to me. Perhaps that was a ploy to get admitted to the keep? Hmm, I wonder." He inhaled sharply through his nose as he tensed up the muscles in his neck. "Bhara, I demand you tell me your name, and what you were doing at the torrapon in the middle of the night. If you continue to refuse, I shall call the Senvosra, who shall not be nearly as patient."

"Fine. I don't know why you keep saying 'Bara'," she said, repeating the name she heard him use. "My name's Kate. Now if—"

"Bhagal Abranir, is there a problem?" The voice, both authoritative and annoyed, came from behind her. As she spun around, Kate saw a dark-haired man, perhaps her senior by a decade, who bowed his head gracefully towards her. Like the first man, he was wearing tights, but he wore no tunic, his long linen shirt cinched with a leather belt. A silver medallion dangled from a thick chain at his neck, and a number of bright silver rings graced his fingers.

"Nay, Aldrish, I was simply trying to learn who our mystery woman is. I must say, she has been quite rude so far."

"Indeed?" the newcomer queried. "What has she told you?"

Abranir crossed his thick arms and glared at Kate. "Very little. There's something rather odd about her, and in my opinion she should be turned over to the Senvosra at once."

The dark haired man nodded sharply, as if grasping the situation fully. "Well, Bhagal Abranir, your concern is duly noted, but also unnecessary. Bhara Kate is my guest, and I had been expecting her for some time." He paused, and tipped his head slightly as he glanced in her direction. With hair the color of the darkest chocolate, a gracefully angular nose and chin, and eyes like a grackle—bold and slightly dangerous—it was impossible not to find him attractive, even in these circumstances. "As it turns out," he continued, "Kate encountered some difficulty on her journey—but she is safe now, eh?"

Abranir made a sound of disgust deep in his throat. "Aye, Aldrish, if you say so." It was obvious he didn't believe a word of it, but at the same time, he seemed unwilling to challenge the statement.

"Indeed. I assure you, you need not trouble yourself with this matter any longer."

"Very well," Abranir replied curtly, shaking his head. "I leave it to you to look after her. But do warn her to take more care in how she conducts herself next time. She needs to know her place here, and act accordingly." With that, he stormed off, waving his hand over his shoulder to indicate his annoyance with the whole affair.

Without acknowledging Abranir's final comment, the new man regarded her carefully. "Well, Kate, I must say, I am very glad to see you are recovered," he said in a low voice. "Would you care to join me for breakfast?" His abrasiveness of a moment ago when dealing with Abranir had entirely disappeared as he addressed her.

Although confused before, now she was dumbfounded. Never had she felt less in control of her situation, and it made her both uneasy and annoyed that she couldn't explain where she was or what was happening. Worst of all, she found herself entirely at the mercy of a complete stranger who, inexplicably, already knew her name. "Who are you?" she demanded.

He blinked once. "Oh, my dear, I apologize. Of course you would not know who I am." He gave his head a tiny shake, as if stopping his train of thought. "My name is Aldrish Rynar—though privately, you should call me Rynar—and I am pleased to be your host for your stay in Loraden."

"Aldrish?" she repeated the odd name as she gazed at the heavy medallion resting against his shirt. For silver, it practically sparkled like a diamond, and it was hard to avoid staring at it.

"Aye. That is my title—it's the ancient word for chancellor. I look after the Vosira's—that is, the king's—affairs, and advise him on most matters."

King? Chancellor? "What? Is this some sort of joke?"

He regarded her with a serious expression. "Is that amusing to you?"

"Uh—" she began, and started shaking her head. "Okay, fun's over. What the hell's going on?" Kate asked, her skepticism rising. "How do you know my name? Did someone put you up to this?"

He had been staring at her, but with a quick jerk of his head he stopped himself and cast his gaze away. "Of course, it is my business to know everyone in the keep, but in fact, even though you've just arrived, you've been known to me for some time." He leaned closer, and as if suggesting there were secrets better off not being spoken here, added, "as for the rest, there will be plenty of time for us to talk later." Changing the subject rapidly, he asked, "are you hungry?"

As soon as he asked the question her stomach rumbled. "Yeah, actually I am, but—" she found herself mentally tripping over what he had just said. "I don't understand. You need to tell me where we are, and what's going on. Why are we dressed like this?" The last thing she could remember was standing in the backyard of her mom's house in the rain. How could she have ended up here? Was her crazy family behind all of this?

"Ah, as I said, we shall have plenty of opportunities later for questions. For now, come along with me." To emphasize his point, he pivoted on his heel and began walking rapidly down the long hallway, past fat candles flickering happily on their pedestals and long tapestries tracing out unknown tales in silver and bright colored threads. Not wanting to be left behind, she followed, though his pace forced her to jog to catch up to him.

"Seriously. Where are we going?"

"My quarters. I already have breakfast on its way."

He led her to a staircase of white marble, the steps cushioned by a runner of blue wool. Without looking behind him, he raced up a flight, leaving her to navigate the steps while holding the hem of her dress off the floor. It was easier said than done, because she no longer had her hands available to hold onto a banister or otherwise keep her balance, and there wasn't a lot of light to help guide her. Meanwhile, once he reached the top step, her new acquaintance turned to wait for her, encouraging her pick up the pace.

With a few steps to go, she heard a voice around the corner call out to him.

"Aldrish—what are you doing here?" Approaching them was another heavy-set man, roughly the same age as Rynar, who was wearing an elaborate tunic of silver, blue and green brocade. He had dark hair pulled tightly back in a braid and a gleaming silver torc at his neck.

Rynar snapped around to greet the newcomer. "Good morning, Vosira." He quickly nodded towards Kate, who had finally reached the top step. "This is Bhara Kate. She arrived in Loraden last night."

Vosira—the king? Things were moving way too fast, and she couldn't make sense of any of it. Who were these people, and why were they wearing these costumes? Instead of responding to the new introduction, Kate found herself unintentionally staring at the man, unable to muster even a polite greeting, since she was preoccupied with trying to figure out if she had met him or the Rynar character before. She recalled that her Aunt Reyna had been involved in a local renaissance festival, and wondered if she had hired these men. Maybe they rented out the castle that the rich guy built at the edge of the city? It was just like her family to do something like this to help her deal with her grief.

"Aye, is this true? Well, then, I am pleased to meet you, Bhara," the Vosira said, with a twinkle in his eye, and not appearing to notice her hesitation. "Rynar, you were planning to bring this lovely woman to join us at breakfast this morning, were you not?"

"Ah, Vosira, Kate has just arrived, and I had hoped for a quiet meal—"

"Nonsense!" As he raised his hands to smooth his hair, the Vosira smiled broadly at her, and she could see the dull yellow of his teeth, which contrasted with the thick, gleaming band of silver on his collarbone. "I won't be able to survive a moment longer without her in my company. My dear, come with me." He held out his hand, palm upwards.

She rolled her eyes at the overacting. At the same time, unlike these men, she had no theatrical training and wasn't sure what she was expected to do next. "I—uh..." she attempted, looking to Rynar for cues. In response, he nodded for her to accept, though the look in his eyes suggested this was the last thing he wanted. Confused, she stammered, "all right…Vosira," and she smiled nervously, feeling incredibly self-conscious as she took his outstretched hand. Normally she wasn't particularly shy, but given that these strangers had the advantage of knowing what was going on, she found it difficult to be herself.

"Excellent. Come along with me. I would love to hear of your travels." He had dropped her hand in favor of wrapping one arm around her back, with his hand resting suggestively on her hip. "And Rynar," he said, looking disapprovingly at the man's simple linen shirt, "do go and change into a proper tunic before joining us."

As her previous escort frowned and turned away to do as ordered, the Vosira pulled her a bit closer. "You are quite a delightful discovery. I anticipate the opportunity to get to know you better."

Even though she knew it was acting, his open advances unnerved Kate. Never one to seek out this kind of attention, she longed to shove him away, and under normal circumstances, she wouldn't have hesitated to do so. Expecting someone to jump out at any moment to tell her this was all a joke, she decided it was best to play along so she wouldn't look as foolish later.

To her relief, their destination was only a short distance away. He guided her towards an arched wooden door that was deeply-embossed with decorative carvings of flowers and trees. It was flanked by a pair of men wearing studded leather armor who were standing crisply at attention. That caused her to do a double-take. Armor? The prank was becoming more elaborate with each twist. She wasn't able to give the costumes sufficient scrutiny, for with smooth and precise movements, one of the men reached for the iron handle and pulled open the door, ushering her and the man known as the Vosira through without forcing them to slow their pace. Just inside the doors was a large chamber with a sizable hearth, carved wooden chairs and a heavy table. They did not stop here, however, but headed towards a second door, and another pair of guards.

This room was just as spacious, with curtains of deep blue wool and silver embroidery drawn across a window near the door. In the center of the room was a long table, which was dotted with a dozen sputtering candles, and at each setting, a wooden tray and silvery goblet. Along one wall was a sideboard displaying a row of ceramic bottles and a lush bouquet of roses.

A number of strangers sat quietly at the table, all turning to stare at the Vosira and his new guest as they entered the room.

Vosira Bedoric took his place at the head of the table, nodding with a polite smile to an attractive dark-haired woman who had looked up when he walked in, and then he absently waved to a servant to seat Kate in an empty chair near his own.

As she sat down, she turned her attention to the woman the Vosira had greeted, the only other female in the room. This woman was close to Kate's age, and wore an emerald velvet gown accented with bright silver jewelry and a sparkling diadem wrapped around her sable curls. The way she smiled back at him, Kate assumed she must be his wife, an insight reinforced when she leaned over to scold a rambunctious curly-haired boy of about five who bore unmistakable physical characteristics of both adults. Seeing how warmly the woman had greeted him, Kate was appalled by the Vosira's earlier actions. Had he really flirted with her moments ago, with a wife such as this just down the hall?

Then she reminded herself that this was all playacting—they each had their roles to perform, after all. That helped her relax a bit.

In addition to the royal couple and their son, at the table were seated several men of varying ages, and all of them were glaring at her. This detail set her on edge, and she laughed nervously, unsure what to do next. Based on their curious glances to one another and then to the Vosira, each man clearly was expecting some sort of introduction or explanation for her presence, yet no one dared to ask for one. Instead, they began to discuss her arrival in murmured tones to each other, with not-so-subtle nods and gestures in her direction. Most unsettling, Abranir—the disagreeable man from a short time before—was one of them, and he shot a series of squinting glances between her and the Vosira, as if trying to decide whose idea it was for her to be there.

"Okay, enough's enough. You guys got me good. Who's hiding the camera?"

Several of the men frowned at her words, and their consternation increased. "Vosira, who is this woman? She speaks in riddles." The question came from a man with thinning grey hair sitting directly across from her. "And why is she—"

His question was interrupted by a quick breeze that caused the candles to flicker, as the door behind her opened again. She noticed with unexpected relief that Rynar had entered the room, now clad in a green woolen tunic with embroidery similar to the needlework on her own gown. She had only met the man moments before, but she already felt more at ease with him there. He had been both charming and kind, and he at least seemed to have some idea what was going on. He shot her a quick smile as he slid into the chair between her and the Vosira.

"Ah, Aldrish Rynar, how good it is that you have chosen to join us, after allowing me to escort your lovely guest to breakfast," Vosira Bedoric announced magnanimously as he nodded to his advisor. "Would you do us the honor of introducing your companion to everyone else?"

"Aye, Aldrish, please do." The sarcastic comment came from the man who had begun to speak a moment before. "After all, it is so unlike you to have a female guest." Like the others, he had been staring intently at her from the moment she had entered the room, though he had done a poor job of pretending otherwise by sipping frequently from his goblet. As he spoke, she noticed that he had taken great care to comb his hair in such a way as to disguise a bald spot, but could not hide his half-rotten front tooth as easily.

Smoothly, Rynar sidestepped the sarcastic comment by ignoring it entirely. "Vosira Bedoric and Bhavosa Bryll," he said, addressing the couple at the head of the table, "this is Bhara Kate. She has traveled a great distance to visit us, and is very new to our land and our customs. As she is my personal guest, I hope everyone will treat her accordingly." He shot a withering glance at Abranir, the man who had first accosted her in the hallway, who narrowed his eyes and then sullenly nodded.

Rynar then coasted into quick introductions of everyone else, for Kate's benefit. After pointing out that the young boy was Ruill, the Charvos, which, as he explained meant 'heir', he then directed his attention to the weasel of a man across from them. "The man who kindly keeps track of my social life," he said, his own sarcasm oozing from every word, "is Bhagal Tashin." Without pausing to give the man a chance at rebuttal, Rynar then reminded her that the man beside him was Bhagal Abranir. After skipping an empty chair, there was a man her own age whose thick, curly brown hair was pulled tightly from his square face; this man Rynar introduced as Bhagal Pyrsac. The elderly man to her left with a shock of white hair sprouting from his scalp was Bhagal Jamra, who smiled and nodded as his name was mentioned, though he continued to look straight ahead rather than turn to her; beside him, a hulk of a man with a scraggly beard was Castellan Solerav, and finally, seated near the end of the table and apart from the others, was Bhagal Koldren, a man in his fifties with thick, wavy hair peppered with silver, and whose face was marred by an old but still very obvious scar that ran from his upper lip straight down to his chin. The rest of the chairs stood empty, and already feeling overwhelmed by the small group, she silently hoped that no additional people would show up.

Once the introductions were complete, Tashin immediately spoke up. In a sugary voice, he asked, "so Bhara, you are not from Sarducia?"

"That's right. I'm from Texas," she rebounded, with equally false sweetness. None of her instincts suggested this was a man she could grow to like. He didn't even look friendly, with bony cheeks protruding from his narrow face, and thin pale lips.

"Never heard of it. How did you come to be here?"

"It was a bit of a surprise, actually." She felt her confidence slowly return. Just keep playing along, she told herself, and it will all be fine.

"That is an odd answer."

She shrugged. "So we're even. This is an odd place," she replied with a smirk. Nothing like a sparring partner to bring out the best in her personality, she acknowledged to herself as she fought back the urge to laugh.

"Never mind him," Pyrsac said, with a genuine smile and nod of his head. His facial features were plain, but his eyes were a startlingly bright blue, and his beard was short and neatly trimmed. "I am pleased to make your acquaintance, Bhara Kate."

Jamra then, cocking his head, leaned in her direction. "Aye, good morning to you, Bhara, and welcome to Sarducia," he said, his voice pleasant and friendly. As she turned towards him, she discovered his eyes were clouded over with a milky film. No wonder he had not turned to look at her when Rynar introduced him. "I hope you are enjoying your visit?" he asked, his words suggesting genuine interest even as his eyes stared blankly over her shoulder.

"Yes, thank you," she fibbed, having had little occasion to enjoy anything since waking up a short time ago.

"That is good to hear," he said. "You know, there are so few charming young women around these days. I am so glad you have decided to visit us."

She smiled bashfully. "Thanks." His friendliness was well appreciated.

Servants began to bring platters of food to the table. After missing at least one meal, Kate would have been willing to eat just about anything, and the huge loaves of bread, egg custards and baked meat pies looked delicious.

With gratitude she nodded to the boy who served her generous portions of everything she requested.

As everyone ate, the conversation was light, with Bryll commenting on the state of the orchards, and Tashin complementing her on the late roses blooming in the courtyard gardens, some of which Kate had already noticed in the room. Rynar said little, focusing on his meal rather than engaging in conversation. She was happy following his lead, and tried to be as inconspicuous as possible.

Finally, Vosira Bedoric wiped his mouth on his sleeve, and looked to those at the table. "I believe there are several matters of business for us to attend to this morning?"

"Aye. This arrived this morning from Hansar." Tashin leaned over and handed Bedoric a rolled-up parchment bearing an intact seal.

The Vosira cracked open the seal and examined the contents, making a face of disgust. "Blast it all, there are still more demands. That queen has no regard for Sarducia's limitations. Clearly, this woman means to bleed us dry," he said, stabbing at the parchment with a fat index finger. "Such blackmail cannot be tolerated."

Castellan Solerav sounded surprised at the comment. "Blackmail, Vosira? What do you mean?"

He replied, in a mocking voice, "apparently Sarducia's tariffs on Hansar's goods are still too high." He pushed the crumpled parchment in Rynar's direction. "I can scarcely believe Tylnea's audacity—she demands we reduce the tariffs at once."

"Again?" Jamra asked, his blind eyes staring straight ahead. "We reduced them considerably in the autumn, did we not?"

"We did, but now she wants more. She also wants us to double our shipments of glysar." Vosira Bedoric gulped a half-goblet of wine, which was promptly refilled by a boy standing at his side. "She's threatening to refuse our ships in her ports if we do not comply."

"I assume she also insists once again that we disband the Sarnoc?" Abranir asked.

"Aye, naturally," the Vosira said, with a sigh. "She thinks we can control what the people want to believe. She's no better than the damn Sarnoc themselves in this regard. While I agree with her in principle, I'm not ready to turn half of the country against me."

"As if she really cares about our faith either way," Koldren spat, and wrinkled up his face, causing the scar to become more prominent. "It's a bid to control Sarducia, plain and simple, and she's going to be dissatisfied no matter what we do in this regard. She recognizes that the Hidden God movement divides our people, and she finds that beneficial to her own interests."

"That may well be," Solerav replied. "But there is truth to what the Prophet says. We all know that the Sarnoc serve only to weaken our kingdom, after all. We would be better off without their interference."

"Nay, Solerav, they do not weaken us." Jamra countered, his voice more forceful than Kate expected. "The Sarnoc are the very reason the gods have not forsaken us, as they have so many other lands, including Hansar." He cleared his throat, and then added in a low voice, "our biggest mistake was barring them from the city."

"Oh Jamra," Solerav replied with an annoyed sigh. Rolling his eyes in an overly dramatic gesture that was lost on the other man, he added, "you really need to come to your senses on this matter. You know as well as any man in this room that the Sarnoc are nothing like they once were."

A sharp cough from the Vosira forestalled any reply, and then Rynar spoke up. "Jamra, you have been warned before about such dissent. You would be well advised to hold your tongue."

"Aldrish, I know the laws of this kingdom as well as you," Jamra snapped back. "I have been a member of the Council for a great many years, and served as Vosira Parmon's first Aldrish. I think I've earned the right to speak my mind."

In what seemed to be a clever attempt to defuse the situation, Pyrsac jumped into the conversation, turning to her with a smile. "Speaking of the Prophet, Bhara, have you been introduced to his teachings? Some of them are quite scandalous, but I find them fascinating."

Before she could stumble through a response, she felt Rynar's hand on her arm. "Pyrsac," he replied on her behalf, "the lady is from a distant land and has no knowledge of such things—though, to be sure, most of the people in her country also worship just one god."

It was an odd thing to say, and she shot him a glance, but once he had spoken, he busied himself with buttering a slice of bread.

"Is this true, Bhara?" Vosira Bedoric asked, and was leaning forward eagerly.

Everyone seemed anxious for her reply. "Well, I suppose so." She had no idea why it mattered. All the same, her response pleased everyone except Jamra, who simply shook his head silently.

"Bhara, I trust the Aldrish will bring you to the square, so that you can hear the preachers speak the words of the Prophet, and judge his teachings for yourself," the Vosira offered. "He has many interesting opinions on our relationship with the gods. Indeed, I am sure the Aldrish would be pleased to explain why the Prophet holds such promise for our land." He paused, watching the man now poking at his meat with his knife. "Aldrish?" the Vosira prompted.

"Indeed, Vosira."

"Is there something else on your mind? You are rarely so reserved."

Rynar leaned closer to the Vosira. "Aye, but I did not want to raise it to the Council yet," he said, speaking so quietly that had Kate not been sitting beside him, she would not have been able to make out the words. "Perhaps we can discuss it later."

The Vosira felt none of his advisor's need for discretion, and loudly replied, "this is hardly the Council." He laughed. "Come man, we have no secrets among us. It must be important if it distracts you so. What is it?"

Rynar hesitated for a moment, taking the time to make eye contact with each person in the room. After a quick sigh, as if annoyed that he would have to speak publicly about his concerns, he nodded. "Very well." He turned away from the Vosira, and continued. "I received some unsettling news from one of my men in the city."

"News, Aldrish? Do tell," the Vosira requested.

Rynar waved to the boy to refill the Vosira's goblet, and then cleared his throat. "I had a credible report that the Dosedra was seen in Loraden last night."

Although the news meant nothing to Kate, it obviously was of immense significance to everyone else in the room. The men turned to each other in shock, several murmuring to themselves.

Meanwhile, all of the color faded from the Vosira's face, replaced by a sheen of perspiration, a slick spreading across his forehead and cheeks. When his wife placed her hand on his shoulder, gazing at him with a mixture of surprise and concern, he did not turn to her, and for a good minute he sat silently, his thick hands gripping the edge of the table. Even when Bryll finally leaned over to speak to him, he acted as though he could not hear her. Then his head began to sway slightly, making Kate wonder if he was about to faint, but then he licked his lips and found his voice.

"How is it possible?" he finally asked in a rough voice. "My brother is still alive?"

After glancing at the Vosira, who did not appear composed enough to speak further, Abranir addressed Rynar. "Aldrish," he began tentatively, "Queen Tylnea told us he died many years ago. Who is this source, and could they be mistaken? No one in Sarducia has seen the Dosedra in a long time."

Rynar nodded, his expression solemn. "Aye, of course, the news is hard to believe." He spoke softly, almost as if he tried to reassure the others with his news. "My source felt certain of the man's identity, and I am inclined to believe it as well. However, maybe we should accept it as a rumor for the time being." He leaned forward to catch the castellan's attention. "I have instructed Senvosra to search for him, and they will contact me if they find him."

"I do not understand," Solerav replied, his eyes bright and accusatory, though his anger did not seem directed at anyone in particular. "If he somehow survived, why wouldn't we have heard news of this before now?" He shook his head. "This must be a mistake. I cannot believe he would suddenly appear, not after all this time, and not after how he left Sarducia so long ago."

"Aye," Koldren added. "I agree. If he is alive and returning home, why would he not tell us?"

"What if it's true? Tashin replied. "Perhaps Tylnea misled us intentionally? It doesn't seem difficult to imagine them conspiring together. After all, the queen must know about Arric's treachery. Perhaps she has been giving him shelter all this time." As he said this, his eyes darted towards Kate, as if blaming her somehow for the situation, but then he returned his attention to the end of the table. "It would be just like her to do something devious like this, telling us he had died so she could keep him in hiding until she judged the timing was right to send him home."

"Listen to you all. Your paranoia is ridiculous! Need I remind you all that when the Dosedra left Sarducia, he led our troops in battle?" Jamra interrupted. "If he's still alive, there's no reason to jump to all of these conclusions. Perhaps he simply wants to return to his home. At any rate, it certainly doesn't mean he's a traitor!"

"You know as well as we do that he didn't leave Sarducia for altruistic reasons, Jamra. And given all he has done, is it any wonder we would question his return?" Solerav shot back.

"He left to fight the Mosumi, at Tylnea's request!" Jamra's face was flushed, and he slapped his palm on the table for emphasis. "If anything, it was a diplomatic choice. How could he have known that Tylnea would turn on us afterwards?"

Tashin scrunched up his thin face in disgust, and for a moment it looked like he was going to spit on the floor but thought better of it. "Aye, and Froida was a disaster! All those men lost—and until now, we thought the Dosedra one of them! After everything he did there, if he still lives, he must be held accountable."

"Clearly we have a different view of Froida," Jamra retorted. "Perhaps it was Tylnea's treachery that condemned his men? We have never had a satisfactory accounting of what happened in Froida, and if the Dosedra is alive, there may be many other things we do not know about what happened. At any rate, you know the Sarnoc do not agree with the version of events you've laid out."

"You make a good point. What if it's the Sarnoc who are behind this?" Tashin crossed his arms. "Vosira, I don't like this situation at all. If he is alive, action must be taken immediately!"

Bedoric had not spoken again, and remained visibly shaken by the news. At the comment posed directly to him, he rubbed his cheeks with his palm. "Tashin, if it's true, I—" he started, and then swallowed heavily, and pounded his fist once on the table. "Nay. I cannot believe this report. It's been what, eight years since we were told he had been killed?" he asked, turning to Rynar. Seeing him nod, the Vosira continued. "How could he have survived without our knowledge, for all this time? It's impossible. We have men in Tylnea's court. They would have told us." He took a sip of his wine, and exchanged glances with Bryll. Then he returned his gaze to the men around the table. "Blast this whole mess. I wish we had even a shred of information we could use." Although he had just cast his doubts over the report, he was still perspiring. Kate watched him run a finger along the edge of a wooden platter, and then raised the finger to his torc. This was not the visage of someone acting in confidence, and he confirmed his doubts by asking aloud, "what if he has returned to challenge my rule now, after all this time? As you all have suggested, what if he has been working with the

Sarnoc, or Tylnea? How can we deal with this, and end his treachery once and for all?"

The men in the room all replied at once, their voices raised to try to be heard over the others. Rynar raised his arms to quiet the debate, but none seemed to notice him until he stood up and clapped his hands once over his head. "Men, calm yourselves. I agree with the Vosira. We must first confirm the reports. Until then, it's pointless to speculate on why he has returned, or what he may be intending to do now." He spoke with measured words, his tone reassuring. "Vosira, I would recommend you proceed with caution. If he resurfaces, at that time you will be able to demand that he account for his time and explain the false reports. For now, though, we must not panic."

"Indeed. We still do not know for certain that it was him," Koldren pointed out. "What if your informant was mistaken?"

"Aye," Bedoric agreed, although his tone sounded tentative. "We can hope for that."

The room fell silent as everyone watched Vosira Bedoric tug at the torc at his neck. He then drained his goblet, and turned back to Rynar. "Aldrish, if it really is him—if somehow, after all this time he really has returned to Loraden—" he paused, appearing to collect his thoughts as he placed his palm against his chest, "what do we do first?"

Rynar tapped his lips, not at all surprised that the Vosira had deferred to his judgment. "Ah, well, there is but one appropriate response. You must welcome him back with open arms." At these words there was noticeable disagreement, and once again several men raised their voices in challenge. With one hand raised, Rynar quieted them all. "Hear me out, men. We have already established that we have no idea why the Dosedra might return after all these years, and lacking such information we cannot allow him to cause problems for his brother. Consider this: he will be able to do much less damage if the people think his brother welcomes his return. We cannot give the impression that we were caught off-guard by his reappearance, or worse, that we have reason to fear him. In fact, I believe we should immediately honor him at a celebratory quantrill at which our Vosira demonstrates how pleased he is that his brother has returned safely and heroically from the battlefield."

"That's insane," Tashin grumbled. "You know as well as the rest of us that the Dosedra is nothing but trouble for us all. Best we throw him in a cell and be done with it."

"Aye," Abranir said quickly. "We need to put out a call to arrest the Dosedra—for our own safety."

Vosira Bedoric glanced to those men, and then to Rynar. He wiped his forehead with the back of his hand, and then looked down at the table. "Nay, the Aldrish is right," he announced, finally pulling himself together. "He may have shamed himself with his actions in Froida, but he is still a son of Parmon. Perhaps he has returned because he has nowhere else to go, which means he has no choice but finally accept my rule." He placed both palms on the table. "If we welcome him, we may be able to convince him to share critical information about Tylnea, which he certainly will refuse to do from the dungeons. We are better off not letting him know we consider him a threat." He nodded to Rynar. "It is good that you brought this to our attention. If your information is accurate, then we must not delay. See to it that preparations to host a grand feast in his honor begin immediately. And Aldrish—if he truly is in the city, you must find him!"

CHAPTER 4

"Do you remember anything from the time you arrived?"

Rynar had directed Kate into a suite just a couple of doors down from the room they had just left. It consisted of two generously-sized rooms separated by a wall with a fireplace that opened into both spaces. For such a large suite, it was sparsely furnished, the central feature being the heavy wooden table piled high with large leather-bound folios, a thick stack of papers held down with round stones, and a cluster of white feathers in a tin cup. The stone floor was cushioned with a thick carpet embroidered with vines, and the long wall across from the fire wore a wide tapestry depicting a variety of animals all delicately embroidered onto the dark wool.

"What do you mean? I, uh..." she fumbled. It was an odd opening question, given everything that had transpired in the other room. "I woke up in that room, and found the dress..."

Without replying to that statement, he waved her towards a wide chair piled with pillows, and then began to rummage through the items on the table. Then he asked, "did you speak to anyone else besides Abranir before I found you in the hallway?"

She settled herself amidst the cushions. "No. He was the first person I saw."

"Ah, good," he replied, his back towards her. "That is one less problem then." With a single powerful sweep of his arm, he pushed three massive folios bound in leather to the table's edge, and rifled through a stack of loose papers.

Growing exasperated by the situation and lack of information, she was unable to relax, and watching him digging through his papers made her even more anxious. "What's going on here, really? Did my aunts put you up to this?"

As soon as she spoke he gave up on whatever it was he was looking for and pivoted around, leaning against the table. He crossed his arms and lowered his eyes to inspect her more closely. Yet he didn't answer her questions. "When speaking to others, you just gave your name as 'Kate'?"

That was another odd question that she wasn't sure how to answer. "Uh, yeah, that's my name, after all. But why aren't you answering my questions?"

He stared at her, his lips pressed tightly. Then he took a deep breath and appeared to calm slightly. "Perhaps no one knows, then."

"What do you mean? What doesn't anyone know?" She stood up and crossed her arms, just as he had done. "Would you please tell me where I am, and what all of that—" she said, gesturing in the direction of the room they had left, "was all about?"

Rynar clucked his tongue. "You really have no idea where you are?" Then he cocked his head to one side. "Did no one tell you about Sarducia before you traveled here?"

"Who would have told me? As far as I know, this place shouldn't even exist. I couldn't have known I was coming here, other than—" she hesitated. Something had happened to her, and whatever it was, it all started with the voices in her head, and then there was her glowing ring. She was about to say something about all that, but then she had second thoughts. She didn't know this man, or what he wanted with her. Her instincts told her to stay silent for now. "Honestly, I don't have a clue about where I am or how I got here."

He didn't seem to notice the stumble. Instead, he wrenched his mouth to one side, as if puzzling something out, and then stepped over to the hearth where he bent over to stir the coals. After a moment he shook his head. "Ah, sorry, they're cold, and there is no time to light a new fire." He turned back to her, and continued. "Well, seeing as this is all new to you, allow me to explain. First of all, this is very much real. We are right now within the royal keep," he gestured to the walls around them, "which is in the city of Loraden, in the kingdom of Sarducia." As he spoke, he watched her carefully. "Back there, at breakfast, I had to share the unfortunate news with the Vosira that his brother has returned. In fact, I need to leave in a few moments to try to find out where the Dosedra might be now."

"You made it seem like it was a rumor."

"Aye, but it's not. I'm certain he appeared in the city last night, and I'd like to find him before he, or the Senvosra, do something stupid. It could be a dangerous situation."

"Senvosra?" Kate repeated. "That man, Abranir—he mentioned that word before. What is it?"

"That refers to the royal solders. They are not known for their gentle handling."

She didn't like the sound of that. "So what's the big deal about this dos... dos... whatever that is? It didn't sound like anyone liked the news."

"Dosedra. And nay, there are none on the Council who would welcome that man, except perhaps Jamra, and even he knows better than to challenge the Vosira on this topic." As he continued, Rynar remained where he stood, his eyes never leaving her. "This is what you need to understand. Vosira Parmon was murdered eight years ago, and afterwards there was considerable confusion because he had not proclaimed an heir between his two adult sons. There was a heated dispute over who would become heir, but as the older son, Bedoric had the support of the majority of the Council and ultimately assumed his father's place. After that, Arric became Dosedra—which means simply, 'one who does not inherit'—and he didn't take it well. He immediately left for the court of Queen Tylnea of Hansar, where he signed up to lead the fight against the Mosumi tribes who were making trouble on Hansar's border.

"After that, not even a year later, the Vosira received the news of a massive battle with terrible casualties on both sides. Some of the Hansari and Sarducian troops might have survived, we were told, had the Dosedra not abandoned his men in the thick of battle. We heard stories that a disgruntled Hansari soldier killed him in retaliation, but it seems that information may have been inaccurate. There were tales of him being a particularly vicious fighter, so it's not difficult to imagine what he might do if he still holds a grudge against his brother."

What kind of political intrigue had she stumbled into? "There was some concern that he would be working with someone called the Sarnoc. Who are they?"

"Really?" The question seemed to genuinely surprise him. "You do not know about them either?"

From the way he shook his head to himself, she guessed that her ongoing ignorance of this land was trying his patience. "Why would I? Like I said, until this morning I didn't even know this place existed."

He let out a breath through pursed lips, as if buying time to decide on how to respond. "Very well, then. It's important that you understand this as well. We have four gods: Yoren, the keeper of the dead; Jorell, the god of order; Cira, the goddess of disorder; and Kerthal, who oversees all life. The Sarnoc are the guardians of that faith, serving as teachers, healers, and judges, and they are quite powerful, both in a political sense and more—" he said, and drew a breath, "shall we say, 'esoterically'."

She tried to make sense of that. "Do you mean magic?"

"Hmm, I suppose you could say that, depending on how you define it. There was true magic here once, but most of the knowledge has been lost over the centuries. The Sarnoc possess what little information there is on the subject, and guard it carefully as the representatives of the gods' will and authority."

"It sounded like you don't believe any of that."

"Oh, I do, but it's complicated." He glanced down at the floor for a moment, as if collecting his thoughts, and then looked back up at her. "The Sarnoc were implicated in Vosira Parmon's murder, and Bedoric forced them out of the city. After that, it was dangerous for anyone on the Council to openly support the Sarnoc. Then this Prophet appeared, teaching that there was one god and the Sarnoc aren't necessary, and that gave Bedoric another excuse to further undermine the Sarnoc's authority." He caught her eyes, and added, his voice lower, "I think the Hidden God rhetoric is foolish, but I keep that to myself."

"So let me get this straight: the Vosira worries that his brother has returned and is working with these Sarnoc to overthrow him?"

"Aye, that's one way of putting it. Dosedra Arric was very close to the Sarnoc before he left. Given his history, I cannot rule it out."

"You make it sound like he might try to kill his brother."

He frowned. "Aye, it's distinctly possible. He certainly has the potential to do great harm." He went back to digging within the pile on the table. "This is why we have to welcome him back, and watch him carefully. Perhaps he wants nothing at all but to be home again, but that is hard to believe.

CHAPTER 5

"The Aldrish gave me strict instructions to look after you." After receiving a message that confirmed the Dosedra was in the city, Rynar rushed off to manage the situation. After a contrite apology, he deposited Kate into the hands of a stout woman named Lillia, whose smile rivaled Kate's own mother's. "And I take my duties very seriously," she added.

"What do you mean, 'look after me'?" Kate challenged. "I don't need a guardian, you know."

That made the woman laugh. "Oh my, the Aldrish didn't exaggerate one bit. You really have come a long way to Loraden, haven't you?"

"You could say that," Kate said, amused by the understatement.

"Ah, then, come, allow me to show you around the keep."

As Lillia led her down the hallways, Kate learned that in the keep, equal attention had been paid to defense and comfort. The building itself had been constructed in the shape of a square, with fortified outer walls a foot thick with had narrow windows barely wider than her head. Meanwhile, the inner walls had wide windows that overlooked a large courtyard garden below. Despite the cold, imposing structure, the residents had gone to great lengths to make it feel cozy with thick rugs, tapestries candles everywhere.

The hallways were also filled with activity. Servants bustled about filling vases with fresh-cut flowers and plumping pillows in cozy alcoves. Others carried piles of clothing or stacks of firewood. Soldiers in blue, swords at their waists, stood guard at doorways. And they passed a number of people of all stations who were all in a rush to get where they were going.

Along the way, it was impossible to avoid hearing rumors of the Dosedra's surprise appearance. The topic was on the lips of nearly everyone they passed. At one point Kate and Lillia passed two ladies sitting on an upholstered bench who were complaining that there simply wasn't enough time to put together a proper quantrill in a single day.

Just before midday, Lillia ran into a friend of hers who was escorting two young girls, perhaps six or seven years old. As the two women shared news, Kate introduced herself to the two girls, who were excited to tell her about their new pony.

After several minutes, Lillia gently interrupted the animated conversation. "Girls, you have taken far too much of Kate's time."

"No, it's fine. They're adorable. Navina hasn't ever been on a horse before, is that right?"

"She will never stop talking if you let her," Lillia cautioned. "In any event, it is time we return to your quarters. The Aldrish was quite clear that I was to make sure you were prepared for tonight."

After promising they could tell her more about the pony later, Kate tore herself away, and reluctantly followed Lillia back to the room she had been previously assigned. Since all of the rooms looked alike on the outside, she had to count doors once they reached the landing, so she could be sure to find it again later. Second floor, turn left, eighth door from the stairs. "Are you sure that this is the same room I was in before?" she asked when they entered. Unlike the dark, cold space she had left, now the windows were open, there were fresh candles on the table, flowers on the mantel over the fire, and a stack of wood beside the hearth. There was also a tray with fruits, cheeses and a small pie that was still warm and filled the room with a delicious aroma.

"Partridge and potatoes," the maid informed Kate as she leaned over to smell the pie. "Once you've eaten, we'll get started."

"Aren't you going to join me?"

"Join you, my lady?"

Kate pointed to the food. "Lunch time, right?"

Lillia chuckled. "Oh no, I have much to do. I still need to get your evening's garments and assist you in dressing. I shall eat shortly. Please, have a seat."

Her jaw fell open. "Really? So you're not just here to show me around?"

"Oh goodness, no. You must have a maid to look after your needs, and I was honored that the Aldrish requested me."

A maid? Kate had never had anyone wait on her before, other than at a restaurant, and suddenly she felt very awkward. How could she sit there and eat while her companion swept ashes from the hearth? Instead of eating, she asked, "so what exactly is this is quantrill, anyway?"

"Ah, it's a formal banquet for all of the Bhagali. Indeed, the cooks worry that there won't be enough variety of meats, since they haven't had the time for the butchering, but they are doing the best they can. They have all of the charnok preparing the wine, and if there is enough to drink, I am confident no one will fault the menu." Lillia turned around and clapped her hands together to dust them off. "Now, please, eat up," she said, admonishing Kate. "There is still much we need to do before you're ready."

CHAPTER 6

Iron chandeliers stuffed with fat candles dangled from the ceiling like hungry spiders, imbuing the cavernous room with a warm glow. Whitewashed stone walls were festooned with lengths of blue and golden fabric. Rows of stout wooden tables marked off the room's perimeter, with enough seating for a hundred or more people, and were arranged to leave an open space in the center. Music spilled from one corner of the room, and laughter and conversation filled every table and corner.

Dozens of men and women had arrived before Kate, and now they either sat along the narrow tables or stood in tight bunches, engaged in animated conversation. As she watched them, she was awed by the display of elaborate clothing and jewelry. Most of the men wore tunics of rich brocade and velvet, with broad shoulders and wide sleeves, over knitted leggings and pointy embroidered slippers. The women, meanwhile, wore long gowns with fitted bodices decorated with colorful needlework. Both men and women wore bright rings, chains and brooches of silver, and nearly everyone wore their hair long, the women pulling it off their shoulders and adorning it with flowers or combs, while the men neatly secured their hair either in ponytails tied with silk cords, or tightly bound in a queue.

Kate wore a gown of stiff green and silver brocade, with sleeves that were attached by ribbons to the bodice, all layered over a spotless white linen shift. Her body had been spritzed with fragrant water, and Lillia had performed miracles with Kate's shoulder-length auburn hair, sweeping it up into a pair of tight braids secured to the base of her neck with curved combs. While there was no makeup as Kate knew it, still Lillia had used a bit of powder on her cheeks and a thin brush and a pot of what looked like ink to line her eyes. Kate's only regrets were that there was no mirror to view her transformation, nor a camera to record it for posterity.

Never before had she felt so entirely out of place. This was a world so different from her own that it was impossible to take it all in. As she absently chewed on her thumbnail, she watched a young man leaning suggestively towards a girl whose bland smile and hands folded in front of her, along with regular glances to one side, indicated she spoke to him out of politeness rather than romantic interest. A table over, two men were loudly laughing at something told to them by a third man, who appeared already drunk and unable to stand without leaning against the table.

She wished that Rynar, that man she had met earlier, had accompanied her here. Instead, her escort had been a teenaged boy who couldn't muster the courage to speak to her. As soon as they had passed through the double doors of the hall, he led her to a table and then promptly disappeared, folding into a cluster of boys his age across the room. Now, not knowing what else to do, and feeling unusually overwhelmed by the situation, she sat quietly in her seat, dragging her fingertips against the rough fabric of her gown.

What was she expected to do now?

She gazed down at her ring, wondering if it would begin to glow again if she removed it now. Hiding it in the folds of her gown, she slid the ring off. Nothing happened. The mysterious beam of light was gone, and again it seemed to be an ordinary ring. She wondered if her mother knew anything about it—had she any idea what the ring could do? Kate might never know the answer to that question. With a frustrated sigh, she put the ring back on and returned to staring out at the sea of strangers.

Not all of the guests were complete strangers to her, of course. The Vosira and his wife Bryll sat at another table close to her own, though Kate doubted it would be appropriate for her to skip over and engage in small talk as if they were old friends. Instead, she watched Vosira Bedoric drain his goblet and wait for a boy standing behind him to refill it. From what she could see, the boy's entire job was that single task, and it appeared he would not remain idle for long. Bryll, on the other hand, was preoccupied with the antics of their son, who was alternating between fidgeting in his chair and banging a metal platter against the tabletop. Her beauty and grace presented such a contrast to her husband that it was a bit shocking. Bedoric might have been handsome in his youth, but it seemed that the allure of rich food and drink had put on the pounds and contributed to his sloppy habits.

A newcomer interrupted her casual observation of the royal couple. A young woman with flushed cheeks and chestnut hair already escaping its braid took a seat across from her.

"Good eve, Uncle Tashin," the girl said, her voice a bit winded, as if she had rushed to the hall.

Kate whipped her head around. While her attention had been focused elsewhere, she hadn't noticed that Tashin, the man from breakfast with the snide manners and bad teeth, had already taken a seat beside her.

"About time you arrived," he greeted the girl with a sour frown.

"Sorry, uncle," the girl said, her eyes downcast. Then she turned to Kate and her expression brightened. "Well hello!" she said in greeting. "I'm Arwyn. Are you new to Loraden? I don't believe I've seen you here before."

"Bhara Kate is a guest of the Aldrish," Tashin explained, as if the fact already bored him. "Apparently that fact granted her a seat at our table."

"Really? A guest of the *Aldrish?*" Arwyn suppressed a giggle with the back of her hand as she pronounced the title. "Surely not?"

"Why's that funny?" Kate looked at Arwyn and then to Tashin. "He seems nice enough."

Arwyn leaned across the table. "That's true, but," the girl shifted her eyes to one side and then the other, and then asked in a conspiratorial whisper, "just how well do you know him?"

"Not that well at all, actually. I'm new here, and I just met him. Why?"

Arwyn glanced at her uncle, and then grinned. "Oh, good, then perhaps you won't mind me asking. Is it true what everyone says about him?" She took Kate's confused expression as a sign to continue, keeping her voice low. "It's common knowledge that the Aldrish never associates with women. You rarely even see him speaking to any of the Bharani here, and when he does, certainly it never goes further than that. In fact, more than once I've heard that he..." she paused for effect, "hmm, how should I say it? That he... prefers men."

Even though she had spoken softly, somehow her uncle overheard the gossip. "Girl, hold your tongue!" Tashin snapped. "Or shall I assume you are actively trying to fall into disfavor at court?"

"Oh uncle, you've heard it too. Everyone has," Arwyn said, rolling her eyes. "Don't tell me you never wondered about it."

He glared at her, and was about to reply when Bhagal Abranir approached him with a question.

Tashin suitably distracted, Arwyn explained, "Don't you worry about my uncle. He takes everything so seriously, but his bark is worse than his bite—most of the time anyway. But tell me, do you think what they say about the Aldrish could be true?"

"Well, I can't say either way." Kate's mind flicked through the brief memories she had of him. There really hadn't been time to judge his character in general, much less something like this—as if it mattered anyway. All she could muster was a weak, "I don't really know him that well."

"See? And I doubt you ever will, either," Arwyn concluded with a wink, and tipped back her head with a giggle. That received a stern glance from Tashin, even as he continued his own conversation. She grinned, and then, as if to redeem herself, she quickly changed topics. "Where's the Dosedra?" she asked the pair of men. "Everyone's been talking about his miraculous return all day, and I can't wait to see him. Is he not planning to attend his own quantrill?"

Tashin leaned back. "Bhagal Abranir was asking me the same thing," he said, as Abranir nodded once and turned back to his own seat. "I was told he would arrive before his brother, but it appears he is late—just as one might expect." He rolled his eyes. "Indeed, that assumes I expect anything from him at all, which I do not."

"That seems a bit harsh," Kate replied.

His eyes widened. "Indeed, Bhara? Do you know something about the Dosedra that you have not told us?"

"No, but it seems to me that everyone's being really hard on someone whose only crime is not being dead."

Her response made Tashin laugh. Well, it wasn't so much a laugh as a fluttering of his thin lips and a choked sound from his throat. "You are a stranger here, and know nothing of our history or the relationship between the Vosira and his brother." He stared at her for a moment, as if examining her more closely. "A piece of advice—don't get involved in this matter."

"I don't intend to. I made a comment, that's all."

"And, uncle, say what you want about him, I still can't wait to see what he's like." Arwyn glanced in Kate's direction and then held her hand over her mouth to stifle another giggle. "I wonder if he's handsome, or if he's fat like his brother." With Arwyn's comment, Kate's own eyes darted to the Vosira. Between speaking to a long line of people greeting him, and giving orders to his servants, he drained his cup without stopping to wipe drops of wine that dribbled down his chin.

Meanwhile, Arwyn's uncle narrowed his eyes at her. "Hush, girl. You really must learn how to speak with more respect, or else remain silent. Your constant gossiping will only embarrass us both, and likely get at least one of us in trouble with the Vosira."

Rather than reply, Arwyn tipped her head back and let out a dramatic sigh, and then turned so she faced into the crowd, with her back to her uncle.

"Oh good grief, girl." Tashin snorted and then, shaking his head in frustration, left his own seat to speak to a man at another table.

Kate admitted to herself that she had shared a general curiosity about both men. Aldrish Rynar had certainly been kind, but she had sensed a bit of hesitation, as if he didn't feel entirely comfortable talking to her. Meanwhile, the Dosedra's mysterious reappearance had been popular gossip, but no one knew anything about him or why he had returned. From the little Lillia was willing to say (for she remained largely tight-lipped about the whole thing), conjecture was rampant.

Arwyn's exclamation broke her train of thought. "Quinsa! I haven't had any in ages."

A young man was at Kate's side, filling her goblet with a blue liquid. "You mean the wine?"

"Of course. It's made from gaminberries, so it isn't served often. I heard it was the Dosedra's favorite."

Kate swirled it around, feeling a bit skeptical about consuming a bright blue wine—all she could think of were the slushie drinks that stained your lips and tongue blue. After watching Arwyn, and ascertaining that this quinsa did not have the same effect, she took a small sip. By allowing the beverage to roll on her tongue, she concluded that the slightly bitter flavor was actually quite pleasant, almost more like a Belgian ale than a wine, and she tipped the goblet back.

"Careful—quinsa is much stronger than regular wine," Arwyn advised. "It will make your head ache if you drink it too fast."

Smiling, and taking her new friend's advice, she set the cup down reluctantly, realizing that as tasty and refreshing as it was, she would likely end up drinking far too much of it. It was at this moment that young men presented the first trays of food to those seated at their table. There were slabs of meat and roasted fowl, a doughy meat-filled pie, and crumbly cheese, along with roasted vegetables, breads and rolls glazed with honey. Kate found herself wanting to try a little bit of everything.

Meanwhile, Tashin returned, and his fingers toyed with the knife that lay before him on the table. "So, Bhara Kate," he said, pronouncing her name sharply, as if taking a bite from an apple. "Perhaps you might explain how you know the Aldrish?"

Already annoyed by his snide tone earlier, and now forced to acknowledge him, she jerked her head in his direction. She was on the verge of speaking her mind when the Aldrish himself appeared and slid onto the bench beside her. "Bhagal Tashin, surely I need not remind you that this is a celebration, not an interrogation?" As the older man glared at him in response, she noted Rynar's expression was smug, one of conquest.

Before she had a chance to be questioned further, and before she had an opportunity to find out more about this strange place from Rynar, there was a flurry of movement at the Vosira's table, with several servants, two of the Senvosra, and several courtiers all crowded around. Rynar simply leaned back, his arms crossed, and waited to see what would happen next.

The Vosira stood up. As he did so, the boys with the trays retreated to the back of the room, men and women took their seats, the musicians put aside their instruments, and the room fell silent.

"Welcome, Bhagali," he began. Despite the quantity of quinsa he had already consumed, his voice was deep and quite steady. "Tonight is a very special occasion, as I bring you surprising and welcome news. For years we believed Dosedra Arric, my brother, had died in Froida. Tonight I am happy to announce that the news was wrong, and my brother is still alive!"

Although the information was scarcely a surprise to anyone, many people whispered comments to one another as they heard the news confirmed.

The Vosira continued. "I have gathered everyone here on such short notice to congratulate my dear brother on his return to Sarducia after a long and difficult military campaign in Froida." He showed none of the uncertainty or nervousness of the morning, which surprised Kate. Perhaps the wine emboldened him? "Without any further delay, allow me to be the first to welcome home the son of Parmon, my brother, Dosedra Arric." He turned, and extended his hands in greeting, though the gesture was unmistakably languid.

As he gestured towards the doors, the musicians broke out in a lively tune as two liveried men pulled open the double doors to admit the newcomer.

It was the Dosedra. The royal prince everyone had believed dead.

He entered the room with his head held high, a serious expression on his face. The response from the crowd was mixed. While the majority pounded on tables in welcome, some—like Tashin—remained silent. Everyone watched as the Dosedra embraced his brother, though the gesture was both formal and dispassionate.

Kate compared the two royal sons. The Dosedra was several years younger than his brother, perhaps in his early 30s, but they shared a remarkable resemblance. The men both had long, dark wavy hair, though oddly only the younger man's hair was dusted with silver. They also shared the same strong cleft chin and straight nose, though the Dosedra's face was marred by two heavy scars, one across his forehead and another that followed the line of his chin. Setting himself further apart from his brother and other men in the room, the Dosedra had eschewed a stylish brocade tunic in favor of a pale blue linen shirt with full sleeves and embroidery on the cuffs and neckline, over which was a leather doublet in deep blue. Whether the choice was born from ignorance of Loraden fashion or defiance of it, his clothing nonetheless showed off his robust build, which, as a soldier, was slender and muscular.

The Dosedra then took a step back. In a voice that was similar to Bedoric's, both deep and confident, he greeted his brother. "My lord Vosira, and my dear brother, it is good to be back in Loraden, among both family and friends."

"Aye, brother," Bedoric replied. "It has been a long time indeed since you have graced the great hall. It is our honor to welcome you home, and celebrate your safe return."

"Indeed. I wish to thank you and the lovely Bhavosa for this wondrous quantrill, and the opportunity to reconnect with old acquaintances. I apologize for giving you so little advance warning to plan such an event." It was a generous comment, but to Kate's ears it sounded almost sarcastic, as did his next statement. "For the future, I look forward to a long career in your service and the opportunity to start a family, here at home." He bowed his head. When he did so, a lock of hair pulled loose and curled just above his eyebrow. "Thank you again, brother. It is good to be back in Loraden."

The Vosira nodded once, but did not smile. "Aye, brother." He paused, and then raised his goblet over his head. "Á Dosedra!" he shouted, and the room clamored in repetition. Then, as quickly as that, he flicked his right wrist in the direction of the musicians, signaling them to continue with the entertainment, and with his left hand motioned for his serving boy to bring more quinsa.

Stepping from the table, the Dosedra began a circuit of the room, pausing at each table, starting across the room from the table at which she was seated. Each of the men nodded to him in respect, and she guessed they were introducing themselves or wishing him well, but rarely did any of the men display genuine joy in seeing him. In contrast, a number of the women, particularly but not exclusively the younger ones, smiled and blinked their eyes at him as he approached, vying for his attention without speaking directly to him.

After a few minutes it dawned on her that every action seemed scripted, each individual carefully enacting their role based on unspoken protocols. The only time there was any variance was when the Dosedra approached a few of the older men, who actually had short conversations with him, though the content of each chat was lost under the volume of the music.

Eventually the Dosedra approached their table. Arwyn squirmed a bit in anticipation; in response, her uncle placed a firm hand on her shoulder. Kate decided the girl was perhaps a little nervous, but primarily curious. As the Dosedra bowed to those at her table, Kate was surprised how ordinary he appeared. He might have been passably handsome as a youth, but years of life outdoors had left his face darkened and damaged, with the prominent scars and deep lines at the edges of his eyes.

He first recognized Tashin, offering him his hand without invitation.

"Welcome, Dosedra. You are well?" the grey-haired man muttered, his brief statement notable for its insincerity.

"Aye, Bhagal Tashin, I am indeed. I hope you are also in good health?" His tone and minimal inflection suggested that like Tashin's, his words were purely formulaic.

Tashin then nodded and gestured towards Arwyn. "You are acquainted with my sister's girl, Bhara Arwyn?"

The Dosedra nodded to the girl and then smiled, causing her to lower her head slightly, though Kate saw a slight hiccup in the girl's shoulders. It was obvious that the slight attention had pleased Arwyn, and this made Kate smirk. "You were much shorter the last time we met," he said to the girl with a wink, and that caused her to giggle. Then he raised his chin a bit as he addressed the man beside Kate. "Aldrish."

Rynar still sat with his arms crossed, something no other man in the room had dared. The other men had responded with appropriate deference, but not Kate's companion. "Dosedra," he replied smoothly, with an exaggerated nod of his head.

For a second the Dosedra's eyes snagged Kate's, but he did nothing to acknowledge her, and she realized he was doing nothing more than registering her presence and calculating whether she was worthy of his time. No one introduced her, and before she could summon up the courage herself, he moved on, nodding to two more men before stiffly stepping back to his brother's table.

As the Dosedra took his seat to the left of his brother, she wondered if others recognized the strained relationship between the two men. This was a royal celebration, a prince returning from war. Yet to her everything seemed 'off.' Although she already knew the Vosira was concerned about his brother's return, she had not expected that it would be so obvious. Then again, she sensed it was mutual. She watched as the Dosedra ignored the food and wine served to him, and instead sat with his arm propped up on the table and his chin resting on his hand, his eyes taking in the crowd before him.

The Bhavosa reached over to tug on her husband's sleeve, and he laughed, pushing back his chair. Then they slipped away from the table and into the center of the room to join the dancers. Yet the Dosedra remained seated. For someone who had returned home triumphantly, she thought he looked rather uncomfortable, and rather than enjoy himself, it seemed that he struggled to look amused and attentive to the conversations of those around him. No matter what he did, there was an air of sadness and uneasiness hovering over him. She could understand why the Vosira might be uncomfortable with his brother's return, but it seemed less clear why the Dosedra would share those sentiments. If he didn't want to be here, why had he returned at all?

She looked to Rynar for an explanation, but he had disappeared. Annoyed, she turned to Arwyn.

Her new acquaintance shared her observations. "He looks rather miserable, don't you think? I wonder why he's not happy to finally be home, after being gone for so many years."

Kate nodded, relieved to share this insight with her new friend. "Yeah, I heard about that, and I was thinking the same thing."

"Uncle, what's wrong with the Dosedra? This is his quantrill, after all. I heard he used to be a great dancer."

"Don't be rude," Tashin replied. "Anyway, he's entitled to do as he pleases, I suppose, even if it does make the Vosira look foolish. After all, Bedoric went to some considerable effort—and expense, I might add—to put together a quantrill in less than a day."

"But is he not glad to be home?" Arwyn asked. "I don't see why anyone would be unhappy to come home after spending years on a battlefield!"

"Aye, well, you're just a girl. You wouldn't understand such things. Really, Arwyn, you should mind your manners and not ask such impertinent questions."

Arwyn made her now-familiar pouty face and spun around to watch the increasing number of couples who had drifted into the center of the room to dance.

Again Tashin leaned closer to Kate, who wished he would likewise pay more attention to the dancing. "The girl does have a point, you know. After so much time, and after everything that he did, it is probably best that he not revel in it." He exhaled sharply, causing her to lean away as he spoke to her, a combination of annoyance that he shut down Arwyn's conversation only to try to prod her into discussing the same topic, and revulsion at his terrible breath. "Even when he was a boy I could see it in his attitude. I knew that one day he'd bring shame upon us all." He frowned and shook his head. "I can scarcely believe that a Sarducian prince would turn his back on his own men. I'd just as soon banish him permanently rather than pretend to celebrate false accomplishments. But what's done is done, I suppose."

When he finished his rant, Kate nodded politely, unsure what to say in response. Instead, she turned her attention back to the dance floor. As she watched, a blonde woman approached the Dosedra, leaning over the table as she spoke to him. As she watched, they engaged in a lively conversation for several minutes, and then he stepped around the table. Clearly not everyone was afraid of the returning prince.

"Oh look, he's going to dance," Arwyn exclaimed.

"Aye, it appears so. Girl, if you know what's good for you, you'll be out there shortly as well," Tashin chided her. "I see Charnok Ulnar watching you. It would not be good to keep him waiting on you."

She rolled her eyes. "Oh, very well, Uncle." As she sprung, quite unladylike, from her seat, Tashin leaned towards Kate again. "Ulnar has favored her all summer. She's getting quite old to still be unwed, so it would be best for her to make him happy."

Old? Could Arwyn even be sixteen? She shook her head and contemplated her goblet of quinsa.

***

A few minutes later, a hand on her shoulder made her jump.

"Shall we dance, Kate?" It was Aldrish Rynar. Giving her no chance to protest, he took her hand led her to the center of the room.

"Do not concern yourself with the steps," he suggested as they waited for the music to begin. "Just move as I do, and watch those around you." Still holding her hand, he turned to his left, and she to her right, so that they faced the same direction behind several other couples, and from there the dance moved them rapidly around the circumference of the room. Several times she had to circle around another dancer, including the attractive Pyrsac, who flashed her a wide smile, and once, Bhavosa Bryll, who gave her a friendly nod of approval.

"You are a quick learner," Rynar observed as they stood in place to repeat the first section of the dance. "I'm quite impressed."

"I've always liked dancing," she replied, smiling at the handsome man who took such an interest in her.

"Ah, I am pleased to hear it," he said, as the music ended. "Then I can convince you to try another?"

The next dance not only caused them to pass close by others on the floor, but forced them to change partners several times as they worked their way through a line of dancers, which by now included nearly every able-bodied man and woman at the quantrill. Following that one was a dance that brought the couples nose to nose a number of times, causing a lot of giggles throughout the crowd. For a fleeting moment, as she and Rynar spun around, she thought she spied the Dosedra looking in her direction, but she turned away too fast to be sure.

Several dances later, and slightly out of breath, they escaped the crowd, sitting at the edge of the room away from the musicians, where it was slightly easier to talk.

Rynar nodded to a servant who brought two goblets of quinsa. "This is better than enduring old Tashin, is it not?" he asked with a wink as he handed one of the goblets to her.

"He's not that bad, is he?" she lied out of politeness, but rolled her eyes with a smile.

That made him nod, with a quick grin. "It depends. As the Bhagali go, he is one of the most able men on the Council, though we don't always see eye-to-eye on political matters. As a dinner companion, however..." He didn't finish the comment, instead using that moment to sip his quinsa. "You deserve better, and I apologize for leaving you with him."

"So do you make it your job to rescue women from boring conversations?" she teased.

"Only the most interesting ones, my dear Kate." He tipped his head in the direction of the head table. "I see my Vosira continues to enjoy himself," he said sarcastically, referring to the way the man was lurching to one side, with a goblet in one hand and a pastry in the other. His dancing, she realized, had ended after the second tune, though his wife was still out on the floor. "I do not understand why he allows drink to cloud his mind and make him appear so foolish." He scanned the crowd, and added, almost too casually, "I wonder if his brother takes after him?"

"You don't know?"

"Ah, no, I know little about his habits, as I wasn't acquainted with him prior to his departure for Froida all those years ago." He finished his goblet and set it on the table behind him. "There will be plenty of opportunities to talk about this later. For now, how about another dance?"

***

"You're not welcome here."

The man's voice was loud and carried over the musicians and all of the conversations in the room, causing most people to stop and stare.

Kate and Rynar both craned their necks to see what was happening, though the rapidly gathering crowd blocked their view.

Apparently someone responded, for the first man continued. "I will not. I have every right to speak my mind."

There were more indiscernible accusations and responses, muffled by the numerous conversations of those in the crowd. Another man raised his voice above the din of the crowd, calling someone a coward, and everyone fell silent.

"Oh gods," Rynar mumbled under his breath. "Koldren, of all men. I do not believe it. Stay here," he cautioned her and then headed towards the disturbance.

Kate glanced to the head table, where, like everyone else, the Vosira was standing, trying to see what was happening. As she watched, he raised his hand towards the group of Senvosra soldiers at the door, suggesting they should not interfere.

Even so, the argument was escalating rapidly, as several others joined in, though she could only catch bits and pieces. One man shouted, "Everyone else sees it that way!" though there was no reference to what he referred to. By now the musicians had stopped playing, and nearly everyone in the hall had gathered around to witness the incident.

"That's a lie!" another man replied, though not as loudly. "That's not what happened. If you—"

That comment, whatever it meant, simply set off more shouting, now from a number of men in rapid succession. "When we go to war with Hansar, it will be on your shoulders!"

"Other men would have destroyed the rebels."

"Why are you here, and not any of your men?"

The accusations flew fast, and by now no one in the room—not even Kate—had any remaining doubts about the nature of the argument, or who was the object of the hostility. A group of Bhagali, clearly having had too much quinsa, had decided to speak their minds to the Dosedra. From what she had learned, the accusations seemed justified, though it seemed inappropriate to air their grievances at the very party celebrating the man's return. Then a thought occurred to her. What if Rynar, or the Vosira, expected this to happen? Had this been the plan all along?

There was no time to contemplate a conspiracy, as the argument continued to build.

"You live only because you abandoned your own men to the Froidans." It was a new voice. "You had no right to return here."

"And I swear to you that none of that's true!"

"Liar!" There was a sudden movement, and it looked as though someone swung a punch, which was met with an equal reaction. Only the swift movements of other men in the crowd were able to stop a full-fledged fight from erupting.

Rynar had been standing beyond the edge of the crowd observing, but now he slapped his hands together. "Men, stop this immediately!" He now worked his way to the middle of the crowd, and climbed up onto a bench. "The Dosedra had every right to return home. After the Council has had time to meet and discuss matters further, we will decide if any action needs to be taken. For now, we are celebrating his safe return, as the son of Vosira Parmon and brother to Vosira Bedoric. That is all that any of you need concern yourselves with tonight."

A woman called out from one of the tables. "Ask him if he'll accept the words of the Prophet."

"Aye. Aldrish," a man nearby agreed. "He must agree to follow the Prophet's teachings."

The crowd had dispersed slightly, perhaps because of Rynar's statement, or perhaps because they realized the Aldrish would not allow the argument to end in bloodshed. Turning to the man demanding his religious conversion, the Dosedra shook his head. "Nay, Bhagal Avir, I will do no such thing. I still believe in our gods, and the work of the Sarnoc, who strive to protect this land."

"Bah," Avir replied explosively. Pointing his finger at the Dosedra, he was undeterred. "What will you say about your gods and the Sarnoc when the Hansar navy lands on our shores and lays siege to Loraden?"

"Enough." Rynar had stepped down from the bench and now was pushing the men apart. "This is not the time or place for such a conversation. Avir, please return to your wife," he suggested, waving his hand to the rear of the room. "And Koldren? I know you're not fond of quinsa. Why don't you join me for some ale, at my table?"

CHAPTER 7

At the end of the evening, Kate was grateful for Rynar's offer to escort her to her room. Arwyn had been right—the quinsa was deceptively strong, and she felt rather dizzy. Walking down the hall was simple enough, but she stumbled a few times on the stairs. Why did the women have to wear these long dresses, anyway? They just made things more complicated. She expected she could revolutionize this world with a few pairs of blue jeans.

After she tripped on her hem the second time, Rynar offered her his arm for support. When they reached the landing to the second floor, he hesitated. Taking a step away, he observed her for a moment, more out of amusement than concern, as if trying to decide how much quinsa she had consumed. "You seem to have enjoyed yourself quite a bit this evening."

"Is that your way of saying I'm drunk?"

"Not at all. Still, I may be able to help with the dizziness, if you wish to accompany me back to my quarters for a moment."

In her intoxicated state, she found herself reading ulterior motives into his request, and she hesitated. Was he hitting on her? With a quick grin, she wondered if maybe Arwyn was wrong about him. "I'm not sure. I mean, I don't know you that well."

"My dear, if I understand your meaning, I wish nothing of the sort from you," he said, an amused look on his face. "Come, join me for a short while."

When they arrived at his quarters, the room was dark, but Rynar coaxed a fire from the coals, which this time had not gone cold, and then lit a couple of candles. From her chair, she noticed that he had taken the time to tidy up the piles of parchment and books on the table, and now a tray with a thin ceramic bottle and two small wooden cups took up much of the cleared space. Before speaking, he filled the two cups and brought one to her, and then pulled up a stool and sat facing her.

"What do you think of Loraden so far?"

She opened her mouth as if to answer, but then leaned back without responding. The question seemed too difficult in her current state of mind. Instead, she took a sip from her small cup. She expected wine, but this was different, like a tonic. It was bitter, but not at all unpleasant.

"I imagine it is much different here from what you're used to," he said, filling in the silence.

"Yeah, it is," she agreed, her words slurring a bit. Before she could offer more details, she felt the room starting to spin, and she closed her eyes.

"Drink up," he admonished her. "It will make you feel better."

"Why, what is it?" she asked, as she cradled the cup between her hands and looked inside at the pale yellow liquid.

"It's a tea made from the bark of arginon bushes," he said. "It's an old Sarnoc remedy for when you've had too much to drink."

"Oh." A magic potion? Whatever it was, her queasy stomach and achy head offered all the encouragement she needed. She tipped the cup back and drank the rest of it. Then she leaned her head back against the chair and took a deep breath.

Taking the cup from her, he set it on the stone hearth beside him. Then he got up and shuffled papers around, or at least that was what she heard, as she continued to sit quietly with her eyes closed. She was certain that if she opened her eyes she'd throw up.

A few minutes later she felt the warmth of his fingertips as he gently cradled her chin. "How do you feel now?"

She opened her eyes, and blinked a few times rapidly. The onset of a headache had been forestalled, and she realized she was no longer dizzy or queasy at all. "Wow, you know, I feel a lot better." She tipped her head from side to side, and rolled her shoulders. The soreness in her neck she attributed to her recent stress had abated as well. "That stuff worked really fast."

"Aye, it does." He pulled the stool closer, and sat down again. "Now. I need to explain some things." He leaned forward. "Tomorrow there will be a long Council meeting and I will not be available until late in the day. If I had a choice, I'd prefer to spend the day with you. But with the Dosedra's return, and that incident at the quantrill in particular, I expect it will be a long day."

"Why?"

He tilted his head forward slightly. "Why—what?"

Boldly, she asked, "I mean, why would you rather spend the day with me? You don't know anything about me."

He seemed taken aback by the question. "You're my guest, and new to Loraden. Surely you'd like someone to show you around the city proper."

"Of course I would, but why would you take the time, given your position and all? I guess what I'm asking is, why are you so interested in me?"

"Ah. My dear, you traveled from quite a different place to be here. I simply wish to learn more about you, and help you acclimate to our customs. Unfortunately, so much has happened all at once, with your arrival and now the Dosedra's, and I cannot afford you the attention your visit deserves." He leaned forward and stirred the fire. "I'm certain you have many more questions, but they will have to wait until I deal with the other matters."

Although she was still a bit suspicious of his motives, on the surface his explanation made sense, so she decided not to press further. Instead, she asked, "do you really think the Dosedra is dangerous? From what I could see, he's rather unpopular. It didn't seem like he was looking for trouble as much as everyone else was. So maybe he's not the threat you expected him to be?"

He leaned back and squared his shoulders. "Aye, it seemed much the same to me, but the sons of Parmon should never be underestimated. It will be interesting to hear his own version of what happened in Froida, and where he's been all these years."

She yawned. Rynar took that as a signal and stood up, dusting a bit of fireplace ash from his tights. "My dear Kate, it's late, and you must be exhausted after such a busy day. It was selfish of me to keep you awake with this conversation."

"I'm not that tired," she said with a grin, though she had to admit to herself that it was becoming difficult to keep her eyes open.

"Aye, you are." He stood up and offered her his hand. "Come with me." He led her into the adjoining room, where a large bed took up the wall across from the fire. "Why don't you sleep here tonight? It's warm, and I'll be close by in case you need anything."

Sleep… here? Was he propositioning her after all? "And you?"

"Don't worry about me, my dear. I have a bit of work still to do, so go ahead and make yourself comfortable." He reached inside a wardrobe. "I have extra blankets," he said, and to demonstrate tossed a couple of blankets to the stone floor. "I'll make myself comfortable out there."

"You mean, on the floor? No, that's silly. I don't want to take your bed." Confused, and perhaps a little disappointed, she half-heartedly offered, "I can return to my own room."

"If you prefer. I shall be working either way." He scooped up his blankets and returned to the other room, where he pulled out a chair at the table.

She turned in his direction, and then back to the bed, which, piled as it was with pillows, looked far more inviting than the simple mattress in her own room. She was absolutely exhausted from this long, confusing day, and she didn't think she could manage a hike back to her own room, so she took him up on the offer.

CHAPTER 8

They could hear his voice a block away.

Standing atop a large wooden crate was a stick-figure of a man shouting out to the crowd. "We must root out the evil within our midst!" He bellowed in a surprisingly deep voice as he gestured with his arm around the square. "It is all around us, and we must learn to recognize it and banish it from our lives!"

***

That morning, she had awoken to an empty room. Wearing only her linen shift, she wrapped a blanket around her shoulders and stepped to the outer chamber. It didn't take long to notice that not only had Rynar already left for the council meeting, there was no evidence that he had ever even slept in his quarters.

Uncertain what to do with herself, she had helped herself to some grapes on a tray and then stepped over to the scattered papers and books on the table. There was a wide sheet of parchment spread out in the center, with small handwriting covering the top half, and a broken goose quill caked with dried ink off to one side.

It looked as though he had been in the middle of writing something but then had left in a hurry.

The script was difficult to read, but remarkably, the words themselves were not foreign to her. From the few words she could make out, it appeared to be a brief recounting of the Dosedra's return. Rubbing her chin absently, she wondered if the account was really worth staying up all night to compose.

It was then she noticed the first dress she had worn was laid out across a chair, and she quickly slipped it back on, grateful for the feel of the soft wool against her skin. Once properly attired, she turned back to the tray of food and procured a hunk of bread, scooping a dollop of the soft butter to spread on it.

Walking over to the window, she opened the shutter and gazed down into the courtyard, where a dozen soldiers engaged in training exercises. Even from the fourth floor she could easily hear the men shouting, the clang of metal against metal, and the thud as swords hit shields. The activity was more than likely a routine, mundane element of life here, but to her it was unexpected and exciting.

Even after all she had seen so far, Kate still hadn't come to terms with where she was, or how she had arrived here. No longer did she think it was a pretend world created by her family, yet at the same time, how could it be real? She wasn't enamored by the garderobes that served as toilets, with the wooden bench with a hole cut out offering a significant challenge to someone wearing a long dress. With the windows shuttered, most rooms were dark, smoky and a bit stuffy from all of the candles and torches, and she wondered why none had glass. If this was a dream, why invent such details? In many ways she felt trapped, and although the adventure was intriguing, with so many unanswered questions, it also remained rather intimidating.

She was occupied with these thoughts, and absent-mindedly nibbling on the bread, when Rynar charged into the room.

As he rushed past her to reach a large wooden chest, she had to jump backwards to avoid him knocking her over. "What's going on?"

"We must go into the city," he announced, and retrieved his scabbard and belt. He waved for her follow him as he went into the main room, hurriedly buckling the sword around his waist. "I need you to get ready as quickly as possible."

Sensing the urgency of his request, she slipped her feet into her leather slippers. "Is something wrong?" she asked as she tied them at her ankles.

"Aye." He glanced over to the table, and slid the document he had been writing under others. "The Dosedra left the city before daybreak, and has not returned to attend the Council meeting."

"What does that mean?"

He stared down his nose at her, just as a teacher might do to a recalcitrant student. "Surely it is not that hard to understand?" he replied curtly, stepping already to the door and waving over his shoulder for her to follow him. "He's up to something. Let's go."

***

Now they were in the city beyond the walls of the keep, and she was staring as the man standing atop the crate drew a crowd around him.

With silent determination, Rynar grabbed Kate's hand slowly and led her through the press of the gathering crowd in the open-air marketplace. They passed rows of wooden stalls filled with various goods for sale: vegetables at one table, cheese and bread at others. There was a man who had metal trinkets spread out on blankets and hanging from crossed poles, and another who had burlap sacks filled with beans and grain. Waiting for an opening in the crowed, they were forced to pause momentarily beside a table with trays of glassy-eyed fish that stared blankly at the spectacle in the square, the blood of their predecessors creeping like rust across the wooden facades of the market stalls, and fish guts pooling in the street.

Meanwhile the man continued his preaching. He was dressed in old clothing with frayed edges, his shirt sewn from a roughly woven cloth, and hanging loosely from his shoulders. In this regard his attire was not dissimilar from many in the crowd, which was a mix of merchants, townspeople and farmers. Unlike the others in the square, the man's head was shrouded in a heavy black hood that hid everything except his large roman nose that protruded from the hood like a shark fin.

"Every day they turn a blind eye to our troubles," he called out to the group of people who congregated around him, his tone one of anger and accusation. "Just yesterday Abelin's wines turned to vinegar, and this morning Jalyk reported sheep dropping dead on the hillside, and I need not remind everyone about our broken mill wheel. But have the Sarnoc done anything to help us? Do they help us feed our families or ensure the harvest comes in?"

In response, one of the men in the crowd, an elderly man wrapped in a woolen cape and supporting his weight with a wooden staff, managed to find the strength to make a fist with his free hand, and now was shaking it over his head. "Nay, brother, they ignore us!"

"Aye, of course they do. When was the last time the Sarnoc and their healers came to Loraden to tend to the sick and help the poor? Do you remember, good mistress?" he asked, and pointed to a girl with a brown scarf wrapped over her head who clutched a linen sack against her chest. She quickly averted her eyes, but shook her head all the same.

"You see? It is as I tell you. They have abandoned us, just as their gods did long ago."

"It isn't true!" This came from a red-faced woman standing beside a towering pile of salt-stained wooden crates, a large silvery fish cradled in her arms like a baby. "It wasn't their fault they had to leave us. It was the Vosira's doing."

"Aha! So the Sarnoc have a defender in our midst?"

"Aye, and another," a burly man called out from the perimeter. He held a pitchfork in his calloused hand, and his face was streaked from perspiration. "Mavano, I'm tired of hearing this drivel every day. Good men and women are here to do business and feed their families. You need to stop this nonsense and leave us alone."

"What, have you joined the ranks of the Senvosra now?" Mavano asked, followed by the crowd's knowing laughter. "Good people, do you hear this? I speak the truth—the very truth your Vosira and his Council have proclaimed by exiling the Sarnoc—and yet after all this time some people still wish to see me cast aside!" The hooded man pointed to his heckler. "You're a fool if you still believe they want to help us!" This was met with a chorus of whistles and shouts, and feeding off the energy of the crowd, Mavano continued, "no matter what a few misguided folks say, we all know the truth. The Sarnocs' time has passed. You must see the truth in what I say!"

"Mavano," the man with the pitchfork called out again. "You know where I stand on this. You need to stop all this nonsense and go home."

"Or what? Again, will you call the Senvosra to haul me off? Or do you plan to do it yourself?" The crowd erupted in boos. "You see? The people of Loraden are sending a message to the Sarnoc. We don't want them back in our lives, ordering us around, telling us who we can marry, which crops the farmers must plant, and how much cream to churn into butter. Most of all we do not want them telling us which gods to worship, or how to do so."

Rynar had managed to squeeze in beside Kate, and Mavano noticed him. "My friends, look here! If my eyes do not deceive me, it is the Aldrish himself, joining us." He pointed in their direction, and shouted out, "Aldrish, you agree with what I say, do you not?"

As if Mavano's words were inconsequential, Rynar waved him off, and redoubled his efforts to push through the crowd. "Come on," he whispered to her, "these crowds often get unruly, and we should not be caught in the middle. And I have no desire to engage that madman."

The preacher wasn't going to let him escape so easily, however. "Join me, Aldrish, and tell these good people how you came to accept the teachings of the Prophet. Coming from such a man as yourself, how can anyone deny the truth of your words?"

"Nay, not today. I am on important business." He tugged on Kate's hand.

In response, the man on the crate laughed, shaking his platform so hard she was sure it would come apart. "Aldrish, you of all people cannot spare a few moments to tell these people the truth of the prophet's teachings? How he has predicted all the evils that we face today? How he alone has recognized the dangers we face? Surely nothing can be more important than that!"

"It seems you are doing well enough on your own," Rynar replied sourly. "Let us be."

Some people snickered, and another man called out, "you do not need the Aldrish to help you make dire projections for our future, do you, Mavano?" The heckler stood on the periphery, where he would not be trapped by surging bodies. Seemingly aware of this, he turned to yell to the crowd, "your prophet is a fraud."

These comments led to a spurt of shouts and jeers, as the man must have expected, and then a scuffle broke out behind Kate and Rynar.

"Just as I feared. We must hurry," Rynar warned her as he turned to push his shoulder past a fat woman with greasy hair and two young children clinging to her skirts. "People have been injured here in the past."

Newly sensitive to the volatile situation, she willingly followed Rynar's lead as he shouldered his way through the rest of the crowd. She could not avoid witnessing the rest of the interaction, however, for the crowd was now too large for them to traverse the square easily.

"Good man," Mavano had turned his attention to the new heckler, and shouted out from his perch, "you are wrong. The Prophet is the only truth, and only he can free us from Sarnoc lies."

With these words many in the crowd—by Kate's quick estimates, easily over two hundred people—cheered loudly, though quite a few also shouted insults back at him.

"The Prophet will protect us." It was an elderly man talking to his wife. Another woman around Kate's age, in a well-worn linen dress with a shawl tied around her shoulders, cupped her hands over her mouth and shouted, "down with the Sarnoc!" which started a matching chant from the people closest to her.

As the chants grew in intensity, Rynar and Kate were able to escape the square by heading up a narrow alley. They passed by rows of stone houses, many of which leaned precariously in one direction or another. She longed for a camera to capture the image of the comical structures. In the streets, dogs and cats hunted for garbage, and they passed horse and donkey carts, goats tied to posts, and even a pair of chickens that darted across their path. There were water troughs, crates filled with hay, and piles of excrement, and in a couple of places, foul water streamed down the road like an open sewer. This might be an interesting place, but it wasn't particularly pleasant.

When she least expected it, the maze of dark streets and alleys opened up, and a wide river stretched out in front of them, its banks shored up with high walls of the same grey stone from which the keep had been built. Stretching across was a wooden footbridge with carved railings, and beside the bridge was a series of steps that led down to the quay.

Upstream from where they stood, Kate could see the city walls in the distance, and in the other direction, a short ways downstream, was the keep itself, with the river flowing into a tunnel underneath.

"The keep is built over the river?" she asked as she stared at the remarkable sight.

"Aye. There are several wells to pull water straight from the river. It is quite efficient, and it guarantees fresh water should we ever be forced to defend the keep from an invading force."

Taking her hand, he led her down to the quay below. Tethered to posts were a series of wooden boats, much like Venetian gondolas but twice as wide. They all were unpainted, but polished, with a platform raised in the front and a covered seating area.

"What's going on?" she asked as Rynar waved for her to take a seat on a bench in the middle of one of the boats. "Where are we going?"

The Aldrish nodded to a fair-haired young man who stepped onto the boat. "I need you to transport Bhara Kate upriver." Then he explained to her, "I need to send you out of the city. You will be safe with my aunt in Terralin."

"What?" His statement unleashed a flood of emotions. Anger. Fear. And inexplicably, failure. "You're sending me away?" The sudden displacement was almost as disconcerting as her initial arrival, and she jumped back to her feet, causing the boat to wobble on the water. "Just like that?"

"Aye, my dear," he said with a fleeting smile. He seemed nervous, clenching his hands into fists several times. "I have no choice. It is for your safety."

"Yeah, I heard you. I don't understand. Why wouldn't I be safe with you? Who would want to hurt me, anyway?"

He furtively glanced over his shoulder, as if expecting someone to be standing behind him. "I give you my word that it was not my intention to do this, but I had no choice. You must go with the riversmith, who will see to your needs now."

As if on cue, the man on the boat introduced himself. "I am Davor," he said, with a bow of his head. He was younger than her, tall and lanky, with his tanned forearms sticking out of rolled-up sleeves. "You will be safe aboard my craft."

"No, that's not right." The sudden announcement still shocked her, and she wasn't willing to capitulate. The last thing she wanted to do was be shipped off to the middle of nowhere. "I don't want to leave."

The wind whipped at Rynar's shirt and hair as he nodded once. "While that may be what you desire, your fate is elsewhere." Again, he glanced over his shoulder, and his hair blew in his eyes. "Don't worry. I will see you soon." Without further delay he spun on the heel of his boot and headed back into the maze of alleyways.

As she stared at his retreating figure with her mouth open, the river craft quickly pulled away from the dock, giving her no options other than to fall back onto the bench and settle in for the journey.

CHAPTER 9

Considerably lower than the streets on either side, the view from the river offered little opportunity to sightsee as they slipped through the city, but that mattered little to Kate, who sat on the bench with her arms crossed, silently fuming.

She knew she had no right to expect anything of her new acquaintances. After all, she had appeared in this strange land without explanation or means to care for herself. Without money—without even as much as a change of clothing—she was entirely at the mercy of those who wished to assist her. Logically, she accepted this, and felt gratitude to Rynar and Lillia in particular for caring for her over the past day.

At the same time, she bristled whenever someone else, particularly a man, made decisions on her behalf. Growing up as the only child of a single mom, she had learned self-reliance and independence early on, and sometimes her willingness to challenge authority got her into trouble.

And right now, she was angry, and stubbornly didn't want to do what she was told.

"Davor," she began, seeing that they were about to approach another wharf, "let me off up ahead."

He replied without turning around. "Bhara, I wish I could comply, but the Aldrish commanded me to take you out of the city. I dare not question his orders."

"What if I jumped out?"

Davor plunged the pole down deeper, and the craft slowed. Turning to face her, he said, "Bhara, please do not make this difficult for me. I am obliged to see you safely beyond the city walls."

He didn't say whether he would stop her from jumping or not, however, and this omission made her wonder what would happen if she tried. "Did you know about this ahead of time?"

"Know about what?"

"Rynar's plan to send me away."

The young man looked startled. "Why would the Aldrish discuss his plans with me? I am a riversmith, nothing more."

She frowned. "So you don't know what's going on, then?"

He took a moment to watch her before responding. "Nay, I know nothing more than you. However, if the Aldrish believes you to be in danger, then it is worth listening to his counsel. He is not known to be careless in his actions. For him to escort you to the wharf personally must mean it was a matter of great importance to him. And, if it helps any, you truly are safe here on the river, so you should relax. We have a long journey ahead, and there's no point in fretting the entire way."

Kate gnawed on her thumbnail, trying to figure out what to do. She had no idea what Rynar had planned for her, and although his rapid disposal of her onto this boat felt initially like a rejection, she knew it had to be more complicated than that. Things were happening in this strange place that she had no context to understand. All she could go on was that, so far, the odd man had shown no inclination to harm her. Wherever she was headed, whatever this Terralin place was, surely it was no worse than throwing herself into the river. She needed to keep her wits about her and do what she needed to do to survive until she either got some answers or found her way back home. Reluctantly she decided it was worth going along for the ride, so to speak, and see what came of it.

At about the time she came to this conclusion, they slipped through the river gate in the outer city wall.

"This is the main channel of the Amberia River," he explained. "From here, the river will become much wider, and no one on the banks will be able to harm us."

She nodded, and watched how Davor stood on the boat's bow, with his legs slightly parted for balance, his shirt sleeves rolled up past his elbows. He looked like Tom Sawyer, minus the straw hat. He held a thin silver-tipped wooden pole upright in the water to steer the craft, and as they continued upstream, she could see no form of propulsion, despite the small boat slicing through the swift current as if it offered no resistance at all.

"To your left is Monmora Hill," he said, gazing towards a steep rocky outcropping. It was quite high, the summit hidden by clouds, and its base grew right out of the river bank and seemed to stretch for miles into the distance.

"If that's just a hill, I'd hate to see what you call a mountain."

"Ah, well, the Carpasic Mountains are just beyond Monmora." He raised one arm to point off in the distance. "You can see the faintest outlines of them at the horizon."

She cupped her hand over her eyes and gazed in the direction he indicated, and could indeed see a mountain range poking through the clouds. "How far away are they?"

"I know not, Bhara. I have never gone beyond Loraden, other than along the river."

**

Not long after they had passed Monmora, they entered a dense forest, with huge old-growth trees looming over them. Here sunlight barely poked through the thick growth of trees that stretched their limbs, like arms, overhead.

"We are now officially within the Arsdala," he announced. "The forest stretches down the very center of the island, and we will remain within the forest the entire way until we reach Terralin." With one hand remaining on the pole he had been using to steer the craft, he crouched down to reach a flask carefully stashed under a ledge, and after uncorking it with his teeth, took a deep swallow of its contents. "Most people call the forest Lockleaf, though. It's common knowledge that if you wander into the forest un-welcomed and unprepared, you'll never find your way back out. The trees lock all trespassers within their grasp. Only a lucky few are ever able to leave again."

"That's a great story." She gave an uneasy laugh. "Of course, the trees don't really lock anyone inside..." She hesitated when she saw the serious look in his eyes. "You're joking, right?"

He shook his head. "It's an ancient forest, Bhara, and very dangerous for travelers."

"But if it's as large as you say—surely people would have to travel through it sometimes?"

The riversmith looked thoughtful. "Aye, there are a couple roads that run through the forest, and a few villages along those roads. I stay on the river, so I wouldn't know those routes personally. Except for those who live here, most people avoid the roads, because the fhaoli are notorious."

"Fhaoli?" she repeated, stumbling over the odd term.

"Outlaws." Davor shifted his weight to steer the boat around a rock. As if for her benefit alone, he quickly added, "we are safe here. The only way to avoid them is to travel by river, because even the fhaoli won't attack riversmiths."

"Well, that's a relief then," she said, not really meaning it. His words caused her to feel anxious, even a little trapped. "I could see why outlaws would make the forest dangerous. Though it still sounds like you're saying that the forest is magical or something."

He dipped the pole a bit deeper. "Perhaps it is, in its own way, just as all of nature is magic. But if you expected me to say there was some sort of spell on the trees, then nay, there is none that I know of."

"I'm glad to hear that. You know, I've been expecting you to tell me that you've been using magic to power this boat, because it looks like you're hardly doing anything!"

In response, Davor frowned, and abruptly steered the raft to the bank, allowing it to crunch to a halt on a narrow shelf of gravel. "Did you think this easy for me, Bhara?" he snapped.

She hadn't meant to insult him. "I'm sorry—I didn't mean anything by that. It's just that we're making good progress against the current, without you as much as breaking a sweat."

"Aye, but it's not magic." He lifted his pole from the water and held it up so she could examine its tip. "Glysar," he said, pointing to the silver metal, "allows this to work. Although I need not paddle, the effort drains me all the same. Indeed, nothing comes freely, Bhara. Only with intensive Sarnoc training was I able to learn how to transfer my energy directly to the kelash pole."

"That's impossible—" she began, and then thought better of it. Her being here at all was impossible; everything else seemed to pale in comparison with that primary fact.

In response to her exclamation, he shrugged, and pushed the boat back into the river. "Watch, and decide for yourself." As a demonstration, he didn't immediately send the pole into the water as he had been doing, and as a result, the craft began to drift rapidly back downstream, spinning almost out of control. She gasped, grabbing hold of the bench. Quickly Davor closed his eyes and dropped the pole, silver tip first, into the river, and with no other show of physical exertion, suddenly it was as before, a straight course, smooth, and to her perspective, effortless.

"It *is* magic." She surprised herself at her willingness to accept the reality of what she experienced.

"I suppose it's all a matter of perspective," Davor conceded as he dropped the tip back into the river, and their boat again began to move. "To me, there's magic in musicians' songs and in the birth of babies. I just don't think of what I do in the same way."

***

"Is that another boat?" she asked, seeing something in the water a distance ahead of them. It was difficult to make it out in the twilight.

They had been on the river all day, and after the previous day's adventures, she discovered the few hours' sleep she had received the night before had not been nearly enough. At Davor's urging, and possibly thanks to the wine he had encouraged her to drink, she had curled up on the wide bench and fallen asleep for the better part of the day.

Now it was nearly sunset, and another boat was approaching them rapidly.

"Aye, it is indeed," Davor said. "And it's odd—there is a waypoint ahead." He leaned forward, as if it would help give him a better view of the distant craft. "Riversmiths do not travel at night, and at this time of day there should be no others traveling downstream in this stretch of the river." He raised one hand over his eyes and strained to see upstream. "It makes no sense." Rather than propel them forward, he held them steady, allowing the pole to remain in the water so they did not veer off course or crash into the banks, which were steep rock walls. If there were to be an ambush, there would be no better place for it.

She recalled the urgency with which Rynar had sent her from the city. "Do you really think we're safe here?"

"Aye. There's no one in Sarducia that would threaten a riversmith. But it's odd all the same," he added, never taking his eyes away from the approaching craft. He continued to stare at the oncoming boat. As it drew closer, he began to laugh heartily. "Ah, Bhara, there is no need to fear. It's the Pasadhi!"

Not knowing what that meant, she looked ahead to see a man dressed in a green tunic steering a craft identical to the one Davor commanded. He quickly brought it alongside theirs.

"Well met, Pasadhi Sebachin," Davor called out. "A bit late to be on this stretch of the Amberia, is it not?"

"Aye, that it is. It's a good thing that I do not require daylight to ride the river," the other man said, and then turned his attention to her. "Welcome, Kate."

When he addressed her by name, she became immediately suspicious. "How do you know who I am?"

"Your arrival was hardly a surprise," he said, and recognizing her confusion, added, "the Sarnoc sent me to bring you the rest of the way to Altopon."

As she tried to make sense of that statement, something even more unlikely happened: the river suddenly stopped flowing. It was as if it had frozen solid, with the boats locked in place. Dumbfounded, she looked over the side of the boat.

"You might close your mouth, Kate, before something flies in," Pasadhi Sebachin joked.

"Wait. What just happened?" She couldn't stop staring at the water. It was troubling enough to have this man appear out of nowhere, but what was going on with the river?

"Ah, don't worry, it's just a small trick." Sebachin held out his hand to her. "Truly, it's nothing to worry about, but come now, the Sarnoc will skin me alive if you're not there by sunrise. Hurry, so Davor can get some sleep."

What was she supposed to do now? Should she go with his man? Would she be in danger? Could she be punished in some way for disobeying the Aldrish? Or was this the plan all along? She was angry that Rynar had shared so little information that she was incapable of even weighing the pros and cons sufficiently.

Follow your gut, she told herself. For twenty-seven years she had survived following her instincts. And right now her gut—and Davor's reaction—suggested that this friendly man in green presented no threat.

Grasping Sebachin's hand, she allowed him to help her climb from one craft to the other. Once she had taken her seat on a pile of pillows in the middle of the new boat—this one had no bench—the water returned to normal, and Sebachin tossed a sack towards the riversmith.

"Your services are greatly appreciated, Davor. If you check, there's some fresh food for your return, and a bit of extra coin for your trouble."

Davor caught the bag easily and peered inside. "Ha! The cakes are still warm! Do the Sarnoc know how you spoil us?"

"It's our secret," Sebachin said with a chuckle. "Good eve to you Davor, and send my greetings to your sisters." Then they spun around and returned to the course she had been traveling with the riversmith.

Kate turned and waved to Davor as she and this odd man in green floated in the opposite direction.

CHAPTER 10

"Where was he supposed to take you?"

She was still a bit taken aback by this stranger's sudden appearance, and found it hard to answer. Finally, she said, "some place called Terralin, I think."

"Really?" He seemed surprised. "That's a pretty small village. Why there?"

"Aldrish Rynar thought I'd be safe there, I guess. He mentioned his aunt lived there."

"Interesting. Well, he must have had his reasons."

"I suppose, but he didn't tell me much of anything. I guess you're not taking me there, then?"

He laughed. "Hardly. I have a different destination for you."

"Really? Where are we going now?"

"We're going to Altopon, the Sarnoc city."

"Are you sure? I don't know if Rynar—"

"Never mind him. You're in good hands now." He smiled and pointed to a basket beside the bench. "We'll be on the river through the night. There's food, if you're hungry. And plenty to drink."

She eyed the basket but shook her head. "No, I'd rather you tell me who you are."

He responded easily. "That's simple enough. I'm Pasadhi Sebachin. You need never use my title, though. Outside of formal occasions I prefer people to call me Sebachin—or even, just Seb."

"So you're one of these Sarnoc I keep hearing about, then?"

"Nay, I am Pasadhi." He shifted his weight between his feet, and tipped the pole slightly away from him. "Why don't you pour us a drink, and I will explain what that is."

Resigned to her situation, she reached into the basket and fished out a stout ceramic jug. From it, she filled two wooden cups. After handing one to him, she took a sip and smiled. "Mmm, it's water, plain water." She drained her cup and quickly refilled it. "I was beginning to think my choices were wine, ale, or wine. I figured if I stayed there long enough, I'd die of dehydration."

He grinned. "Outside of the city, our water is pure, and plentiful, and people take great care to store it in clean casks. It was once that way in Loraden as well, but Sard habits are ingrained, and they are not always so..." he looked at her and winked. "As they would say in your world, 'sanitary'."

She looked at him oddly, and laughed. "That sounds about right."

"Good, so you do have a sense of humor. I am happy to see it. It would be much harder for you if you didn't, you know." His green eyes sparkled as he talked. "I have reason to believe that you're also strong-willed, which will aid you a great deal."

"Really? Why's that?"

"Our world is very different from yours, as you have already discovered. It takes a lot of courage to stand up for yourself and find your way, but it seems like you'll be able to handle it." He looked at her closely, squinting for a moment, and then smiled. "Even so, I sense that the transition has been difficult for you. It often is, between worlds so unalike as yours and ours."

Her eyes opened wide, and she sat back, as if to better see him. "So you know about my world? Do you know how I ended up here, in Sarducia?"

"Kate, I am Pasadhi." He stared at her without blinking. "I know quite a bit about it."

"Oh, really?" She released sigh, relieved that finally she might get some answers. "I figured someone had to know something. So—what's going on? Is this all for real?"

"Ah, well..." He sipped from his cup as he held the pole one-handed. He paused. "It's real enough, but I can't say much more than that."

"What? Why not?"

"Ah, well..." he seemed a bit uncomfortable, and shrugged one shoulder, as if a bug was crawling down his back. "You see, I agreed not to say anything on this topic before we reached Altopon." Seeing her about to protest, he quickly added, "It's not that I'm trying to keep any information from you, I promise you that. It's simply that the Sarnoc asked me not to discuss it until we can assure our privacy and your safety."

"Wait. I thought you said I'd be safe with you. Are you suggesting we're in some sort of danger here?"

"Nay, I didn't say that. This just isn't the time or place for that conversation."

Exasperated, she threw up her arms and made a frustrated sound in her throat. "Are you kidding me? You know how I ended up here, but you're not going to tell me anything?"

He nodded. "Aye, for now. I'm truly sorry." He had a pained expression, as if he wanted to say more. "To be honest, I don't wish to keep this information from you. I'm simply asking you to wait a little longer. I know it must be frustrating for you, because it is for me as well, but I did give my word."

She dropped her arms to the pillows. "Fine." She glanced out onto the water, and then turned back to him. "Do you promise we'll get to talk about this later?" Seeing his nod, she continued, "can I ask you other stuff?"

"Sure. Like what?"

"Well, who are you, exactly? Do you work for the Sarnoc?"

He threw back his head and laughed. *That's* funny." He continued to giggle for a moment, and finally said, "we Pasadhi work for no one."

She tried to process what he said, but it made no sense to her. "So who are you then? What's a Pasadhi?"

He calmed himself after his fit of laughter, and finally continued. "Well, as best as I can describe it, I serve the Goddess Kerthal."

The gods again. "Don't the Sarnoc serve her as well?"

"Aye, but they serve all the gods in a general way, much the same as everyone does, but with a focus that defines their particular roles. I'm different, more of a personal servant, a direct link between the Goddess and the people of Sarducia."

She scrambled to put it into terms she could understand. "So you're like a priest, then?"

He thought about it for a moment. "As far as I know what you mean by that, then I suppose it's a reasonable analogy to a point, but it's not quite the same either."

"So there are others like you?"

He shook his head. "No, I am Pasadhi. There is only one."

"You said, 'we' a minute ago."

"I did. All Pasadhi of the past are linked with me through the energy within the land, and all the knowledge is shared through that connection." He steered the craft around a tree limb that had fallen into the water. "I just draw on my own inner awareness to tap into the knowledge."

That was a lot to take in, but she kept pressing for more. "So there's one of you, but there are four gods, right? So if you serve Kerthal, then there are there others like you, to serve the other gods?"

He shook his head. "Although it seems odd to me, there are not. Perhaps it's because in many ways I serve all the gods, but Kerthal in particular. Or perhaps there are those like me elsewhere, in the lands that are protected by the other gods. This I do not know."

"I still don't understand how you're different from the Sarnoc—not that I really know anything about them, really."

"Ah, well, I'd wager that you already know considerably more than most people." He reached for his cup. "Even though the skills have eroded over the centuries, they are quite powerful, more than most people even imagine. If some people in Loraden knew the extent of it..." he whistled, shaking his head.

"Some people? Do you mean Vosira Bedoric?"

"Hmm. Well, he knows a great deal about the Sarnoc, and I think it's for that reason that he distrusts them so greatly. That, and he blames them for his father's death, which is likely why he promotes the nonsense about the Prophet." He rolled his eyes and again shook his head.

"Foolish, foolish man. He should know better." He looked at her carefully. "You will not tell him what you learn at Altopon, I expect."

It was neither a question nor a request, but a statement of fact. Kate's mouth opened to respond, but she wasn't sure what to say.

"You are honorable," he explained. "I can see it in your eyes." He drained his cup. "Are you sure you're not hungry?"

She hadn't been thinking about food, distracted by everything that had happened since leaving Loraden, but at his question, she realized she had not eaten in many hours. "Maybe a little?"

He waved to her to open the basket. The moonlight was just enough for her to inspect its contents. There was a loaf of dark, grainy bread, a small ceramic crock of butter, a sizable block of pale cheese, and purple berries nestled in a smaller, tightly woven basket. "Eat as much as you wish," he invited, reaching down for a couple of berries. "I'm not terribly hungry." She gave him an 'are you sure' look, but he waved at the food. "Please, help yourself. While you eat, let me know if there's anything else you wish me to explain."

As she tore off a piece of bread, she reminded him, "you haven't really told me what the Pasadhi actually is."

"Did I not?" He snorted a laugh. "Sarnoc Vaj tells me I tend to get off topic." He put his fingers over his mouth, and tapped it, thinking. "It's difficult to explain, especially to someone who hasn't met Sarnoc yet. Hmm. Well, I don't have what I'd call 'skills' that I learn and practice as Sarnoc do, but I have this innate control over the elements. So I can do things like this." He leaned over towards the water, and it started swirling at the base of the pole, like a whirlpool, and the raft began to spin with it. As they made a complete 360-degree circle, he brought the craft back to its original route. "I can't drown, although I had more than one chance as a child before I actually learned how to swim. Fire can't burn me, and the weather is little more than is a bit of air and water to command."

"How's that possible? How can you not drown?"

He shrugged. "I suppose if I wanted to, I could. It's just that I'd force the water away from me before that could happen. Anyway, it's just who I am. I call on the life-force of the land, and the energy within the elements, and I make things happen."

"That's amazing." And Davor said there was no magic.

"Not particularly. Really, it's simply different. And I should also point out that although I live among the Sarnoc, I am not one of them. I suspect Sarnoc Vaj desperately wants me to adopt Sarnoc discipline and be more like the others, but it's not in my nature. I can do things better if I don't think too hard about what I'm doing. When I really concentrate and focus, like they recommend, I don't always get the right results. And yet, being Pasadhi is still quite daunting, since the Sarnoc come to me with questions. Even though I can't do many of the things that they can, I'm the one who understands how those things are done. I can also sense underlying truths about items, and about people. The contradiction is quite perplexing."

"Have you always been Pasadhi?"

"Nay, it's only been three summers now." He ran one hand through his curly hair, pushing it behind his ears. "Though from the time I was small, I always knew there was something different about me. I was always sensitive to everything, such as being able to feel things in rocks, plants, even the river. I knew when someone came to our village to cheat us, and I could tell which husbands were cruel to their wives. It all seemed so normal for me, but no one else shared those senses, so I tended to keep to myself. My mother didn't know what to do with me, because I would just wander off into the woods for days on end, rather than do my chores. No one expected that I'd have a vision of Kerthal, and then be named Pasadhi. They all just thought I was lazy. You see, there had been no Pasadhi in Sarducia for many seasons, and no one knew what the signs of the new one would look like." He smiled again. "It's nice to be able to talk about this with someone other than Sarnoc. You seem to be genuinely interested."

"Well, it's fascinating, even if I'm not sure I understand half of what you told me. And to be honest, it all sounds a little weird. I mean, you can control the elements? That's really hard to take in." She tipped her head back and gazed up at the moon and the stars that shone so brightly here without the fog of electric lights. "It's like so much other stuff here, I just don't even know where to begin to figure it all out."

"You'll understand it soon enough," he predicted. "Give it some time."

"Maybe. Can I ask you something else?"

He shrugged. "Sure."

"Well, I was wondering if you knew the Aldrish."

The question seemed to surprise him. "Aldrish Rynar? Nay, I have never met the man. I hear the Vosira relies heavily on his guidance, though."

She thought back to the breakfast meeting. "Yeah, that seemed to be the case."

"Why do you ask?"

"Well, when I arrived, he acted like he knew who I was, and made such a big deal out of me being there."

"He treated you well, I assume?"

She nodded, and tried one of the berries, which although round, tasted like a very sweet blackberry. "He was very kind, and took good care of me, so I can't complain about any of it, but he was also a bit odd, if that makes sense, as if he wanted something from me, but I couldn't figure out what. And even after everything that happened, and the quantrill, I don't know if he even slept last night."

"Aye, that matches what I've heard about him, that he's a pleasant fellow, but very driven, and hard to get to know or understand."

That made her laugh. "Well, you may not have met him, but it sounds like you know him pretty well anyway."

CHAPTER 11

A pair of towers, spiraling up into the clouds, shimmered in the dawn sun against the base of a tall mountain.

"Welcome to Altopon," Sebachin announced.

They had spent the evening trading tales—she told him about the quantrill, and he shared stories from his childhood. For a few hours, as darkness enveloped them on the river, it was easy to forget where she was, and as the boat bobbed up and down, she finally dozed off again on the pillows.

Now that the sun had risen, the shiny towers served as a stark reminder that this was not the world she knew.

He pointed to a large stone standing upright on the bank just ahead. "That's one of the torrapon stones. If you look, you'll see more off to the distance."

Torrapon. She had heard that word before. "What are they?"

"I suppose the easiest way to explain them is that they're boundary markers. The ancient Mosumi peoples used them to mark off sacred spaces. Some torrapons are small pavilion structures, like what you'll find outside of Loraden, while others are much larger. This one encircles Altopon. Rather than a wall, it's the torrapon that provides the majority of the city's defenses."

"A stone circle provides defense?"

He nodded. "You can't pass through the stones unless invited by Sarnoc or myself."

"Can't?" she repeated. "Or shouldn't?"

He turned towards her, and the sun washed over his features. He had the greenest eyes she had ever seen, and he had a nice smile. "If you do not have good intentions, the stones will prevent you from passing through."

"You're serious?"

He nodded once again. "Aye. You should always respect a torrapon when you come across one."

"Point taken. So what are they, exactly? Other than just defensive structures, I mean."

"Ah, well, the torrapon isn't actually here for defense. Its primary purpose is to focus energy. Torrapons are also the locations where the gods' powers are the strongest, so they can serve as portals between worlds."

"So is that how I—"

"Aye." He winked at her. "Patience, Kate. We will have time to discuss this soon enough."

He steered the craft towards a long, floating wooden dock that was lashed to pillars along the bank of the river, at the base of a steep hill. Other crafts similar to his were already tied up along the dock. After he maneuvered the boat into position, he waved to a young man cleaning his own river craft. "Well met, Tovandar."

Tovandar raised his head. "Ah, Seb, good to see you out on the water again. It's been a while, has it not?"

"Aye, the Sarnoc keep me busy. This is my friend Kate. She will be visiting for a while."

He brushed thick pale blond hair from his eyes. "Welcome to Altopon. Watch out for that Pasadhi, he's quite the ladies man around here."

Kate turned to Sebachin and raised an eyebrow.

He rolled his eyes. "It's just a joke—right, Tovandar?"

The riversmith took one look at Sebachin's pained expression and cracked up. "Point for me, Seb."

"What?" Kate looked between the men, not understanding.

"Come on, Tov, poor Kate here is a visitor to Sarducia. She doesn't understand."

Tovandar grabbed a sack from the boat and climbed up on the dock, offering Kate a hand to do the same. "Don't worry, you won't fall," he assured her as she placed a foot tentatively on the dock. "The riversmiths just like teasing your friend here. It's hard to embarrass him, but we like to try."

"I'll get even, don't worry!" Sebachin called back at him.

Grinning, Tovandar helped her climb onto the bank, and then led her to a wide stone staircase that was built into the hillside. "It was a pleasure meeting you, Bhara Kate," he said, nodding his head politely. "I do hope you'll enjoy your time here." At the base of the steps stood a young man with red hair, and wearing a grey tunic, his hands folded in front of him as he waited for their arrival.

"Kate, I'll be joining shortly," Sebachin called out from the dock. "I need to tie up the rivercraft and do a few things first. Laliri Tanvi will escort you from here."

"You're not coming?"

"Sure I am, but I need to tend to the boat. I'll be along soon, I promise."

"I don't mind waiting."

"Aye, but the Sarnoc might. You're in good hands here, so there's nothing to fear."

"All right," she said. She was skeptical, but as pleasant as he had been, she agreed to extend her trust a little further.

The steps were quite steep, and when they reached the top, Kate got her first full glimpse of the Sarnoc city. To her left was a wide road that led downhill to a city spread out in the valley below, tucked in at the base of another mountain, and bordered on the side opposite the river by what looked like another dense forest. In front of her, at the top of the rise, was a series of large buildings punctuated by the two white spiral towers she had seen earlier. In the center was a building capped with what looked like a massive sapphire sparkling in the sun. Beyond the large buildings lay manicured gardens and further off, an orchard.

"Wow." She stopped to take it all in. "It's beautiful."

The youth smiled, but said nothing. He waved her to follow him down a gravel path towards the buildings, and then across a lawn of fern-leaved yarrow, until they reached a small circular garden sheltered by trellises. "I welcome you on behalf of the Sarnoc, and will inform them that you are here." Without further explanation, he bowed his head once and then simply walked away.

She tried to swallow her anxiety and wear a brave face, a task made even more difficult by the vision before her. She stared at the building with the blue dome and then the towers. What was most remarkable about all of the structures, as well as the giant stones of the torrapon, was that everything appeared to be constructed from the same pale stone that shimmered ever so slightly in the morning sunlight. And in contrast to the dingy city of Loraden, here everything was clean, bright, spacious, and green.

Where she stood was also remarkably quiet. She reached up to a vine twisting up the trellis, pulling it a bit closer so she could inspect the unusual purple pods hanging from it. That's when she discovered that inside the trellises, the garden had a single inlaid stone path spiraling inward. After looking around and seeing no one nearby other than a few sheep off in the distance, she found herself compelled to walk the path, leaning over to smell a clump of pale blue flowers.

As she reached the center of the garden, where a single tree stood to mark the spot, she suddenly felt the presence of someone else behind her. Whirling around, she found herself face to face with a man in a tunic of white silk, embellished with silver embroidery along the cuffs and hem, and belted with a length of green cord. His hair was a dark blond, though greying at the temples, and he wore it long, in a thick plait down his back. His eyes—a piercing blue that threatened to delve deep into her soul and uncover all of her secrets—wordlessly confirmed his identity as Sarnoc.

Still, he introduced himself to her. "Greetings, Bhara Kate, I am Sarnoc Vaj." Before she could ask him anything, he turned back down the spiral path. "Come with me."

She had a dozen questions she wanted to ask, rapid fire, but she had to channel all of her energy into following him, as his long strides made his pace much faster than she was accustomed, and he showed no inclination to match her own speed.

He led her across the lawn to the domed building, and to a pair of tall wooden doors flanked by two young men, both unarmed and, like the boy who had led her to the garden, wearing grey tunics. Unlike Loraden keep's dark smoky hallways, they continued their rapid pace down a bright corridor with walls of silver-flecked rose marble. Overhead, the rising sun streamed down from an arcade of glass windows—the first glass that she had seen in Sarducia. The floors were also marble, and the walls were left bare.

Several times they passed more of the young men in tidy gray tunics, and each time, although they never spoke, the youths would bow their heads in deference to the Sarnoc.

Moments later he was conducting her through double doors inlaid with dozens of sparkling stones.

"This is the Sarnoc great hall, and audience chamber," he explained. "Here all Sarnoc and laliri—our novices, the ones in gray—come to share news and learn from each other." It was this room for which the brilliant blue glass dome served as a roof and skylight, allowing sunlight to brighten the entire chamber without being blinding. In the center of the round room was a slender marble pillar that in turn supported a series of walkways and galleries overhead. The walls were covered in the same shimmery stones she had seen on the outside, the tables and chairs were fashioned from a pale carved wood, and the floor was white marble.

Rather than remaining in this spectacular room, Vaj continued through one of the archways and down a hallway into a smaller chamber, where he lit a small glass lantern, and then pushed open a door to a stairwell.

There could be no doubt. This was one of the towers she had just seen. The base was quite wide, though the stairs themselves were narrow. Like a seashell, it twisted upon itself, climbing forever higher, with walls of tightly-fitted stones, carved to fit the curve of the staircase. As she began to climb, to her right at all times was the spine, the stem from which each step sprung. To her left, hanging from small iron rings set into the wall, was a rope serving as a handrail. After years of use the rope had been rubbed smooth from a great many hands, and the stone steps were polished as smooth as glass, each with a slight depression where feet had worn down the surface. She grabbed the hem of her skirt and took the first step, and then switched hands, uncertain whether the rope or a hand on the spine would steady her better. She didn't relish an ungraceful, and likely painful, descent back to her starting point. Occasionally a tiny window punctured the bare walls, just large enough to allow in a wisp of fresh air. With the curvature of the tower, they did not provide enough light to illuminate the stairwell itself, forcing her to rely on the light carried by the Sarnoc.

Sarnoc Vaj took the steps lightly and surely, his tunic concealing what must have been an exceptionally healthy physique. He would make a great marathon runner, she decided, dismayed more than ever that she could not keep up with his pace.

The tower was quite tall, and it didn't take long for her legs to grow heavy, and she gasped for fleeting breaths. When she paused for a moment to rest, she found herself cut off from the light of the Sarnoc's lamp. In the dim stairwell, she tottered. She didn't like dark, confined spaces, and she struggled to keep going, her breathing growing more labored from her exertion now tinged with anxiety.

Suddenly the space she occupied filled with a bluish-green glow.

«You must hurry. I cannot sustain the light for long.»

The sound of the voice startled her, and she stumbled on the next step, catching herself with her hand on the rope. She looked over her shoulder, but there was no one there. Where did that voice come from, she wondered. It couldn't have been the Sarnoc—it was as if it had been spoken right into her ear.

«Please continue up the stairs, towards my light. I am not far ahead.» The voice instructed her, yet now she realized that the words had not been spoken at all. The voice came from within her head. Telepathy?

She did not pause to rationalize this thought further, but instead took his suggestion and picked up her pace. The blue light followed as she ascended, extinguishing itself in the stairwell behind her. Soon she caught up to him, and once within the glow of his lamp, the blue light faded. Vaj said nothing at her reappearance, but resumed the climb, albeit at a slower pace, with a few pauses to allow her to catch up.

Eventually they reached a dark landing at the top of the staircase, where a pair of doors greeted them. Her legs were rubbery from the steep climb, and the Sarnoc allowed her a moment to recover and again catch her breath.

As she did so, in the flickering glow of his lamp, she examined the wooden door in front of her. It was a single polished surface, the surface so smooth it reflected the light. There were neither hinges nor a handle or knob. As she wondered how to open it, Sarnoc Vaj solved the mystery. He placed his hand, palm flat, against the door's surface. Effortlessly, it gave way to his touch, swinging smoothly and completely open. "We   have   arrived."

CHAPTER 12

They entered a semi-circular room with a row of tall, skinny windows and a round table in the center, with a fire blazing in the fireplace. Sarnoc Vaj waved her to one of the wooden chairs cushioned with white pillows, and as she sat down he reached to the silver decanter in the center of the table, pouring a pale rose-tinted liquid into two of three crystal goblets, one of which he placed in front of her. Then he sat across from her, folded his hands on the table and sat silently, watching her.

"That was you speaking to me in the stairs? In my head?"

«Aye. Sarnoc can communicate without speech, by touching the minds of their listeners.»

He had done it again. "So you can read my mind?" She was instantly apprehensive at the invasion. "I never thought anyone could... that something like that would be possible."

«It is not,» he reassured her, using the same form of communication. «We Sarnoc can speak through minds, but we cannot gain access to what another is thinking. Only another Sarnoc could answer me in the same way as I am communicating with you now. Even then, it is simply an ancient form of communication, particularly useful over distances. I assure you, one's private thoughts—the Sarnoc's, or another's—are never endangered.»

Her worries only moderately eased, she considered this information. "And the light?"

«A skill, you could say, that we learn over time. It takes effort to cast light at any distance from ourselves, so it is used only when necessary. However, both skills are little known outside of Altopon, and should not be discussed outside of the city.»

More of the 'non-existent' magic, she mused, but did not challenge him on the point. Feeling awkward and a bit intimidated by his form of communication, she sat there, staring at the beverage she refused to sample. When she eventually looked up at the Sarnoc she noticed he was watching her intently. Even though he had seemed friendly enough until now, she suddenly sensed that this tower served as an effective interrogation chamber, and was even now waiting for her to incriminate herself. Had she done something wrong? What was he waiting for her to do?

Finally, she couldn't contain her curiosity any longer. "Where are we, exactly, and why did we come all the way up here?"

He continued to watch her. After a delay that to her seemed overly long, he said aloud, "Given the nature of what we need to discuss, Pasadhi Sebachin suggested that we meet here." With that comment, he again fell silent.

After several minutes of silence, in frustration she pushed herself out of the chair and walked over to the closest window, where she could look out over the grounds of Altopon, including the spiral garden, which from above was impressive in both size and precision. To one side, she gazed over farmland houses. In the other direction, she could see the river snake away in the distance, only to be swallowed up by the thick forest. Far off along the horizon she thought she recognized the Carpasic Mountains that Davor had identified the day before, and wondered if she was staring in the direction of Loraden.

"So this is all for real?" she asked aloud.

"Why would it not be?" Sarnoc Vaj replied.

"I'm still having a hard time believing it's not just me dreaming it all." She turned back to the table.

"I assure you that this is no dream, Bhara," he replied.

"Are you going to explain what's going on, then?"

He sat with his hands folded on the table. Very calmly, he replied, "what do you think is going on, Bhara?"

"What? How am I supposed to know? I show up in this strange place and I have no idea what's happening to me."

He didn't respond, but instead seemed content to sit and watch her.

"Oh come on. I don't have a clue about what's going on, and you're just sitting there, not saying a thing."

He blinked. "What would you like me to say?"

She turned her head from side to side, frustrated by the interaction. "I'm just wondering why we had to come all this way if you're still not going to tell me anything."

"I never said I was unwilling to talk to you, Bhara Kate."

"So why are we here? I feel like I'm just a puppet that's being handed off from one person to another, and no one thinks that the puppet herself has something to contribute. It's all just a game where everyone is trying to control me."

"No one here is attempting to control you."

"Really? Then why am I here?" As she spoke, she meant the tower, or maybe Altopon more generally, but as the words left her mouth, she realized she was really asking why she was in this strange land where there were a thousand questions without answers.

"That is a good place to start. What do you remember about traveling to Sarducia?"

"Well, to be honest, not all that much," she conceded as climbed back into the chair, and crossed her legs under her. "It was the middle of the night, and there was a thunderstorm. I went out into the rain and I think I was struck by lightning. And the next thing I remember, I woke up in the keep."

"Is that everything?"

She nodded. "I don't really know what happened."

Sarnoc Vaj sipped at his beverage. "You have left out a few details, I suspect. Do you not trust me to keep your secrets?"

Secrets? "You mean, the fact that my ring was glowing?"

"Do you not think that detail to be important?"

Was he scolding her? "Well, maybe. It was weird."

"And what else?"

She stared at the table, and ran a fingertip along the base of her glass, but dared not taste it until she had a better sense for what was going on. She didn't want to tell him about the voice she had heard. "I remember waking up, and someone had wrapped me in a blanket, but I was still outside. I don't know where I was, but the people were speaking a foreign language."

"Do you know who they were?"

She shook her head. "No, I never saw any of them. I just remember feeling very cold."

"And what else do you remember? Why did you go into the rain?"

"I don't know. I think I threw the ring outside."

"You said it was the middle of the night. Why were you awake at that time?"

"I don't know... I guess I just woke up. It was the storm, maybe."

"You can tell him, Kate." Sebachin said from the doorway.

"What do you mean?" she asked him, unnerved by his sudden presence. How long had he been standing there?

He was leaning against the doorframe. "I experienced the same things, once. It gets easier if you just admit it." He winked at her as he stepped into the room and took a seat.

She then stared at the two men, who could not be more different in appearance or demeanor. They in turn remained silent, as if waiting for her to do something. "This again? Don't you get it? I don't know what you want me to tell you." She alternated her gaze between the two men. "Do you expect me to say something in particular, or are we all just going to stare at each other all day?" Apparently that was exactly their plan, for neither replied. Sarnoc Vaj had a bland expression, a blue ribbon poker face, but Sebachin had a bit of a mischievous look in his eyes which reassured her just a bit. "Damn it!" she finally exclaimed, bringing her fist down on the table so hard it nearly toppled the delicate glasses. "Why won't you tell me anything?" She pushed herself out of the chair and walked back to the window.

Then she spun around. "From what I've learned about this place in the past couple of days, it sounds like the two of you are about the best people around to give me some answers." She leaned against the wall and crossed her arms in front of her. Although she wasn't about to admit it to these men, being here in the tower terrified her. It felt more like a prison than a place for casual conversation, so remote that no one would ever hear her if she called out for help. She also couldn't shake the fact that the door had no handle or hinges. Was it their intention to extract some sort of information from her—information she was certain she couldn't provide—and then lock her up here? If so, she might not be able to stop them, but she wasn't going down without a fight. "I don't know what you're expecting from me, but if you want my cooperation from here on out, you need to start explaining what's going on. Frankly, I'm getting pretty tired of being shuffled around and never having a clue about what's happening. I didn't ask to come here, and I'm not going to play any more games until I get some straight answers." There, she said it.

In response, the Sarnoc's eyes seemed to widen a bit. He brought his hands up from his lap, clasped them together and then covered his mouth, as if trying to prevent himself from replying to her.

Sebachin, however, burst into laughter. "Kate, come back over and sit with us," he said as he threw his head back and laughed more. "Sarnoc Vaj is sharing some of his private stock of arbishi with us, and it would be a shame if I drank it all before you got to try any." He lifted one of the glasses of the pink beverages and held it out to her. "Come on, have some. I think you'll like it."

It was impossible to be furious around this man. She sighed and stepped forward to accept the glass. "Hmm," she murmured after she had taken a sip. "That's really good."

Sarnoc Vaj nodded his head in appreciation. "It is a rare beverage, made by Mosumi in very small batches, and only when the arba flowers bloom. I hoped you would like it." He waved his arm towards the chair she had recently vacated, the full sleeve of his tunic making the gesture appear quite graceful.

"Mosumi?" she repeated, as she sat down. She had heard the word before, but wasn't sure what it meant.

"Aye," the Sarnoc replied. "They are the ancient people of Sarducia, who lived here before the Sards conquered them centuries ago. Most of the Mosumi intermarried with Sards over the years and no longer identify themselves as such. Some escaped and now live in Froida, many days' journey over the ocean. In a few remote areas of Sarducia, you can still find communities that hold to the old traditions, but they are rare."

"The Mosumi are our heritage," Sebachin added. "Only those with Mosumi blood can become riversmiths, healers, or Sarnoc."

"So you're both Mosumi, then?" They nodded. "And the people who live in Loraden?"

"The Vosira and most of the Bhagali are Sards," the Sarnoc explained. "As are most of the people on the island. In truth, there are very few people in Sarducia with sufficient Mosumi heritage to become Sarnoc—or Pasadhi," he added in deference to his colleague.

"Wait a second, this doesn't make sense. Aldrish Rynar told me that the Dosedra was fighting the Mosumi. If you need to be Mosumi for all these things, isn't it a problem if someone is trying to kill them?"

"Aye, it is indeed," Vaj agreed. "No one will deny that we have a complicated history. The Mosumi of Froida share our ancestors, but they fled at the time of the conquest. Now they live a semi-nomadic life." Then Sarnoc Vaj changed the subject. "Bhara Kate, you are quite outspoken and confident for someone who has just recently traveled between worlds."

"Yeah, well. That's just how I am."

"Aye, and it was not intended as a criticism." He laid his hands flat on the table in front of him. "I am immensely relieved to learn that you are well-suited to face the challenges ahead. Someone more timid would find it difficult."

"I told you," Sebachin replied. "She will do well."

Kate, however, was shaking her head. "What do you mean?" She narrowed her eyes. "What challenges?"

Sarnoc Vaj shook his head. "I wish I could answer that, but in truth, I know no more than you do. What I do know," he continued quickly, holding up a hand to prevent her protest, "is that you are here to accomplish something important, at a time when Sarducia itself is facing her own challenges, and possibly even a war with Hansar."

"No, you're mistaken. I didn't even know this place existed a couple of days ago. What makes you think I can do anything?"

"Kate, you're here," Sebachin offered. "It seems Goddess Kerthal chose you for a reason."

"I don't know about that. I don't know anything about this place, and it's not like I have any sort of special skills. I just work at a marketing firm. I think you may be expecting more of me than I can manage."

"Nay, I don't believe that for a moment. At any rate, it's not a question of what you've done in the past, but what you're capable of doing." Sebachin stretched his hand across the table to her, palm upwards, as if seeking hers in return.

She eyed the gesture suspiciously at first, but then slowly stretched out her hand to grasp his. As she did so, he held up her hand, as if showing off her ring.

Vaj nodded.

Confused, she turned her gaze to the ring, which seemed to have just the slightest glow, as if there was a cold fire inside the metal. Then she realized that the Sarnoc was holding up his right hand, where the same thing was happening to his own ring, a wide silver band set with a clear cabochon crystal similar to hers.

"So you recognize the similarity, then?" Vaj asked. "Both are made from glysar."

She released his hand examined her own ring more closely. It was the same glow it had emitted the other night. "I don't understand. Isn't it just silver?"

"Not at all. Glysar is entirely different. It is a precious metal found only in Sarducia, with special properties not found in any other substance. It was once quite plentiful here, and is widely used on our island—and coveted by those beyond our shores."

"No, you're wrong. My ring's just silver." She stared at it. "It has to be."

Her statement caused the Sarnoc's lip to twitch, as if he was holding back a smile. "You know that's not true. Silver doesn't shine as that does, nor does it possess the same energy within it."

As he said the final word, she inhaled sharply. His words had sparked a memory. When she was about eight, she and her mother had gone on a picnic. When her mother had dozed off on the blanket, Kate had reached out to touch the ring, but it shocked her. At the time she thought it was just static electricity, but now she wondered if it was something else.

Seeing her expression, Sarnoc Vaj added, "so you know I speak the truth."

"No, that's impossible..." It was her mother's ring, something she had worn every single day since Kate could remember. How could it be something from this land?

"You used the ring to travel here, did you not?" Sebachin asked gently, as if trying not to spook her further. "It worked because it's glysar. That's one of the many things glysar can do. The kelash pole I used on the river had a glysar tip, and every torrapon stone has glysar embedded within it."

She was still staring at the ring on her hand, which suddenly had taken on an entirely new, and rather mysterious, aspect. "So I could use it to go home again if I wanted?"

Sebachin nodded. "You must be in a torrapon, but aye, you could use it in that way. With some concentration you should be able to locate the energy lines to take you home." He put a hand on her shoulder. "Having said that, I should warn you to be careful, for the travel will drain you, and you might find it difficult to return. You should not travel until you are certain that you're ready."

"Well, to be honest, I never asked to come here, and I was yanked right out of important things at work—"

"Truly, Kate? You really want to leave?" Sebachin sounded genuinely disappointed.

"Bhara, I hope you will reconsider." Sarnoc Vaj's demeanor had softened, but he remained serious. "For you to travel here so abruptly, and without prior planning or intent, there must have been a reason."

The voice in her head, the call... "It's not like I had a choice in the matter."

Vaj walked to the door. "You represent something very interesting, Bhara, though what that may be is not up to me to explain to you. That is something for you to work out on your own."

"But..."

"Keep following the path in front of you. If you pay attention, you will always have signs that show you which way to go."

And with that, and a simple nod to Sebachin, he left the chamber, pushing the door closed behind him.

"Wait—what do you mean?"

"You won't get anything else out of him on the subject," Sebachin explained, and poured her more of the pink beverage. "The Sarnoc tend not to answer your questions so much as they leave you with more."

"It sounds like you're speaking from personal experience."

He grinned and took a sip of arbishi. "Perhaps."

"So what do you think's happening to me, then? You promised I'd get answers here. Or will you walk out as well?"

He chuckled at the comment. "Ah, if I wanted to end our chat, I'd have to ask you to leave first. You see, these are my quarters."

"What?" She glanced around. "Really? All the way up here? That seems... inconvenient."

"Not at all. It gives me the solitude I need for study, prayer, and reflection—and it keeps me from being under the watchful eyes of Sarnoc all day." He nudged her glass closer. "Drink up. You'll have few opportunities to ever sample arbishi, and you don't want this to go to waste. For all I know Sarnoc Vaj means to return to fetch his bottle."

She took another sip. It was so light, slightly sweet, and heavily fragrant. "I don't think I've ever had anything like this before." Then a thought occurred to her. "What does it do?"

"The arbishi?" Seeing her nod, he shrugged in return. "Arba flower tea is known to help focus the mind, so I suppose arbishi would have a similar effect. Nothing other than that, as far as I know. Certainly nothing harmful, I assure you." He cocked his head to one side. "Kate, did you think we would try to drug you?"

The shocked tone in his voice made her feel a little self-conscious, and she stared at the table.

"Listen to me," he said, reaching for her hands. "On my word, you never need to fear the Sarnoc, or truly, anyone within these walls. Elsewhere in Sarducia, I cannot make the same promise, but you're safe here."

CHAPTER 13

The Sarnoc gardens had given way to a wide expanse of unmanaged wildflowers and grasses, the meadow untouched by humans other than a small footpath that wound through the field. As the sun glinted off tall stands of goldenrod and fluffy Queen Anne's lace, and a variety of purple flowers she didn't recognize, she couldn't help but smile. This was something she understood, a world not so different from her own, and for the first time since she had arrived she felt like herself, unhindered by the expectations or demands of others. Standing quietly in place, she spotted a hare dashing through the thick growth, and a pair of eagles circled overhead, swirling with the updrafts. Ahead, the trees were lush and inviting, and not as imposing or sinister as Lockleaf had seemed from the river.

Sebachin had shown her to her room, a bright space with french doors that opened into a garden. Inside the wardrobe was a new gown, made of lightweight wool like her current dress, green with floral stitching down the arms, around the square neckline, and all along the full skirt. There were also clean undergarments and leather shoes that tied around the ankle. She stared at the clothing in amazement, suspecting it would fit her well, and having no idea how such a thing was possible since she had only arrived a few hours before.

Free of the Sarnoc for the time being, and having no obligations on her time, she quickly washed up and changed, and slipped out through the tall glass-paned doorway into the garden. She wanted to put space between her and all those she had met, even if just for a short time. While no one had harmed her or done anything to make her feel unsafe, still she found it difficult to trust anyone here. There were still far too many questions left unanswered, too many agendas unidentified. Why was she here? Why was everyone so interested in her? And what was she supposed to do next? It was still bewildering that she was here at all. Had her absence from work been noted yet? Had any of her aunts gone to the house to check on her, and reported her missing? They had to be worried sick that she had disappeared, particularly so soon after mom's funeral, and must be thinking the worst. Never in a million years would she have wanted to put them through this pain, but unless she could figure out where she was, how she had gotten here, and how to return, there was nothing she could do to spare her family.

She stared at her ring, and then removed it. Again, nothing happened. Even though Sebachin said she could use it to return home, she had no idea how to make it work.

The path she followed led her to a patch of trees, and soon she lost sight of the towers, alone in woods that might well have been in her own world. For a few minutes, she had no one staring at her, asking questions, or directing her about like a lost child.

After about a mile, she decided she had gone far enough. Just as she was about to turn back, out of the corner of her eye she spotted a small building nestled within the trees. It was a round hut, made of weathered stone that recalled the massive torrapon stones Sebachin had pointed out earlier, with a thatched roof and a zig-zagging row of small windows made from rounds of different colored glass.

There was a single door, and it stood open.

Curious, she crept up to the opening and peered inside.

Rather than a house, it appeared to be a workshop. Inside, there was a large crescent-shaped table and shelves under the windows bearing dozens of jars, boxes and books. At the rear of the room stood a kiva-style fireplace with a hungry fire licking the base of a cauldron. Along the table there were all kinds of bottles and bowls of different colors, knives and wooden utensils, and small bundles of plants.

Most notable, though, were the three women who were busily at work within the room.

One, a young woman with long dark hair that hung in a tangle of curls down her back, had a stoneware pitcher full of honey, and was pouring it into small jars stuffed full of herbs.

A second woman, remarkably slender and tall, who wore her pale hair coiled loosely at the nape of her neck, was adding ingredients from a mortar to the cauldron, and then returning to crush more with a heavy stone pestle.

The third woman, a pixie of a girl with large eyes and closely-cropped hair, alternated her attention between a large leather-bound book and the contents of a deep bowl.

In a stark contrast from the women she had seen in Loraden, all three were barefoot. They wore brightly-patterned blouses and full skirts made from batiked fabrics, rather than wool or brocade, and the garments sparkled from silvery beads and threads woven into the design. They wore glysar bangles and bells around their ankles. And their faces were tattooed with blue spirals that started on their necks and curled along their hairlines like vines of indigo.

One of them, the tallest of the three, was softly humming to herself. As Kate watched, the woman's humming took on words, and she began to sing. The melody was light, though the words meant nothing to Kate, but it was a lovely tune that reminded her of music she had heard from an Irish band that sometimes played in town.

As they worked, the three women danced around each other, spinning and twirling, operating always in concert as if everything was choreographed. It was almost as if they were one being. It was like watching the flames of a campfire darting about, so many intricate movements, but always as one.

Kate couldn't take her eyes off of the scene playing out in front of her, and she longed to join them, but held back, not understanding what she was witnessing.

She was so engrossed in the dance of the women that she never sensed the presence of a newcomer, and jumped when she felt the light touch of a hand on her arm. Whirling around, she turned to face the intruder.

"Oh, it's you." She smiled at Sebachin, and turned back around to watch the women dance.

Except the hut, and everything inside it, was gone. In its place was a stand of oaks that, from the looks of them, had been there for centuries.

"Wait—what just—" she exclaimed, and extended her arm out to touch the doorway that had been there just seconds before. She stumbled forward, over what would have been the threshold, and ran her fingers over the rough tree bark of the closest oak to verify that it was solid and not an illusion. "There were three women here," she said, so confused she couldn't order her words into a coherent single thought. "There was a cottage here... and now it's all gone?"

"Aye."

"I saw them. I know wasn't imagining it. There were three women in a round stone building. They were so focused on their work that I don't think they knew I was there."

"Oh, they knew. You wouldn't have been able to see them otherwise."

"So you know what I saw?" She looked over her shoulder, hoping they had reappeared, but there was nothing behind them but the trees. "They were real?"

"Oh, aye, they were real. Come, let's head back and I'll explain." As they walked shoulder to shoulder up the narrow path, he continued. "They are what we call Isa, the twilight ones. As far as I can tell, they exist here but in a kind of in-between state. They existed since before Altopon or the Sarnoc, and the only constant is that no one can see them unless they choose to be seen, which isn't very often."

"That kind of sounds like our stories about fairies."

He tipped his head back and made a squinting face, and then nodded. "Aye, if I understand rightly what you mean by that, then they are similar. Who knows, maybe they're even the same? They exist within the space between worlds rather than in one in particular, and they move to and fro as it suits them. They are said to possess great magic, but they rarely share it with humans. Most of the time people's only interaction with them is receiving a surprise gift on a doorstep, usually medicine or other healing materials, that could have come from no one else."

"You saw them, though? It wasn't just me?"

He shook his head. "I just saw you leaning against a tree, but the way you were captivated by something, I had a feeling they were there."

"Really?" That struck her as strange, given how he had described his role here. If anyone would be able to see them, wouldn't it be him? "Why was I able to see them, then?"

Sebachin shrugged. "I don't know. I know little about them, as I have only seen them once, for just a moment, just after I was named Pasadhi. I've sought them out since that time, but they have never reappeared to me. The fact that they don't perceive you to be a threat is a good sign, and worth considering further."

***

As they came once again in sight of the Sarnoc complex, a man in a white tunic emerged from the garden and began walking quickly in their direction. He held up his hand in greeting as he approached.

"Good day, Sarnoc Garnell," Sebachin called out to him. "We were just out for a walk."

The man reached them, and stood facing them on the path. "I heard of the Bhara's visit and was hoping to steal a bit of her time."

"Aye, Sarnoc." He turned to her. "We can delay the rest of our tour until after lunch, if you'd like. I need to finish up something for Sarnoc Vaj anyway."

Tour? She found his choice of words interesting, since she had wandered off by herself. Was that his way of deflecting further questions? She chose not to say anything about it. "Well, I guess that would be all right." She wondered what this Sarnoc had planned for her.

"Bhara, I do not wish to keep you long."

Seeing she needed additional reassurance, Sebachin added, "you're in good hands, Kate, don't worry. I'll come looking for you shortly." Turning to Garnell, he asked, "Sarnoc, will you be taking your meal in the courtyard today?"

"Aye, we will head there shortly," he said.

Sebachin nodded, and waved to her as he turned to jog back in the direction of his tower.

"I guess I'm all yours, then," Kate said.

"Excellent," Garnell said with a nod, and pivoted towards the Sarnoc buildings. "How has your visit to Sarducia been so far?" he asked as they entered the gardens. "You haven't been here long, if I understand correctly?"

"No, it's just been a few days." So much of it was a blur of new faces, strange occurrences and experiences she had yet to fully understand that it felt much longer. "It's been a bit of a whirlwind, though. I still don't understand most of what's going on."

"You've been treated well so far?" They passed under a trellis, and he paused to twist an errant vine back onto the wooden slats.

"Yeah, especially for a stranger that appeared out of nowhere." As they headed towards the buildings, Kate looked up to the sky, and idly noted, "clouds are moving in."

"Aye, the weather is shifting. The Pasadhi told us our sunny days will come to an end for a while. Rain tonight, most likely." They resumed their walk, and he said, "I understand your mother died recently. I wanted to extend our condolences."

She licked her lips. "Thanks. But how did you know?"

"The Pasadhi told me."

And how did he know, she wondered. Instead of saying anything, though, she just nodded.

"Do you have other family?"

Seeing no reason to hide it, she answered truthfully. "Yeah, I have several uncles and aunts, but I don't think they're all actually related to me." Every time she thought about them, she had to fight back a wall of emotions she still couldn't completely unravel.

They had reached paving stones that led into the courtyard. He held out his hand to guide her around the first one, and then knelt down beside it. "It's still cracked. I'll need to see if one of the laliri can replace it." Then he raised his head. "About your family. What do you mean? How would they not be related to you?"

She thought the paving stone had sidetracked him, and was surprised by the question. "Well, I've known them all my life, and they care for me as if I was their own flesh and blood, but I think they're just friends of my mother's. But they're my family all the same, you know?"

He nodded, as if the answer pleased him, although Kate couldn't imagine why it mattered. "And your father?" he asked.

"I don't have one." She caught herself. "Well, I guess I had one, or I wouldn't be here. But I don't know anything about him. My mom told me he died a long time ago."

"Indeed? That's a shame."

"It's all right. My mom made up for it."

"Aye, she must have been a strong woman, to raise a daughter on her own."

"Yeah, she was. Speaking of which, do you mind if I ask you something?"

"Of course not. What would you like to know?"

"I was just wondering, why aren't there any women here? I've seen a bunch of men, you and the other Sarnoc and laliri—and Sebachin—but not a single woman."

"Oh." The question seemed to catch him off-guard. "Really? You truly don't know much about us, do you?" Seeing her shake her head, he continued. "There used to be many women here, long before the Sardic conquest of the island."

"So there were female Sarnoc once?"

"Nay, not exactly. Many women served as healers and riversmiths, but the most skilled did not become Sarnoc, but instead became Na'isa. While Sarnoc were the scholars, Na'isa were the true magic users. But that is all in the past now."

He was poised to continue, but Kate interrupted him. " 'Na'isa'," she repeated. "Are they the same as the Isa?"

The Sarnoc turned his head. "You've heard of the Isa, then?"

"Uh, well, just—Sebachin told me about them." She didn't want to explain what she had seen, as if it had been just for her.

"Ah. Tradition holds that the Isa has many forms, and the Na'isa were just one. The Na'isa were the warriors, the ones who turned their powers against the invaders. According to our ancient tales, they were quite fierce. Yet the Sards, even without magic, were able to defeat them, though no one ever found out how that was done. After that, many of our ancestors fled the island or went into hiding. While, in time, the remaining Mosumi were able find a way to live alongside Sards, the

Vosira feared the power of the Na'isa could return, and they forbade any women from being trained by Sarnoc. Indeed, vigilantes often sought out young Mosumi girls and put them through a battery of painful tests to discover if they displayed any hidden talents. If they did, they were immediately killed."

Kate was appalled by the tale. "They tortured them to see if they had magic?"

"Aye, I'm afraid so. Even today, tradition prevents girls from being trained by Sarnoc for any of the Mosumi pursuits."

"It's not a problem that I'm here, though, is it?"

He laughed. "Of course not. Women are allowed to visit Altopon—and plenty live in the city. Some even work among us, though they are few in number. So if you find yourself being pampered a bit, you now know why." He winked at her, and to illustrate his point, used a small knife on his belt to cut the stem of a stately crimson sunflower, which he handed to her with a flourish.

"Thanks." Hearing Garnell's explanation helped her understand quite a bit about this world's culture. Their history had deep roots in patriarchy, even misogyny. No wonder so many men had displayed scorn and distrust towards her, as she wasn't intimidated by male dominance and authority. "Has there never been an attempt to change things?"

"From time to time, there have been incidents with families whose daughters act out in some way. Most of the time it's a girl whose brother unknowingly teaches her how to use a weapon, or who asks a healer to teach her to read. Such moments are generally ended swiftly by the local community, though in some cases the Senvosra intervene with harsher penalties."

"What do you mean? Girls can't learn to read?"

"It depends on the family. Some members of the Bhagali, as they come from strong Sardic roots, allow their daughters to study letters, but it is uncommon, and it's almost unheard of in the countryside. It is men who rule in Loraden, and women are encouraged to take up other pursuits."

"I noticed that." Hearing this history, Sarducia wasn't quite as amazing as she had thought. It seemed even more restrictive and repressive than medieval Europe, which it resembled in so many other ways. At least in Altopon there was a little room to breathe, though she suspected even here there were limits.

The direction their discussion had taken brought their conversation to a temporary lull, and for a few minutes they continued to walk through the garden in silence. Then she asked, "Do you think I was in danger back in Loraden?"

He shrugged. "It's impossible to know for sure. Things have been rather volatile of late, particularly with the growth of this new Hidden God movement, which is a source of many fights in the city. More troubling, though, is the return of Dosedra Arric. We do not know his reasons for returning, but we fear he plans to stir up trouble with his brother, and while the Vosira is no friend to the Sarnoc, we also fear a conflict on our own shores might provoke the Hansari queen to attack."

"I think Aldrish Rynar might agree with that."

"Aye, he might indeed. It was quite fortunate that he sent you out of the city when he did, so you didn't need to be caught up in that, and I'm glad we were able to bring you here. Now that you're here, are you enjoying your time at Altopon?"

"Yeah, it's not been too bad. It's so beautiful here, and peaceful."

The Sarnoc nodded. "It is much different from Loraden, that's for certain. As long as I've lived here, I still appreciate how much the city sparkles."

"It does, doesn't it?" she said with a smile, glad she wasn't the only one who had those thoughts.

"All of the Sarnoc structures are built with a stone that contains flecks of glysar. They say the ancient ones did this to strengthen the buildings and give them power, but sometimes I think they did it because it's so pretty to look at."

Back at the Sarnoc buildings, he led her inside a building she had not yet seen. "This is the Sarnoc wing," he explained as he flanked Kate. "Come this way."

They walked through a doorway into an open colonnade that overlooked a courtyard patio and garden, with a fountain in the center. "These are the Sarnoc quarters," he explained, making a circular gesture with his arm to indicate a number of doorways punctuating the colonnade, and he led her to an area carpeted with herbs and clover, where a wooden trestle table had been set up. "On nice days we often come outside for meals."

The table was laid with bright silver plates and glass goblets, with fresh flowers and herbs in the center, a basket of warm bread, and two golden bottles on a tray. A young man in grey greeted them.

"Well met, Kyril. This is Bhara Kate, who has come a great way to visit with us." To Kate, he asked, "Bhara, is there anything in particular you might like to eat?"

She shook her head, not even knowing enough of the options to make a request. "Anything will be fine."

Garnell nodded once and gave instructions to Kyril, and then turned his attention back to her.

"He's laliri," he explained, as he politely pulled a chair out for her. "They split their time between study and service to the Sarnoc. In time, if they master their training, they too will become Sarnoc. We prefer this system to employing servants as they do in Loraden, as this way, everyone has the opportunity to serve and be served, and it shows that none of us are better than anyone else."

"Isn't that like the charnok?" she asked, having just a bit of knowledge gained from observing the young men at the quantrill.

Garnell took his seat across from her. "Charnok do indeed assist the Bhagali, but they do not do menial tasks such as cleaning and preparing food as the laliri do."

"Ah, I see. I'm sorry, it's just all very strange for me having servants around. I'm not really used to having people whose job it is to help me bathe or get dressed or clean my room. I do all of those kind of things for myself."

"Truly? You are not of the Bhagali in your world?"

Kate laughed. "Oh, hardly." While she reached into a basket overflowing with small loaves of bread, she realized he was still staring at her in surprise. "Oh, it's not a big deal. I'm pretty ordinary, really."

"I find that surprising. May I ask what your life is like?"

"Really? Well, I go to work in the morning, and then after work I'll have dinner, and then maybe watch—" she was about to say, 'watch TV' and realized he would have no reference, and that would be too difficult to explain, "or do my laundry. Sometimes I go out with friends, and there's one family member or another who's dragging me out with them."

"You said you 'go to work'," Garnell repeated. "What do you mean by that?"

"Oh. I have a job at a marketing firm, and do research for them." She realized none of that would mean anything to him. "Basically, when people want to sell things, they hire my company, and we figure out the best ways for them to do it." From the look on his face, even that explanation wasn't resonating with him. She glanced around the table. "Okay, so let's suppose you grew flowers like those," she said, pointing to the bouquet on the table. "And no one knew who you were, but you wanted to make sure the Bhagali wanted to buy your flowers more than anyone else's. You'd come to where I work, and we'd work on finding ways to tell everyone that your flowers were the best."

"But how would you know they *were* the best? Who decides that?" the Sarnoc asked.

"Oh, well, no one. That's not the point. You just want people to believe it, so they think yours are better in some way than someone else's."

"So you'd lie about the flowers, then?"

"Well... I wouldn't say it's lying, exactly. It's taking pride in your work, I guess you could say. There's nothing like that here?"

"Indeed not, and I must say, that is a very odd system. I cannot imagine it working here." He uncorked one of the bottles and filled her glass. It was a pale golden color, and effervescent.

She lifted it to her nose. "Is it cider?"

"Aye, apple and pear."

She took a sip, wondering at the rich flavor.

"So tell me more about your time in Loraden," he asked, though it seemed to be a friendly question, not the interrogation of Sarnoc Vaj. "Did you meet anyone interesting?"

"Well, really, everyone's interesting. You're all so much different from the people I know back home." She poured more of the cider, and a couple of drops spilled on the table. "But I did meet the Vosira and many of the other Bhagali."

"Pasadhi Sebachin said as much." He reached over and dabbed at the cider she had spilled with a napkin. "What were your impressions of the Vosira?"

She knew political conversations could be dangerous, so she measured her next words carefully. "He's definitely a character. I don't know if I got to know him well enough to say more than that." Before she could tell him any more, she heard another voice call out from across the courtyard.

"Here you are!" It was Pasadhi Sebachin. "You've eaten?"

She shook her head. "No, we just got here. He was just asking me about the Vosira."

"Ah, Sarnoc Garnell, this is no time for so many questions!" He said it playfully, but Kate sensed that he was cutting off a more serious conversation than she had figured it to be. "Sarnoc Hissil was looking for you in the apothecary."

The Sarnoc reached up and smoothed his hair, as if to suggest the interruption was of little consequence. "Aye Pasadhi, thank you," he said graciously. "I should see what Hissil needs. Bhara, I look forward to talking with you again later."

CHAPTER 14

"Can I ask you a favor?"

Kate and Sebachin had spent two days exploring the city beyond the Sarnoc complex or relaxing in the gardens. He took her to a pub where they shared mugs of citrusy beer and plump rolls filled with spiced meat and cheese. They visited a hidden spring-fed pool downhill from the Sarnoc gardens where they spent an afternoon swimming. A few times he had research to do for the Sarnoc, and he'd haul one of the massive codices into the solar and show her the illuminations in the margins as he sought passages on the giant parchment pages.

Now it was late afternoon, and they were sitting on a stone wall at the edge of the city that overlooked the river, drinking from a flask of water Sebachin had brought along, and sharing a small basket of sweet orange berries he had purchased from a stall in the market.

"Of course, Kate. What can I do for you?"

"I want to go back and find those women again, the Isa."

"Aye, if you wish. You're free to come and go as you'd like. I should warn you, they don't often make themselves visible."

"I know, maybe that's why I want to go. For the past couple of days I haven't been able to stop thinking about them, and I just wonder what they're all about, you know? I can't really explain it. Maybe I just want to see if they're real?"

"It's getting late—why don't we go first thing in the morning? After all, Sarnoc Vaj will be unhappy if we're late for supper. He's gathering all the Sarnoc to meet you tonight, you know."

"I know, but he said nightfall. That's still hours from now." She hopped off the wall. "There's plenty of time. Come on, let's go before the Sarnoc come up with something else I need to do, and I never get the chance."

"Fair enough." He uncorked the flask with his teeth and used a bit of the water to rinse his hands of berry juice. "Then let's go, but let's hurry so we don't have to walk back in the dark."

***

Just as before, the round hut appeared among the trees, looking like an ordinary, albeit ancient, stone dwelling. There was nothing about it that suggested magic was involved, and had she not been here before, she wouldn't have suspected anything unusual.

As they approached, Kate pointed, and mouthed, "can you see it?"

He nodded, his eyes wide, and covered his mouth as if to silence his own surprise.

Slowly, taking care to move as quietly as possible, they moved closer. Like before, the door was open. She mouthed, "stay here," and pointed to the ground. Then she pointed to herself and the doorway, signaling that she wanted to get closer.

Closing one eye, he gave her a look that said, 'are you sure?' but Kate nodded. She wasn't satisfied with just finding the hut this time. She needed to know more. Seeing her determination, with the flick of two fingers, Sebachin encouraged her to approach.

Again, Kate stood at the doorway. Inside were the same three women that she remembered from her previous visit. Instead of working, they were clustered together at the center of the table, all holding metal goblets in their hands, and they were singing. They again wore festive clothing, with scarves of colorful silks in their hair, and they reminded Kate a little of gypsies. She stood there transfixed, listening to their song. It was rhythmic, and although she could understand none of the words, she sensed that it was a song of celebration. As she watched, they began to dance, raising their arms and twirling around. As they moved, lifting their bare feet and spinning around each other, she could hear the sounds of tiny glysar bells they wore on their ankles.

This continued for a minute or two, and then the woman with the long curls waved for her to come inside.

She glanced back at Sebachin, who was close enough to see inside, but remained behind her in the trees. For someone who could stop the flowing of a river, he seemed transfixed by the Isa and their music. When she returned her attention to the hut, this time it hadn't disappeared. Now, all three women lifted their arms and beckoned her to approach.

Memories of fairy tales swirled through her mind, with the sinister intentions of magical beings. If she entered the hut, would she ever escape? She knew nothing about these Isa, who were mysterious even to Sebachin. Logic dictated that she remain outside with him, but their song beckoned to her. With trepidation, she stuck one foot across the threshold. When nothing happened—when she wasn't turned to stone or killed on the spot—she took another step forward.

Immediately the three women spun around the table to greet her.

"You have come!" said the woman who had beckoned her to enter.

"Welcome!" said the second, the pixie girl.

"We waited for you," the third woman, the eldest said.

"We have waited so very long." The first woman offered her a goblet, holding it out with both hands across the table.

Kate nodded in thanks, unable to find words suitable for the moment, and grasped it with both hands. It was glysar, with many symbols and designs engraved upon its surface. She sniffed its contents, and then looked inside. It was not wine, nor ale, nor did it smell even like spirits.

"We know you did not come alone," the first woman said.

"Do not worry," said the second. "We recognize his spirit."

"He is wise," said the third. "And kind. He will not betray us."

Kate was still holding the goblet, and didn't take a drink. She was a bit unnerved that the three women were speaking as one individual. "He's a friend. He just wanted to see you for himself."

"As do all men."

"They think we hide from them."

"In reality, they are blind to us."

Kate nodded, assuming this was what Sebachin had explained earlier. Again she looked into the goblet, which now she felt awkward holding.

"It is tala," said the first woman.

"We wish to celebrate," said the second.

"It is our best. Please drink." the third announced.

They all raised goblets, and with their free hands, signaled for her to do the same.

Before she did, she looked over her shoulder, and saw Sebachin still just beyond the door. If something happened to her, at least he'd witness it. She raised her goblet with the others, and then following their lead, took a sip.

It was alcoholic, but it was not a recreational beverage. One sip, and she could tell there was magic at work.

Her vision blurred and cleared, and Kate immediately knew the women's names. The first woman, with the long hair, was Tamysa; the second, the youngest was, Ovia; the third, the oldest of the three, Caris. And just as quickly as she had this knowledge, they recognized it, and rushed forward and collectively wrapped their arms around her, embracing her as they would a sister.

Kate was overwhelmed by the gesture, which felt genuine and full of love. When she glanced back at the door, it was closed, though none of the women had gone near it. It was as if the entire world beyond the walls of this small hut had disappeared, as if they were a vessel afloat in the heavens.

They released her, and for a few seconds, she imagined she was being wrapped in threads of golden light that flowed from their fingers. It was an amazing feeling, for in those moments it was as if she was floating, without a single worry or concern, and she wondered if this was a hallucination. Nothing real ever felt like this. Every pain and fear she had ever experienced in her life melted away, and she was drawn into a state of perfect contentment and safety, the way she only felt in dreams.

"What are you doing?" she finally asked, stumbling over the words even as she spoke them.

They joined hands, encircling her with their arms, and guided her into the open area in the center of the table, the inner curve of the crescent.

"We wish for you to remain here, with us."

"But it is not your time to do so."

"You have much to do here."

"She has told us to release you."

"This is your destiny. Do not fear."

"You shall follow the path the Goddess made for you."

Kate barely heard them, but their words were bouncing in her brain, finding permanent hold in her thoughts. She was swimming in their light, in the energy of these women, and at that moment believed she would never need anything more than that.

Then the light faded, and she found herself standing alone, the arms of the table curling around her. It was hard to know how long she had been inside the cottage, but it appeared the sun was low on the horizon. Then she saw a silver light descend from above and felt a tingle beginning at the crown of her head that quickly moved through her body. When she raised her arm, she noticed that once again, her ring was glowing brightly.

It was at that moment that she lost consciousness.

CHAPTER 15

Wind pulled at her dress and twisted her hair into knots. Nausea kept her close to the ground for several minutes, and even lifting her head made her dizzy.

Opening her eyes slowly, Kate discovered that she was lying face first on rocky ground. As she sat up, the queasiness subsided, and she pushed herself up onto her feet. As she did so, she realized she was standing on a wind-scrubbed hillside near a battered tree that grew sideways. The sky washed with gold and peach tones, suggesting there was little daylight left. Examining her surroundings further, the only other notable thing nearby was the remains of an ancient cottage at the base of the hill. The building was ancient, with gaping holes in the walls. The roof had caved in long ago, and weeds carpeted the floor. She thought she could see a second cottage in the distance, though it appeared to be in no better condition than the first.

She had fleeting memories of where she had been moments ago, and looked at the remains of the stone hut with curiosity. It had none of the magic of the one of the Isa, and looked for all purposes like an old cottage that had been long ago abandoned to the elements.

The Isa. Had that really happened, or was it a dream? Looking around, she wasn't sure about anything now. This wasn't Altopon, and Sebachin was nowhere to be found.

Just then, someone grunted behind her.

Alone only a moment ago, she spun around to confront the new-comer. The sound came from a trio of sheep that had climbed down the hillside and now were investigating her sudden appearance.

"So I suppose this is your house now?" she asked the animals. The ram lifted his head and stared down his nose. Then he shook his head and led a rapid retreat back up the hillside.

Realizing even the sheep had better things to do, she climbed down the hillside to the cottage, and sat against one of the walls. She gathered her legs close to her chest due to the chilly winds, and waited.

What had happened? How did she end up here? And, perhaps most importantly, was there any way to determine where 'here' was? There was nothing to indicate whether she was still in Sarducia or somewhere in her own world, though it scarcely mattered until she could find someone to help her or some sort of clue to find her way home. Had the Isa sent her here, and if so, why? What was she supposed to do now? She remembered that Sebachin had been just outside their cottage. He would know by now that she was gone. Would he come looking for her?

Drops of water splashing against her cheek interrupted her thoughts. "Rain?" she said aloud. "Oh, that's just great."

She had no time to devise a plan, as the rain quickly turned into a downpour. Thoroughly angry about her situation, she scrambled to her feet and let out a scream of frustration. Already chilled by the winds, and now soaked by the sudden shower, she realized she needed to find shelter, and quickly. She left the cottage for an overgrown footpath leading downhill. Walking across the hillside was treacherous: the sun was sinking towards the horizon, leaving precious little daylight for navigation, and rainwater coursed down the little path, causing her to nearly lose her balance in the slick mud. The whole process was compli-cated by the fact that she was wearing her beautiful dress supplied by the Sarnoc, a garment distinctly unsuitable for hiking.

As if agreeing with her decision to leave the cottage, the storm was short-lived, and although the rain continued to fall, it turned into little more than a drizzle.

There was barely enough light to see the path, which was little more than a scratch on the rocky ground, but soon she made out the sound of the ocean, so she kept aiming for that. Eventually, she spied a small cluster of buildings in the distance. Inspired by a chance to find shelter from the rain and wind, she started jogging in that direction, disregarding the mud that splattered her skirt at each step.

The first building turned out to be a stable, but beside it was a salt-stained stone structure with a tattered sign hanging above the door. The faded inscription was illegible, but she could make out a hand-painted image of a tankard, and expressed silent gratitude for the universal symbol. Having no money, she wouldn't be able to purchase anything, but at least it would be dry inside, and perhaps someone could tell her where she was and how to get back to 'civilization,' however loosely defined that might be out here.

With no reason to hesitate further, she pushed the door open and walked inside, trailing streams of water behind her.

The main room was barely brighter than the darkness outside. Even in the dim light of candles and a fire in the hearth across the room, it wasn't hard to discern the roughness of the structure, with the tables made from old wooden planks, perhaps recycled from another building, and a floor that was bare earth and dusty—other than the spot where she stood, which was turning rapidly into a pool of mud. But it wasn't the décor, but the stench—a combination of mildew and stale beer, and something else she didn't want to guess—that nearly sent her back out into the rain. Becoming used to dark rooms was one thing; the odors of this world were something else. She lingered, however, because despite its many flaws, the inn was warm and dry, and as cold and tired as she was, that trumped all else.

The inn was nearly empty, with just a few strangers occupying a table in the corner closest to the fire. As she shook rain from her arms and hair, the men turned their heads in her direction and mumbled something to each other.

One of them, tall and thin, kicked back his stool and walked over to her, greeting her with an expression that appeared to be a combination of curiosity and concern.

"What in Kerthal's name happened to you? You must be freezing." Without waiting for a response, with slender fingers he unpinned a simple glysar brooch. While she wiped her wet face with her sleeve, he removed his cloak, shook it out, and draped it over her shoulders. Then he pushed open the door and looked outside. "Bhara, where is the rest of your traveling party?" he asked in a gentle voice that demonstrated genuine concern. "I hope you did not meet with trouble on the road?"

She had to think quickly. This world was still foreign to her, but she realized that to these men, a young woman, traveling alone, would raise suspicion. "Something spooked our horses, and in the commotion, I fell." Even her ears it was a pathetic lie, but it was the first thing that came to mind. "After that, everyone scattered, and I lost track of them." Given the rising chill that set her teeth chattering, it was hard not to sound weak and pathetic, but she sensed it would be safest to infer that she was with others who would be looking for her.

"Oh dear, were you injured?" This information seemed to trouble him, and his eyebrows pinched with concern as his hand came to rest on her shoulder.

"No, I'm fine." She sucked in a breath between her teeth as she pulled the cloak closer. "Just wet from the rain, and a little cold."

"Of course, you must come over to the fire." While his hair was still dark, his thin beard was turning grey, and it was hard to place his age. Nevertheless, in a fatherly gesture he placed his arm around her shoulder and guided her to the seat closest to the fire, and used an iron poker to stir the coals until there were new flames. "How long have you been traveling?"

"Uh—" she hesitated. "I've lost track of how many days it's been since…" she scrambled for something. "Since we left Loraden." There, that would work, she hoped. It wasn't so far from the truth anyway.

"Such a long journey, eh?" he asked as he pulled out his stool, and then slid his full mug of ale over to her. "Wherever your companions are, it will be foolish to try to find them in weather like this, but perhaps they will reach the inn themselves in due time. So, for now, please join us, and I'm sure you will soon be reunited with your party."

Kate stood at the edge of the table and examined the mug, and then back to the stranger who had offered it. She then eyed the other three at the table—all of whom were staring at her now—with trepidation. Although she had no idea what to do next, she knew survival was her biggest priority; after that she'd see what else she could manage.

Taking her hesitation as fear, the man nodded to her. "Go ahead. It will do you good."

Nervously, she sat on the stool he had pulled out for her, and then she took a sip. The ale, weak though it was, tasted heavenly, and refreshed her a bit.

"Why would you be visiting this wretched place?" one of the man's companions asked her. Compared to the first man, who was slightly built, this one was a giant, with thick arms and a broad chest. He had a red beard and wiry hair to match, and as he leaned forward to scrutinize her, he swept hair from his eyes. He was indisputably less congenial than his companion, and his words sounded more like an accusation than an honest query.

"She's become separated from her party, and just found her way here," the first man explained before she could do so. "I don't think she knows where she is," he said, looking to her for confirmation.

As she nodded, the second man replied gruffly, "Aye, well, let me help you out, as if it would matter. You are in Bhoren, my lady—what there is of the place, forsaken as it is." He tilted his head to get a better look at her. "That's rather fine garb for travel over the mountains," he said as he lifted the cloak with one finger to get a better look at her dress. Then he narrowed his eyes. "The Bhagali rarely have reason for a journey to this coast. Women such as yourself, even less. What might your business be?"

Kate knew caution was dictated, but she couldn't stop shivering, and it was hard to devote the concentration necessary to come up with a plausible story. Wanting to change the subject and downplay her situation, she said, "look, I didn't mean to bother any of you—I just needed to get out of the rain."

"Are you in some sort of trouble?" This time it was a younger man who spoke, his voice soft and with a touch of innocence; it was a contrast to his bulky companion. He leaned forward, displaying jet-black hair and almond-shaped blue eyes, and she realized he was much younger, perhaps in his early twenties.

"No, I'll be fine, I swear. It was really just the sudden storm that caught me off-guard."

The fourth man had been leaning back in the shadowy corner, his hood shielding his face. He pulled his stool forward. With one hand, he pushed the candle towards her, and she caught sight of a large signet ring on his middle finger. "Hmm, interesting." He kept his voice low as he spoke, and then he paused. With sardonic humor he continued. "Aye, of course. How could I expect anything less?"

He leaned over and whispered something to the giant redhead, who in turn tipped his head to look at her more closely. "How in Kerthal's name...?" he began, a look of surprise on his face. "Oh, aye, she's the one, all right. I'm surprised I didn't recognize her right away."

"What do you mean? I don't know any of you."

"Be that as it may," the large man said, as he eyed her cautiously. "I suppose it's good to see that you've recovered from your illness, Bhara." He turned to his friend in the shadows. "Curious how she turns up so unexpectedly each time we meet, eh?"

The hooded man nodded in agreement. "I was thinking the same thing."

Kate looked from one man to the next. What were they talking about? They couldn't know her—she had never seen them before tonight.

The first man also seemed confused by the comments of his friends, and he tipped his head to examine her features more closely. Then he sucked in his breath. "You're right. It's her." He rubbed his lips thoughtfully. "Perhaps she truly does not remember us."

"Ah, do you really think so?" the red-haired man replied, his eyes never leaving Kate as he took a sip from his mug. "Well, at least she's here alone."

"Aye, but we must be on our guard, given the company she keeps." Then the hooded man turned back to her. "You attended the recent quantrill with Aldrish Rynar, did you not?"

The quantrill? Oh crap. So they weren't just toying with her. They really had seen her before. Her heart began pounding at the base of her throat.

Before she could reply, the young man spoke again. "Truly? You know this woman?"

"Nay, I know her not," the hooded man admitted, "for despite having seen her on two previous occasions, we were never introduced." He dragged the candle back to the center of the table. "It is time we rectify that. Your name, Bhara?"

She took a deep breath. So far no one had tried to harm her. She needed allies, if she was going to figure out where she was and how to get back to people she knew, so she decided to take a risk. "My name's Kate, and yes, I was at the quantrill. Did I meet you there? I must admit, I've met so many people in the past few days that it's entirely possible I've forgotten. Or maybe you're Senvosra, and saw me in the keep?" she added, using the term for the royal soldiers that had been all over the keep.

The hooded man laughed, and as he did, the hood slipped back. She immediately recognized the face, and she sucked in a quick breath, followed rapidly by jumping from the stool, knocking it over in the process.

"Nay, I am not Senvosra." Her sudden response seemed to amuse him further. "I surmise that you now recognize me as well."

"Dosedra Arric," she whispered, so quietly that her voice barely carried over the table. "I had no idea…"

He bowed his head politely. "I understand. Usually I would say that I was pleased to make your acquaintance, but…" he held his tongue as he pulled the hood back over his head, "I'm not at all certain I should be, this time."

She nodded, recognizing the awkward nature of this encounter, and wrapped the borrowed cloak tightly around her. This was definitely an unfortunate turn of events. In the few days she had been in Sarducia, she already knew that this man had few friends here, least of all his own brother, the king. Rynar had even hinted that he might be dangerous. And yet… here he was, and she was alone, with no clue how to proceed, and no one to speak on her behalf.

Without putting much thought into it, she stepped backwards, towards the door. Distance was her greatest ally now. Unfortunately, her exodus was quickly stalled when the red-haired man blocked her path with a couple of well-timed steps.

"Perhaps you would be so kind as to explain why you're following us, Bhara?" he asked. His question was politely posed, but clearly meant as a demand.

"What?" She stammered, coming completely undone at the ludicrous assumption. "I don't have any reason to follow you—why would I want to do something like that? I don't know any of you, other than the Dosedra... well, I know who he is, but like he said, we never met." She realized she was babbling, and tried to abandon the conversation before things got any worse. "I'm really sorry that I bothered you, and I think I should just get going. Let me check to see if it's still raining and then I'll be on my way..."

Finding her plea unacceptable, the red-haired man shook his head, pointing his arm towards the table, commanding her to return. "Bhara, I am quickly losing my temper," he stated, his teeth bared. "Your actions are far from innocent, as proven by your pathetic attempts to escape. Before you go anywhere, you owe the Dosedra an explanation for why you are here tonight."

Kate held her breath, entirely paralyzed with uncertainty. "But I—I don't have one. I didn't know he was here. I just wanted to get out of the rain." She was shaking visibly now, though she wasn't sure whether it was still from the cold or from newfound fear. Be strong, she told herself. It took everything in her power not to completely break down in tears, but she kept her head up and stood her ground. "Just let me go."

The young man with the black hair scrambled from his stool and caught her gently by the arm. "Never mind him," he said, and reached for her hand. "None of us will harm you. Please, come back to the table."

"No, I need to go."

"Nay, lady, please," he entreated. "You're freezing. I can hear it in your voice. You won't survive the night if you go back outside now in your wet clothing, and there is no other decent shelter for a half-day's journey. Come, on my word, you will be safe with us. Tell us your story, and maybe we can help you out." He blinked his eyes slowly, doing his best to appear non-threatening. "I'm Nyvas," he offered with a bit of a grin. "You can trust me."

"Now, boy," the red-headed man cautioned her new champion, who even now was leading her back to the table. "Do not say too much to this one. We still don't know her motives here."

Nyvas winked at her. Then he turned to Dosedra Arric. "What could she do?"

The Dosedra shrugged. "Ah, at this point, she knows plenty already. Names aren't likely to make anything worse."

Taking that as his cue, Nyvas continued with his introductions as he bent down to right the stool she had knocked over. Pointing over his shoulder at the man who had blocked her path, he said, "that's Fantion. He keeps us all in line," he added with a slight smile. "Of course, you have already met Lysander, having relieved him of his cloak. And as I said a moment ago, I'm Nyvas."

Fantion placed one hand on his shoulder. "That's enough for now."

"Aye," the Dosedra said, his voice remaining low. "Bhara, even from where I sit, I can see you're shivering. You have need of dry clothing, and from your account, a place to sleep for the night as well." Before she could protest, he had already stepped to a door at the back of the room, where a rapid knock got the innkeeper's attention. After a short conversation involving the parting of several coins, he rejoined the others at the table. "He says he has a small room upstairs that you may use for the night," he said to her without further ceremony. "His wife will provide you with dry clothing for the evening as well."

"You're not going to force her to tell us why she's here?" Fantion asked his friend.

Forestalling a response from the Dosedra, she replied, "honestly, this is all just a misunderstanding. I promise to leave you alone."

To that comment, the Dosedra just nodded and waved her off, as if it was all a minor inconvenience. Glad to be able to escape the awkward interaction, Kate murmured thanks, and when the innkeeper reappeared moments later, she quickly followed him out of the common room, sighing with relief as she climbed the stairs behind him.

CHAPTER 16

The innkeeper's wife, a stocky woman with thick arms and a wrinkled face who introduced herself as Noresa, showed her to a tiny room, and helped her dry off and change into dry clothing. Gone was the green woolen gown from the Sarnoc, and in its place was one of Noresa's own dresses, a simple tunic of worn, faded brown linen, a bit baggy at the arms and waist and about two inches too short. All in all, it wasn't especially attractive, nor was it as warm as her own gown, but it was clean, and most important of all, it was dry. Best of all, her shivering quickly came to an end as she sat close to the fire.

However, her moment of solitude was short-lived. When she asked for something to eat, Noresa muttered something about her husband having no manners, and before she could mount a protest, the innkeeper's wife promptly shooed her back out of the room, sending her back to the common room below for a meal.

As a result, she found herself slowly descending the stairs, decidedly reluctant to rejoin the Dosedra and the others, but her growling stomach wasn't going to let her be picky about the company she kept. She decided she'd sit at a different table, which would at least mitigate some of the awkwardness of the previous encounter. Hopefully tomorrow, after a good night's sleep, she would be able to figure out a way to get back to Loraden, leaving the Dosedra and his secrets to this godforsaken place.

When at last she reached the bottom of the steps, the men heard the creaking boards, and their hushed conversation ceased as they turned to look at her. In silent response she shrugged as she crossed the room and pulled out a stool at another table.

"Bhara?" Lysander called out to her, cueing her for an explanation.

She sighed. "Noresa said if I was hungry I should come back down here. Don't let me bother you."

"It's an inn," Nyvas pointed out cheerfully. "That means you have as much right to be here as we do." From a platter of fresh food that hadn't been there when she first arrived, he tore off a hunk of bread bigger than both of her fists and held it out to her. "Why don't you join us?" he offered, casting a defiant glance towards Fantion and the Dosedra as he did so. She wondered what had been said about her during her brief absence, and it appeared there had been a difference of opinion. "We have plenty of food, and it wouldn't be polite to have you sit alone in a place like this."

At first, Fantion looked resentful of the situation. Then he rubbed his beard, and with a shrug hopped up to fill another mug of ale from the cask in the corner and then set it in front of an empty seat at their table. "Aye, might as well," he said, waving her over. After he took a drink from his own mug, he looked around the room at the unoccupied tables. "It's not like you have your pick of companions here." Looking to the Dosedra, he added, "you know, this is the quietest inn I have ever seen—you would think even Bhoren could turn out a few men on a night like this."

"It does seem odd that there is no one else about," Dosedra Arric agreed.

Swallowing what was left of her pride, she relocated to the spot where Fantion placed the mug, and watched as he pulled a short knife from his belt and began carving into a block of pale cheese. As she pulled up the stool, he offered her the first slice.

The cheese was firm in texture, but a bit grainy, similar to cheddar, but with a stronger taste. As hungry as she was, it was exquisite. While she ate the cheese, silently accepting an additional chunk when Fantion offered it to her, the Dosedra reached for some of the grapes on the platter. Snapping a large bunch off from the main stem, he split the cluster into two and placed half in front of her.

While the others ate, Lysander had not touched the food, instead chewing on a jagged fingernail. Then he stood up and fed another log to the flames, remaining close to the hearth to allow the fire to warm his hands. "I recall the innkeeper said nearly all the rooms were taken," he said when he sat down again. "I've seen no other visitors. Who occupies the other rooms?"

The men looked at each other and shook their heads. "We should remain on our guard," Fantion agreed. Noticing the Dosedra's mug was empty, he hopped up again to refill it. When he slid it in front of his companion, the Dosedra raised an eyebrow.

"It's hard to be on my guard with a bunch of ale in my stomach," he pointed out.

"Aye, that's true. But you have pushed yourself hard these past few days," Fantion replied, with a chuckle. "You deserve a little relaxation."

"Perhaps so," the Dosedra agreed, and lifted the stoneware cup to his lips.

Although she remained silent, she was paying attention to the casual interaction between them. Who were these men, and why were they all here? Rynar had been distinctly annoyed with the Dosedra's disappearance, so putting two and two together, she figured that this excursion was unsanctioned. What was the Dosedra up to? She wasn't the only one who was feeling curious, however. She felt his eyes on her, and knew he had been watching her as well.

Given the lack of trust between them, it seemed no one's questions would be readily answered, if at all. She recognized that her best course of action was to stay out of his way, and find her way back to people she knew as soon as possible.

Her thoughts, and the men's small talk, were both disrupted when the outer door to the inn slammed open and seven men entered the common room, their bawdy voices preceding them, and their heavy boots thundering across the wooden floor. Flinging wet cloaks over one table, the newcomers chose a pair of tables across the room from Kate's small company, and fell onto the benches.

One of the men slammed his fist onto the table. "Innkeeper! Your best ale!"

Fantion, whose back had been to the door, turned around, and his eyes caught the uniforms of the men. He swiveled around quickly, and leaned forward. "Senvosra." he whispered under his breath. "Damn."

As she watched, the Dosedra abruptly pushed back from the table and leaned once more into the shadowy corner, tugging his hood forward to shield his face. Lysander bent over and whispered something to him. In response, the Dosedra shook his head. She heard him explain, "that one on the far right—his name is Gilam, and he served with me for a time." The Dosedra rubbed at an imaginary itch to hide his face, and then clenched and unclenched his fists. "This is not a coincidence."

Despite the Dosedra's concerns, the Senvosra were so far oblivious to his presence. Instead, one of the soldiers tipped the cask. "It's nearly empty," he announced to his comrades. "Innkeeper!" he called out as the others beat on the tabletops. As he tried to rouse the innkeeper, one of the other soldiers noticed Kate and whistled at her.

"Look at the fine bird that flew in," one called out.

"Hey girlie, if you want a real man, come over to our table."

With no ability to control it, her face burned with embarrassment, which was made worse when one murmured something off-color to the others, leading them all to laugh raucously.

As the hoots continued, Lysander observed in a whisper, "the lady draws their attention to us all."

The man who had been beating at the door to the kitchen called over to Fantion, who sat closest to the kitchen. "Hey you over there— where's Tamil?"

"Is that the innkeeper?" Fantion replied casually.

"Aye. Where's he at?"

He pointed to the door. "He wanted to turn in for the night, I fear." He grinned sheepishly and made a gesture of helplessness. "We are on our last beers ourselves."

"Hey, that's no good." The man kicked at the door. "Hey, Tamil! Come on out." He kicked again, and resumed pounding. "All we want is something to drink, and I know you want our coin." He did not hear the latch slide, and almost kicked the innkeeper in the shins when the man reluctantly opened the door again. "Old man, we need some ale."

The innkeeper, looking first to the soldiers' table and then, anxiously, to the Dosedra's, eventually nodded. "Aye, very well. I will fetch more." He shuffled back through the doorway, towards the kitchen.

Suddenly the Dosedra, who had raised his folded hands to his mouth as if to further disguise himself, dropped his hands and smiled. Without lowering his hood, he stood up and announced to his companions, with enough volume that he might be overheard by the others, "if it's all the same to you, I think I'll try my luck with the lady." His smile broadened as he took one of Kate's hands in his own, and in a coarse voice, said, "come with me, my beauty. It's time for some fun."

"What?" Kate asked with surprise, yanking her hand back and recoiling from his touch. "I don't think so."

The Dosedra grabbed her wrist and this time, clenched it tightly. "Do not fight me," he commanded, in a hint of a whisper. Then, loudly, he added, as he cupped his other palm under her breast, "I think I'm in for quite a treat, don't you?"

From the grin on Fantion's face, she worried that they had the wrong idea about her. With a sick knot in her stomach, she wondered if they thought she was a prostitute. Panicking, she wanted to call out for help, but words froze in her throat, doubting that anyone in the room would be sympathetic.

Meanwhile, the Dosedra's grip on her arm was like a manacle, and he held her firmly as he forced her towards the stairs. "The girl is quite spirited, isn't she?" he said, speaking up above the din of the common room, but keeping his face turned away from the others. "I will get my gold's worth with this one."

"Aye, my good man, she is indeed a lively one," Fantion responded, also quite loudly. "Enjoy yourself," he added in a suggestive tone of voice. "Not too much, though—save a little for the rest of us!"

A combination of anger and fear swelled in her throat. Was their earlier kindness just a prelude to this? Although she knew of men who treated women in this way, never had she been on the receiving end. She started to kick at him, but with her soft shoes, it did little good. "Stop!" she shouted. "What are you doing?"

"Look at her," Fantion pointed to the others. "She's a fighter, isn't she? With a girl like that..." he began in a robust voice, but finished with a whistle. "She's some prize. Hurry back, so we can all get a turn with her!"

The soldiers appeared to enjoy the drama, and their own shouts and whistles proved none would come to her aid—in fact, they seemed to approve of the Dosedra's actions. Arric transferred his arm to her shoulder, and then his hand slipped to her backside—much as his brother had done, Kate recalled, though this was much rougher—and he pulled her close. This brought a new chorus of hoots from the soldiers. Then he grabbed her face and kissed her, his touch rough and sloppy, summoning loud laughter and calls of approval from below.

Frightened and outraged by the assault, she continued to resist. When she struggled, he compensated by gripping her arms tightly so she couldn't pull away. When he finally stepped back, she took a deep breath in order to scream, but as soon as she opened her mouth, he kissed her a second time. Then he shoved her up the stairs, and out of sight.

CHAPTER 17

As soon as the door closed behind them, the Dosedra released her, and then and fell against the door with a sigh.

"What the hell are you doing? How dare you!" She scrubbed her mouth with her sleeve and tried to put distance between them. Her eyes were wide with a delicate combination of anger and fear, and her trembling had returned. "I'm not a, a—" she attempted, but couldn't force out the words. "Don't you dare touch me!" Retreating rapidly in the dimly-lit room, she stumbled against the bed and fell backwards, and it took her a moment to regain her footing and stand back up. "Who the hell do you think you are, anyway?"

He tipped his head away from the door and stared at her, as if shocked by her response. When he recovered from his surprise, he replied, "I am Dosedra." Then, as mindlessly as she would have switched on a light switch, he knelt down to stick a reed in the coals, and then lit the candles on the table. "I meant nothing by it," he added, in a surly voice. "It was the best thing I could think to do under the circumstances."

"The best thing?" she repeated, her voice elevated. "So was that all—" she scrambled for words—was it all just an act?" As he shrugged his shoulders, she was relieved that he wasn't about to force himself on her, but that left her appalled by the callousness of his actions. She again wiped at her mouth, wanting to make sure he understood her disgust. "I can't believe this—did you really think it would be all right? Or did you just not care how I might feel about it?"

"Bhara, on my honor, I assure you that it was necessary," he said, his words harshly spoken. He demonstrated no sympathy for her position, and in fact, as if to validate her own fears, he added, "That is enough explanation for you."

"Oh sure, your 'honor'." She had crossed her arms, and now she tightened her body and clenched her fists. "I've heard lots on that topic."

"Indeed?" he said, turning his head slightly, as if seeking clarification.

Fuming, she ignored his query, and instead asked her own question. "So, is this how you always treat women, then—as objects that serve no purpose but to do your bidding?"

He narrowed his eyes. "What are you suggesting?"

Memories of the argument at the quantrill, and of everything she had heard about him, reinforced her complaints. Again refusing to respond to his question, and keeping her arms tightly folded, she said nothing, but gave him a venomous stare.

He squinted at her, as if unaccustomed to having a woman speak to him in such a manner. "Bhara, it didn't seem like such a great matter at the time." He made a sour face as he spit out his words. "And rest assured, I didn't enjoy it."

"Well, that's good, because the feeling's mutual." She glared at him with absolute disgust, and when she next spoke she couldn't help herself. To hell with caution. "You had no right to do that to me." She tried to keep her anger in check but it just spilled out. "You know, I was kind of hoping everyone was wrong about you, but now..." She snorted and rolled her eyes. "Damn, you're just revolting."

As if she had slapped him, he jerked his chin in response to the insult, but said nothing in response. Instead, he cracked open the door to peer outside, but after a moment pushed it shut again, muttering to himself as he shook his head. Then he snapped his head back to face her, clenching his teeth. "Bhara, I do not know who you are, but again let me remind you that I am Dosedra." Now he glared at her. "You need to learn some respect."

Her eyes nearly popped from their sockets when she heard that. She craned her head in his direction, her jaw open, disbelief washing over her face, and she dropped her arms. "Respect? After all that, you think I owe you respect? You've got to be kidding." Had she been in striking range, Kate would have slapped him, but instead she held her fists tightly at her sides. Then, after several shaky inhaled breaths, she flopped in an un-ladylike manner onto the mattress—which, filled with old straw, was low to the floor, and not particularly soft—and crossed her arms again defensively. "You're really a piece of work."

He remained against the door, but turned his head away to avoid looking at her. Several minutes passed without either saying a word. Finally, after again looking outside, he broke the silence with a sigh. "The hallway is clear," he reported dispassionately. As an afterthought, he asked, politely but with appreciable bitterness, "Bhara, is there anything else?"

She nodded. "Yeah." She lifted the cloak from her mattress, where she had left it earlier. "Thank your friend Lysander for this—at least he knows how to be a gentleman. As for this room—" she said, gesturing with a snap of her hand, "I think it's best not to be in your debt, no matter what your friends say." She gathered up her soggy dress that was hanging over the back of a chair. "I'll look for somewhere else to sleep."

He snorted at the suggestion. "Where in Kerthal's name would you go on a night like this?"

"I have no idea, but I imagine that even the stables would be better than being beholden to you."

He opened his mouth to reply, but a knock at the door forestalled his words. No longer cautious, he yanked open the door to Nyvas standing outside. "What is it?" he snapped.

The young man stared with wide eyes, and seemed surprised by the tone. "Uh, is there something wrong?" he asked, attempting to appear more innocent than he likely was. "When I went to our room, you weren't there."

"Nay," the Dosedra said, his voice low. He gave her a surly glance, adding, "the lady and I were just having a bit of a disagreement about my handling of the situation downstairs."

"Oh yeah, that's what it is, a 'disagreement'," she replied sarcastically. "Apparently he thinks he can assault women whenever he pleases regardless of how we might feel about it."

"Assault? What in Kerthal's name—" the Dosedra began, but then he rolled his eyes and grunted, a sardonic smile curling his lips. With a flip of his hand, he announced, "Bhara, I'm finished with this. If you need anything else, Nyvas will assist you." He tossed the boy Lysander's cape and stormed out of the room.

Nyvas remained in the doorway. "My lady, pardon me for intruding. May I come in?"

Throwing her hands in the air as a sign of defeat, she said, "sure, whatever." She dropped back down on the bed, her dress still folded over one arm. "Do whatever you want."

He nodded appreciatively, and, after closing the door, approached, and knelt down beside the bed. "It's not my place to do so, you understand, but I'd like to apologize for what just happened."

"Thanks, but it's a little late for that."

He smiled. "Please understand—the Dosedra had to act quickly, before one of the Senvosra decided to cause trouble for us." He blinked, and she was taken aback by how long his eyelashes were. His genial disposition offered such a contrast to his companion that she struggled to imagine how the two men could get along. "Believe it or not, he'd hate to think he had offended you."

"Yeah, I'm sure he would." She didn't believe a word of it. "From what I've heard, I'm probably lucky that he didn't go farther with his little game." She shook her head, and sighed, rapidly losing her composure. "Oh god, I really can't deal with this right now." She took a deep breath to try to calm down.

Her words made him frown. He smoothed the blanket on the bed and then sat beside her. "Is there something else wrong? If you're in trouble, I'd like to try to help you if I can."

She dropped her arms, allowing the wet dress to fall to her lap. "I don't know, maybe. I'm not even sure I know what's going on. So much has happened in the past few days that I don't think I'd even know if I was in trouble." She looked towards the door. "He definitely didn't make things any easier, that's for sure."

Nyvas listened to her carefully, his blue eyes never straying from her face. "My lady, believe me, despite what just happened, our Dosedra would never harm you. I don't know what you've heard about him, but on my life, I promise that he's a good man. While I hate to make excuses for him, I know he's had to deal with some difficult matters of late, and it may be that the strain has affected him."

She considered his words. "Well, he's not the only one."

"Indeed?" Nyvas leaned back on his hands. "What really brings you out to Bhoren, Kate?"

His informal pronouncement of her name softened her mood. Here was someone who was trying to show her a bit of kindness, and just in time, for she needed a friend right now. She knew she couldn't tell him the truth, but maybe she could get out of the situation gracefully. "It really doesn't matter now. I just need to get back to Loraden." She really wanted to return to Altopon, where she felt safest, but knowing that the Sarnoc were not universally appreciated, she decided to hold her tongue where they were concerned.

"Well, I believe that can be arranged." He said it confidently, as if there was no question of his assistance.

"Really?"

"Oh, aye, I shall speak to the others about it. You have my word on that." With a hand that was calloused from physical labor, he reached for her own, which was balled up in a loose fist on top of the clothing. "You are new to Sarducia?"

"How did you know?"

"It's not so hard to see that you are different—though," he continued quickly, "that's not a bad thing. You need to have faith, Kate, and believe that there is good to be found here in our land." Squeezing her palm lightly, he added, "and even in our Dosedra."

"I don't know about that. From what I've heard about him, and from what he did tonight, it's hard to believe he has any redeeming qualities."

"Then perhaps you should not believe all that you hear." He sought her eyes, and smiled, causing her to grin ever so slightly. "I noticed that you didn't have a chance to eat much. Shall I bring you some of the food we have left?"

Though the recent incident had distracted her, now she realized that what she had eaten hadn't taken the edge off her hunger. "I'd rather you didn't go to any extra effort..."

"It's no bother. I'd be happy to fetch something for you."

Before he could open the door, though, she had to say one more thing. "It was stupid of me to yell at the Dosedra, wasn't it?"

The young man shrugged. "You had every right to be angry—he was rough with you, and never sought your permission before he acted. But besides that, you responded honestly, without pretense, and that's an admirable trait. So in my opinion, you shouldn't have to change who you are, just because of who he is." He smiled, as if amused by his own comment. "I'll be back in a moment." Quietly he slipped out of the room and pulled the door shut behind him.

Now alone, Kate's anger largely evaporated. Something about the young man's demeanor, and his kindness, had a calming effect on her. Instead of remaining frustrated at the Dosedra, she began to focus on her situation. The Isa had sent her away... but why here? It was odd that of all places, she had ended up exactly where this prince had turned up, in a backwater of a town if there ever was one. Perhaps she was meant to meet him again. If so, how had she screwed things up so badly, and was there any way to rectify the situation and get out in one piece? There had to be a reason for her ending up here, and the sooner she could figure it out, the better.

One thing was for sure. Sarducia was a lot different from home, particularly for women, and from now on she needed to be more careful when dealing with the strangers around her. She had been warned about the Dosedra—yet already she had challenged him, putting herself in danger. What a foolish, reckless thing to do. Despite Nyvas's reassurances, she sensed she had been fortunate that the young man had appeared before the situation deteriorated further.

Wondering if it still rained, she went to the narrow window and unlatched the shutter. Outside, the wind had once again intensified, and distant flashes in the sky indicated that a new storm might be blowing in from the ocean. Gazing at the ramshackle buildings along the road, she accepted that there wasn't any other place she could safely go tonight, and despite the threat she had made, she really didn't want to stay in the stables. The inn was far from comfortable, but it had to be worlds better than that. At the same time, she didn't want to run the risk of running into the Dosedra again, so she remained torn with indecision.

She stared at her mother's ring, tossing it to the mattress. Like before, nothing happened. "Please, get me out of here," she said in a whisper, trying to coax the magic to happen again. Sebachin said she needed to be in a torrapon, but it had worked at her apartment—why not here?

Her thoughts were disrupted by another knock at the door, and she quickly slipped the ring back on her finger. Expecting Nyvas, she pulled the door open casually. To her surprise, outside was Dosedra Arric, standing there alone, holding a tin plate piled with bread, meat and cheese in one hand, and an apple wedged under his arm.

"Nyvas said you were still hungry." He did not look at her as he stepped past her and placed the food on the table beside the candles.

Why in the world had he returned? "Thanks, but you shouldn't have bothered."

"Don't be foolish. I never intended for you to go without your meal." He reached into his shirt and pulled out a flask. "It's just water, but it's all I have handy." As she reached for it, he placed his free hand on her arm, and before she could jerk it away, he said, "I must apologize for what I did. You have my word that it will never happen again." Then he sucked in a breath, and continued quickly, before she could interrupt. "Nyvas said that you were hoping to return to Loraden?"

When she nodded, utterly speechless at his altered demeanor, he continued. "My companions and I expect to depart for the city in the morning, since our business here is complete. Rather than see you travel alone, we would be pleased to serve as your escort—assuming your companions haven't reappeared by morning, of course." The way he spoke the last sentence suggested he had guessed the truth—there was no one looking for her.

She blinked in surprise. It was neither what she had expected, nor what she would have chosen, but it was the only offer on the table. "That's very nice of you," mimicking his polite tone as she spoke, "but I'd rather you not make any special arrangements on my behalf. I'm sure I'll be fine on my own."

He drew in a slow breath. "Bhara, please be reasonable. There are no others traveling in our direction—other than the Senvosra, perhaps, but I cannot imagine you would prefer their company."

"Maybe I would."

"I do not believe that." He leaned against the doorframe, and dusted imaginary dirt from his shirt. "Truly, you should join us. It won't be an easy journey, but I promise that I will personally see you safely back to the city. And while you clearly do not trust me, my companions will make the same pledge. Will that do?"

She threw her hands up in resignation. "Fine. Since I don't have any other options, I accept your offer." As soon as she said the words, she wished she could take them back... but there it was.

"Good, then it is agreed." He reached for the door latch. "It has been a long day for us all. Sleep well tonight, and we shall see you at dawn."

CHAPTER 18

She couldn't escape the battlefield. All around her bombs exploded, and dozens of mangled, twisted bodies and dismembered limbs lay piled on the muddy ground. In the middle of thick smoke she searched for signs of life, lifting the bloody corpses in a desperate hunt for survivors, but in the maddening way of dreams, she was able to do nothing but repeat her futile efforts over and over without success. Then there was a huge bang, and she was sure it was the bomb that would kill her.

She awoke with a jolt, her heart pounding.

Utterly disoriented, she sat up and struggled first to remember where she was, and then to reassure herself that it was only the thunderstorm that had startled her awake. Even when she finally recognized the dingy room of the inn, she was not comforted; everything around her was alien and unsettling. As she lay back on her pillow, lingering images of men dying around her feet plagued her sleep for the rest of the night, and she flopped around restlessly.

Rising in the morning after such a sleepless night was bound to be unpleasant, and it was made worse by someone tugging at her arm. She lifted her heavy head to find Noresa, the innkeeper's wife, frantically trying to get her attention.

"My lady, the men are in the stables, preparing the horses." She returned Kate's dress to her, now warm and dry from hanging by the fire.

Once she had slipped her gown on, Noresa held out her leather slippers. "They sent me to see what was keeping you."

She had not lied. By the time she entered the cramped stables, the men had saddled up, their supplies tied to their horses. When she walked in, no one spoke, though she briefly caught the attention of Lysander, who gave her a quick nod before returning his concentration to a buckle on his saddle. Nyvas kept his head lowered, as if focused on the saddlebag he was packing, but she could see him grinning to himself. However, Fantion, who was tying back his mop of red hair, glanced at her only briefly, and he seemed displeased.

"Ah, very good." This came from Dosedra Arric, who waved Noresa over, and gave her a coin from his pouch. "Now we can depart," he said, as he led his horse, a sizable gray mare with a broad head, into the yard beyond, the other men following behind.

Once outside, the Dosedra called out to Kate. "Bhara, can you ride?" The question came in lieu of a greeting.

His actions the night before, although partially forgiven, were not easily forgotten. Despite being a city girl who had only gone riding once (on her thirteenth birthday) pride inspired her to say, "of course I can."

"Glad to hear that," he announced. "You will be riding with me."

"With you?" she repeated. "I'd rather not."

"Then you will have to walk, for Trill, my battle-mare, is the only horse that can handle two riders over the distance we must travel. Come, climb up." He stood beside the horse and held out his hand to assist her. "You will need to pull up your skirt and then straddle the horse. It's not particularly dignified, but it's the only way you will stay in the saddle."

She assessed the horses and their riders. It was true enough—the other horses were small and a bit on the thin side, and would not possess the strength of his large mare. "Fine, whatever." There was no saddle horn, so she slipped her foot into the stirrup and grabbed onto the saddle with both hands. As she quickly discovered, she had neither the upper body strength nor coordination to pull it off, making what seemed simple in theory impossible—and rather embarrassing—in practice. After a couple clumsy attempts that were complicated by her long dress, she had to admit that she was unable to climb into the saddle on her own.

The Dosedra placed his hands on her hips, but she slapped them away.

"Just give me a push," she said, too annoyed for anything else. "I just need a little more momentum to get my leg over."

He nodded silently, but then she heard a chuckle behind her. She turned to see Fantion step beside the horse, on the other side. "In all my days I have never seen a woman who was this reluctant to be around Arric," he said as he offered his own hand to her. "Perhaps you will humble him."

"Me?" The Dosedra said, suddenly laughing. "You have a few lessons to learn on that score as well, my friend."

She wanted to offer a few choice comments herself, but she bit her tongue. She was determined not to provoke a new conflict this morning, and promised herself to do her best to get through this experience with as little trouble as possible.

There was still the matter of mounting the horse, though, and even with his help, she was still unable to master the combination of lifting her leg over the saddle without becoming hopelessly tangled in the dress.

"Allow me," Nyvas said. "Sander, would you stand on the other side?"

As Lysander did as his friend requested, Nyvas leaned over and locked his fingers together. "Place your foot here, and I will give you a boost up," he told her, "and then Sander will help you with your skirt."

Feeling less of a need to prove herself to these two men, who seemed less inclined to ridicule her, she agreed, and with their combined efforts, she was seated properly on the first attempt. "Thanks."

"It was nothing," Lysander assured her, and returned to his own horse.

Once she was settled on the horse, the Dosedra placed his own foot in the stirrup and in a single fluid motion, pulled himself up onto the saddle behind her. His quick movements betrayed his skill as an expert rider, no doubt one honed during his years as a soldier. A fact, Kate reminded herself, that she would do well not to forget.

Meanwhile, Fantion asked him, "shall we return through Camwall? It is the quickest route."

"The mountains will be difficult riding for the young lady," Lysander said.

In the daylight she had her first chance to examine their clothing. While the Dosedra was wearing a simple linen shirt, an unadorned leather doublet, and wool trousers, all of his clothing was well-made and sewn to fit him. Lysander, on the other hand, had a torn pale tan shirt pieced together from rough fabric under a faded woolen doublet that had been repaired several times, and his trousers were baggy, hanging loosely on his thin frame. Turning her attention to the others, Kate noted that Fantion and Nyvas also wore clothing that was serviceable but ragged, as if they owned nothing else. Fantion's trousers were constructed from goatskin with makeshift patches on the knees, and Nyvas's shirt was a shabby grey fabric with a torn hem and frayed cuffs. They also all had woolen cloaks, though the one the Dosedra wore was the only one that was without holes or torn hems. All of this struck her as odd, because they treated one another as social equals, not as she would expect from poor men in the company of a prince.

"Perhaps," the Dosedra replied, in reference to Lysander's suggested route, "but the lady's comfort cannot be a consideration right now. There seem to be too many troops in the direction we came, so our only option will be to follow the Elsasir River through the Muras, something I had hoped to avoid. Still, with such a route we may be able to elude the Senvosra entirely." For her benefit he added, "the Muras is the swamp to the north. In fact, even now we are at its edge."

Swamp? She thought of the swamps she knew about, and considered all the potential dangers, including snakes, alligators, and biting insects. Then again, encounters with wildlife would be just one of many problems. There was likely to be mud, quicksand, and water. Lots of water. "Won't we need a boat?"

"Boats cannot pass through the growth," he explained impatiently. "We will ride when we can, and lead the horses when we cannot." In words heavily laced with sarcasm, he added, "it will not be easy for a woman, but I suspect you'll manage it well enough."

Even as she worried about her ability to keep up with them, she resolved not to be made to look like a fool. "I'll be fine. Let's get going."

CHAPTER 19

The Muras was not at all what she had expected, but also not what she had hoped. If someone had broken a water main, flooding an entire forest, and then abandoned it all to stagnate, it would be still a bit better than the Muras. Under the shady canopy, ivy and moss clung to the trees, while in areas where the trees thinned, thick stands of horsetail and briars popped up randomly. Where there was a passable route—if one could consider any route through the Muras truly passable—the ground was soft and spongy. Birds of all sizes zigzagged from tree to tree, and insects filled the air with their cacophonous shrill whistles and chirps. The air was thick with humidity, with a pervasive stench rising from the rotting leaves and other organic matter in the water. The smell of decomposition combined with the lack of a breeze meant that the simple act of breathing was unpleasant.

They had been riding for the better part of the morning. Even as their horses were splashing through murky water, Fantion and Lysander rode on ahead, seeming not to mind the environment, and were engaged in a lively banter. Nyvas rode closely behind them, but remained silent. This left the Dosedra and Kate to bring up the rear.

Riding with him meant close physical contact, something she wished she could have avoided. Memories of the previous night were still fresh. She chose not to speak to him unless it was required, and even then she spared no extra words. On this point they seemed to agree, for he was likewise reticent, and only addressed her when he needed to give instructions.

As much as she disliked riding with him, she soon discovered that there was something much worse. The first time they had to dismount, she sank her feet through a crust of dark scum into ankle-deep water, and she mumbled every epithet imaginable. The water was disgusting, and she cringed when she pulled out her foot, now coated with sludge. Several hours into the journey, her dress was soaking wet halfway to her hips, sticking to her skin and tugging at her shoulders; her feet were cold and blistered from sliding around in her damp shoes; and her calves felt like stiff, solid tubes of cement. Even on so-called dry land, she stumbled on rotting logs and various other debris, and she lost count of the times she stubbed her toes against rocks. As if the persistent damp wasn't enough, gnats swarmed her face and arms, and more than once someone spotted a snake curled around a water-logged tree stump in their path.

Adventures were one thing; this was pure misery.

Despite her discomfort, she did her best to keep pace with the men, and she struggled not to complain as she slogged through several inches of water that reeked of sewage. Back home she enjoyed an occasional hike, but never anything as arduous as this. Still, her pride clung to her as closely as the damp air, and she refused to admit that she couldn't handle it.

After several hours of travel, she noticed that even Fantion and Lysander, who had been chatting throughout the morning, had finally fallen silent, and now walked with their shoulders hunched and their heads down, their arms slack and the horses' reins hanging limply in their hands. Dosedra Arric was behind them, looking equally glum and uncomfortable. It seemed as though everyone was tired, bruised and sore—the strong men were just as miserable as she was, and struggled equally. It wasn't much, but she allowed the realization to cheer her a little all the same.

Just as Kate took a moment to appreciate the fact that she wasn't alone in her misery, one of her leather shoes came untied, and the thick mud sucked it right off of her foot. "Oh, that's just great," she grumbled as she tried to balance on one foot long enough to pull her shoe free.

"Need some help?" Nyvas asked, but before she could answer, he had already retrieved it for her, and dumped out the mud. "Lean on me," he offered as she struggled to put it back on her foot. She was determined that whatever else happened, it wasn't coming off again, so she tied the lacing around her ankle with a knot. Just to make sure, she retied the other shoe's laces as well.

"Thanks," she said, once the task was complete. "You came by at just the right time."

"Aye, so it seems." He smiled at her, and then looked up. Already the other three men were quite a distance ahead of them. "Come on, let's get moving."

"Right—just keep moving." She spoke more to herself than to him, and as the words came out of her mouth, her voice sounded almost mechanical.

"Cheer up," he consoled her. "We don't have much longer to walk today. We'll set up camp before sunset."

"Well, I guess that's something." She was discouraged by the idea that there might be several more of these torturous miles ahead. With each step, her toes clenched against the dampness, and at the pace they had been traveling, her shins burned so badly she couldn't walk faster if she wanted to. She privately wondered how much longer she could hold out.

"I know it's difficult for you, but I promise that Arric would not have pushed all of us so hard if he hadn't thought it necessary," Nyvas offered. "He just wanted to get as far from Bhoren as he could before nightfall."

"Whatever." Nothing she had seen of the Dosedra today had improved her opinion of him.

Nyvas sensed her frustration. "He did it for our safety, Kate. You understand that, do you not?"

Her head hung down as she tried to focus on the task of walking. "To be honest, I don't understand anything about what's going on. Least of all why he has to run away from his own soldiers." After his disappearing act in Loraden, she wasn't surprised men had followed him, but surely no one would harm him.

Nyvas grunted. "They are Senvosra. That means they are the Vosira's men, not his."

"Same difference, isn't it? I mean, he's a prince, right? I don't see why he'd be so worried about them. It's not like they'd do anything to him, would they?"

"That's hard to say, because I don't know what Bedoric would do. Nor does Arric, I'd imagine. What I do know is that he's far more worried for me and my friends than for himself."

She shrugged but didn't reply.

Nyvas was undeterred by her silence. "You do know what we are?" He had lowered his voice, as if he worried that even with the distance between them, the others would overhear.

Based on their appearance, they clearly weren't members of the Bhagali. Farmers, perhaps? That didn't match with the casual manner in which they interacted with the Dosedra, though, so she had already discounted that. Then she figured that perhaps they had been soldiers that had served with him, though Nyvas did not seem at all right for that vocation, and was likely too young anyway. As he brought up the question directly, she realized that she really had no idea who they might be or what their relationship with the Dosedra was. "No, I guess I don't."

"We are fhaoli." He said it without emotion, as if it was utterly normal to make such a pronouncement. "Do you understand what the term means?"

She remembered what Davor, the riversmith had told her about fhaoli. "You're outlaws? That doesn't make any sense." Rapidly she tried to piece together what he was saying, but in her exhausted state was unable to understand. From what she knew of history, outlaws would never interact with royalty in this kind of intimate fashion, as if they were equals. As she kept walking, she turned to look at him, measuring Nyvas's appearance as if it was for the first time. "You're serious?"

He nodded. "Aye." After a moment's pause, he continued, "so now perhaps you can understand why he's so worried that we might be discovered by the Senvosra. According to the law of the land, we have no rights whatsoever." He paused for a moment to let the idea sink in. "Being fhaoli means that if we're caught, the soldiers can do anything they wish to us, as if we were nothing more than wild animals." He spoke with such solemnity that it caused a shiver to run up her spine. "Arric worries that the Senvosra will kill us on the spot if they find us." He paused to skirt around a low branch. "The funny thing is, Fantion's not nearly as concerned about our safety as he is about the risks the Dosedra has taken to be with us."

She hadn't really expected this development, and wasn't sure what she thought about it. These men were criminals? Suddenly all of the things she had heard back in Loraden started to make sense, and she understood why Rynar had been so worried for her. She wondered what kind of trouble she had landed in this time. "Yeah, I guess that makes sense. It wouldn't be good for his brother to find out he was here, would it?"

"Nay, it would not."

CHAPTER 20

"We've gone too far this way—we need to go back," the Dosedra announced. They had been stumbling in heavily wooded, muddy terrain for hours, and with his pronouncement he sounded equally annoyed with the situation, and confident with the assessment. Without another word, he tugged on his mare Trill's reins to turn her around.

The others followed his lead without question, but Kate hesitated, shaking her head. He had made this decision without a map or compass, and it seemed rather arbitrary to her. In the twilight, she strained her eyes to see what would have caused the Dosedra to reverse course. She called out, "why are we going back the way we came?" Having come as far as she had, she wasn't inclined to backtrack now.

"You do want to camp on dry land?" the Dosedra snapped over his shoulder, his patience threadbare.

"Of course I do, but how do you know there's any in that direction? It's just the same that way as any other. There's been nothing but mud for hours now."

He sighed. "Just trust me."

In response, she rolled her eyes. In fact, she was still fuming privately when, after only a few minutes, the Dosedra led them up an incline, following a dry creek bed overgrown with grasses and small bushes. At the top of the hill, the trees opened to a small meadow. Unlike the swamp, this land was dry, the soil was sandy rather than rocky, and the entire field was covered with soft grass that swayed lightly in the breeze. A tall granite cliff sheltered most of the clearing, blocking the wind and concealing their location. Had she designed her perfect campground, she scarcely could have done better.

As the men began to secure their horses to the trees around the edge of the meadow, she boldly walked up to the Dosedra. "How in the world could you have known this clearing was here?"

Rather than respond, he waved her away with a flick of his hand, and busied himself with unpacking their supplies, tossing bedrolls on the ground and then untying a leather sack.

She stood there a moment, furious to be dismissed in such a cavalier manner. Meanwhile, Fantion worked his way along the fringe of trees looking for firewood, Lysander unsaddled and brushed down the horses, and Nyvas dug a shallow pit for a fire. No one spoke to her, gave her directions, or explained anything. It was if she had disappeared entirely. Was her question so unreasonable?

She shook her head and leaned against a tree. Never had she missed her own home, her shower, her bed, more than she did right now. Then, after taking a deep breath and resolving not to sink too deeply into self-pity, she approached Lysander. "Can I help you with the horses?"

"Nay," he replied gently. "We have things under control. Though," he added after a moment's consideration, "you might check with Arric in case he needs anything."

Before she could respond to that, Nyvas, who was digging the fire pit, tugged at her skirt. "I could use some kindling for the fire," he suggested quietly. She nodded and gathered up dead leaves, pine needles and small twigs. He used everything she gave him to get the fire started, but when she turned back for more, he caught her hand. "That's enough. Fantion will bring more. You need to rest." To encourage her, he pulled lightly on her fingers, and she gratefully sank to the ground beside him.

With the weight of her body blissfully off her feet, she wasn't sure if she could ever convince herself to walk again. Her feet and legs hurt more than she ever imagined possible, and her back and thighs ached from the time spent on horseback, a situation she had made worse by trying to avoid leaning against the Dosedra. As the fire grew quickly under Nyvas's expert coaching, she sat as close as possible, grateful for the warmth. Realizing the heat would also dry her shoes, she yanked them off and placed them on a stone at the edge of the fire.

After he finished with the horses, Lysander joined them. The older man waved his long fingers over the fire to warm them as he shook out his damp brown hair. Then he set up a simple wrought-iron tripod above the flames and hung a small cauldron on the hook in the center, filling it with water from a leather pouch. As she watched, he unrolled the top of two other leather bags, and from them, tossed bits of various herbs and dried meat into the water. "After the rough journey, I decided we needed a warm meal to restore our energy," he explained when he noticed her attention. "It won't be much, but it's better than choking down plain jerky." He rubbed his thin beard, adding, "I suspect you in particular could use a hot meal tonight."

"It looks good." She appreciated the momentary kindness. "But don't go to any extra trouble on my account." She felt a nudge at her arm, and turned to see Nyvas handing her a flask.

"Do not let him fool you, Kate," he said, shyly but in a joking manner. "He lives to fuss over us all."

"Thanks." She offered him the best smile she could muster under the circumstances. Then she lifted the vessel to her dry lips. She swallowed a mouthful before noticing it wasn't water. She coughed as it went down her throat. "Is that whiskey?"

After dropping an armload of branches by the fire, Fantion stepped beside her and took the flask. "It's havar," he said curtly, before he swallowed some of the liquor himself. He started to walk away, but stopped. "Bhara, may I have a word with you?"

"Go ahead."

"Nay, I meant privately." He held out a broad, calloused hand. "Come, walk with me."

Her slippers were still damp, but unwilling to walk barefoot in the darkness, she pulled the soggy leather back over her toes with a groan. Then, waving away his hand, she tried to stand up on her own. Even after such a short time resting, tight, sore muscles resisted her efforts to stand. It took her a moment, and she grimaced against the discomfort, but eventually she pulled herself to her feet and limped behind him.

He led her towards the trees, far enough that only minimal light followed them from the campfire. Deep shadows clouded his features, accentuating ridges and furrows on his forehead and around his frowning mouth. "I wished to speak to you about Arric."

Immediately on her guard, she replied, "what about him?"

"He's in a foul mood this eve."

"Aren't we all?" she replied before considering her tone. More softly, she added, "I'm sorry, but really—we're all exhausted and sore, and our clothes are soaked with putrid water—"

He did not look at her, instead shifting his gaze back towards the camp. "It isn't the swamp that troubles him." He slapped his arms against his sides, and then continued, his voice deep and bitter. "What in Kerthal's name caused you to act so spiteful towards him all day today?"

"Oh, I see." She tried to focus her eyes on the shadowy outline of a tree rather than look him in the eye. "Did he send you to scold me?"

From the sound of it, he gritted his teeth, fighting back his first instinctive response. "Nay, my lady, he hasn't said a word to me about it, but I've known him all my life, and I can tell when something is bothering him. Honestly, after all he's done for you, it angers me that you cannot speak to him with a civil tongue."

"Oh, right. You have a problem with the fact that I don't like him. I suppose you'd prefer that I fawn all over him, like the women at the quantrill did?"

"Nay, my lady. I care not a whit whether you like him or not. It simply seems to me that you should not be so rude towards him after he placed your welfare above his own."

At this comment she made a half-laugh through her nose. "You've got to be kidding."

"You didn't notice, then?" He shook his head, as if disappointed with a student who hadn't learned her lesson. "All day he tried to set a pace that you could manage. It was slower than he wanted to go, but he recognized that you were struggling to keep up with the rest of us, and tried not to push you any harder than necessary."

"Don't give me that. Everyone found the swamp difficult. And anyway, I never asked for any favors."

"Aye, I'll grant you that. Still, you're a member of this company just as I am, or the others," he reminded her, "and he does not want any of us to suffer on his behalf."

"Uh huh." She glanced towards the glow of the fire. After a day like today, this confrontation was the last thing she needed. Longing to return to the fire and collapse, she really wanted this conversation to end as quickly as possible. "You're obviously talking about a different man than the one I met last night, and who couldn't say a nice thing to me all day today."

That caused him to lose his temper. "Blast it, Bhara. Do you not hear what I'm telling you?" He was trying to keep his voice low, so it almost sounded like a growl. "If you could just forget what happened in Bhoren for a moment, you'd see the truth in my words."

She sighed. Obviously he had more energy than she did. "The problem is, I can't forget that so easily. I don't know what it's like here, but where I come from, what he did just wouldn't be acceptable. I'm sorry, but I can't overlook it, no matter what you say." She rubbed her forehead, fighting back the first twinges of a headache. "Is this all you wanted, then?"

The tall man pounded his thigh in frustration. "You truly don't grasp what I'm telling you, do you? Then understand this, Bhara. Out of concern for you, he has asked to change horses with me tomorrow. To you, that's nothing, but for him... Bhara, you need to realize that Arric never allows another man to ride his battle-mare. He personally trained Trill from the time she was a foal, so that he could rely on her in battle. You might have noticed how perfectly she responds to his commands. He and that animal share a bond, and he doesn't take that lightly, or entrust her to anyone else without good cause. For you, though, he would make this sacrifice, so that you need not ride with him again."

Oh, great. All she needed now, as serious fatigue weighed down every limb, was a guilt trip. "So what you're saying is that I should just act like last night never happened, and that the way he made me feel doesn't matter? That he's just a great guy and why can't we all just get along, and all that?"

"Nay, Bhara, I just hoped you'd understand." With a grunt, he started to turn back towards camp, but then spun back on his heels.

"Ah, there is one more thing. You should watch yourself. I thought it was a mistake bringing you along in the first place, and I'll gladly leave you behind, right here in this swamp, rather than have you jeopardize his safety or well-being. Do you understand me?"

His words incensed Kate. "Look, I didn't ask to come along—it was all his idea. And to be honest, I'd be more than happy to leave you to your precious Dosedra if I had any other options at this point."

"Is that all?" he asked, impatiently.

"No, it's not," she shot back, seizing the moment to vent her frustrations. "To tell you the truth, I'm cold, exhausted, and everything on my body hurts, and the last thing I needed was a lecture from someone I hardly know. But more than that—I'm not inclined to blindly follow someone just because of his position. You all agreed to follow him into this hellhole without so much as a map. And now, even though we're completely lost, all you care about is making sure he's not in a bad mood? To be honest, after everything he's done, he's probably brought it all on himself." Realizing how ridiculous the situation was, Kate tried laughing but the effort nearly brought tears instead. "Look, I'm so tired I can barely see straight. All I want is to get out of this swamp, and I don't see that happening in my lifetime. So please, just leave me alone."

She expected Fantion to shout back at her, but instead he shook his head and smiled. She could tell, because in the dim light his teeth glowed brighter than anything else. In response to her diatribe, he simply said, "I cannot make you more comfortable, but if it helps your opinion of Arric, he promised that we'll leave the swamp early tomorrow."

"Yeah, sure. Why can't you all just admit that you don't have a clue as to where we are? We'll probably still be wandering around in here a week from now."

"Well, I don't know where we are, that's true enough—but rest assured, Arric does."

She rolled her eyes. "Oh come on. You don't really believe that?"

"Oh, aye. Did you not know?" Now he sounded distinctly amused. "We travel with a Sarducian blood prince. He has the land-instinct, which means that he cannot get lost anywhere on the island. He always knows exactly where he is."

"What? That's impossible."

"Nay, it's true. Both he and his brother have this ability. How else could he have found this clearing? Even better, he believes the land extends for many leagues in the direction we need to travel, so we shall have a dry journey in the morning. This is why he wanted to double back earlier—so we could camp here. If we had kept going the way we had been, we'd have run into a lake."

She was still skeptical, but she could hear the confidence in his voice. "You're serious?"

"Of course I am. I promise that he knows exactly where we are, even if you and I do not. He felt terrible that he had led us in the wrong direction for a short time, but I'm blaming that on fatigue."

Awed by this information, she smiled wanly. Although logically it made no sense, it wouldn't be the first inexplicable thing about this place. At any rate, it was a huge relief to know they weren't really lost. "Wow, I don't know what to say." She felt a bit ashamed of her earlier comments. "I guess I owe you an apology."

Fantion grasped her hand pulled her back towards the fire. "Nay, not to me. Perhaps, however, Arric would listen if one was offered."

"I don't think so." There was hesitation in her voice now.

"Bhara, we have a long journey ahead of us. I'm not asking you to become friends, but it will be easier for everyone if you could at least be civil towards him." Interpreting her shrug as agreement, he led her back to the clearing.

When they returned, both of them noticed the Dosedra was missing.

Fantion asked, "Sander, where did..."

Lysander pointed to an area of shadows. "He said he wished to be alone. I tried to offer him some food, but he refused to take any of it."

"We'll see about that." Fantion fetched a cup of Lysander's stew, and a wedge of the bread packed by Noresa. He started towards the area his friend had indicated, but paused, and snatched up the flask of havar as well.

CHAPTER 21

"I hear you might like some company," the Dosedra said, seating himself on the ground beside Kate, who was finishing her stew. His voice betrayed both exhaustion and reluctance, and she wasn't sure how to respond.

She looked to Fantion, who nodded once. Lysander and Nyvas, sitting on the other side of the fire, seemed to be engaged in a separate conversation, though their glances in her direction betrayed their interest. She turned back to the Dosedra, who was picking at his own stew with a wooden spoon. His wavy dark hair was clinging damply to his forehead, and mud streaked his scarred face. What had Fantion told him? She wanted to bury the hatchet, so to speak, but how? Not knowing where to begin, and with him sitting so close to her, she froze.

When she didn't say anything, he sighed and put his wooden bowl in the grass beside him. "Clearly you dislike me," he said as an opener. "Is it just because of the incident back in Bhoren? Or perhaps you have other reasons?"

Kate cast her eyes to the dark sky above where they sat. Limited moonlight spattered the ground within the forest, and even the stars seemed dim. Eyeing the hilt of the knife on his belt, she wasn't sure she could speak her mind. Instead, she just said, "you must be imagining things. It's just the swamp. I'm tired, and it was a really long day."

He grabbed a fistful of the tall grass, yanking it from the soil. "Nay, it's more than that." He tossed the grass away from his legs and then pulled out a second clump. For a few moments he said nothing else, and the buzzing of insects and the crackle of the fire roared in her ears.

Then he turned back to her. Very quietly, just above a whisper, he asked, "was it Bedoric who sent you, or the Aldrish? Have you learned enough about me yet?"

"What?" His accusations caught her off-balance, just as he would have intended. She had been sitting cross-legged, slumped forward, but this caused her to straighten up. "You think they sent me to spy on you?"

She watched as he rubbed his palms on his thighs, contemplating a response. When he finally spoke, it was with great deliberation. "If you mean to ridicule me, I do not wish to hear it. Believe me, Bhara, I have given this matter a great deal of thought today. You had a reason for traveling to Bhoren, and you could not have completed such a journey, especially in so little time, without assistance—perhaps from the Senvosra? Anyway, in the unlikely event your reasons were honorable, I hoped you would offer an explanation if I gave you an opportunity." For the first time, he looked directly into her eyes. "For the record, I am on a mission of personal relevance, nothing more."

There was nothing she could say. He would hardly believe the truth—that she had traveled because of some sort of magic within her ring, and other than that, she had no other explanation. True or not, it would sound pretty ridiculous to blame everything on a piece of jewelry, yet that was the best she could offer.

When again she didn't respond, he pushed himself up. "Bhara, I am weary from the journey, and regardless of your reasons for being here, I have no energy left to battle with you." He looked over to his friends, and she followed his gaze. Fantion and Lysander pretended not to have overheard, but Nyvas was staring in her direction.

She said nothing, and, still sitting, turned her gaze to the ground. At that moment a strong northern wind soared through the treetops, and the cool air hit her damp dress. Involuntarily she hunched over, and as the chill set off a wave of shivering, she once more caught herself wishing she were home.

"Take off your dress."

His words caused her to forget her discomfort, and she raised her eyes. "What?" she exclaimed.

Dosedra Arric hesitated, and then bent down towards her. "I spent most of eight years in the borderlands, where it rained all the time. If you try to sleep in that heavy gown, it won't dry, and you will be so stiff in the morning you won't be able to walk. That's assuming, of course, that you're lucky enough not freeze to death." He reached to his throat and unhooked his cloak. "Keep your shift on, and then wrap yourself in this."

"I don't need your help." She was being stubborn, even though inwardly she knew he was right.

"It's not a request. Here—I'll hold it up so you can have some privacy."

She sighed, but realized he was serious. Already he was holding the cloak out like a broad curtain, his head turned away. "Fine," she agreed, and quickly, and not a little self-consciously, she stripped the dress from her shoulders. When the colder air hit her damp, bare skin, she gasped, and grabbed the cloak. It was soft on the inside, like brushed flannel, and as soon as she had wrapped it around her, she felt better.

"Give your dress to Sander, and he'll hang it where it can dry." He nodded to his friend. "Should you need anything else, I am at your service. No matter what you think of me, I am not a heartless man." He turned to walk back into the trees.

Cynically, under her breath she said without thinking, "So that's what you tell yourself."

"What do you mean by that?"

He heard her? "Nothing."

"Nay, lady, tell me what you meant."

She shivered again, though this time it had nothing to do with the weather. Even so, she pulled the cloak tighter around her shoulders. She wanted to be brave, but she found it difficult even to speak. Finally, in hushed tones, she found the words. "I've heard the stories, same as everyone. How you abandoned your men to die. Then you came home and expected everyone to call you a hero."

He swallowed, but when he spoke again, his voice cracked slightly. "Who told you such things?"

"You don't deny them?"

"Ahh..." The Dosedra, choked with frustration, raised his arms in the air, curling his hands into fists that would pound the murky clouds above him. His actions caused her to flinch, and she thought he would strike her. Then he let his hands drop. "You have it all wrong, Bhara. I never abandoned anyone." He shook his head, unwilling to go into further details. "And I'm certainly not looking to be called a hero."

"Whatever. I heard differently."

"What did—" he began, but stopped, and instead just said, "what you heard was a lie, but I am not here to argue the point."

"So why are you here, then?" she challenged him. She had no idea why she was pressing the issue, but she continued anyway. "If you have nothing to hide, why are you in the middle of a swamp, running from the Senvosra?"

"Nay, Bhara, it will not go that way. I shall not answer any more of your questions until you explain why you are following me."

"Don't be ridiculous. Why would I want to follow you? I don't even know you."

He snorted derisively. "If you're not following me, then how did you come to be in the torrapon the night when I met with Fantion and Sander?"

"What are you talking about? I never—" Suddenly the memory of laying in the grass came vividly back to her, so clearly that she even remembered the voices of the men who found her, and the soft blanket one of them had used to cover her... a blanket that was exactly like the cloak she now wrapped tightly around herself. Even now, she caught the scent of rosemary in her nostrils. "That was you?"

He raised an eyebrow, as if surprised by her response. "Aye, of course. I carried you back to Loraden even as I returned home myself, and the guards at the gate said they would see you safely home. I assumed, from the way you looked at me at the quantrill, that you remembered me but didn't want anyone to know."

She sighed, suddenly feeling deflated. It explained why the men had acted so strangely when she entered the inn, and even why he had ignored her at the quantrill. "I had no idea. I only remember bits and pieces from that night." Seeing the skepticism in his eyes, she reiterated, "honestly, no one told me a thing. If I had only known that it had been you..." Now she was annoyed for an entirely different reason.

He nodded once. "Then why were you in Bhoren?"

Her brain was working hard to piece everything together. No wonder he thought she was following him. Suddenly she was angry that no one—particularly Rynar—had shared this piece of information with her. Had she known, their interaction at the inn might have gone much differently.

"Look, as I said last night," she began, "I only went into the tavern so I could get out of the rain. I had no idea who you were until I saw you at the quantrill. I certainly would have had no reason to follow you." It was the truth. She hoped it would be enough.

He snorted again, perhaps a little amused, but also clearly doubtful of her story. "It makes for a good tale, Bhara, but I'm not so easily fooled. Even if you had left the city immediately after the quantrill, you could never have reached Bhoren so quickly unless you traveled with Senvosra. Even the four of us, riding hard, had only arrived earlier in the day." He folded his arms across his chest and shook his head, his mind made up. "I just wish I could determine why you refuse to speak the truth."

Nyvas overheard their conversation as he walked by to fetch another flask from his saddlebag. "She did not ride from Loraden," he said confidently. Coming closer, he added, "Arric, surely you remember the story of Imryll, who flew between the furthest-most points of Sarducia in just one day?"

"That's nothing but a legend, Nyvas." The Dosedra rubbed at his eyes, exhaustion rapidly claiming him. "Do not make excuses for her. The only explanation is that she's working for my brother."

"Nay, not him." Nyvas countered confidently, and knelt beside them. "She is definitely here for a reason, but not in Bedoric's service. I do not see any signs that she will betray us. If she had intended to do so, she would have done so by giving you up to the Senvosra back at the inn." He looked into her eyes. "My guess is that she's been caught up in matters she scarcely understands, and is doing her best to make sense of it all—just as you are doing." As she nodded to him, he smiled quickly and then turned back to Arric. "I mentioned the story of Imryll because I think it could explain how she got here."

"What do you mean?" Arric asked.

As he continued, Nyvas seemed much older than his appearance suggested. "As you recall, Imryll did not believe in the gods of our land, and challenged all the people's most sacred beliefs. One day he defied the gods and entered a torrapon alone, trying to show his village that there was no power within the stones. For such a transgression, the gods decided to teach him a lesson. As a display of their power, they sent him to each of the four corners of the island in a single day. After that, he became a disciple of the gods and, as tradition says, he was the first Sarnoc."

Dosedra Arric sighed and rubbed at his eyes. "Aye, I know the legend, and truth be told, it would bear repeating in Loraden these days. Still, what could it possibly have to do with her?"

Still kneeling, Nyvas offered her the flask. "She had to travel somehow. It makes more sense to think she traveled via torrapon than to imagine she walked—or rode—" he added in jest, referring to her difficulty mounting the horse, "all the way there. After all, you found her in a torrapon the last time, did you not? And there is a torrapon just outside Bhoren."

She stared at him, speechless that he had figured it out—in fact, he seemed to understand more than she did. The Dosedra, however, kept shaking his head as if he didn't believe a word.

"Arric, most people dismiss tales of Sarnoc powers, but I know you think differently. And if I'm right—" he said, again looking into her eyes, until she was forced to turn away, "then there's a lot more at work here than just the ambitious graspings of your older brother."

"Bah, that's all preposterous. I appreciate the different perspective, Nyvas, but the simplest explanation is that she's a spy."

"Perhaps," the boy conceded, "but I think that for now, we should give her the benefit of a doubt."

The Dosedra threw up his hands in defeat, and abruptly pushed himself to his feet. "Fine. If you wish to trust her, then so be it. I'm going to sleep."

CHAPTER 22

"Why don't you ask him why he returned?"

"Hmm?" she replied, half-asleep. It was still dark, and she could barely make out the features of the man crouched down beside her. As exhausted as she had been, she had slept poorly on the ground, and despite being wrapped up in the Dosedra's woolen cloak, she had been shivering most of the night. All of that, and the ache in her legs, didn't put her in the best of moods. "What in the world are you talking about?" she mumbled, as she pulled the cloak over her head.

"You should ask Arric why he returned to Sarducia," he said softly.

Slowly she processed the fact that it was Nyvas beside her. She squeezed her eyes shut and pried them open again. Then she shook her head and propped herself up, with her elbow on the ground and her chin leaning on her palm. Really, all she wanted was to go back to sleep. "I appreciate your wanting to help, but—" she hesitated, and looked to either side of her. None of the other men were on their bedrolls, and in fact, the blankets appeared to already be packed up. "Honestly, while I'll take your word for it that he's not an evil man, it's not that easy for me to move on, after everything I've seen and heard. It doesn't help that he's convinced I'm a spy."

To her surprise, rather than upset him, her comment made Nyvas smile. He reached over and squeezed her shoulder lightly. "Just remember what I said," he urged her, and with that he walked over to where Lysander was cooking breakfast over the fire.

"Ugh." It felt like she had just fallen asleep, and she wondered how it could already be morning. For several minutes, she remained wrapped in the cloak and stared at the sky, which offered up no indication that the sun was rising any time soon. When she finally decided to get up, the muscles in the backs of her legs were tight and painful, her hips and thighs ached in unexpected ways, and it was difficult to walk. Just the idea of sitting on a horse made her wish she were dead. She stumbled to the branch where Lysander had hung up her dress last night, and then she disappeared into the trees, where she took care of her personal needs and then got dressed.

When she returned to the fire, Lysander handed her a cup with warm porridge, and as she took it, he placed his other hand on hers for a moment. He was trying to be kind, she realized, and didn't pull away, allowing the warmth of his touch to seep into her skin. The gesture helped restore a bit of her confidence and energized her somewhat, though she was still too tired to converse with anyone, so she just nodded her head to him and sat down to eat. As she took the first bite of the sticky paste, she grimaced, but she ate it just the same. Despite its unappealing consistency, it didn't taste too bad, and it did take the edge off her hunger pangs.

Meanwhile, Lysander seemed cheerful enough, humming to himself as he returned to the fire and scraped the rest of the porridge into his own cup and then used a bit of water from his flask to rinse out the pot. Nyvas also appeared refreshed and ready to tackle another day's journey. A few minutes later, emerging from the woods with Fantion, the Dosedra took a seat across from her, at edge of the fire. He too looked worn out, his dark head sagging on his shoulders as if he barely had the energy to hold it up. Even his hair, newly-washed in a nearby creek, hung limply at his shoulders. Fantion sat beside him, eating his own porridge, but did not appear to share his friend's fatigue.

When it was time to depart, the Dosedra quietly announced that she would again ride with him. She wondered why he had changed his mind, but with a shrug, she agreed, and allowed him to lift her onto the horse. She hurt so much in so many different places that she didn't have the spirit left to protest.

They rode for a while without a single word passing between them. She couldn't address what had been said the night before. Although she continued to ponder Nyvas's suggestion, she had no idea how to raise the subject, and had no inspiration for alternate conversation. Making things easier, at least, the Dosedra likewise remained silent.

Twice they had to dismount to maneuver through thick trees, and she was careful to keep her distance, both to avoid conversation and so he wouldn't notice her limping. Each time it was possible to ride again, the Dosedra called out to her to join him, and without speaking she mechanically went through the steps to climb onto the horse. At least by now she had figured out how to mount the horse with only minimal assistance.

The second time, once they were again on horseback, he finally broke the tense silence between them. "Bhara, I have a matter to discuss with you, if you're willing to humor me."

"What is it?" she asked, defensively, uneasy about the direction the conversation would take.

He sucked in a breath, as if it was no easier for him to talk to her than it was for her to reply. "You say you're new to Sarducia, yet it appears you were easily convinced to see me as an enemy. Was it the Aldrish that turned you against me, and if so, could you tell me what he told you?"

"I don't know what you're talking about," she hedged.

He was undeterred. "We are well past playing games, Bhara. I know you were the Aldrish's personal guest in the keep, and that he escorted you to the quantrill. I know little of the man myself, but what I do know is enough to make me question his motives. You may keep whatever secrets you are bound to honor. I simply wish to know what he has said about me."

The question made her uncomfortable, and she hesitated. The question required her to make judgment calls she felt unqualified to make, and to take sides in a conflict in which she preferred to remain neutral. But she had to tell him something, so she stuck to the truth. "There really isn't much to say. I heard about how you left to fight in some war after your brother became Vosira, but then abandoned your men, and disappeared. No one knew you were still alive until you showed up in the city."

"I see." By the way he snapped the reins once, she sensed he was becoming impatient. "What did the Aldrish say about me leaving Loraden?"

Would he throw her off the horse if she said the wrong thing? Or something even worse? An involuntary shiver ran across her shoulders and down her back. Rynar had warned her that the Dosedra could be dangerous. "Do we really need to talk about this now?"

Without warning, the horse stopped so suddenly that she was amazed that she didn't fly right over Trill's head. "Do not play games with me. You cannot deny your association with the Aldrish. Before we go any further, you must explain how you came to be his guest in Loraden and what he has told you about me."

"Why?" It was her turn to lose her patience. "What does it matter?"

"Bhara," he said, spoken as if there was gravel between his teeth, "What does the Aldrish know about my journey, and why did he send you?"

"Don't you understand? I don't know any of that. And I wasn't looking for you—I just ended up here. I don't even know why I'm in Sarducia, and even the Sarnoc can't explain it."

He sucked in a breath, and then, in a softer tone than he had ever used with her, asked, "you spoke to Sarnoc?"

Did she dare tell him the truth? She quickly weighed the pros and cons in her head, and decided to take a chance. "The Aldrish sent me out of Loraden after you left. The next thing I knew, my trip was diverted and I was meeting with Sarnoc and the Pasadhi. And then I ended up here. Honestly, it makes no more sense to me than it does to you."

"Hmm." He flicked the reigns lightly to coax his horse forward again. They rode in silence for a while, and she felt sick to her stomach.

Finally he broke the silence again. "Bhara, even if everything you say is true—and I'm not saying I believe you—one fact remains. You were terrified when you realized it was me back at the inn. Why is that?"

She felt like there was chalk in her mouth. "Rynar told me that you might be dangerous."

"Did he, now?" He breathed loudly, causing her to tense up. After a few moments, he asked, more softly, "did you truly believe I would hurt you?"

"I—I don't know. I guess so. I didn't know what to think then—" or, she realized, what to think now. She could feel her heart racing, and really wanted to climb off the horse.

"Huh." In a surprise gesture, he placed his left hand lightly on her forearm. "I appreciate your courage in telling me this." Then he lifted his hand to her chin, and gently guided it to the right, so she would turn her head, and he leaned out so they could almost have eye contact. "I swear to you, Bhara, in the name of the goddess Kerthal—if you're being honest now, you have nothing to fear from me." He guided Trill around a rocky outcropping, choosing to go left even though it seemed clear to the right. As they passed by, she noticed that a tree had fallen directly over the other path. "The stories about me are untrue. While I'll be the first to admit that I've done a great many things I'm ashamed of," he shifted his weight in the saddle, pulling away from her slightly. "I've never abandoned anyone under my command, or harmed anyone outside of battle."

"Why does everyone say that you did, then?"

"Well," he said, "it's not an easy story for me to tell, Bhara, but—" He hesitated. "It's a fair trade, for sharing what you've told me." He flicked the reins once, and Trill began moving again. "First of all, I made some grievous mistakes as a young man, and running away to Hansar— to the Queen, no less—was probably the worst of them all. At the time, I jumped at the chance to lead the Queen's forces against the Mosumi rebels. I had the opportunity to do something I thought was important, I didn't have to watch my brother become Vosira, and at the time, it seemed like a way to get my revenge on him for how he had treated me. So I went to Froida, where I was scarcely more than a mercenary, though for a short time I did command the troops the Queen had convinced my fool brother to send over." He shifted his weight on the saddle before continuing. "The night of that battle, when they said I ran away, we had been fighting the Mosumi for several days in the snow. There is no way for me to know how bad the battle really was, or how many died that night, because..." he raised his hand, and when she turned her head again, out of the corner of her eye she watched him rub the scar on his forehead. "He came out of nowhere with that axe. I should have died, Bhara. The blade cut deep into my skull. I should have died right there, and a part of me wishes I had. But I didn't."

He fell silent for a moment, and reached back into the saddlebag for his flask. He first offered it to her, but she shook her head. After he drank for a moment, he corked it and returned it to the saddlebag.

When he didn't continue, she gently prompted him. "What happened?"

"Forgive me for hesitating, but I've only told the story once before, to Fantion and the others. It's not an easy tale to tell, and not something that I would tell to a stranger."

"Please tell me."

He hesitated, and for a moment it seemed like he wasn't going to comply. Then he cleared his throat, and a little hoarsely he continued. "I was certain the god Yoren had come to claim me, for all around me there was this blinding light and music. That is all I can remember, the light and music. Then it was spring, just like that. The rest of winter had just passed me by as I lay there, with a mortal wound that—wasn't. And when I woke, it was with the Mosumi in Froida. They had healed me. After everything I had done to them, all of the men I had killed—they healed me."

"Why did they do that?"

"I knew not. All I knew was that I was far from the battlefield— well inside Froida, in fact. They had nursed me, their enemy, back to health, and then carried me all the way back to their chieftain. Every day I asked why they would do such a thing for me, wondering what their motives might be. It made no sense. And then, after spending some time as their prisoner, their chief befriended me, and everything changed. Even though I was technically his captive, to be honest, I've never been so happy in my whole life. I learned that the Mosumi had never wanted to attack Hansar, but instead the whole conflict had been a result of Queen Tylnea trying to extend her borders and influence into Froida and other lands—much the same as she's trying to do to us now. When I matched that information with some other information Tylnea had given me, I realized in the end that I had fought on the wrong side, and I was deeply ashamed of what I had done."

As he spoke, she felt herself shaking. It wasn't the tale she expected, yet she believed every word. It wasn't the kind of thing someone would make up. "Nyvas said I should ask you why you came home."

"He did?" he seemed surprised. "Hmm." He considered the request. "Very well, but I'd rather this not be repeated in Loraden, so can you keep it between us?"

"Of course." She agreed, and then realized that this request suggested he was willing to trust her—a status she wasn't sure she had earned.

He continued, as if he was telling the story for his benefit more than hers. "I had been in Froida for several years, and living with the Mosumi. As the years went by, Tylnea's anti-Mosumi policies made me increasingly angry. Finally, I decided I had to confront her on it. So as much as I wanted to stay in Froida, I felt it was my duty to try to end the conflict between her and the Mosumi people.

"Of course she didn't want to hear any of it. When she rejected my recommendations for a cease-fire, my plan was to head back to Froida, but I met a Sarducian trader on the docks. Idle curiosity led me to ask him how my homeland fared, and that was the first time I heard of this nonsense about a 'Hidden God,' and that Bedoric was on the verge of outlawing the Sarnoc entirely. With that information, I decided I should come home and see what I could do." He sighed. "You know, when I think about it, the Aldrish was right. I did abandon my people—but it was the Sarducian people, not my troops. I should never have left my homeland. I should have stayed here to challenge my brother. From what I can see of it now, he's made a terrible mess of things."

"I had no idea about any of this." She suddenly felt like she had been played.

"Of course not. As I said, no one knows, other than the four of you with me now—and no one else needs to know. I just wish I hadn't been such a selfish, foolish young man all those years ago, because all of this could have been avoided."

He grunted, a sound deep in his throat, the sound of anger and frustration. And then, without warning, she felt his knees shift, and his arm tightened around her waist, and then Trill burst forward, tearing through an opening in the trees.

"What the hell?" She grabbed Trill's mane as she bent down against the horse's neck, trying to reach around it. Branches clawed at her arms, and thorns scratched her scalp, and she closed her eyes as she prayed she wouldn't fall off. She had no idea how fast her heart was pounding as they covered what seemed like several miles at rocket speed, cruising over rocks and shrubs, dashing around larger trees, and galloping across an open field.

Breathing was difficult until Dosedra Arric finally reined in Trill and they came to a halt, with the others far behind.

As they sat there, perfectly still, he continued his story, though his voice was softer, almost as though he was talking to himself. "I have to find a way to restore the old faith in Loraden, and help some of the people my brother has wronged—starting with my friends traveling with us. It is the only way I can make amends for all the suffering I caused in the past, and thank the gods for sparing my life. The whole point of this journey was to look for an old friend who could have helped me with that, but he passed on years ago, so I must return and face my brother alone."

She tried to imagine herself in a similar situation, but it was impossible. "Dosedra, I'm sorry." She wished she could say something more profound. "I shouldn't have assumed the worst."

He exhaled heavily, a sound of disgust coming from deep in his chest. "Nay, I deserved it. You had no way to know anything different, and on the surface, I must have appeared as cruel and cowardly as they said I was." With those words, he leaned over and rested his head on her shoulder, a gesture that made her catch her breath.

For a few minutes they sat in that position, both silent. Trill shifted her weight once, but otherwise none of them moved.

Out of the blue, he lifted his head and said, "I truly am sorry about the other night. I treated you with great disrespect, and I regret it deeply."

"Thanks. And I'm sorry I questioned your judgment yesterday. I had no idea you really knew where we were, all along."

It was remarkable, for he actually laughed at that. "Ah, so someone told you about the land instinct. Fair enough, then."

CHAPTER 23

As the day progressed, the weather turned sour. A light drizzle fell from the clouds, chilling everyone, and making things worse, they were forced to dismount again.

"Blast this weather," Fantion grumbled at one point as he shook the water from his curly hair and then bent over slightly to block the worst of the rain from his face, scowling the whole time. Water rolled down his nose and he flung it away with a flick of his hand. As he splashed through the pooling water on the ground, he said, "the swamp was bad enough, but rain as well? By the gods, I don't think I'll ever be dry again."

Arric, whose own head was covered with his hood, grunted in agreement, and slapped his friend's back as he stepped past him. Nyvas and Lysander seemed to tolerate their misery no better, and neither would speak unless necessary. As for Kate, the pace had utterly worn her out, and the blanket she used in lieu of a proper cloak was soaked through. Worst of all, her stamina simply could not compare to theirs. More than once the men had to stop to allow her to catch up. Oddly, no one complained, and once she thought she even caught an encouraging smile from Fantion, but she felt terrible about it all the same.

Once they were again able to ride, she gratefully allowed Dosedra Arric to lift her into the saddle. Once he was seated behind her, he gathered her into his cloak and pulled it close around them both as best he could. She didn't protest this new intimacy, for she was entirely chilled now. Once she caught herself dozing off, and she jerked herself awake before she could fall from the horse.

"You're not accustomed to such strenuous travel," he observed. "I apologize for pushing everyone so hard, but we need to keep going so we can find a safe place to camp tonight."

He had not offered any explanations the day before, and the fact that he trusted her with one now was gratifying. Perhaps they had reached some sort of understanding. "I'll be all right."

"Nay, Bhara, I sense your exhaustion. It's also obvious that you're not used to riding, and you must be terribly sore, but under the circumstances, it can't be helped. Just a little further, and we will reach the confluence," he said with confidence. "Travel should be easier then, and we will have a dry place to camp."

"Thanks, but don't worry about me." She wanted to be cooperative now that she understood their situation better. "Just keep going."

"Aye." He felt her shift her weight against him. "Bhara, I don't mind if you try to nap while we ride. I will not let you fall."

Despite her best efforts, and despite the constant bump and sway of horseback riding, once he had made this suggestion, she couldn't help herself, and she soon slipped into a light slumber.

***

Late that afternoon, after two days of trudging through the swamp's thick mire—and just as Nyvas had promised to her the night before—they emerged from the Muras. It was a gradual transition from water to thick mud to solid land, but eventually Kate recognized a difference in the vegetation. The terrain was no longer forested, and instead they rode through tall, flowering grasses that stretched across the gently undulating foothills. Even better, the sun emerged and warmed them after a day of damp that chilled them all.

It was then when she learned her first lesson about what it meant to be fhaoli. When they crested a hill, she saw it first.

"Is that a fire?" she asked aloud, and pointed to a dark plume several miles off to the south.

Lysander was riding beside Trill, and shaded his eyes from the sun as he stared in the direction she pointed. "Aye, and a large one at that." He turned to Arric. "What do you think? Should we see what it is?"

"It's a long way off," the Dosedra said with a frown, and tugged once on Trill's reigns to halt her progress on the rocky ground. "I hate to spare the time, and it would mean a long ride across open land." He gazed at the sun. "Ah, and I had hoped to reach the edge of the Arsdala by nightfall. If we were to go, it would mean camping out in the open tonight, and that would be dangerous with all the Senvosra around." He called out to Fantion, who was several yards ahead. "What are your thoughts?"

His friend turned his horse and stared out into the distance. "Aye, Arric, it looks bad. I'd like to find out what's happening as well, but you're right, we'd be rather exposed." He was frowning as well, and appeared genuinely concerned. "I hate to turn our backs on it, though, because these things are rarely random occurrences."

"What do you think is burning?" Kate asked.

"It could be anything. Sometimes farmers burn their fields after the harvest, or perhaps someone's clearing a briar patch," Fantion explained. "It could even be a cottage fire, though from the looks of it, it's more than that."

"You seem pretty worried about it."

"Aye, and for good reason. There have been several village fires lately, and if this is one of them, it would be good to lend a hand if we could."

"Oh blessed Goddess, do you think it could be Ryvenor?" Lysander said with a sudden gasp, his hand over his mouth. "Coming from this direction, I didn't realize until now we were so close." He looked at Fantion with panic in his eyes. "Yvora."

The Dosedra nodded. "He's right. Ryvenor is the nearest village in that direction." He clucked once to Trill so he was next to Lysander, and placed his hand on his friend's arm. "Sander, Fantion might be right. It could just be farmers clearing their land."

Nyvas had said nothing up to this point, and kept his eyes on the smoke. "It's still burning, whatever it is." Just as he made the observation, a thick roll of black smoke spun up into the air, as if something new had exploded in flames. "That is no farmer's fire—it's far too large for that. Someone should go. I'll do it, Sander, if you want."

"Nay, I wouldn't ask anyone else to go in my place." Lysander's horse was already prancing, strangely recognizing the fear of his rider. "Arric, I'm sorry to leave you, but I must check on my sister. If I can, I'll return tonight."

The Dosedra slapped his thigh. "Sander, if Yvora's in danger, we should all go with you."

"Nay, Arric, as you've already said, it's too risky. How would you explain it to the Senvosra if you were caught with us?" As he saw the Dosedra about to challenge him, he quickly added, "it's best for everyone if I go alone." With that, before anyone could argue further or make other plans, he kicked the horse with his booted heels and the brown gelding and cloaked rider charged across the hillside, flying towards the smoke.

The others remained silent on the crest of the hill, watching him ride off as if pursued by demons. Finally Kate whispered to Dosedra Arric, "what do you really think happened?"

He turned Trill back to the path they had been following. "I don't know. A fire as large as that could mean the entire village is burning." He was visibly upset with the idea. "I've seen such things many times before, but not in Sarducia, where we haven't known war in centuries."

"Senvosra," Fantion suggested and spit on the ground. "Either that or bandits. Though these days, I'd put a wager on it being soldiers."

"Bedoric is using his men to maintain order in the villages now?" Arric asked. "Do the Bhagali not police their own lands?"

"Aye, but the Bhagali tend to overlook fhaoli," Fantion explained. "When men are arrested, there are fewer hands to bring in the crops, which means lighter tax revenues. Having fhaoli around means their chests are heavier at the end of the season. Bedoric, though, has more soldiers these days than he's inclined to garrison in Loraden, and he empowers them to do his bidding in the countryside. More often than not the Senvosra use this damn Prophet to justify fights or some random act of destruction."

"So that's the way of things, then. I feared as much." The Dosedra sighed, and pounded on his thigh. "Damn, I wish Sander didn't have to face this alone."

CHAPTER 24

Fantion gazed up towards the treetops that prematurely ushered in the night. After a lengthy ride, they had reached the Arsdala, a dark forest that stretched across half of the island, and offered significant concealment and protection. "Who'd have ever thought I'd be happy to be back in Lockleaf?" he said, using the forest's nickname with a chuckle. "This is the first time I've felt like I could breathe in days." To Kate, he added, "the Senvosra tend to avoid the trees, so we're less likely to be pursued now. I've heard some say that the forest is cursed, and if they want to believe that, it suits us just fine."

Although there was still daylight left, soon after entering the trees, Arric decided upon a campsite that consisted of a small opening in the middle of a patch of thorny bushes. However, because they were still relatively close to the road, they collectively agreed that a fire would be dangerous. As much as they all wanted one, they didn't want to take a chance of being discovered by the Senvosra, so it meant a cold night ahead, with only dried jerky strips and stale bread for supper. And although the rain had stopped, the wind was gusty. As they ate their meager dinner, they sat huddled together, the horses hobbled close to where they would sleep.

After their meal, Fantion and the Dosedra excused themselves to slip into the trees to talk privately, leaving her alone with Nyvas to lay out their blankets.

"You're worried about Sander." She didn't know much about these men, but after a few days it was obvious that the two were particularly close.

In the fading daylight, Nyvas's angular features seemed more pronounced, and something about the shadows of his face made him look quite old. "Aye, if anything has happened to his sister and her family, I don't know if he could stand it." He spoke softly, with pain evident in his voice. "They are his only family, and they mean everything to him."

"Do you think things could be that bad?"

He unrolled one of the blankets with a snap, and to her it looked like he was struggling to keep up a facade of congeniality that covered an underlying seething anger. "It's anyone's guess. It all depends on what caused the fire, but honestly, none of the reasons I can think of are good." He took a deep breath and reached for another blanket. "And then there's the fact that he's gone. Riding out alone always brings additional risks. It would have been best for him to stay with us in Lockleaf, but where his sister's concerned, there's really no point in arguing with him or holding him back. I just hope he's safe, and nothing has happened to his sister or her family. If the Senvosra have harmed any of them..."

She placed her hand on his arm. "Try not to imagine the worst. I'm sure he'll be fine."

"Thank you, Kate. I hope so." He looked up and gave her a weak smile. "It's hard to remain positive right now, but I know it's all in the hands of the Goddess, and I have to believe it will work out. Hopefully he'll be back soon."

Kate thought to how far they had traveled since they last saw Lysander, and how they now camped in the forest in complete darkness. "How will he ever find us now?"

Nyvas didn't hesitate. "Oh, you don't need to worry about that, at least. He'll find me." There was no doubt in his voice as he said it. "So we shall wait for him." He held out a strip of jerky. "Are you still hungry?"

"No, go ahead." She sat on her blanket, which Nyvas had insisted she lay out between his and Arric's, for protection and warmth, he said.

Then she leaned back on her hands. "I just wish we knew what was happening with him."

"Aye, so do I."

Fantion and Arric returned soon afterwards. Unlike the previous evenings, tonight they would take turns guarding the camp. Despite all the stories about Lockleaf, apparently the fear of discovery was greater because they could be tracked much more easily in the forest than in the swamp, and there was more traffic through this part of the woods both by soldiers and common folk, some of whom would have hostile intentions.

Nyvas volunteered for the first watch, claiming that he wouldn't be able to sleep anyway, and no one argued the point. As he sat at their feet, sword and knife at the ready, she and the others curled up close together to try to get some sleep.

They hadn't been asleep long when they heard a horse bluster. When she heard the sound, it was soft, and seemed to be out in the trees, leading her to surmise that it wasn't one of their own. "Is that him?" she asked, in a loud whisper.

"Shh," Arric gently admonished her, rolling over to cover her mouth with a finger. Leaning close to her ear, he explained, as he quietly reached for his sword, "we don't want to announce our presence until we know for sure. Let him approach."

Nyvas was already on his feet, and the other two men were close behind him, all silently moving. Oddly, although Fantion and Arric had weapons at the ready, Nyvas had already sheathed his sword. Moments later, she heard a whip-poor-will call, and then the men relaxed their sword arms. Immediately after that, Lysander slipped into the tiny clearing with his horse, barely visible in the light of the newly-risen moon. She could hear both man and beast breathing heavily. As Arric took the reins of the horse and led it to be with the others, Nyvas greeted his friend with a short exclamation, and then embraced him.

"Sander?" Fantion approached him with a flask of water, and Lysander took it readily, swallowing easily half of its contents in a couple of gulps. Then he wiped his gloved hand across his forehead and leaned against a broad tree trunk.

"It was Ryvenor, just as I feared," he finally said, panting, his voice low and rough. "Burned to the ground. Completely destroyed."

"And Yvora?" Nyvas asked with a grimace.

Lysander tipped his head back and tried to catch his breath. After a moment, he replied, "she's unharmed, as are her boys." He drank again from the flask, and as he did so, Arric struck a flint and set a twist of pine needles alight, which he used to light a torch so they could see each other. "She had quite a fright seeing me gallop into the middle of it all, I must tell you." He allowed himself to grin despite the grave situation. "They were lucky, all things told. She and the children escaped without even a singe."

"What about Tomar?" Fantion asked.

Sander shook his head. "He's safe, but he's fhaoli now, I think. She didn't know for sure, but she thinks so, and of course he's long gone now." He paused to think, and then continued, "that would mean a dozen newly outlawed, plus the five from the beginning of the summer. That's nearly all the men in the village." Again he took a drink. "They all took off for the trees as soon as the Senvosra appeared. It'll be hard on Ralli and Wylan, though, especially Wy—he and his father are very close." He emptied the flask and returned it to Fantion. "You can well imagine that Yvora was mad as a hornet that I showed up when I did, since the soldiers had just left. She was sure I'd be arrested and hanged in the square before day's end."

Dosedra Arric's eyebrows furrowed as he considered the news. "The Senvosra started the fire, then?"

"Nay, it was the men of the village. It was planned." He took a moment to suck in a breath. "They were expecting arrests, Yvora said, and the village agreed it was the best they could do. The goats had already been chased into the hills, and the chickens into the trees. The boys will try to catch them all tomorrow, I suspect."

It made no sense to Kate. "They burned their own homes?"

"Aye, Sander, what would make them do that?" Arric seemed as confused as she was.

"It's on the list," Fantion explained. "Ryvenor was suspected of harboring fhaoli. That's one of the edicts from a few summers ago. Any families found to have fhaoli living among them have their belongings confiscated by the Senvosra, and everyone is arrested and punished as the Senvosra see fit—even the children. Since so many were already outlawed, everyone knew it was a matter of time. So the people of Ryvenor burned their own homes to create enough confusion to allow the men to escape."

"Aye, a village without people is a dead village," Fantion said. "It's becoming a common tactic. This way, at least the men remain free, and no one gets arrested. And they'll have a chance to rebuild."

"But... if all of the village's men are fhaoli now..." Dosedra Arric began. "Won't they just face future raids?"

"Ah, well," Fantion said, "welcome to the cycle of life under Vosira Bedoric."

***

"I'm really sorry, Sander," Kate said.

He had been kneeling so that he could roll out his blanket, and now he sat back on his heels, nibbling on a bit of bread and drinking heavily of the havar Fantion had just offered him. When she approached he pushed back damp strands of hair from his face. "Ah, I appreciate your concern, but there's nothing you can do about it."

"I know, but it's still really horrible."

"It's the way of things. At least my family is safe. Tomar—my sister's husband—and the other men will be joining us in Lockleaf for a few days, and then when it's safe we'll all go help rebuild the village. It's really nothing new for us, as this happens at least once a season. I just worry about Yvora because she's heavy with child, and doesn't need the grief now. I would have sent her to the Sarnoc, but with all the Senvosra on the roads, that's almost impossible. Instead, she's talking of coming to Lockleaf with Tomar to give birth, since I'm here." He made a low, grunting sound. "You cannot imagine how angry it makes me to think she would have to birth that baby in the woods. She should be in her own home—but now she has nothing." There was a catch in his throat, and he covered his mouth and turned away for a moment. When he faced her again he trembled slightly. "Worst of all, it's likely my fault."

"What do you mean?"

"I went there, to Ryvenor, when Yvora became ill early in her pregnancy. Tomar was worried because she wouldn't eat or drink anything, and she wouldn't see another healer. I had to go. Afterwards, we got word that while I was there, some travelers recognized me and reported it when they returned to Loraden. So the whole village lost their homes, and it's because of me."

"It's not your fault, Sander," Nyvas said as he walked up behind him, and placed his hands on his shoulders. "You did what had to be done." Without a word Lysander reached up to cover the young man's hands with his own long fingers.

"Perhaps so, but it's still hard to know why it happened, and not be able to do anything."

"Sander, I shall speak to Bedoric about this when I return," the Dosedra promised.

"Nay, Arric. It would be better that you say nothing. Ryvenor needs to be left alone. If we're lucky, they'll have until spring before the Senvosra return. If they can get new homes built, they may have a chance to make it through the winter, but if Bedoric has a mind to send more soldiers, they will suffer greatly for it."

"Very well," he agreed, but sounded doubtful. "I will send coin to your sister, though."

To that comment, Sander nodded. "That will be greatly appreciated."

CHAPTER 25

The next day, after a much shorter day of travel, and a much warmer one than the previous days, Arric dismounted and led them into a clearing in the shadow of a sheer rock cliff. With boulders in front of them that limited access to the area, it was a more isolated and defensible location than anywhere they had been for days. "Shall we make camp here?"

Kate was surprised by the suggestion, since they had a late start, and it was still a good two hours or more until sunset.

Apparently she was not the only one caught off-guard. "Are you sure?" Fantion asked as he circled his own horse back around. "We can probably travel another league before nightfall."

"Everyone is drained, including the horses, and I doubt we will find a safer location for the evening if we press on." In a low voice the Dosedra added, "Sander's a wreck. I wouldn't want to wager on whether it would be him or the horse that would collapse first."

"Aye, that's true enough." His friend shrugged as he glanced back at Lysander, who seemed lost in his own thoughts. "Well, it works for me. This is more riding than I've done in years."

Kate appreciated that comment, and after Arric helped her down from the saddle, she joined the men in stretching out aching limbs and shoulders. No one seemed immune from saddle-soreness, making her wonder if any of them rode horseback as often as she first thought.

As Arric and Fantion unpacked the bedrolls and other supplies, and Nyvas gathered wood, she crouched down beside Lysander to help him prepare their meal. Without a word he reached into his pouch and handed her packets of dried meat wrapped in leaves and twine, the small bag of dried herbs, and the last of the carrots Noresa had packed for them.

"We'll need water," the Dosedra said. She nodded to him, and unhooked the leather pail from Nyvas's horse, as well as an empty leather flask. "There's a stream that way, just down the hill." He indicated the direction with a jerk of his head since he was busy cleaning the dried mud from Trill's hooves. "Would you mind filling my flask as well?"

"No problem." With a skip, she headed down the incline. Even though she ached all over, the pain abated a bit now that she felt she was part of the group rather than a reluctant—or worse, distrusted—guest.

The water of the stream was clear and cold. She scooped up water in her cupped hands, and after drinking deeply, splashed water on her grimy face. The water felt so good after days of mud and muck. She took a deep breath as knelt on the bank. There was little time to delay, since they needed water for cooking. Still, she stole a moment to use the pail to pour water over her head and scrub at it. Then, after shaking her head to release the excess water, she then filled the containers, and headed back up the hill.

On her way back she passed Nyvas and Fantion leading the horses to the stream. "Good idea," Nyvas remarked at her damp hair. "I think I'll do that myself."

When she returned to camp, Arric was sitting on the ground, his face buried in his saddlebag, rummaging for something.

"Ah, here it is," he exclaimed. "I feared I'd lost it in the swamp." He pulled out an item wrapped in blue wool, something long and thin. As he unrolled the fabric on his thigh, she saw the unmistakable glint of glysar.

"What is it?" she asked from the other side of the fire, as she emptied the pail into the cooking pot.

He cradled the shiny cylinder in his outstretched palms. "It's an ioni flute."

She stepped around the fire. "It's beautiful." It resembled a silver flute from her world, but without the keys, and it was a bit shorter and thinner. In the sunlight it shone as if on fire.

"Legend says the secret of how to make ioni flutes came from the gods," he said, as he warmed the luminous metal in his hands. "This flute is generations old, and I believe it's one of the best that was ever made. Though perhaps you and the others should be the judge of that."

He placed one end to his lips. A single note beamed forth, pure and unwavering. He blew into the flute a second time, this time filling the irregularly shaped holes with the fleshy pads of his fingers. Without further hesitation, he filled the flute with his warm breath, and from the instrument came a simple, haunting melody, with the notes slow and deliberate, hovering in the lower register.

As he played, she returned to the cooking pot, cutting up the carrots and dried meat with Lysander's knife, and then she added the seasonings. When she carried the stew to the fire, her attention was on the music, and she almost dropped the pot the first time she tried to hang it on the hook.

Returning with his horse, Nyvas pushed his dark hair from his eyes, and stole a glance at the Dosedra. "I had no idea he could play like that," he whispered to her as he crouched down beside her. "If I had known, he would've had that flute out every night, Senvosra or not."

She smiled, and nodded in agreement. As the Dosedra played, his eyes were closed, his energy focused entirely on the flute and the music that came from it. The stiffness he carried with him every moment—as if he was always prepared for an attack—had vanished. "It's incredible," she whispered back to Nyvas. "Who'd have thought it possible?" She leaned back on her feet. "It's really hard to believe he's the same man that I met a few nights ago." She chuckled, mostly to herself. "What's the song called, do you know?"

Lysander walked up behind her to stir the pot. "Ah, he doesn't name most of his tunes."

"Wait—that's his own music?" Seeing Sander nod, she shook her head in disbelief. "The surprises never end with him."

With a gentle nudge from Lysander, as the stew bubbled, she grabbed her blanket and spread it out by the fire. Sitting quietly, she could give her full attention to Arric's music. As he continued to play, her head began filling with images. It was easy to imagine a field of wildflowers in the spring, with warm breezes and children playing. She felt the ice-cold shock of jumping into a spring-fed pond in mid-summer, and eating fresh peaches right off the tree, the juice dripping down her cheek. There was dancing, and merriment, in a hall brightly-lit with torches, with laughter and rejoicing. By hearing his music she half-believed she was sharing his intimate memories.

As he continued to play, one song melting into the next, she almost forgot that she was in the middle of nowhere. Illogically, the music seemed to help revitalize her sore feet and diminish her aches. Maybe the flute really was god-given, or if not, perhaps the talent of the performer had been. She lost track of everything around her, and for the first time since her mother had died, she let go of grief and fear. Even as a few tears fell down her cheeks, she experienced a sense of inner calm, as if all her worries were set aside for the moment.

Eventually, however, Lysander broke the spell. At the end of the next tune, he softly called out, "food's ready."

In response, Arric set the flute in his lap, his eyes closed in contemplation, his fingers quietly absorbing the last of the gentle power within the metal. Finally content, he rolled the flute into its protective wrappings and carefully placed it back in the saddlebag. Then he walked past where she sat, ruffled her hair playfully, and reached for one of the bowls sitting on a rock beside Lysander.

As he passed, his touch sent a wave of goosebumps down her back, and she bit back a smile. In her current position, with her chin resting on her hands, and her elbows propped up on her knees, she neither moved nor dared to look up at him.

"Aren't you hungry?" he asked when he passed by her again. She now glanced up and saw that he was holding two bowls. "May I join you?"

In some ways, things had been easier when she thought him heartless. At this moment—now that she no longer feared or despised him—she found it infinitely more difficult to talk to him. Kate closed her eyes, trying to summon her confidence, and nodded.

He sat beside her, crossing his legs under him. Whether or not he sensed her awkwardness, he did not acknowledge it.

"It's been a long day, aye?" he asked gently, reaching for one of her hands, and placing a bowl in it. "Sander said that under no circumstances was I to let you fall asleep before you finished that."

Her eyes opened a crack. His words were kindly spoken, and it made her smile. Smelling the aroma of the warm broth, she scooped up a mouthful with the wooden spoon and began to eat.

"You've been rather quiet this evening, Bhara." He had started on his own stew, and finished his mouthful. "There's nothing wrong, I hope?"

"No, Dosedra, not really. I'm just tired."

He tipped his head sideways to gaze at her. "Aye, fair enough." Then his eyes fell back to her bowl. "You've stopped eating."

With a smirk she took another bite.

"While I'm sitting here, there's an issue I've been meaning to discuss with you," he announced gravely. "It's been bothering me, and I think we should resolve it now."

Her anxiety returned with a vengeance, and her head shot up. "What is it?"

"It's all this formality," he said, gazing at her, and then he winked. "In public, it must be different, but while we're out here, please, just call me Arric."

She smiled with a sigh of relief, glad nothing was wrong. "Then you'll have to call me Kate."

After they ate, Arric was coaxed into performing again, and when he played a couple folk tunes, Fantion offered his voice to sing the words. It was a funny pairing, since the flute was so pure and light and Fantion's voice was rough and slightly off-key. Still, it was an entertaining evening, the first she had known since the quantrill. As they sang, she reclined on her blanket, and before she knew it, she was fast asleep.

CHAPTER 26

"These are the foothills of the Carpasic Mountains," Arric explained, as much to his male companions as to Kate. "We rode around them on our way to Bhoren, but we will cut through them here."

This new day led them down a road that seemed little more than a faint line etched into the rocky cliffs. To make up time, Arric had chosen a more direct but also quite challenging route, with a path strewn with jagged rocks and small bushes with thick roots exposed from years of erosion. The treacherous passage required careful movements to avoid injuring the horses. Many streams found their source high in the mountains, and frequently the cold springs spilled down the hillsides and over their path, making the rocks slick. For a long stretch the path was particularly dangerous, meaning they had to dismount and walk, lest they and their horses go sliding down the hillside.

When they reached a spot that was unusually wide, enough that two horses could stand side by side without fear of tumbling over the edge, Arric called a brief rest. Lysander asked to search for a particular healing plant native to these mountains, and Arric gave him leave to hunt for it. "Hurry back," he admonished, as Lysander scurried down the incline, Nyvas at his heels. "We still have a long way to go today."

Kate sat on a boulder near the horses. Secretly she hoped the men would take their time, because today more than any day before, her feet were killing her.

Meanwhile, Arric bent his body forward and backwards in an attempt to stretch out the muscles in his back. As he did so, he said to Fantion, "I've been thinking about Sander and Nyvas a great deal these past few days. They are good men, to have agreed to accompany me on this foolish quest of mine."

"Aye, that they are." Fantion dismounted and approached a stream of water spilling down from somewhere higher up on the cliff. "Watching them together, though, sometimes I wonder about their relationship—if you know my meaning," he said as he filled his flask. "They have always been friends, but lately..."

"I suspected as much the first day I saw them together. Perhaps they have spoken the Oath of Alisavi?" Arric turned to look in the direction they had disappeared. "Being fhaoli, it's good they can share such closeness with each other."

"What's the oath?" Kate asked. She had pulled off one of her shoes and was rubbing a toe she had jammed against a rock. It was hurting quite a bit, and between that and all her blisters, she had been limping all day. Looking at the blisters on her heel and ball of her foot, she wondered if it was possible to get a blister on top of another blister.

"In ancient Sarducian tradition," he explained, "the Oath bound two people together for all their lives and beyond. Even today it's seen as a promise to the goddess Kerthal to live out your life with one person. Although we have ordinary marriage rites, some people choose to affirm their relationship in this way since it is considered more meaningful. Unlike regular marriages, few who speak the Oath ever remarry if their partner dies."

"It does not bother you?" Fantion asked as he drank from the newly-filled flask. The water dribbled down his beard, and he wiped it with his sleeve, and then offered Arric the flask. "After all, pairings such as theirs are not generally acceptable in Loraden."

Arric held the flask in his hand without drinking. "Like I said, I am happy for them both. Oath or not, I respect anyone with that kind of bond, regardless of who they are. It's a rare thing to find someone you can truly care about in that way."

"Aye, 'tis true enough."

Turning to look at Kate, Arric abruptly changed the subject. "How long have you had those blisters?"

She pulled her skirt over her feet. "They're nothing. Don't worry about it."

"Ah, Kate, you should have said something." He stood with his hands on his hips, and shook his head. "Is it easier for you to ride?"

Shrugging, she replied, "marginally, but one way or the other, something's going to hurt."

Still dissatisfied, he coaxed her into giving him a better look. "You've had those for days, haven't you?" When she didn't answer, he added, "you should have told me. Well, Sander should be able to help. When he returns, I'll ask him to tend to you, aye?" He caught his tongue in the pocket of his cheek, and made an odd face as he handed her the flask.

Surprised by the way he spoke to her, she hid her smile by the mouth of the flask. He stepped over to the same small waterfall Fantion had used to fill his flask, and filled his hands with the spring water. He splashed it on his face, and then used a small handkerchief to dry his face and hands.

She watched him intently. She wondered what was on his mind that had caused the peculiar expression, but she remained silent.

Fantion, meanwhile, had busied himself with examining the horses' hooves, to make sure the rocks had not caused any damage that would surface later. Continuing their previous conversation, he asked Arric, "Tell me this, old friend. Do you think you'll ever take the Oath? There was that woman, before you left—"

"Merel? Aye, that might have turned out well, but I left, and she married someone else." Arric wiped his hands on his trousers, and then quickly added, "and anyway, the borderlands were notoriously deficient in eligible women." It was an attempt to make light of the matter, though neither man actually laughed. "It is for the best, as I do not see myself as the marrying type."

"I wouldn't be so sure, Arric. I bet your brother started making plans for you as soon as you returned," Fantion replied with a chuckle.

"Indeed, he probably has already arranged a politically-expedient marriage for me. Can you see me married to the ugly daughter of some

Hansari lord?" He held out his elbow, pretending a woman was at his arm. "What am I thinking? Bedoric hasn't been making any such plans. He would leave this matter to his meddling Aldrish."

"With that man planning your future," Fantion added, "you'll be lucky to enter into a marriage that does not bring you endless misery. From what I hear, he keeps to himself and refuses to marry, an altogether peculiar choice for a man of his position, so perhaps it is impossible for him to understand anything about being happy. My guess is that he'll find the oldest, most wrinkled hag on the continent for you."

"Surely that's not true," Kate said. "He was very kind to me. I can't imagine that he'd want to make other people's lives miserable."

Both men turned to her. "That's quite a favorable report, Kate. Maybe he does have a way with women, then? Or at least one, perhaps?" Fantion winked, causing Arric to smirk even as she blushed.

"I'll be keeping an eye on you, then," Arric announced to her playfully. "Perhaps you'll be the one who finally melts that man's heart."

"I don't think so.." She tried to protest, but her words were cut short when Fantion, actually grinning at her, tossed her a second flask.

"Don't worry yourself on that score, Kate," he comforted her. "Arric hasn't been around long enough to learn that the Aldrish has no heart." Then he pointed to the flask. "Help yourself. It will take the edge off the soreness."

She grimaced as she swallowed some of the havar, but she suspected he was right about it helping, and took another drink. As she did so, in what seemed fair play, Arric asked his friend, "how about you? Anything between you and that woman you've mentioned..."

"Halia?" Fantion said, a bit surprised. He rubbed at his beard, twisting his mouth to the side. "Ah, I fear it will never amount to much, what with a price on my head and all."

"You know, I respect your decision to stand up to my brother," Arric said. "If only I had done as much years ago."

Fantion nodded. "Well, when it all started, someone had to stand up for the Sarnoc and challenge that foolishness. Who knew back then that Bedoric himself would turn out to be one of the Prophet's followers, and he'd punish those who argued with all that nonsense?"

"But what a price to pay..."

"Aye, my friend. Being fhaoli certainly isn't the life I wanted for myself, but at least I didn't lose my head to one of the Senvosra's swords."

Kate was startled by the news. "Wait—are you saying you were outlawed for speaking against the Prophet?"

"Aye," Fantion confirmed with a sigh. "Not long after Bedoric became Vosira, this Hidden God nonsense began. He ordered the removal of Sarnoc Sofinar from the Council, and banished him from the city. He claimed that it was because Sofinar was involved in Parmon's murder, but no one believed that, and it was pretty obvious that he just didn't want a Sarnoc around. It wasn't long after that he banned all Sarnoc from the city. It was a terrible decision, and as it turned out, I was the only one on the Council who openly spoke up against it." He laughed lightly as he toed at a rock protruding from the cliff. "I remember saying I could not serve a Vosira who turned his back on the gods, and stormed out of the meeting, and that was that. Within the day I was named fhaoli and they confiscated my lands."

He swung his head up, and, speaking more to himself than to Arric or Kate, cast his gaze to the sun. "I won't be marrying Halia or anyone else in this lifetime. Though the gods know I desire her, I cannot live outside the safety of the forest, and she cannot live here with me. Lockleaf is no place for women."

"Nor men, in truth," Arric said in sympathy.

"Aye. That is more true every day."

Arric walked over to Trill, and scratched the mare's gray forehead. Then, reaching in one of the saddlebags, he pulled out a small parcel of meat and offered it to Kate.

She took a small piece, surprised that it wasn't jerky. "Where did this come from?" She started to hand it back to him, but he encouraged her to take more.

"A couple of fat hares stumbled into Nyvas's snare last night after you fell asleep," Arric explained. "It was his first chance to set them since we started back, but I'm glad he did."

She nodded, and gratefully accepted another slice. A week ago the idea of eating rabbit might have repulsed her, but now it was one step short of heaven after their sparse provisions the past couple of days.

After their brief snack, Fantion looked up at the sun, which was sliding towards the west. "Shouldn't they have returned by now?"

"They have been gone longer than I had expected," Arric said. "I hope they did not run into trouble..." Then he caught sight of the two men climbing up the incline. "Thank the gods—there they are."

"Something's wrong," Fantion guessed, as he noticed their hurried pace. His mouth twitched, and he waved Kate over to the horses.

When he reached them, Lysander struggled to catch his breath. "Senvosra—a dozen men."

Nyvas, just as out of breath, was right behind him. He added, "they were behind us on the main road, headed towards the city. We got caught on the wrong side of the road, and had to hide until they passed."

"Were you seen?" Fantion asked.

"Nay, we were careful, but they're heading this way."

"We must leave this footpath," Arric said grimly. "Since they are on the road, and we're higher up, it will be difficult for them to catch us, even if they spotted us. Still, I think we should leave the ridge. We need not make it easy for them, aye?" When he was greeted with nods from everyone else, he announced, "then that decides it—we will have to travel further to the north." He looked to the sky. "We have time to put some distance between them and us, but we must hurry."

Leaving the ridge, however, was not as easy as Arric thought it would be. Going down the incline was difficult enough with the horses, but making matters worse, each of the men had to take a turn at slashing through thorny vines and picking out a route that would take them around trees and boulders. This meant that Kate needed to take the reigns of each man's horse in turn, doing her best to maneuver both herself and the beasts through the tangle. Worst of all, her feet continued to ache with every step, but she said nothing about it.

It was Lysander's turn with the knife, cutting a path through the woods. He struggled against an ancient thicket of greenbrier, with stems nearly as thick as his fingers. They all had to halt along the narrow path as they waited for him to hack at the vines.

"So I suppose this detour means no grassy meadow for our camp tonight, eh, Arric?" Fantion said, obviously teasing, though he sounded a bit disappointed as well.

Arric scrubbed at his cheeks, where a scraggly beard had grown out. He had earlier confided to the others that his untidiness aggravated him. So it was no surprise when he responded, "And no time for a shave."

"I'd give anything for a nice hot bath," Kate said.

"Baths are overrated," Fantion said with a laugh. "Though in truth, it's been a long time since I've had one. What I really miss is my hammock. I hate sleeping on this damn rocky ground. I'm too old for this abuse."

"Aye, my friend, it catches up with us—" Arric began, but stopped in mid-sentence when Lysander cried out.

Standing behind Nyvas, Kate was unable to see what had happened. The boy, however, quickly tossed the reins of his horse to her. He frantically pushed through the thorns, oblivious to how they scratched his face and hands, trying to reach Lysander as quickly as possible. Then Fantion shouted to her to reverse course and head towards a small clearing they had left moments before.

Kate, not very good with horses even in the best of situations, struggled to convince both Lysander's and Nyvas's mounts to follow her out of the trees without a lot of room to turn around. They kicked out in frustration, and swung their heads back, but she spoke calmly and pulled firmly on the reins, and they finally cooperated.

Back in the clearing with Arric, she worried when the others did not emerge from the trees.

"What happened?" she asked.

"Sander got caught in the vines, and I think the knife slipped," Arric said, his eyes on the trees where they had just been. "I don't know for sure."

"Aye, he's cut," Fantion confirmed as he led his mare into the clearing. "I saw it happen, but I could do little to help him, not with those damn vines snagging my cloak in every direction. I just hope it's not serious."

A minute later, Nyvas led his friend out, his left arm over his shoulders while his other hand helped support Sander's bloody right arm. Lysander was pale, and he had clenched his teeth against the pain.

"Clear a space for him," Nyvas called out. "He needs havar, and we need to wrap his arm." Instead of his usual boyish demeanor, he now commanded the others with calm authority.

Fantion pulled a flask from his saddlebag. Kate, meanwhile, called to Arric. "Give me your knife."

He stood motionless, staring at her in confusion.

"Your knife, come on." She was impatient now, and held out her hand.

Arric pulled the blade from his belt, and she immediately took it, using it to slice fabric from one of her wide sleeves, thinking to use it as a crude bandage. She stepped over to Lysander, who was now sitting on the ground, one arm cradled in the other, his eyes squeezed shut against the pain. Nyvas held Fantion's flask to his lips, coaxing him to swallow a few sips.

"Leave it to the healer to be the one who gets injured," Lysander joked, though his voice was weak.

She considered the situation. She knew nothing about Sarducian medicine, or their form of healing, but she knew basic first aid. "Can I see it?"

"You should look away," Nyvas said, trying to protect her. "It's a deep cut, and pretty ugly." He looked towards Arric. "You've seen battle wounds—maybe you can help?"

One glance at Arric told Kate all she needed to know. His frown indicated that while he wasn't afraid of the sight of blood, his knowledge of proper wound care was meager at best. "I think I can handle it."

At the moment, Lysander had no patience for social niceties, so he held out his arm, grimacing as he did so. Across his left forearm was a long, deep gash, bleeding profusely. It was obvious that he had been holding a vine in his hand, and somehow he had slipped, his blade slicing his flesh on the downstroke, rather than cutting the vine. Given how sharp these men kept their knives, she was surprised he hadn't cut it clean through to the bone. She wiped at it with her skirt, to clear away some of the blood. To Nyvas, she held out the fabric she had cut from her sleeve, and instructed, "fold this, and then hold it tightly against his arm, putting pressure on either side of the wound, to slow the bleeding. Oh—and help him keep it raised, like this." She demonstrated by holding her own arm against her chest. To the other men, she said, "it could have been a lot worse. He'd probably do better with stitches, but I'll try to bind it without any."

She looked around, trying to decide what she needed. "I'll need more fabric to clean it and stop the bleeding, and the least dirty stuff you can find to make into a bandage, to cover and wrap it. Linen, if you can get enough, rather than wool." Arric had pulled an extra shirt from his pack and was already cutting it into strips. "Boil it all first so it's clean."

Then she remembered her mother's herbal lessons, and began scanning the ground. "Yarrow. Anyone know it? A small plant with soft fern-like leaves? Or shepherd's purse, the plant with the little heart seedpods? They'll help."

"I know them both," Nyvas said. "It's too late for shepherd's purse, but I saw some yarrow not too far from here." He looked down at his friend. "Kate, take over and I'll fetch it."

While the men worked on a small fire, she applied pressure to Sander's wound, holding it above his heart, and praying her efforts would be enough to stop the bleeding. Already the cloth she was holding was soaked with blood. She had to breathe deeply to banish her own queasiness.

Nyvas quickly returned with a sizable pile of leaves. She crushed the leaves between her palms, and then applied the fresh herb to the cut and quickly covered it with another handful of linen. "Can you make a strong tea with the rest?" As she shifted her hands, Lysander noticed the blood and started to fuss. "Don't look at it," she admonished him. "We're going to stop the bleeding for now. You'll be okay." As he protested, she said, "close your eyes, and breathe deep breaths. You need to calm down." So he was a healer, she thought to herself. In her world, they always said doctors made the worst patients. That truism seemed to apply here as well.

A short time later, Nyvas circled around to the other side, and placed a poultice of tea-soaked fabric over the cloth she was already holding on Sander's arm, allowing the liquid to slowly seep downwards to the wound. He understood that the plant would help staunch the blood flow.

When the makeshift bandages were ready, she pulled the bloody cloth away. It was nothing short of a miracle, but the bleeding had largely stopped, and the wound didn't look quite as bad as she thought it had before.

With a second bit of cloth, she started wiping away blood. Then she grabbed a flask. "This will hurt," she warned, "but it's all I have to clean it." He nodded, squeezing his eyes shut, and then she wiped a cloth soaked with a bit of havar lightly along the edges of the wound, trying not to get any directly in the cut. Still, he groaned loudly, and gnashed his teeth. "Sorry, it can't be helped," she said sympathetic to the pain he felt.

He nodded. "I know," he said weakly.

Nyvas knelt beside her and offered a small ceramic jar to her. "This will help with healing," he suggested.

She uncorked the container. It was a green salve. She sniffed the contents. She guessed it might contain comfrey, but the other ingredients were a mystery.

"We use it when no healer is available," he explained. "There's plenty more, so use what you need."

Once she had dabbed the salve around the cut, she tied the bandage tightly over the wound, taking care to pull the edges of the cut as closely together as possible as she did so. "You can't use this arm for anything until it heals over," she told him. "Understand? You can't move it at all, or the wound will open up and start bleeding again. You'll need to ask one of us for help for anything you'd otherwise use the arm for."

He nodded feebly, his eyes half-closed.

"Keep it elevated, over your heart." She used the rest of the fabric to make a sling, and she tied his arm against his chest. "It's not going to be comfortable, but this should help." She turned to Nyvas, kneeling beside her. "This all will have to be done several times a day until it heals. And hang on to the yarrow, we might need more later."

Nyvas's blue eyes took in the information. "He'll be all right?"

She nodded. In truth she was far from certain, but she was unwilling to confide that. It was a nasty wound, and the chances of infection—or tetanus, she realized—were extremely high in these circumstances. She had done all she could, and now, she supposed, it was all in the hands of the gods to decide. The gods. She had just recognized them as having sway over their lives, and she spared just a moment to let the novel concept sink in.

"Thank you," Lysander mumbled. "How is it that you know so much about dressing wounds?"

Kate shrugged. "I don't know that much, really. Just enough common sense to get by." She held out her own arm, and showed them a pair of scars. "I put my hand through a glass door when I was thirteen. This is more or less the same as what my mother did for me. It gave her a reason to teach me a bit about herbal medicine, and after that I learned everything I could from her."

"Well, I'm grateful to her for doing that," Lysander said, as he inspected the wrap. "You did well."

The day was already drawing to a close, and Fantion suggested they remain in the clearing for the night, even if Senvosra were close, as traveling now would be even more risky.

The men left her with Lysander as they went off to set up camp.

"Thank you again," he told her, once they were alone. "Even though I'm a healer, I could have done no more for any of you. After all our travels, I have no strength to heal another person, much less myself. I'm grateful that you joined our company."

Embarrassed, Kate smiled a bit sheepishly. "I really didn't do much. I just wish you could go somewhere to get stitches and sterile bandages. Boiling water or not, that bandage is filthy, and it might get infected."

"What do you mean, infected?" he asked, unfamiliar with the term.

"You know, a bacterial infection, when it becomes inflamed and fills with pus. If it gets infected and it's not treated, you could lose the arm, or even die."

"You say that so casually." His eyes were wide, and he seemed horrified by her description. "Do such things happen often in your world?"

She looked at him with a curious expression. Surely infections were common in Sarducia, without the benefit of modern medicine? "It used to happen all the time, although we now have medicines that can prevent it." What she wouldn't give for a good antibiotic now. She always used to take such things for granted, but no more. "Isn't it the same here?"

Lysander shook his head. "Not really. At least not for a minor injury like this."

"Minor?" she repeated with surprise. "You consider this a minor injury?"

"Aye. Usually there's a healer who can mend a wound like this before anything like that could happen. I'm glad we had the salve, with herbs that do the job as well, just more slowly." He sighed. "I just wish I wasn't so tired, or I'd heal it now myself."

She took her sleeve and wiped his forehead, for he had been sweating for some time. When they called him a healer, she thought they meant he was some sort of rudimentary physician, or an herbalist. "What else would you do? How could you heal a wound like this and avoid infection?"

"Ah, usually something like this would be easy. I would just apply my energies to the wound, and it would mend."

"I don't understand. What do you mean?"

"Well, if I had my strength, I'd bring my energy to focus on closing the wound and repairing the damage, and it would happen, and heal."

"What—" she stared at him. "Do you mean, immediately?"

"Aye, more or less. If I were at my peak, this would already be just a bad memory." He grinned weakly. "A good healer, fully rested, can even prevent a scar from forming, but most people are happy to have the bleeding stop and the pain go away." He closed his eyes, clearly unaccustomed to the ache such a wound caused. "I suppose you have no remedies for the pain?"

Suddenly she felt inadequate. "Sorry, the best I can do for now is havar. I wish it were more." She handed him the flask, already opened for him.

"Ah, do not apologize. What you did is plenty, for without your help I might have bled to death." He took two long pulls at the flask, and his eyelids fluttered for a moment. "I am in your debt, Kate."

CHAPTER 27

Rain already began to sprinkle on the company as they sat eating their first true meal of the day around Fantion's hastily-built fire.

Arric had wandered into the trees and appeared to be pacing restlessly at the edge of the clearing, as if sensing the trees held him prisoner. Without warning, he returned to the fire and announced, "I'd like to reach Loraden tomorrow night. There is far too much to do, and I am losing precious time here in the forest."

"Tomorrow?" Fantion whistled, and looked to the sky, where the sun was dipping to the west. "It is still a good two days' ride from here, longer if we still have to blaze a path through the damn briars." He looked at Lysander, who had fallen asleep beside the fire. "Plus you know as well as I that he cannot travel in the morning."

"Fantion's right," Kate seconded. "Sander can't get on a horse right now. The strain would force the wound open again, and that would be really dangerous."

"Aye," this time it was Nyvas, his voice betraying how worried he was for his friend. "He needs to regain his strength so he'll be able to heal himself."

"All right, all right, I hear you all," Arric said, waving his hands in front of him, to quiet their protests. "He shall not be moved until he's ready." He dusted his hands on his trousers. "By tomorrow, or the day after, he may be strong enough to heal himself, but I cannot wait so long." Then he pointed into the trees, in a different direction from the ill-fated one they had originally chosen. "The Jeso Road is nearby." Predicting the responses, he explained, "the whole point of changing our route was to hide from the Senvosra, and that's why it's been taking so long. However, the road is much faster, and I've been gone long enough as it is. I know that every extra day I'm gone, my absence becomes that much more difficult to explain." He turned to Fantion. "I think it's best that you and Nyvas wait here with Sander until he is well enough to ride. With the three of you safely hidden here, Kate and I can travel the road without fear."

"Kate?" Fantion said in surprise. "To reach Loraden tomorrow means a hard ride, and you know we cannot spare any of our horses for her. She should stay here with us."

"Aye, perhaps you're right," Arric agreed.

Kate, however, shook her head. She wasn't worried about remaining in Fantion's protection, but she suddenly had a strong, if irrational, feeling that the plan wasn't right. She had a path to follow, and she somehow knew that it meant sticking with the Dosedra. "I know it sounds crazy, but I need to go back with you."

Rather than dismiss her outright, Arric rubbed his chin in thought. "Aye, it could be done, but it will be a difficult ride, if we share Trill," he warned her. "It will be a much faster pace than we've done so far. You're certain you can handle it?"

"Not at all." She smiled. "But that hasn't stopped me yet."

***

She sat silently on her blankets, hugging her knees.

The threat of rain had thankfully passed for the moment, and the night was much warmer than the previous nights, more like the late summer nights she remembered from home. Just like there, the buzz of cicadas and crickets filled the air, and the sky was clear for the moment, though a haze of clouds hung near the horizon. Stars shone brightly overhead, and when she tipped her head back to look, she took comfort in the fact that they were constellations she recognized. The big dipper hung overhead, just like at home. How was such a thing possible? Even in her world the constellations changed between hemispheres. Here she was in a wholly different world, but the stars were the same. And some, if not all, of the plants and animals. It seemed incredible that two places so unlike one another, with no interaction, could share so much in common.

She had been in Sarducia for less than two weeks, though it had felt much longer. A handful of days among strangers, in a world without technology as she knew it. No computers, cars, or microwave ovens. No airplanes, no internet, no indoor plumbing. Yet she had come to realize that in both worlds the people themselves were pretty much the same.

Her gaze traveled to the forms of the sleeping men, just barely visible. With a waning moon, every night was darker than the last, and tonight, its thick crescent had barely snuck past the horizon. Still, her eyes had adjusted to the faint light just enough to see Fantion laying on his side, facing away from her, a blanket underneath him, and his cloak wrapped around his arms. He seemed to sleep fitfully, as if always ready to spring on an opponent. It hadn't escaped her notice that his sheathed sword was on one side, and his knife just above his head, always. On her other side, Nyvas had curled his body protectively around Lysander, who lay on his back with the injured arm over his chest. Their weapons, too, lay on either side of them.

Across the banked fire was another blanket, but it was unoccupied. She raised herself up a little and tried to get a better look. She thought Arric had been there a moment ago, but it was hard to be sure.

"You can't sleep either?" a voice whispered behind her.

She jumped at the sudden statement. When she turned her head, she realized Arric stood beside her own blanket.

Relaxing her guard, she shook her head. "I was just thinking."

"Ah."

"And you?" she asked in a low voice, worried she would wake one of the others.

He did not respond. Instead, he crossed his arms and, if she saw him right in the darkness, he smiled down at her.

It unnerved her entirely. What the hell was he doing? "Do you need something, Arric?"

With a nudge of his head he signaled for her to join him as he slipped into the nearby trees.

She sat where she was for a moment, holding her hands out in front of her, with an expression that belied her confusion. What did he want? Finally she pushed herself up and slowly felt her way through the trees.

Fortunately he hadn't gone far. "I'm glad you're awake," he said when she found him. "I wanted to talk to you."

"About what?"

"You know we'll be in Loraden tomorrow."

"Yeah, that's what you said earlier. Are you sure we can make it? Fantion didn't think we'd be able to travel that far in just a day."

"Oh, aye, we can do it. That's not what concerns me." He stepped a little closer to her. "Things will be different when we return."

It was an odd comment, she thought. "What things?"

"Ah, you can guess, I'm sure. Out here, I am just a traveler, no different from fhaoli. In the keep I shall be Dosedra. It changes things."

"Oh." She didn't like the sound of that. Riding in a saddle with him for the better part of a week had eased them into a sort of friendship. She had reminded herself often who he was, and his role in this society, but after seeing the worst of him as well as the best, it was hard to imagine him as anything else. "So you're telling me I won't get to see you again?"

"Nay, nothing like that. I just wanted to warn you that I will be different, and indeed you will be different as well. It's the nature of life in the keep, that there are rules and expectations for us all. For me in particular, because I will have duties, social obligations, and guards everywhere I go. Out here we've been traveling companions, but in the city the familiarity must end, and I regret that."

"Thanks for warning me, though I guess it's not all that surprising, really." Something else occurred to her. She remembered the uproar that took place when he disappeared. "You're not very popular there, you know." She remembered the whole scheme to put together the feast at the last minute. "I guess you know by now that the quantrill wasn't really meant to welcome you home."

"Aye. No one wanted me to return to Sarducia, but I can't let that stop me. If I want to resolve this matter with my brother and this whole Hidden God nonsense, there's a lot that needs to be done, and I may be the only one who can do it."

"If that's true, why did you leave Loraden right after you arrived?"

"Ah, well." He yanked at a tree limb, shaking unripe seed pods to the ground. "I was hoping to see an old friend again."

"You mean Fantion?"

"Hmm. Aye, I suppose so, though that's not who I meant." He leaned against the trunk of the tree and sighed. Rather than explaining further, he changed the subject. "You know, I had no idea that things had gotten so bad under Bedoric, or I really would have tried to return home much sooner." He raised his hand to cover an unwelcome yawn. "I worry that in all this time, things may have deteriorated too much for me to have any impact."

"Something else you should know," she began, hoping she wasn't betraying a confidence, "the Aldrish was really worried when you disappeared after the quantrill."

He exhaled sharply. "Aye? I'm surprised he cared."

"He was nearly in a panic about it, or at least that's what I saw. But from what you say, I can't figure out why it would matter to him."

"Interesting. Perhaps they worry that I haven't given up."

"Given up? What do you mean?"

"Ah, never mind that." He chuckled.

"At least I can tell people you didn't desert your troops in battle."

"So, does everyone think that about me, then?" Without waiting for her to reply, he continued, "It matters not. Whatever they're saying likely has some truth to it, so if people dislike me, I have it coming. What's important to me is that you don't get involved in it."

With that, silence breathed a cold breath between them, and Kate shifted her weight between her feet. "I'm sorry to have brought it up, then."

"Aye, well, I shouldn't be burdening you with my problems either."

"It's okay, I just know that the rumors about you are just going to get worse."

"Let them. You know they aren't true now, and that's a start."

"Yeah, I guess so," she acknowledged, as she turned to head back towards the camp.

He wasn't ready to return, however. "So you know quite a bit about me. What about you, Kate? Tell me about where you come from. Is it very different?"

His question rooted her where she stood, as she considered her own reality to be no less complicated than his. "It is," she replied, not having a better response. How could she even begin to explain her world to him?

He must have picked up on the complex nature of the question. Rather than pursue it, he asked instead, "do you have a family?"

It was scarcely easier to handle this subject, but she knew she couldn't avoid it. "It was mostly just me and mom, and she died recently." The memories sent a chill down her back.

"Oh, I am sorry to hear that. You were close to her?"

She twisted her mother's ring on her finger. "Yeah. I don't have any brothers or sisters, and I never knew my father." She didn't want to try to explain her strange extended family now.

He nodded, and leaned against the tree closest to him. "I understand that. It's much the same for me. Bedoric—and now his wife and son, whom I scarcely know—are all the family I have. My mother died a couple years after my father was killed. She was a good woman, but the fever caught her, and Sander couldn't save her. The worst part is that she died while I was away, so I couldn't be there with her at the end."

"That's so sad—I'm sorry." At least she had been there for her mother when she passed away. Then she realized what he had said. "Sander was there?"

"Aye, he was one of the healers in the keep, and a good one. It wasn't his fault she died. Sometimes with fevers, even the best healers can do nothing. My brother, though, blamed him, and—ah, well, you can see for yourself the outcome."

"He was outlawed for that?"

"Aye. Oh, and I don't know if I thanked you for helping him today. What you did was remarkable. I would not have been able to forgive myself if something happened to him on this foolhardy quest of mine." He reached for her hand. "You probably think me foolish for leading you out here just now as well. I suppose all I wanted was to reassure myself that when we return to Loraden, you do not become my enemy."

She squeezed his hand in return. "There's no way I'll let that happen," she promised.

CHAPTER 28

"I assume you had a safe journey back to Loraden, my dear?" Rynar asked as he stared down at her.

Stifling a yawn, she found it difficult to say anything in response. Having just been sent to the baths to scrub a week's worth of embedded grime from her body, she now sat in front of the Aldrish's fire, wrapped in a wool robe and shaking out her damp hair. "It was interesting," she offered, but was unwilling to say anything further about it. Instead, she stared at the flames, uncomfortable in his presence after everything that had happened recently.

The return itself hadn't been without incident. No one had challenged Arric and Kate when they entered the city gates, but at the keep itself, they were forced to endure a number of questions from the Senvosra concerning where they had been and why they looked the way they did. After all, both were filthy, with torn clothing and dried blood from Lysander's injury. Arric had answered all of their questions authoritatively, and the guards didn't challenge his explanations. However, when one of the Senvosra addressed her specifically, asking why she was with the Dosedra, she stammered a vague explanation. As soon as she had finished speaking, a guard whisked her away and put her in the hands of two women previously unknown to her.

After a long, drawn out bath in which the women insisted on scrubbing every inch of her with stiff brushes until she cried out, she was finally allowed to dress, and then they led her to Rynar's quarters. While it felt good to be clean for the first time in a week, she would have preferred to handle her own grooming, and she certainly wished she could be alone in her own quarters now. Since the choice had not been left to her, she wasn't in a particularly charitable mood.

"Where did you go, precisely? I understand you didn't make it to Terralin, as I had instructed." His voice was accusatory, as if she had done something terribly wrong by not going where he sent her. He was leaning against the fireplace, his arms crossed in front of him, and his eyes bore down on her. "I feared you had been killed."

Kate kept her head down, not wanting to look at him. When she didn't respond, Rynar continued. "Were you injured?"

Slowly she tipped her head back to look at him. "No, I'm fine," she snapped. She was annoyed with him, and indeed with the whole situation as it had unfolded, and wasn't in the mood to hide it. Then she dropped her gaze back to the fire. "I don't see why it matters to you, anyway."

"Perhaps you misunderstand the seriousness of the situation. You returned just now with the Dosedra, your gown covered in dried blood and torn beyond recognition, and your feet cut to ribbons. The Vosira will demand an explanation."

"Well, if he asks, I'll give him one," she replied sharply. She was exhausted, her body ached all over, and she could hardly think straight. The last thing she needed was an interrogation from someone she barely knew, to whom she had no obligations. Whatever fondness she might have felt for the handsome stranger had disappeared over the past few days. Arric had been honest and forthright; Rynar was clearly playing at something, and acted as if he held most of the cards.

Her response caused him to clench his fists. It wasn't clear why he cared about her whereabouts so much, but her refusal to offer any answers seemed to enrage him, and he could barely keep his emotions under control. What was obvious was that he was used to getting what he wanted, and wasn't pleased by her lack of cooperation. "Is that all you have to say?"

"Yeah, I really don't want to talk about this now. I'd like go back to my room."

"Aye, of course you would." He taunted her now. "However, before that can happen, you must account for yourself. Two points that must be addressed: first, why it is that you returned in the Dosedra's company, and second, whose blood was on your clothing? You know that the Vosira will want to know what happened."

She lifted her head again and shot him an angry glance. "You mean, you want to know."

"Aye, that I do." He crossed his arms, and circled around her. "And is that so unreasonable? I did everything to look after you when you arrived, and tried to ensure your safety. Yet, even though you knew about the Dosedra's past, and everything he's done, you still chose to be in his company, and you now refuse to explain how that happened, or where you went." He shook his head, disappointed. "That fact alone could mean trouble for you, and I need you to explain yourself before things get any worse."

"I didn't plan any of this," she countered. "You're the one who sent me away. I just happened to run into him on my way back to the city, and he offered to escort me to the keep."

"You expect me to believe you randomly met him just outside the city gates—twice?"

"I don't expect anything." She wanted to fight him back, but instead she found herself starting to drift off, and had to close her eyes and take a deep breath before she could continue. She didn't think she had been this exhausted in her entire life. Riding Trill back to Loraden had sapped every bit of strength, and it was all she could do to walk into the keep and get cleaned up without passing out. Even as she was feeling queasy from exhaustion, she added, "you're free to believe whatever you like."

He exhaled sharply, and watched her for a moment without responding. He must have finally realized that in her current state, she was unlikely to cooperate further. "Very well. As long as you promise that he didn't hurt you, we will discuss it in the morning."

"Of course he didn't hurt me. I'm fine." She was surprised that he had relented so quickly. "I'm just," she yawned again, and leaned her head against the back of the chair, "really tired." She closed her eyes and within seconds had fallen fast asleep.

CHAPTER 29

When she awoke, she was back in her own room. The shutter was half-open, and from the look of the sun she guessed it was nearly noon. She jumped out of bed, her heart racing. In Sarducia she had already come to understand that there was no such thing as 'sleeping late.' In a land without electricity, it was foolish to sleep during the day, when there was natural light. Regardless of how late you stayed up, when dawn came, you were expected to already be awake and ready to start the day.

As her feet hit the stone floor, she expected to feel the sharp pain from the blisters that covered the soles of her feet, but felt nothing. Hobbling on her right leg, she lifted up her left foot.

"What in the world?" She exclaimed as she wiggled her toes. The blisters were entirely gone. Confused, she pushed up the sleeves of her gown—the random briar scratches were gone as well. Even childhood scars seemed a bit fainter, if such a thing were possible. "What the hell happened?"

The last thing she recalled was falling asleep in a chair in the Aldrish's room, but now she was back in her own. As she looked around, everything seemed just as she had remembered it. To her eyes, the only things new to the room were the meat pie and wine sitting on a tray near the fire, and a pair of new gowns in the wardrobe. One was a woolen gown of rust with yellow and green embroidery; the other was a formal gown of dark blue.

She decided on the rust gown, as the simpler of the two garments, and after she slipped it over her head and worked to lace up the bodice, she realized it fit much better than the other dresses she had worn here in the keep, though it was less comfortable than the one from the Sarnoc. However, it was also more flattering, as it had full sleeves that reached to the edge of her palm, and the fullness of the skirt started just below her hips. It was lightly scented with roses, and was as soft as flannel against her skin. Someone had gone to considerable trouble to have this dress made specifically for her. Was this Rynar's doing?

Her mind went back to their confrontation the night before. She had thought him angry then—but perhaps he had simply been worried? After all, he had been looking after her, even if his reasons for doing so were unknown. Despite his efforts, she had for all intents and purposes vanished into thin air. The idea made her laugh, since for once that description wasn't far from the truth.

Back to the more mundane issues at hand, however. As she nibbled on the meat pie, she reflected on her current situation. Without any explanation forthcoming, she was still in Sarducia, a land with expectations that she couldn't begin to fathom. She still wasn't entirely sure what was going on and why people were so interested in her, but perhaps the Sarnoc were right: maybe she could do some good. But to do that, she needed to stop passively floating along, waiting for something to happen to her.

And now was as good a time as any to start figuring things out.

Since Rynar hadn't yet arrived to pounce on her for another round of interrogations, she sought out a pair of slippers stashed in the corner of the chest, splashed some water on her face, and headed out into the hallway before he could catch up to her.

She saw a few charnok gathered at the corner, but otherwise it was remarkably quiet. She circled the hallway, running into no one she knew. There were servants and Senvosra, but not a single member of the Bhagali. In her idle wandering, she went down the stairs to the main level of the keep, and noticing the gate to the gardens was open, slipped inside.

Roses were blooming, bright yellow and red antique blossoms lending their sweet fragrance to each corner of the courtyard garden. A stand of sunflowers sprung up by a small reflecting pool favored by a pair of cardinals. Tall spikes of rosemary cordoned off a small herb garden, with a stone path leading to pale green sage, sprawling tufts of thyme with specks of white flowers, and a great patch of peppermint. In one corner lemongrass whispered in the caress of the light breeze, dancing with the lavender flowers of a clump of skullcap, and dangling from the branches of a pomegranate bush hung small fruits like upside-down jesters' caps.

There were two women working in the garden, both bent down in newly-turned soil the color of rich chocolate. When she approached, they looked over their shoulders at the newcomer.

"Interested in helping us, Bhara?" one of the women asked. She had dark brown hair loosely pulled into a knot high on her head, and her woolen gown was streaked with bits of dirt and dead leaves despite the long apron she wore.

Kate recognized her immediately, and was at a loss for words. Lacking anything coherent to say, she attempted to drop into a curtsy that ended up turning out all wrong, and she lost her balance. "Bhavosa," she finally murmured as she regained her footing.

"Ah, Bhara, it is good to see you again." Bryll smiled warmly at Kate as she wiped her hands on her apron and nodded to her companion. "It's Bhara Kate, a guest of Aldrish Rynar," she explained. Then she waved to indicate her friend, a woman about the same age as herself. Like Bryll, this woman had dark hair, though her features were much plainer. While the Bhavosa had a long, straight, elegant nose set between bright golden eyes, and flawless creamy skin with a hint of blush on her cheeks, this woman was sallow, her plump face showing a few creases at her mouth and eyes. However, her smile was wide, and her expression seemed genuine. "Bhara Kate, this Bhara Gysalia. She is wife to Bhagal Ulvicar."

Kate smiled in return and nodded, though she had no idea who Bhagal Ulvicar was. "I'm pleased to meet you, Bhara."

"And you, Bhara Kate. Welcome to our city. Tell me, have you been shown proper Loraden hospitality?"

Kate chose the gracious way out. "Yes, everyone has been very kind."

Bhavosa Bryll smiled, nodding her head politely in appreciation. "That is good to hear. I would have to take the Aldrish to task if I were to learn he was anything but a proper host and gentleman." She winked at Kate, and then waved her hand to the soil behind her. "We are planting new roses. A couple of the bushes succumbed to some terrible blight, and I hope these new ones will fare better. Are you interested in gardening, Bhara?"

She had always enjoyed working in the garden, her mother's green thumb having rubbed off on her. Not wanting to dwell on sad thoughts of her mother, she forced her eyes to bounce around and take in the effect of the entire garden instead. "Are you responsible for all of this?"

Bryll laughed, a hearty woman's laugh, not the giggle of a girl. "Ah, this represents the work of many. I am just a small link in a long tradition of women working in the gardens. Gysalia and I do oversee what is planted here, though, and I'd like to think I have made my share of improvements over the years. Many of the Bharani come here to assist us. You, Bhara, must consider joining us some morning."

"Yeah, I'd like that. I'm just surprised. I would have thought servants would do all this work."

"Servants?" Bryll said with her lips spread wide in a beautiful smile. "How could we ever trust them to do it all right? Nay, my lady. It is one of the tasks of the Bhavosa to ensure the gardens are maintained. Of course there are servants who help haul materials for us, but we care for the plants, and occasionally get to choose new roses for the trellises."

From behind a hedge of rosemary, another woman stood and walked over to them. "Bhavosa, who is this lovely lady?" she asked, bowing her head politely to her. Like the queen, this woman wore no gloves, though a pair was tucked into the waistband of her apron. Her hair, dark and very curly, was pulled away from her face in a simple ponytail, though several curls had escaped and framed her face with their softness. While Bhavosa Bryll had an elegant beauty about her, this woman, a bit younger, was simply breathtaking. She was tall and slender, with skin as smooth and clear as porcelain. Even with a bit of perspiration dangling at her eyebrows and a smudge of dirt on her graceful nose, this was a woman whom others envied, for she needed no jewels or fancy clothing to outshine her companions.

"Bhara Merel, this is Bhara Kate."

"Oh, the woman who just recently traveled with the Dosedra?" Merel said with surprise. "I have heard of you."

"Really?" Kate replied, not trying to hide her surprise. "I didn't really expect that anyone would know who I was." So this was the woman Arric had been in love with, once, and perhaps still was.

In a second her eyes swept across Kate from head to toe, and she wrenched her mouth to the side. "My lady," she asked, "would you walk with me for a moment?"

Kate nodded, suddenly feeling awkward. "Sure, I guess…"

Meanwhile, Merel tipped her head to the Bhavosa. "Would you mind?"

Bryll gave silent assent with a simple wave of her hand.

Leaving the other two women sitting on a nearby bench, Kate and Merel walked slowly to the rear of the garden, where late summer annuals bloomed profusely. Zinnias, asters, and cosmos, in shades of yellow, purple, pink, red and orange crowded together in a tiny plot along with varieties she did not recognize.

Merel leaned over and snipped a cactus-flowered zinnia between her fingertips, twirling the bloom in her hand. "I have not had a chance to speak with Dosedra Arric since he returned from Froida. I was devastated to have missed the quantrill, but I was not in Loraden at the time." She blinked, and then asked, "how does he fare these days?"

So she was planning to pump her for information? Knowing that, but not fully understanding the stakes, Kate was on her guard. "He's well," she replied honestly, but vaguely. "A bit tired, though, I suppose."

"I understand you spent some time with him since his return. I hope you don't think me too bold, but is there anything between the two of you?"

Kate laughed lightly, feeling a bit awkward to have the question asked of her. "No, not at all. He just escorted me back to Loraden."

Merel hardly heard her words. "I wonder if he's changed much. When I knew him, he was so charming and lively—and so strong." There was a bit of a dreamy quality in her voice as she played out old memories. "You know we were promised to one another once, not long before he left for Hansar. We would have wed, but with his father's death, and then his decision to leave, the timing was not in our favor. I consoled myself by thinking that he put off ceremony because the wanted to spare me the pain of his absence and the unknown dangers he would face. Now that he has returned, I wonder if he's changed much."

As Merel spoke, there was just the slightest twinge in Kate's stomach, and it caught her by surprise. She smiled despite a bit of annoyance at herself. "Not knowing him before, it's hard to say if he's changed, but he seems quite nice. He has been through a lot, though, you know."

"Aye, of course." She had stopped twirling the flower. "He is still… handsome, though, is he not? Those despicable Froidans didn't—"

Kate bit back a laugh. This woman was at least as old as her, possibly older, and yet there was still a trace of adolescent infatuation. "Well, he does have a few scars—you knew he had been wounded, of course— but he's generally in good shape from what I can tell. I mean," she added quickly, lest her words be misconstrued, "I don't think there's anything you'd need to worry about."

She sighed, relieved. "I'm glad to hear it. I was worried, of course, because he had not sought me out since he returned. I thought perhaps he was ashamed." She began to slowly walk again towards the other two women.

"No, I'm sure that's not it at all, Merel." Kate made a point of saying the woman's name, as if it would create a bond between them. She liked this woman, and set aside her jealousy as misplaced. She had no claim on the Dosedra, after all, and never would. The last thing she would want would be to interfere with his personal life. "Why wait for him to find you? Maybe you should look for him. I'm sure he'd be glad to see you, and know you still care about him."

Merel, blushed slightly at the suggestion. "I couldn't do that. You see, I married while he was gone."

"Oh, I see."

"Nay, it is not like that at all. My husband, Bhagal Chirval, died two years ago."

"So what's the problem?"

"I don't know how Arric would think of me as a widow."

Bhara Merel looked, and sounded, as little like a widow as Kate could imagine. "While I'd hardly consider myself an expert where he's concerned, I'm sure he still cares for you, and I doubt what happened in his absence would matter now."

"Why, what a kind thing to say, Bhara Kate." She smiled with a new contentment. They had returned to the other women by this point, and they ceased their whispered conversation. Bhara Merel nodded to Bryll, and asked, "Bhavosa, you have invited this lovely lady to attend tonight, have you not?"

"A good point, Merel." Bhavosa Bryll blinked her eyes once, and then asked Kate, "you will join us this evening, I hope?"

"I'm sorry, I don't know what you're talking about," she respond- ed. "I haven't really had a chance to talk to anyone since I returned. What's happening this evening?"

Gysalia had been wearing a pair of tight leather gardening gloves, and she pulled them now from her fingers, allowing Kate to see the sparkle of a flawless ruby set in a glysar band. "You returned to Loraden at a good time, my dear. There will be a consort from Tralys here to perform for Vosira Bedoric, and the meal shall be quite splendid. Oh, and of course there will be dancing. You certainly don't want to miss it!"

"Aye, Bhara," Merel insisted, "you must join us. I would love to have a chance to speak with you again."

So this partly explained why the keep was so quiet, she realized. Servants were preparing the feast, and maids and manservants were busily preparing the ornate clothing the Bhagali would wear once again. She recalled the hubbub putting together the last quantrill. She still felt fatigued from her journey, but with an invitation from the Bhavosa and her ladies, how could she refuse? "Sure, I'd like to attend. Is there any- thing special I should do?"

"Nay, my lady," Bryll reassured her. "I will send one of my maids to speak to Lillia—she is the maid in your service, am I right?" Seeing her nod, Bryll continued. "She will know how to handle things from there. She can also arrange for you to have an escort—that is, of course, if no man has already spoken for you."

Kate laughed at the suggestion. "That's not likely," she said, find- ing the whole thing amusing. She was still a stranger here, and not many men knew her—and of those who did, she had few fans. "No, thanks, I'll be okay on my own. I really don't need an escort."

All three women turned to each other in surprise. "No escort, my lady, and you yet unmarried?" Bryll clucked her tongue as Merel shook her head in moderate remorse. "Nonsense. You must have a suitable man escort you to the hall. Gysalia, perhaps we could arrange for one of the unwed Bhagali to accompany her?"

"There's Bhagal Tashin," the woman suggested, and grinned when she saw Kate turn a bit pale. "But of course, he would never suit you."

"Koldren's wife died last spring," Bryll noted, as she rubbed the hollow of her throat. "He may be willing to accompany the lady. He usually is a polite man," she told Kate, "despite his behavior at the quantrill, which was quite unlike him. As I recall, he is not keen on dancing—though, seeing as you are new here, perhaps you wouldn't mind."

Gysalia looked skeptical. "Perhaps he would be willing to serve as her escort, Bhavosa, but you would have to ask him personally. He still talks about Arellia every time I see him, and I do not know if he seeks companionship these days. In any event, I wouldn't want to raise the subject with him myself."

"Aye," Bryll agreed, "he may still be a bit sensitive to the idea. Still, there must be someone who would enjoy Kate's company."

"Perhaps Aldrish Rynar plans to escort her?" Merel suggested, sparking the rapid onset laughter of the other two women. "Now, it isn't so absurd, is it? He is her host, after all."

Gysalia initially covered her mouth to try to hide her laughter, but finally gave up the attempt. "Can you really see the Aldrish choosing to socialize with a woman, much less one as fine as Bhara Kate?" She giggled.

"He's not so bad, and he is a good dancer." Kate couldn't believe that yet again, the Aldrish's social life was worthy of so much amusement, and she also couldn't believe that once again she was defending him.

"Indeed, Bhara?" Merel said in surprise.

"She has spent some time with him in his quarters, after all," Bryll pointed out with a playful lilt in her voice. "Perhaps she knows something we do not?" she winked.

Feeling guilty for finding him handsome, Kate blushed, and the other women misread the gesture.

Bhavosa Bryll clapped her hands together. "Bhara Kate, I had no idea!"

"No, no—you misunderstand. I'm not—I mean, he's not…" she stumbled over the words, her embarrassment growing by the second. "I didn't mean to suggest that anything had happened between us, because it hasn't, I mean, it's not like that at all." She began to panic. Rynar was anything but a frivolous man, and it was unlikely he'd take well to the idea that she had spread rumors about him, even inadvertently.

Bryll put her arm around her shoulders. "Never fear, my dear, we're just teasing. We know the Aldrish well. After all, he is my husband's most trusted advisor, and greatly respected at our court. Of course nothing happened between the two of you. It's just not every day that women speak up for him, you see." Turning to the others, Bryll announced, "Nay, my friends, we can do better than the Aldrish, for our new companion here deserves to have a good time." To Kate, she said kindly, "do not worry, my dear. Once the Council session is concluded, I shall arrange a suitable companion for you."

Kate nodded, trying to seem like she appreciated the effort, though really she was beginning to dread the outcome. She really didn't relish another awkward encounter with a strange man, especially if it was another teenager or someone like Tashin. To hide her apprehension, she leaned over to smell a rose.

"A lovely one, that," Bryll nodded appreciatively. She stepped to the bush and yanked a short blade from her belt, cutting a few buds and handing the small bouquet to her. "Take them with you, my dear, and perhaps they will brighten your chambers this afternoon." She paused, and then added, "hmm, one moment." She tapped her lip with one finger, and then wandered a short way down the path, snipping bits of this and that, some sprigs of rosemary and thyme, a cluster of sweet alyssum, and a few additional roses. Then she handed the small but highly aromatic bunch to Kate. "I am pleased that you are a guest here. Until tonight, then?" Her hand lingered on Kate's for a few moments. "I do hope you enjoy yourself here."

CHAPTER 30

"Your escort has arrived."

Hearing Lillia's announcement, she tugged at the sleeves a final time. The blue gown was very different from others she had worn. This had a tight bodice that laced up the back, with loose, flowing sleeves, and a much more revealing neckline, around which were dozens of tiny drops of silver that Lillia had just finished sewing on by hand. They glistened against the deep blue fabric. "Someone left a pouch of these glysar beads for you," she had explained to her earlier, "and I thought they would look lovely on your gown." Winking, she had added, "you have an extravagant admirer."

The maid's announcement felt like a punch to the stomach, but she said nothing. They must have come from Rynar, just as she assumed the gowns had. There was something about that man... he tried so hard to take care of her, yet refused to offer up any explanation as to why. His constant attention worried her, and she wasn't really looking forward to an evening with him. Still, she was back in relative comfort here in the keep, with dry, warm clothing, a comfortable bed, and as much hot food as she wanted, and she was determined that even under the Aldrish's watchful eye, she would have fun tonight. And, as she consoled herself, at least there would be wine.

As she adjusted the dress once more, she declared in a whisper, "it's tighter than the others I've been wearing." She held out the skirt and turned around, desperately wishing there was a mirror so she could inspect the way it looked. "Are you sure it fits okay? Maybe I should wear that other dress—"

Lillia twisted it slightly at the waist of the skirt, to settle it better over her hips. "Ah, my lady, that is exactly how it should fit." She stepped back, to better appraise Kate's appearance. "Indeed, you look beautiful. This style suits you nicely." She reached into a small box on the mantle and pulled out a narrow silver chain. "I think you should wear this as well." She wrapped it around Kate's waist and pulled the ends together with a sapphire clasp.

"I don't know—" she hesitated. Never in her life had she been slim, though the time she had spent in the swamp likely burned off a few pounds. Keeping her voice low, she asked, "you really don't you think it makes me look fat?"

"Goodness, no, my lady. However, perhaps your escort should be the one to judge?"

Kate swallowed heavily, and took a deep breath. Then she raised her head and walked out of her chamber and into the larger room beyond. She was prepared for Rynar, or some pock-faced boy, to be waiting upon her.

It was neither.

As she stepped into the other room, she realized that Lillia had been mistaken—this wasn't her escort. Standing at the mantle of the fireplace, admiring the roses that she had brought back from the garden, was none other than Dosedra Arric.

Even so, her breath caught in her throat, for the transformation of the Dosedra from rough and tumble renegade soldier into an immaculate courtier was astonishing. Unlike his appearance at the "welcome home" quantrill, where he had dressed in tidy but well-worn garments, and clearly had not spared the time to prepare, tonight he had put significant effort into his appearance. Now Arric wore neither a simple linen shirt nor even one of the common tunics, but instead a vest made of very soft midnight blue leather over a fitted shirt of embroidered dark gray silk with full sleeves. The vest was tailored to follow the curve of his chest, lacing up front, with a flounce to accentuate his hips, rather than falling straight down from the shoulders. Complementing the dark vest, he wore finely-knitted tights of pale blue, and blue and silver brocade slippers. On his fingers, in addition to the one large signet ring he always wore, were numerous glysar rings set with gemstones. His hair seemed different—a bit darker, as if he had used some sort of dye to fade the gray strands. It was smoothed down and braided in a neat plait that hung just past his shoulder blades, gathered at the end with an elaborate glysar clasp. He was clean-shaven, and even his fingers were scrubbed, his nails trimmed and scraped to perfect pink crescents.

Throughout her appraisal of his makeover, he had apparently not heard her entrance. "Dosedra?" she finally said to announce the fact that she stood there.

He spun around. "Aye." He took in her appearance with similar awe. "You look breathtaking tonight, my lady."

Blushing, she shrugged off the unanticipated compliment. "Um, thanks, I guess." Then she considered more carefully the fact that he was here. Surely he had stopped by on his way to retrieve Merel? "I'm sorry, but is there something you needed?" she asked, and then quickly added, "I don't mean to be rude, but it's just that I'm expecting—" she paused, not knowing whose name to fill in, "someone else."

"Someone else, Bhara?" he said, seemingly confused, but keeping to the courtly address.

"Well, of course." How could she explain it without sounding stupid? "Bhavosa Bryll arranged an escort for me, and... oh never mind." Damn it all, how was she going to deal with this without sounding insulting? She tried a different angle. "Were you wanting to ask me about Merel, then?"

He tipped his head slightly, as if he did not understand her words. "Bhara?" he said, remaining formal. "What gave you that idea?"

"I just figured, since you'll be seeing her again after all these years..."

"Aye, that is true enough, but what does she have to do with you?" He had pulled a small peach rosebud from the vase and was examining it closely.

"Well, I—" she began, but then, exasperated, threw her hands up into the air. "Okay, just tell me then. Why the hell are you here, Arric?"

He twisted his mouth. "It's 'Dosedra,' Bhara Kate. I believe I reminded you about using the title a couple of days ago?" Rather than angry, he sounded amused. "From what I was told, you were in need of an escort. Or was I mistaken?"

She turned to Lillia, who grinned, revealing her role in pairing them up for the evening.

As she stood there, still a bit confused, he reached over to pull the stem of the rosebud through the tines of one of the combs in Kate's hair.

"No, you heard correctly." She felt the warmth of a blush on her cheeks, which embarrassed her. Normally she wasn't so shy.

"Good." He examined her appearance once again. "The beads look very nice on your gown, by the way." He winked, and at that moment he reached out for her hand. With sudden, uncharacteristic exuberance, he tugged her towards the door. "Come, Bhara, it is time we joined the others. I insist we arrive before the dancing begins. I wish to be the first one out on the floor!"

As he led her down the wide flight of stairs to the great hall, they caught up with a few other couples heading the same direction. With a small crowd forming close to the landing, he stumbled slightly on a step, jerking his arm to maintain his balance. Kate, who was holding onto his forearm, was jostled in the process, and examined Arric's demeanor a bit more closely. "You're drunk," she said softly after a quick appraisal.

"Nay, my lady," he replied, a bit too loudly, "I have had a few sips of havar, but I assure you, I am entirely in control."

"Are you sure?" she whispered as she watched him take the steps slowly, overcompensating for his loss of balance by pausing every couple of steps. As he staggered to the landing, she grasped his arm firmly and forced him to straighten up. "I mean, it seems somehow unlike you."

"It is nothing to concern yourself with, Bhara," he said, not un-kindly, but still, she dropped her hand from his arm. If he wanted to make a total fool of himself by falling head over heels down a tall stair-case, that was his business, but she wasn't inclined to let him drag her with him.

***

As the doors to the hall were opened, she noticed that the room was already rather full. The Vosira and many of the Bhagali were already seated, though the food was just being brought out. Rather than seat the Dosedra near his brother, as she expected, the pair were led to a smaller table along the side. While it was clearly a slight against Arric for them to be seated there, secretly she was relieved to not be in the spotlight. So far the only other occupants at their table were Bhagal Jamra, who smiled warmly as Arric placed his hand on the man's shoulder to announce their presence, and a couple of the charnok, who first stared at them and then, after a glance to each other, reached for their goblets and casually got up to join friends elsewhere.

Arric took a gulp from a goblet at his seat, and flashed her a fleeting grin. Then he skipped over to the minstrels, and began an animated conversation with a man who played the flute. It was not the same kind of instrument as the one Arric had played several nights ago, but she imagined there was enough in common for them to be discussing technique.

Watching him, she realized how out of place she felt, attending a banquet of this nature with a prince. A few days ago he was just Arric, but now—it was just like he said. The formality set a very different tone, and she started to wonder if it was a good idea to be with him, because of both his rank and his reputation. Many of the Bhagali were boldly staring at the Dosedra, some even pointing and making comments. It was like the quantrill the first night, except now people weren't even trying to be subtle about it. Had something happened in their absence, she wondered, or was it simply his disappearance and sudden reappearance that caused tongues to wag?

She glanced to Aldrish Rynar, who had already arrived and was seated tonight at the royal family's table. He was intently listening to Vosira Bedoric, and didn't seem to notice her. She then noticed Bryll, who was ignoring the tale her husband was telling, and instead was leaning forward to chat with a pair of women standing across the table from her, one of them Gysalia. In contrast to her often-sloppy husband, she again noticed how stunning the queen was in her ruby velvet gown.

Also at the Vosira's table, the weasel-faced Bhagal Tashin sat with his arms crossed in front of him, exuding a smugness she could not decipher. He was staring in her direction and didn't as much as drop his gaze when she made eye contact, and knowing his eyes were on her made her nervous. She held her gaze for a moment, as if to tell him she wasn't afraid, and then tried to look away as casually as she could.

The musicians had paused as the Dosedra spoke to them, but in a splash of sound, they began a loud and lively tune. Stepping into the center of the room, Arric clapped his hands above his head, indicating others should join in the dancing. Then he jogged over to Kate, and after draining his goblet, grabbed her hand. "Come, it's time you dance with me!" His words startled her, and he dragged her from her seat without allowing her to refuse.

As she watched the others, she realized that this was a very theatrical dance, with a lot of exaggerated arm gestures and wide steps and spins. It was very unlike the dances she had attempted with Rynar, and it seemed that Arric was not as keen to explain every maneuver. At the same time, he didn't seem concerned if she got the steps right.

"Just have fun," he whispered as she made a mistake, and then he grinned. "Tonight we shall have no worries. It is much better here than the Muras, is it not?" he added, with a wink. Unlike Rynar, who was controlled and precise in his dancing, Arric seemed to care little about what others thought of him, and instead just tried to enjoy himself. He never stopped smiling, and his attention was as much on her as on the music. In return, she felt at ease and happy, and she couldn't help giggling. Unlike the sullen and wary man she remembered from the earlier quantrill, tonight he had transformed into an entirely different person.

As the first dance ended, Arric wiped his forehead with his sleeve, and reached for a goblet on a tray. "You did well," he praised her. It wasn't true, but his words improved her confidence. At least that was the case until the music began again. At the very first strains, he pulled her close, and exclaimed, "it is the Dance of the Ripolas!"

"Oh, no, I don't think so." She remembered the music from the quantrill. It was a fast dance, and intricate, and worst of all, it was very long. "I'd never make it through this one," she argued with a laugh.

"Nay, Kate, you must not quit on me so soon!" He lunged forward and grabbed her wrist, spinning her back into the crowd of dancers. "This is the song of Sarducia. I wish to celebrate being home."

As they lined up to begin, she noticed Merel had managed to appear beside her. The tall brunette with milky pale skin and a long, elegant face, wearing a violet gown with a tight, low-cut neckline. The glances between the former lovers were quick, but unmistakable.

Instantly she became self-conscious. Arric's old flame was a stunning woman and light on her feet, whereas she felt about as graceful as a sack of potatoes.

Oblivious to her thoughts, Arric grasped her hands tightly in preparation to dance, and suddenly she couldn't look him in the eye. As they made their introductory steps, he leaned close. Did he sense her emotions, a peculiar combination of awkwardness and jealousy that weighed on her? What was he thinking? She decided that the best idea was to not to make a fool of herself, so she kept her attention on his feet and tried to mimic his moves. She feared she'd never master these steps, and at least once she almost tripped him, though it didn't seem like he cared.

When the dance finally ended, she retreated back to the table for some wine and a breather, while Arric vanished back into the crowd to find a new partner. Once again she glanced to Rynar, who was now engaged in a heated argument with a few of the Bhagali standing across from him, while the Vosira leaned back and listened with amusement. The Aldrish had not acknowledged her since she had entered the hall, and she wondered if he was still angry with her. While she didn't care what Rynar thought of her personally, she didn't want to be on the bad side of someone with so much influence, as that could come back to haunt her later.

As she watched Rynar, the Vosira caught her eye, and with two fingers he waved her to his table. Here it comes, she thought to herself. At that moment she wished her half-empty goblet held havar rather than wine. After taking a healthy drink of it, she stood up carefully and worked her way over to him.

"You gave poor Rynar here quite a fright when you disappeared from Loraden the other day," Vosira Bedoric said as a way of welcoming her, and waved for her to take a seat across from him.

She noted that Rynar said nothing, but scowled in response, looking much like a wet cat, totally unhappy with the situation but not wanting anyone to know it. Meanwhile, she just smiled politely, and nodded in gratitude as a boy brought her another goblet filled with wine.

"He spent a full day in the city looking for you," the Vosira continued gleefully, clearly aware of the effect his comments had on his advisor, "and by the time he gave up, I think he had enlisted the assistance of a half-dozen Senvosra. Bhara," he added, leaning close so that the others wouldn't hear, "I haven't seen my Aldrish so concerned about anyone, least of all a woman, in all the years we have known each other."

The Vosira's words made her do a double-take. After all, Rynar himself had arranged for her to be transported by boat to a village upstream. While it was true she hadn't made it to his intended destination, he also knew full well that she hadn't gone missing. The only conclusion she could draw from this was that he had lied to the Vosira—but had he done so for her sake, or his? She tried to catch Rynar's eye, but he had turned away, as if intentionally trying to avoid being dragged into the conversation. "I'm sorry, I didn't expect anyone would be worried," she replied generously. "I figured, as a stranger here, no one really paid much attention to what I did."

"Nay, such things would never be true, not for such a lovely lady as yourself," Bedoric said, his words like velvet, and he reached out to lightly stroke her chin with his fingertip. He wasn't much to look at, but in that moment she found herself drawn into his charm. "We missed you here, I assure you. So my dear, where did you go? You were gone such a long time, after all."

Just as Rynar had warned her, she had been put on the spot—and it was here, out in public. The question was so kindly asked, that she almost hadn't seen it coming. Scrambling for a story, she said the first thing that came to mind. "I went to visit a friend, that's all."

"Indeed? So you left Loraden on your own accord?" Bedoric leaned forward, intrigued by her tale—or doing a good job of pretending to be. "My poor dear, you should have let us know you intended to travel. Aldrish Rynar was certain something terrible had happened, since you disappeared without a trace just after that fight in the square."

So that's how Rynar had explained her disappearance? It seemed overly dramatic, given his role in the events. Perhaps he hadn't expected her to return? "I know, it was foolish of me." She glanced at Rynar, whose attention had suddenly shifted to her, but he said nothing. Instead, his dark eyes watched her carefully, without offering up any hints on how she should proceed. Without his assistance, her only chance of success was to keep rolling with the story, as any hesitation would do her in. "I'm sorry I worried anyone. I really hadn't expected that to happen."

"Aye, so you say." He clicked his tongue several times. "It is so dangerous out there for a young woman traveling alone. Surely you knew this, and did not truly think you would get far without assistance?"

She shrugged. Truthfully, she explained, "where I come from, women travel alone all the time. It honestly would not have occurred to me to ask for someone else to join me."

He nodded, appearing to understand. "Very well then, my dear." He smiled, as if he was satisfied, and drained his goblet. Then he tipped his head, and with a friendly grin, asked, "perhaps you would do me one favor?"

"Of course, Vosira." Relieved, she readily acquiesced. Was he going to ask her to dance, perhaps?

He leaned forward. "I was hoping you could clear something up for me. If everything you say is true, and you left alone to visit a friend, then how did you end up with blood all over your lovely gown, and even more, why did you return in the company of my useless brother?"

So there it was, she realized. It was the million-dollar question. Rynar had warned her, had he not?

She swallowed, and tried to collect her thoughts as quickly as possible. She had just fallen into a deep pit, and there was no way out of it now. Rynar leaned back in his chair, as if pretending not to be concerned about the conversation. She could tell he was listening intently, but for some reason was unwilling to participate. Why wasn't he saying anything? Was he hoping she'd dig herself in even deeper? Scrambling now to find a way to spin her tale further, she finally continued. "After my visit with my friend, I was on my way back to Loraden. On my way back to the city, the wheel of the wagon I was riding in came loose, and the driver injured himself in the fall. I helped patch up his cuts, and that's where the blood came from. And as I was helping him, the Dosedra came up on horseback. He lent a hand to the situation, and then gave me a ride into the city." She took a moment to seek him out among the dancers, and smiled as she spotted him. "You know, he's not at all like people say he is," she added. "He was actually quite kind."

"Hmm." Bedoric tipped his head. "That is a very odd account," he declared, and finished off his wine. "I wonder, why did the Dosedra say nothing of this himself in the Council today?"

Rather than concede the point, and surrender the game, however, she shrugged as if it mattered little to her why their stories did not match. "Maybe he was embarrassed. I don't know. It wasn't really a big deal."

Rynar stood up, and walked around to her side of the table. As he did so, the Vosira just leaned back in his chair and studied her, causing her to squirm in her seat.

"Your story is preposterous," Rynar said, casually leaning down to whisper in her ear. "No one, least of all the Vosira, will believe a word of it."

She smiled, and nodded, as if responding to something entirely different. To quickly extricate herself from the situation, she used Rynar's sudden maneuver to her own advantage. "Vosira, I hope that's all? If so, would you mind too much if I danced with the Aldrish?" she asked, batting her eyelashes at him.

The Vosira nodded, and in a rapid shift in demeanor, chortled at her comment. "Of course, my lady. There will be plenty of time later to discuss these matters. Dance with the man—someone needs to entertain him, after all!"

Rynar took her hand led her to the center of the room. "I hadn't intended to dance with you," he muttered.

"What a shame. If you'd like, I'll go sit down again—" she offered, calling his bluff, and took a step towards the Vosira's table.

"You shall do nothing of the kind," he replied, reaching for her other hand. As they stood waiting for the musicians to retune their instruments, he leaned close to whisper, "that was well played, my dear."

She bit back a self-congratulating grin.

"You need to be more careful how you proceed," Rynar suggested, and then as the dancers all came together in a line, he folded both of her hands in his. "The Vosira is not foolish—and his brother is not the man you think he is," he added, but then was forced to cut his comments short. Along with the dozen other pairs of dancers, he lifted her hands high over their heads, their arms forming an archway that would become part of the dance as couples passed under. In such a position it was impossible to carry on a covert conversation.

Curious as to what he meant, she had to wait before she could hear more, for the dance had begun, and her concentration had to be focused on the expected set of movements. Instead of allowing it to worry her, however, she pushed it from her mind as she spun around a petite woman in pale pink who seemed a bit bored with the dance.

The tune ended, and she noticed that Arric had finally worked his way over to Merel. As she watched, there was the inevitable pause as they gazed at each other, taking in the span of eight years. They then embraced each other tightly.

"You see, there is no point in pursuing him," Rynar said.

"Why would you think I was trying?" she challenged him, and immediately returned her attention back to the music, as if Arric was the last thing on her mind. "Shall we try this one?"

Again, the dance separated them, but soon it was their turn to promenade through the archway. She leaned close and said, "you know that those stories about him aren't true."

He seemed unshaken. "So he's convinced you of that, has he? Hmm, I suppose love really is blind."

"You've got it all wrong. There's nothing going on between us."

"Truly?" He seemed skeptical.

"Of course there isn't!" Exasperated, she lost track of her steps, causing the woman behind her to crash into her. With a murmured expletive, as people passed her, she abandoned the dance and retreated to the edge of the dance floor.

Rynar caught up with her, and instead of being annoyed at the abrupt end to the dance, simply took her hand led her away from the crowd of dancers. "My dear, I know you did not randomly run into him outside of Loraden," he whispered. "Indeed, if there's nothing between the two of you, perhaps you can explain why—and how—you were able to locate him from Altopon."

She suddenly felt dizzy. How could he know she was there? And what else did he know? Like a child caught with her hand in the cookie jar, she could only offer a feeble response. "I don't know what you're talking about."

Oddly enough, he didn't press the point. "Never mind that now." At an unoccupied table, he pulled out a bench for her, and then sat beside her. "My dear, you must understand how concerned the Vosira is about his brother's activities, and how urgent it is that we explain your role to his satisfaction, before things get worse." He lowered his voice until it was just barely audible over the musicians. "It is my fault for not explaining this sooner, but I had no idea this would happen." He lifted his eyes and scanned the vicinity, and confident no one was close enough to overhear, continued. "There's something you must know, right now, before things get any more serious between the two of you. Eight years ago, the Dosedra was so desperate to rule Sarducia that many believe he was involved in his father's murder, and that he left Sarducia rather than be held accountable."

"What? That's impossible." Kate's mind flashed back to the man she had gotten to know over the past week, and then her eyes darted out into the crowd, seeking him out. Seeing him dance with Merel, she shook her head. "You don't really believe that he's capable of that, do you?"

He shrugged. "I don't know. However, it matters not what I believe—it's what the Vosira believes that concerns me, and should concern you as well."

"But—"

He held up his hand. "I cannot tell you who to trust, but I would caution you against allying yourself with the Dosedra."

She shook her head. It was all wrong. She desperately wanted to believe that he wasn't the monster Rynar was portraying now. Hoping to see the lie in his eyes, she lifted hers to his, staring into the dark pupils.

He didn't waver, or blink. "Let me ask you this. Did he ever tell you why he went to Bhoren? Or why he chose to do so secretly, and in the company of fhaoli?"

"You're crazy," she argued, in a last-ditch effort to deny the truth. "Wouldn't that be illegal?"

Rynar raised an eyebrow. "So you understand the concept of fhaoli, then. Interesting." He folded his hands in his lap. "My dear, there is no point in denying anything. The Vosira knows where he went, and with whom. Most of all, he knows why." His expression grew solemn as he continued. "What you need to understand is that the Dosedra is playing a dangerous game, and it is just a matter of time before the Vosira takes action against him."

"Now wait a minute. You're making all these accusations, but you're being really vague about it all. Whatever he might have done, I don't see how his trip is anyone's business."

Rynar crossed his arms, and peered down his nose at her. "So he didn't tell you who he was looking for, then?"

"He said he went looking for a friend, and that's all."

"Indeed?" This seemed to surprise him. Continuing, he explained, "I fully expected him to try to sway you over to his side, and have you rally to his cause. You see, he went on that extended journey hoping to find his old friend Sarnoc Sofinar, who used to serve on the Council, until he was banished under suspicion of aiding Vosira Parmon's murder." He smiled to himself. "The Dosedra had just returned to Loraden, yet he rushed out to find that Sarnoc, just like that," he said, snapping his fingers for emphasis. "All without any regard for family, duty or honor."

"You're wrong. There wasn't a Sarnoc there."

"Ah, so you finally admit to being there with him." He smiled, having won the concession from her. "I would expect not. As everyone knows, Sofinar is long dead." He stood up, and tugged at his tunic to straighten it. "Well, I should return to the Vosira, and try to keep him appeased. Enjoy the rest of the evening, but be on your guard. You know Arric's true colors now. I trust you will know what to do."

CHAPTER 31

After Rynar had returned to Vosira Bedoric's table, a number of men had approached Kate, and she had a steady line of dance partners for the rest of the evening. Even though she suspected the Bhavosa had put them up to it, she still enjoyed the dances, and tried to be as graceful as she could be, given her lack of practice. After a number of dances, Rynar reappeared, leading her through several dances without another word of Loraden politics. Perhaps Bryll had been behind that, too.

Throughout it all, she tried not to pay attention to Arric, but he made such efforts impossible. As he danced, he often exclaimed loudly about how much he enjoyed a tune, or he called out to people he knew. Several times he pulled Merel into the middle of the room when the musicians performed a tune unknown to the rest of the crowd, effectively leading her in a solo dance. As drunk and rowdy as he was acting tonight, it was unsurprising that his brother and the Aldrish had such poor opinions of him. At any rate, although she encountered him several times on the dance floor, never again did he ask to dance with her, instead focusing his attention on the beautiful woman he might have married many years ago.

She tried not to feel disappointed by his lack of attention, but it was difficult. Given the exuberance with which he had escorted her here tonight, and the friendship they had built during their travels, she found herself wishing he would spend a little more time with her tonight.

Watching him with Merel brought mixed emotions. She recognized he bore a heavy burden of guilt from both his extended absence and the duties he had performed as a soldier. It was as if he was pursued by his own personal demons, and he could barely outrun them. Tonight, however, he seemed light and carefree, finding a bit of respite from the burden he carried. Seeing him this way, it was difficult to fight the slow bloom of jealousy that grew from the seed Merel had planted earlier today. No matter what she felt for this man, she knew his affections would always be elsewhere, but that didn't make it any easier to swallow.

And what if Rynar was right? What if the Dosedra really was involved in something dangerous, even possibly treasonous? Could he have had a role to play in his father's death? It seemed so unlikely, but then again, how well did she really know him? As she watched him laughing as he spun Merel past another pair of dancers, she realized that she didn't know him well at all.

Tonight it was clear that she was tangled up in a political intrigue, and everyone expected her to take sides. When something as innocuous as a banquet had political ramifications, she wasn't sure if she wanted to play the game.

***

It was quite late into the night when Arric slid onto the bench across from her. He held his goblet out to a boy with pale skin who had been hovering over the table next to theirs, but when he saw the Dosedra's gesture, he rushed over to fill it for him. Draining the goblet in a few gulps, Arric sought a refill, and then smiled at Kate. From what she could tell, he had consumed wine at a pace that rivaled that of his brother.

"Shall I show you back to your quarters, Bhara Kate?" he asked, the question sounding quite formal, as if they were scarcely acquainted.

"Sure, if you want..." As she stood up, aching from all the dancing, she scanned the stragglers in the room looking for the lavender dress. *So that's why he's ready to leave,* she realized with disappointment. Bhara Merel was gone. It was impossible now not to feel a little snubbed by him.

He appeared to be unaware of any reluctance on her part. Instead, as she walked around the table, he draped his arm over her shoulders in what felt quite improper for someone of his standing. He weaved considerably as he moved, and Kate, who herself had soaked up quite a bit of wine herself, was no help.

As they passed the musicians, he hung his head back and began to hum along with the ballad being performed. She rolled her eyes, a bit embarrassed for him, but figured it would end as they stepped out of the room. To her complete astonishment, however, he didn't leave.

Instead, just short of the double doors, he stopped and turned around to the remaining Bhagali in the hall... and burst out into song.

In a loud voice that was slightly out of tune, he offered up a set of off-color lyrics that no one in the hall was likely forget. Mortified, Kate stepped to the side, her eyes averted, and she could feel her cheeks flush with embarrassment. This was so unlike the man she had traveled with that it was becoming impossible to reconcile the two personas. Had the rigors of travel made him seem more serious and responsible than he really was? Were Rynar and Tashin and all the others actually right about him? She didn't have to endure his singing for long, however, for the musicians brought the travesty to a rapid conclusion.

In the silence that followed, those in the room simply stared, dumbstruck. He grasped her hand and spun her around, and then led her from the hall, humming again as they departed.

Then everything changed.

As soon as the servants pulled the doors shut behind them, Arric straightened up and grew quiet. When he next spoke, he lowered his voice, which just moments before had been sloppy and loud. "Bhara Kate, I trust you had a pleasant evening?"

"Uh... I guess." She tried to pull away from his touch but he clutched her shoulder so she couldn't bolt from him. "You certainly seemed to enjoy yourself," she added sarcastically. With all the wine she had consumed, the doubts Rynar had planted had already taken root, and in her present state of mind, her annoyance was difficult to conceal.

"Oh, it was tolerable, I suppose." Perhaps it was the alcohol, but he didn't seem to notice her sharp tone, or if he did, he didn't remark upon it.

"Only tolerable? You seemed to be having the time of your life in there tonight."

"Ah," he exclaimed lightly, twisting his mouth, as if thinking how to answer her. "Aye, perhaps I did enjoy myself, eventually."

Was that a dig against her? She was about to reply in kind, but instead held her tongue, choosing not to make a scene, particularly with him as inebriated as he was. So she just walked with him in angry silence as they crested the stairs.

Near her own quarters, he suddenly glanced down the hallway in either direction and then pulled her to a bench under a window overlooking the courtyard.

What was he doing now? Fearing the wine had taken control, she tried to resist, but he shook his head and raised a finger to his lips. She was trying to decide how to best escape to her room when he smiled at her warmly. "What are you doing?" she asked him quietly as he reached inside his vest. "You're drunk…"

Very quietly, he replied with laughter in his voice, as he pulled something from his vest and hid it in his palm. "Nay, not in the slightest. I've had nothing but weak wine all evening."

What? With a start, she noticed his eyes betrayed a sober mind. It wasn't possible. "I don't understand. Earlier, you smelled of havar, and everyone noticed—well, it was impossible not to notice. You drank heavily all night, more than even your brother. And the way you were acting…" she squinted to get a better look at him in the dim light of the hallway. "You had to be—I mean, I could have sworn you were completely drunk."

"Aye?" He had not stopped smiling, and it was the grin of a child who had gotten away with a great prank. "So you believed it, then?"

"Yeah, who wouldn't have? You were being ridiculous." She stared at him with disbelief. "So you're telling me it was all an act?"

"Aye, Kate, of course it was. I feared that my behavior might distress you, but I thought it best that I convince my brother and all the rest of the Council that the only things I'm interested in these days are drinking and the ladies."

Really? She was impressed. "Well, if that was your goal, I think you succeeded," she confirmed. "Was Merel a part of your plan, then?"

His smile faded immediately. "Nay. She knows nothing about it."

She stared at the rug under her feet, following the pattern of the golden scrollwork with her eyes. She felt like a complete idiot sitting next to him, and wanted nothing more than to run into her quarters and bury her head under the blankets. "Oh." It wasn't a very profound response.

"I do hope that one day she will forgive me for how I acted, but I must not worry about that now." His voice was low, and unexpectedly solemn. "Kate, there are other matters that I hoped to discuss with you tonight." A couple of charnok rounded the corner just then, and he grabbed her hand and slumped his shoulders forward, pretending to sway slightly as they passed by. The boys were impeccably polite, but she could tell that Arric's behavior had not gained him any respect, and in their curt greeting to him, she recognized their disdain.

"The Vosira asked me why I returned with you yesterday," Kate said softly, "and Rynar says I shouldn't trust you. They both seem really concerned about you and your trip to Bhoren."

He frowned. "Indeed. I was worried about that." He dropped her hand, and sat up straight. "It confirms what I'm about to tell you." Again he scanned the hallways, making sure no one was nearby. "There is more afoot here in Loraden than I had anticipated. Worse, I appear to have sorely misjudged the situation, and underestimated my brother's intentions." He had the edginess of a fugitive as he spoke. "Lest you think me mad, there was actually an important reason I wanted to escort you tonight."

At those words, she looked at him carefully, her curiosity raging, but she kept her expression as bland as possible as he continued. "You see, I must ask a favor of you, and I could not discuss it with you earlier with Lillia there." He opened his fingers to show her a small pouch of deep blue velvet, cinched with a silk cord. "For eight years I have carried this, but now I fear that it may fall into the wrong hands." After tugging the drawstring open, he indicated that she should hold out her hand. As she did so, he turned the pouch over, allowing a heavy glysar ring to tumble into her palm. "It was my father's," he explained, in a voice barely more than a breath, as he folded her fingers over it. "I need you to keep it for me, safe and out of sight. No one must know you have it."

She nodded readily as she uncurled her fingers a little, and turned the ring over with her thumb. It was a wide, flat band of the silver metal, polished to a shiny chrome finish and bearing no further embellishments. "Sure, but why?" She examined it as well as she could in the dim glow of wall torches and candlelight. To her eyes it appeared wholly unremarkable; certainly there was nothing about it that suggested it was worth all this trouble. "What's so special about it?"

Once more he looked up the hallway, and down to the other end. With a sigh and a swallow, he said simply, "at this time, its significance matters not. Just promise me one thing: if anything happens to me, you will take the ring to the Sarnoc, and tell them that my father gave it to me before he died. You must do this yourself, and entrust no one to do this in your place." He sought her eyes, as if to seal a contract. "Trust no one else, do you understand? Only you can know about this."

She looked back, into his eyes, dark and deadly sober. Now she was scared. This conversation had taken an entirely new direction. "Something's wrong, isn't it?" She considered what Rynar had told her. "I heard that some people think you were involved in your father's murder."

The comment surprised him. "What do you know about that?"

"Not much," she admitted. "Rynar—I mean, the Aldrish mentioned it, and warned me about spending time with you. And given how you're acting—"

He relaxed. "Ah. Well, it's true that they never caught the bastard, but they were quick to lay blame." He looked right into her eyes. " I had nothing to do with it. I loved my father, and if I ever find out what really happened, I'll be the first in line to deal with the guilty party."

Reassured, she nodded, but then asked, "Are they trying to blame you for it?"

Arric shrugged, and licked his lips. "Aye, it's a possibility." After a night of dancing his neat braid had frayed, and he pushed stray hair from his eyes. "I don't know what is going on here, but something smells rotten to me. That is the reason for giving you the ring. Should something happen to me, I need to be able to trust someone with it. While I loathe having to impose this on you, as we scarcely know one another, there is no one else I can turn to."

"What about Merel?"

"Ah, her again." He tossed his head back. "So you know about her, do you?" he asked.

"Yeah. I met her today, and she told me that you were going to marry her. After seeing you with her tonight, you obviously still care about her."

"Aye, that's true enough, on both counts. Eight years ago, I was in love with her, and perhaps there's still something between us, but it's been a long time." As he explained it, he sounded a bit wistful, as if regretting what might have been. "We've both changed, and I don't know where things stand with her."

"So you can't trust her with this?" She held up the closed fist that held his ring.

"Nay, not her."

"But if you wanted to marry her—"

He sighed. "It's not as simple as that. If it looks as though I am sick with love for Merel, it could buy me some time. It helps that her father, Gevinsin, is one of the wealthiest men in Sarducia, and his lands produce most of our glysar." He cupped his hand over her fist. "This matter is different. It has been eight years, and I don't know if I can trust her. You, however, are different. I believe I can trust you with this, because Nyvas trusts you. That's enough for me."

"Nyvas? What does he have to do with it?"

He smiled. "Let's just say I have faith in his instincts." He squeezed her hand. "Is it a promise, then? You'll keep this for me?"

It seemed like a very small favor indeed. Even with everything Rynar had told her—things she wish she could forget, now—what could it hurt to hold his ring? "Sure, I'll do my best. Is it all I can do to help you, though?"

No trace of inebriation marked his expression as he nodded. "It's enough."

CHAPTER 32

The soldier stiffly led Kate into the large room used for the Council Vosidari sessions.

Given the late hour, the room was dimly lit with a handful of candles on the table, and the fire in the hearth looked as though it had just been started a short time before. Two men sat at a long table of richly-polished wood, with goblets in front of both of them. Rynar immediately stood as she entered, while the Vosira, simply waved for her to approach. "Good evening, Bhara Kate," he said solemnly.

"Good evening to you, Vosira," she said politely, but remained standing, unsure what was expected of her. She noticed that the other seats at the table were empty.

"Ah, yes, very well. Please, lady, take a seat. We do not have all day." At that cue, one of the Senvosra stepped forward and led her to a chair across from Rynar.

Vosira Bedoric, meanwhile, wasted no time. Before she could even sit down, he demanded, in a stern and unkind voice, "tell me who you met in Bhoren." All of the flirtatious personality he once showed towards her was gone. No longer did he seem to be a slightly inept buffoon, and suddenly she understood Rynar's warning not to underestimate him.

As a result, she was at a loss for words, and stood frozen, her hands gripping the back of the heavy chair. She glanced at Rynar, but he used the moment to return to his seat. Like at the dance the night before, he did not look at her.

"Shall I phrase it another way? Who were you with while you were there?"

She shrugged, simultaneously shaking her head. It was an impossible question to answer. Even if Arric was guilty of something of which she was unaware, she decided right then and there that her loyalty was to him, not the Vosira or the Aldrish, and she wasn't going to confirm anything that could put the nail in Arric's coffin—which, she realized might well not be a metaphor. Regardless of what Rynar had told her, she had been through far too much with Arric for her to betray him now. She absently ran her fingers across her chest, where Arric's ring now was hidden, suspended from a thin glysar chain under her gown. If the Vosira wanted more information about his brother, he would have to get it from someone else.

Bedoric uncrossed his arms, and leaning forward, put his elbows on the table. "Come now, Bhara. Do not try to hide things from me. Just tell me the truth about where you were, and who you were with, and this will be over. If you don't, then things will quickly become more difficult for you."

She rapidly looked from one man to the other, expecting Rynar to speak up for her, but although he was frowning, he remained silent. "I don't know what you're talking about," she bluffed. "I told you last night where I went."

"Nay, Bhara. Had you had told me the truth, we would not need to discuss this again, would we?"

She stared back at the Vosira, knowing strength and confidence was conveyed through eye contact. She felt neither quality right now, but if she could pretend otherwise, maybe she could buy herself some time. "I still don't see why it matters to you."

"Bhara, do not play games with me."

"My lord Vosira, please calm yourself," Rynar finally said. "Bhara Kate is just scared. She does not understand the ways of Sarducia. She doesn't feel safe—"

Bedoric slammed his fist on the table. "Aldrish, I am not stupid, nor do I care if she feels safe at my court." He had raised his voice, and his face had flushed red almost immediately. "In fact, if she's found dead in an alley tomorrow it would mean nothing to me. My only concern with this woman right now is that she is trying to meddle in my affairs, and has apparently decided to join forces with the traitor I have for a brother."

Already frightened by the outburst, now she was shocked by his words. Rather boldly, she asked, "since when is he a traitor?"

With a barely perceptible gesture, Rynar shook his head, warning her not to challenge the Vosira further.

"Ah, well, we will get to that in due time, Bhara, I promise you that. As soon as the others arrive, these things will become clear. For now, you have one more chance to revise your story about meeting my brother just outside the city walls." It was not a request, regardless of how it was phrased. "We all know your current story is a false one. Tell me the truth about what really happened after you left Loraden, or I promise, you shall pay the price for your insolence."

She blinked. Something must be terribly wrong. Rynar already knew Arric had been seeking out a Sarnoc—surely there was no point in demanding that she tell them herself. They must be fishing for something else. Without understanding the game at hand, all she could do was shake her head in refusal.

"Kate," Rynar addressed her, his voice calm but missing its usual confident polish. "I know that you innocently entered the Dosedra's company and had no knowledge of his intentions, but Vosira Bedoric remains skeptical. Anything you can offer to demonstrate your innocence would be good to share with us now." When she looked up at him, she realized he was pale and looked slightly desperate.

So she wasn't there for them to collect information on Arric; it was all about her own activities. The Vosira wanted to gauge her own guilt or innocence. "There isn't anything else to say," she countered, speaking honestly. "I only met the Dosedra a few days ago, and I don't know him well enough to be involved in anything. You might think that I know more than I—"

She was saved from having to continue when the door to the chamber opened again, and Bhagal Tashin entered. He took a seat beside Aldrish Rynar, so both men now faced her. The attendant behind

Bedoric brought Tashin a goblet, and refilled the ones in front of Rynar and the Vosira. Nothing was offered to her.

"So we are almost all here now," the Vosira announced, tapping his fingers impatiently. "Naturally, the last to arrive will be my worthless brother."

At this, she caught her breath. She wasn't sure if it was good or bad news that Arric was joining them, but the Vosira's choice of words to describe his brother was not in the least bit comforting. Something must have happened during the day today, and she wished she knew what it was.

"Bhagal Tashin," Vosira Bedoric said, his voice demonstrating none of the bitterness he had just used on her, "we were just giving Bhara Kate one final chance to explain why she was with my brother, and who they visited in Bhoren. Oddly, she claims that never happened, and she also claims that she just met him a few days ago, but of course we know all of these things are lies."

Tashin, whose thinning hair was askew, must have been interrupted from some other activity. Although he had not had a chance to prepare himself for the meeting at hand, he showed no discomfort at the sudden summons. Instead, he made a tight-lipped smile. "My lord Vosira, I tend to believe her." She was shocked. This man was supporting her position? Maybe she had misjudged him. "While I expect she still has information we shall find useful," he continued, "I have no reason to believe she was involved in these matters with the Dosedra, which of course go back many years. She has not been in Sarducia long enough to have been able to make alliances of such import."

"Unless she has been working for Tylnea," Bedoric reminded him. "She could have been in Hansar all this time, waiting for the Dosedra to return."

Tashin shook his head. "Vosira, Kate has neither the appearance nor the accent of someone from Hansar." He turned to glare at her. "And she is just a woman, after all."

"We shall see." Bedoric turned his head to the guard at the door. "Go see what is keeping my brother. I am anxious to get started." With these words he grinned with delicious anticipation.

She stared at the table, the burnished wood soaking up the light of the candles and fire in the hearth, and the torches at the door. Under the table she rubbed her hands, and she felt a bit queasy. Something was about to happen, but what? She tipped her head up to catch Rynar's eyes, but he now refused to look at her, as if ashamed that she had not disavowed the Dosedra while she had the chance. Tashin, however, was once again watching her intensely, and that caused an involuntary shiver to run down her spine. What was going on?

Finally the door swung open to admit the Dosedra into the chamber. His shirt was unlaced at the neck, and he had not combed back his hair, which tumbled in unruly clumps at his forehead, and hung loosely between his shoulders.

"Found him in the library, my lord Vosira," the guard explained.

"Reading anything interesting, brother?" Bedoric asked with a bit of a chuckle.

Arric shook his head. "Nothing at all, actually," he responded quickly. "Apparently several of the chronicles I had hoped to read are missing." He stood behind the empty chair that lay between Kate and Vosira Bedoric, his hands tightly gripping the leather back of the chair. "Brother, if you had given me warning, I would have dressed properly for the Council meeting."

She stole a glance at him but did not look at him directly. All the same, she bit her lip, trying not to smile at his brashness.

Vosira Bedoric, however, did not find his comments amusing. "Brother," he repeated, but layered with sarcasm. "This no Council meeting." He motioned to the chair. "Now if you would take your seat, we have important things to discuss."

Arric nodded politely at her, as one would do to a casual acquaintance. "Bhara."

She nodded in return, but said nothing.

As he sat down, she felt his knee brush against hers. At first, she thought it was an accident, but he pushed it closer, as if hoping his touch would give her courage—or perhaps it was the other way around. Either way, it was a subtle enough gesture that no one else in the room would have seen it, not even the guards that stood behind then at the door.

"Now, finally, we can begin." Bedoric smiled politely to Rynar and Tashin. He snapped his fingers behind his head. "You may leave us," he signaled to the attendant. Then to the guard at the door, he waved his finger, as if beckoning someone else to join him.

"Aye, Vosira," the soldier nodded, and left the room as well. He returned with a second guard, and between them they led in a third man, his head and shoulders bundled under a long cape.

"Now." Bedoric smiled broadly to Arric and Kate, as if gloating over something. "We shall see if the two of you stick to your stories. I must thank Captain Joven for his hard work finding this one," he said, nodding appreciatively to one of the Senvosra. As he spoke, the cloaked man was led to the end of the table, across from Bedoric. "Brother, I believe you may be acquainted with this man?"

At the Vosira's signal, the guards yanked away the cloak.

It was a young man, badly bruised and bloody about the face, with a deep laceration on his cheek, and with his arms tightly bound behind him. He held his head down, and appeared to be in considerable pain as he stood there. Still, his dark hair, slender nose, and freckled cheeks over a wisp of a beard were unmistakable.

"Nyvas?" she called out without thinking, and quickly turned to Arric, who didn't flinch, and instead, in the practiced way of a seasoned soldier, stared at the boy without sign of recognition. Yet, as a response he would not have learned on the battlefield, under the table he reached for her hand, and gripped it tightly.

"Ah, this is quite an interesting development, wouldn't you say?" Bedoric had not stopped smiling, and Tashin shared the expression. "If you know him, Bhara, then I think it is safe to assume my brother has also had the chance to become acquainted?"

Arric turned to Vosira Bedoric, but the expression on his face was intentionally bland, and he made no indication either way.

Rynar, however, was noticeably puzzled. "Vosira, who is this?"

Bedoric leaned to his brother. "Perhaps you would like to do the introductions? I believe Aldrish Rynar is the only one in the room still unacquainted with this boy."

Arric sat straight up. Kate sensed he was restraining himself from attacking his brother right at that moment. Remarkably, however, he kept his voice calm as he replied. "His name is Nyvas, and he is fhaoli." His eyes flickered between the Aldrish and his brother, resting with Bedoric, finally. "I do know him, aye. I won't deny that fact."

The Vosira reached for his goblet, and nonchalantly spun the stem between his fingers. "Of course, brother, you know that to willingly associate with fhaoli is to bring their crimes onto your own shoulders. I assume when you invited him and his friends to join you on your lengthy journey, you also planned on joining them as they met their fate—a fate which, I should point out, is now assured?"

"What do you mean?" Kate asked, her voice trembling. She looked at Nyvas, who had raised his head, and was carefully watching everyone in the room, despite the fact that one of his eyes was puffy, and nearly swollen shut. He was uncomfortable, and in considerable pain, but alert. They had beaten him quite badly, but his spirit seemed intact. "What have you done to him? And what else are you going to do?"

Bedoric shrugged, acting entirely too nonchalant for the topic. "We shall see. He will die, of course, but when, and by which means, will be determined by this meeting. You see, he knows many things that would be useful to me. If he is forthcoming, I will consider offering him a quick and merciful death, more than he probably deserves. If not… well, like I said, we shall see."

"What could he possibly know?" Kate cried out. She would have gotten to her feet, but Arric still held her hand in a death grip under the table. The sight of their friend was obviously disturbing him as well, though he was struggling to hide his reaction. It was as if she had to speak for them both, and she didn't hesitate. "Look at him. He's no threat to you." She turned to Arric, and then to the Vosira. Finally, she tried to get a sympathetic expression from Rynar, but he averted his eyes. "I don't understand. What has he done? Why are you saying he has to die?"

Tashin answered this question on Bedoric's behalf. "Bhara, do not be fooled by him. He is fhaoli, and for that fact alone, his life is forfeit to the Vosira. However, this boy is special." He leaned forward. "When you were in his company, did he never share with you the reasons why he became fhaoli?"

She shook her head. It hadn't ever occurred to her to ask. Surely Nyvas could not have been capable of anything that bad—certainly not something worthy of this kind of drama.

Tashin ran his tongue over his yellowing teeth. "Nay, I suppose he would not, for had he done so, even you might not have chosen to associate with him. Bhara," he continued with a grin, "this one became fhaoli eight years ago. He was lucky for such a fate, however, because by all rights, he should already be dead."

With this comment, Rynar turned to him with surprise. "Tashin, what do you mean?" She could tell he was irritated that information had been kept from him. Preferring to being in charge of a situation, this time the Aldrish was as much in the dark as she was, and it was obvious that he was growing impatient with the game being played.

"Allow me to explain," Bedoric said, and waved to the door again. A guard opened it once more, admitting another man in uniform. "This is quite the party today, isn't it?" he laughed. "Castellan Solerav, would you please be so kind as to share with everyone what you told me this morning?"

Although she had seen him before, the castellan's presence tonight was rather intimidating. He was a brawny man who towered over all the other men in the room, and his spiky black hair simply added to his height. As he stood there, he held his giant hands at his waist, his thumbs hooked in his belt. "My lord Vosira, when my men brought the fhaoli into the city late last night, they thought little of him. To them, he was just one of a group of bandits that attacked the Senvosra at the edge of the Arsdala. He was the only one my men were able to capture, as all the others got away, but they hoped to find out more about the rest when they brought him back to the city."

With those words, she caught a bit of a grin from Nyvas. So Fantion and Lysander were safe? That at least was good news.

"I assumed the Senvosra questioned him, and told you where the others are camped?" Rynar suggested. "You could return for the rest of the fhaoli."

"Aye, that was my thought as well. From what the men tell me, though, they tried to get information from this one, but he would not speak, even as they utilized various means to convince him to do so.

Usually, of course, in such circumstances, the Senvosra then would have killed him outright, but the boy had an unusual demand that saved him from a quick demise." Tipping his head down, he stared at Arric, a frown on his face. "To their astonishment, at the last moment he demanded to speak to the Dosedra."

Bedoric sipped from his goblet, the smile on his face quite joyous for what was undeniably a serious occasion. Why was this so important?

The castellan continued. "Of course, such an odd demand caught my interest, so I personally went to see him myself. 'Who is this fhaoli who knew our Dosedra had returned to Sarducia,' I wondered. To my great surprise, I recognized him immediately." With a shift of his eyes, he gazed upon his captive. "He is taller than I recall, and his hair is no longer blond, but I knew him well as a boy, and I would never forget that face." He was not smiling, but seemed pleased with himself anyway. "Vosira, this fhaoli is none other than Stavan, son of Elric. Behold, the murderer of Vosira Parmon."

With that announcement, Arric released Kate's hand and jumped from his seat. "That's a stinking lie!" he shouted, and kicked over his chair as he leapt towards the castellan, who merely stepped backwards, a smile unmistakable under his beard.

One guard tried to restrain him, but Arric easily knocked away the man's arm. Meanwhile, two other guards struggled to hold onto Nyvas, who used the distraction to kick and bite them. Bedoric shouted for more Senvosra, and those outside the room rushed inside at his command. Kate tried to put her body between the door and her friends, attempting to block the soldiers from entering the room, but the Senvosra roughly shoved her aside, causing her to fall hard against the table. In moments one of the Senvosra had lifted her up and shoved her back into her chair, holding her there with his hands, and two others struggled with Arric to likewise restrain him.

Meanwhile, Nyvas had broken free from his own captor and stumbled towards Tashin. As she watched helplessly, another soldier backhanded him with enough force to break his nose and send him crashing against the wall, effectively ending his efforts to escape. Tashin meanwhile stood up and slid behind Rynar's chair, towards the Vosira, as if afraid to be contaminated by the blood that now gushed from Nyvas's face.

Arric continued his struggle against the guards that held him, and muttered several curses. One of the Senvosra finally subdued him by roughly twisting his arm behind his back. "It's impossible, Bedoric," Arric finally replied, out of other options, and grimacing in pain. "Stavan has been dead for years, as well you know. After you captured him and put him on display in the cage, he was killed and his body ripped apart by the mob. This boy may be fhaoli, but he is not Stavan."

As they spoke about him, the guards lifted Nyvas from the floor. Kate's heart nearly broke from the sight of his abused face. Nyvas now gasped for breath through his mouth, which was filled with blood. The punch had also split his lip, and heavily bruised the previously uninjured eye socket, which now was beginning to swell. Blood ran down his mouth, onto his chest, and spattered the table. One of the soldiers held him tightly, wrenching Nyvas's head back and covering his mouth with a gloved palm so the boy could not speak, causing him to sputter for breath.

Rynar had watched the melee with concern, his right hand against his lips, clenched in a fist so tight that his knuckles had turned white. He too was shaken by the proceedings. "Vosira, it may be the Dosedra is correct. After all, it has been eight years. Perhaps, with all due respect, Castellan Solerav is mistaken."

Bedoric shook his head. "I wish you were right, Aldrish, for it would make things much easier. The boy, however, admitted it himself last night, after a bit of the castellan's own efforts at persuasion."

"You tortured him?" Kate asked, appalled.

"Call it what you will, Bhara, but it was necessary—and successful. Surely you must realize that where my father's murderer is concerned, I cannot allow myself the usual niceties." He glanced at Rynar, who gave him a similar look, nodding very slightly, as if they had communicated something unsaid between them. Then Bedoric stared at his brother, and when he next spoke, his voice was deep and foreboding. "It is fortunate that we did so, for now I understand that you went to Bhoren to devise a plot against me. Arric, since the day I was named Vosira, I knew that you resented the fact that you would not be the one to wear this torc. Others warned you'd cause trouble for me, but I chose not to believe it, thinking you would accept your fate in time." He pressed his lips tightly together, visibly disappointed, and sucked in a breath, nearly shaking from anger. "I never thought you'd do this to me, brother. At least now I know your intentions, and I shall do everything in my power to ensure that you never have a chance to plot against me again." Out of nowhere, he slammed his fist on the table with enough force to knock over his goblet. There was a pause, but in the silence, no one moved to clean up the pool of wine. Finally Bedoric declared, "it is over now."

Arric still tried to get free from the soldiers' grasp, but they held him firmly. "That's all a lie, Bedoric, and you know it. That's not why I went to Bhoren, and I know that Nyvas didn't tell you that. It just isn't true."

Bedoric shrugged, unconcerned by Arric's comment. "Who knows what else he told the castellan? From what Solerav told me, the boy was screaming too much from the pain to tell him anything. Knowing you went to Bhoren, and that you traveled with Stavan—this is all I would ever need to know of your character and your intentions."

Throughout the accusations, Nyvas had been struggling to gain his freedom from the arms of his captor. He had been unable to speak because of the guard's gloved hand over his mouth, and his nose still bled profusely. More than once he grunted slightly as the soldier tightened his grip. Pointing his finger at him, Bedoric announced, "Stavan, as a traitor and fiend, you shall die in accordance with the laws of this land, and this time I will ensure the sentence is carried out in front of my own eyes. Whether or not you suffer further will depend on what you can tell me about your role in my father's death, and what you can divulge concerning my brother's schemes."

The guard dropped his hand, and Nyvas lifted his chin in defiance. He sucked in a deep breath through his mouth, the first satisfying breath he had taken in several minutes, though the effort made him cough. Then, in a muffled voice, sounding not unlike he was trying to speak underwater, he said, "I will tell you nothing. I'm innocent, as is the Dosedra. You are wrong about us both, and you know it well."

"That is quite an impertinent speech, boy." Bedoric's eyes burned with fury. "Very well. Since you refuse to cooperate, your fate is easy to decide." He grinned now. "On the night of the next full moon, flames shall cleanse you of your crimes. That will be a fitting end to such a life as yours."

Despite his pain, and what the Vosira had just said, Nyvas was remarkably calm. "If that is my fate, I accept it. I will not lie to ease your conscience."

With one glance from Bedoric, a guard wound up his arm and punched Nyvas low in the abdomen, forcing him to spit blood across the table, and then he let out a strangled gasp as he collapsed onto his knees.

"Stop it! Isn't he hurt enough?" Kate tried to get up from her chair, only to be pushed violently back into her seat by the soldier.

"Aye, Bedoric," Arric added his own protest to hers. "End this. He's done nothing. You are wrong about him."

The Vosira, however, ignored their protests. "You, Bhara," he said, turning to Kate, "have not escaped my notice. Why couldn't you have just stayed in Loraden—you would have been a great joy to have at court. Instead, you had to wander off, forcing me to puzzle over your own role in this. Despite what my Aldrish tells me about you, it appears you are neck-deep in my brother's treachery. This I will not abide." He once again waved his fingers, and before she could react, the Senvosra who had shoved her back into her chair now slammed his fist down on her left hand, which had been resting on the table.

She cried out in surprise and pain as his fist crashed down like a mallet, shattering a number of bones instantly. The pain was sharp and immediate, and she cried out in misery. Although she didn't want to show weakness now, of all times, the pain was too intense to hide.

Enraged, Arric again tried to get free of the soldiers, and shouted, "how dare you! She had nothing to do with any of this! Bedoric, you should be damned to Yoren!"

"So you admit you wish me dead, then, brother?"

At the guard's action, Rynar had also jumped to his feet. "Vosira," the Aldrish pleaded, visibly shaken by the violence in the room. "I beg you, end this now. Bhara Kate should not have to suffer for their mistakes. The Dosedra is right—she's innocent."

As they spoke in her defense, she could barely hear them. The pain was excruciating as she leaned forward, slowly lifting her hand to bring it up to her chest, trying not to look at the damage, the crushed bones, the torn skin, and the pooling blood. Never had she experienced broken bones, and she was dizzy with pain and shock. Even so, she tried to remain brave, taking her cues from Nyvas, who, despite even worse injuries, remained silent and defiant. Then she caught a glimpse of Arric, who likely would have killed every man in this room excepting Nyvas if he could have gotten his arms free. Instead, one of the guards further twisted the arm he held, causing the Dosedra to choke with his own pain as his shoulder was nearly dislocated.

After a few minutes to gloat over his latest accomplishments, Bedoric finally leaned back in his chair. "All right, I think perhaps this scene has become gruesome enough. My point has been made. Guards, take them away before they bleed any more on the carpeting."

"Where, my lord Vosira?" one asked.

"Ah. Well, that one—" he pointed to Arric, "should be taken to the south tower just here," he indicated a wall behind him, "where I can keep an eye on him until I decide his final punishment. The murderer, of course, shall go back to his cell."

The Senvosra immediately grabbed both Arric and Nyvas and struggled to haul them out of the room. Kate turned her head, tears streaming down her face, and Arric shouted curses towards his brother and kicked his legs in a futile effort to get free.

Nyvas, despite his pain, actually smiled at her as they dragged him past her seat. "Don't worry about us," he whispered as he passed by. "Just stay safe."

The Vosira wasn't done, however. "As for her," he said, referring to Kate, "it's clear she's as guilty as the men. Throw her in with the boy. I have no further interest in her."

A soldier grabbed her by arm and yanked her from her chair, caus-ing it to fall backwards. She screamed in pain as her hand was jostled in the process.

Immediately Rynar spoke up. "Nay, my lord Vosira, not her." Pleading on her behalf, he requested, "release her to me. On my word, Kate is innocent of any involvement in this, and must be spared."

"On your solemn word, Aldrish?" The Vosira twisted his head to face him. "That is quite a show of confidence for someone with such evidence of guilt. If you are wrong, are you prepared to share the same fate as the others?"

As she squirmed in the soldier's grasp, half-crazy from the pain of the broken bones in her hand, she had a hard time following the conversation, but heard Rynar say, "Absolutely, my lord. I will take responsibility for her. I promise you that she will cause no further problems."

"Very well, I will grant you that favor, under the condition that she remain under heavy guard unless she is in your company."

Then the Vosira pointed to her. "Bhara?"

Kate lifted her head, her eyes burning with anger, and stared at him.

"If I hear so much as a rumor that you are working against me, you will share the boy's fate. Is that absolutely clear?" He glared at her. She nodded. Then he looked at Rynar, who did the same.

CHAPTER 33

Bolts of lightning shot up her arm.

Dazed by everything that had happened, she dropped into the closest chair, cradling her injured hand in her lap. Her senses were numbed, and she could barely see or hear, and it took every ounce of her concentration to remain upright.

Moments earlier she had followed Aldrish Rynar to his quarters, needing his support to just make it down the hall without fainting. His room was warm, almost to the point of being stifling, as the shutters were closed and a fire blazed high in the hearth, and she started sweating profusely.

Yet she said nothing.

She didn't know what to do. In the council chamber everything had had a surreal quality to it, as if she had been watching a movie. Never before had she experienced anything like it—never before had she witnessed someone so casually, and cruelly, inflicting pain on others, least of all people she cared about, or herself.

"My dear, may I help you?" Rynar asked, crouching down beside her.

His words triggered despair, and she doubled over in distress, sobbing, both out of pain and fear for her friends. "I'm not the one who needs help."

"Do not waste your tears on them," he gently admonished her, as he wiped her cheek with his fingers. "They deserved what happened to them."

"No, it's not right, they—" she began to argue, but she did so, she made a slight movement that shifted her hand. She gasped as the grating of the splintered bones in her fingers sent a new wave of fire up her arm, and she cried out. Her hand was limp and bloody, and her knuckles were swelling up quickly. Just a quick glance at her disfigured hand made her feel sick. Waves of dizziness made it hard to sit upright, and she could feel her perspiration slick and clammy on her face. Still, she tried to fight it. If Nyvas could bear what they had done to him, then she could bear this. She had to be strong, for their sakes.

Concerned, Rynar reached for the injured hand. "My dear, there is no reason for you to suffer so. Please, let me see what I can do."

Instinctively, she turned, hunching over to shelter her hand, sticky with blood, and intensely painful. "Just leave me alone." Contending with both physical and psychological pain, she pulled away from him. "You can't do anything." Her breathing was shallow, and despite her efforts she knew she was going to pass out. With her eyes tightly clenched, she added, more to herself than to him, "I should be with them."

He pulled up a chair next to her. "Ah, my dear, the Vosira was wrong to force you to be witness any of that, much less cause you to be injured. If I had known his plans—"

"You should have stopped him," she demanded, accusing him of complacency even she fought to remain conscious. "None of it's true."

"What is untrue? Everyone knows Stavan is guilty. I don't know how he managed to survive all these years, but I'm afraid his luck has finally run out."

"No." Another wave of pain cascaded through her body and she winced.

"Kate, I have done my best to advocate for you, but I fear you are making my role all but impossible."

She bowed her head, unwilling to look at him. The slight movement caused her to again jerk her hand, and she sucked in a breath. The pain made it difficult to focus on this conversation, but she stuck to it, hoping to convince him. "You just don't understand what Arric was trying to do..." She stopped with that comment, and closed her eyes. The pain was interfering with her judgment, and she didn't dare say anything further.

"My dear, for some reason you care about our Dosedra—though honestly, he's utterly unworthy of your time. He is as conniving and cowardly as he was eight years ago, and I fear he will try to undermine our Vosira for the rest of his days. He's just angry that he's been found out."

"No." She continued to protest, more weakly, and never opened her eyes.

He placed a finger against her chin, turning her head to face him, and her eyelids fluttered open. "Once a man is named Vosira, and wears the torc around his neck, nothing short of his own death will change that. The Dosedra has never been able to accept that his brother became Vosira instead of him, and that stubbornness will be his undoing." He clucked his tongue. "I'm so sorry. It's always difficult to learn that friends are not what you believed them to be." He reached out and smoothed her hair. "You haven't known these people as long as I have, dear Kate. With time, you will see the truth in what I have said."

As she sat there, it was becoming a little easier to breathe, and she no longer felt like she was on the verge of passing out. "No, I won't." Even though she chose her gut feelings over logical facts, she remained resolute in her loyalty to them. "What's going to happen to them? Will the Vosira really execute them?"

Rynar licked his lips. "Let's not talk about it now," he said in a soothing voice, and continued to brush her hair with his fingers.

In a croaking whisper she pleaded, "tell me." She wanted to demand it of him, but her voice was too weak to make much of an impression now.

He shrugged. "It is difficult to say about the Dosedra. I doubt that Vosira Bedoric will bring grave harm to his own brother, no matter what he's done. As for Stavan, well, he should have died eight years ago, so Bedoric will have no problems ensuring that the sentence is carried out this time." He bent down a little, so he could see into her eyes. "You can do nothing about it. It is the will of the Vosira."

"You have to stop him."

"My dear, it's out of my control. You need to move forward, and try to not let it bother you too much." He reached out and put two fingers on her elbow. "Now, may I see your hand?"

She was still cradling her injured hand against her chest, and despite his request, she did not move.

"Please," he beseeched her, holding out his own hand. "There are broken bones. You cannot ignore such an injury for long, or you'll lose the use of your hand. Surely you would not wish for that to happen?"

"Just go," she whimpered. "You can't do anything about it anyway. Just leave me alone."

"Hmm." He was undeterred. "You might be surprised by what I can do." He continued to hold out his hand. "May I? Really, dearest Kate, I insist. Let me do this for you."

She shrugged. "Fine, whatever will make you go away." She gently placed both of her hands on her lap, the uninjured hand cradling the other. "See?"

He gently uncurled her fingers, causing her to scream as white-hot fire gushed towards her elbow. "Shh, dearest," he comforted her, and as he spoke the words, the pain seemed to diminish slightly. "Just as I thought. That idiot. This was totally unnecessary."

He grasped her arm above the wrist, and very delicately placed the injured hand in his own. As she closed her eyes, there was a flash of warmth that seemed to emanate from the marrow of her bones; it started in her fingertips and slowly spread down to the knuckles, and into her palm, up her wrist, and traveled all the way up her arm.

She sat quietly for a moment, soaking in the warmth, and the pain seemed to dull ever so slightly. Her tense muscles relaxed, and she settled into the chair. Perhaps she dozed off for a little while, it was hard to say. When she opened her eyes again, Rynar was no longer in his chair, but instead was kneeling beside her, her hand still in his, and his head resting against her knee.

He must have sensed movement, for he raised his head. "Is it better, now?" he asked softly, blinking several times, as if he had fallen asleep himself.

Looking away, she wiggled one finger, then the other. Then she gently closed her hand as if to make a loose fist. "Yeah, I think maybe..." she began, but her words melted away. She turned to look at her hand, now. Although there were streaks of blood where the bones had broken through the skin, the pain and swelling were entirely gone, and everything was back in place, as if nothing had ever happened. It was like her blistered feet—she was entirely well again. "What did you do?" she whispered.

If it were possible, Rynar appeared a bit embarrassed. "It was a simple healing, that's all." He stretched out his own fingers in response, as if they had become stiff with the effort. "Broken bones are the easiest for me."

"You're a healer?" she whispered. "You can heal broken bones, just by touching me?"

"Aye, more or less." He stood up quickly, and dusted imagined dirt from his knees. "Although I don't make this fact publicly known."

"But how—" she remembered what Lysander had said, and for a moment allowed herself to be amazed. Then she pictured her friends together, imagining how hard Sander must be taking the news of Nyvas's capture, and this sparked fresh sobs.

"Oh, my dear, you need to rest. It has been an altogether trying evening for you."

CHAPTER 34

Kate felt like a bird in a gilded cage.

For two weeks, she remained in Rynar's care, unable to come and go as she pleased. Where he went, she was forced to follow, whether it was his sword practice in the exercise yard or a council meeting, supper in the great hall or long hours as he worked in his quarters. And throughout this time, there was no change in the status of her two imprisoned friends. Every day Rynar dodged her questions about their welfare, and refused to allow her to check on them, or contact them in any way.

Without fail, each evening she stared out the narrow window, noting the phase of the moon as it rose for the night. Nyvas had been captured just after the new moon, and was scheduled to die at the next full moon. The last three nights she had not been able to see anything but a fuzzy glow due to heavy cloud cover, and despite Rynar's reassurances, she feared the full moon would come and go without her knowledge.

Tonight, as she leaned out, she gasped. The moon was large and bright, and nearly a complete disk in the sky.

"My dear, what is it?" He had decided to forego the evening's dancing in the great hall, and instead pulled several parchments from his locked chest, none of which he would share with her. Now, in the light of a half-dozen candles, he labored over the documents. "Is something wrong?"

"It's tomorrow, isn't it?"

"Hmm?" he replied absently, scarcely paying attention to her. "What is?"

She let the curtain drop over the window, and fell into a chair beside him. "You know what I meant," she replied angrily. "Vosira Bedoric said Nyvas has to die at the full moon."

Rynar lifted his head to look at her. His expression was solemn. "Aye, that's tomorrow night."

She stared at him, her eyes filled with anger. "You still haven't done anything to stop it."

He pushed the documents to the side, and folded his hands on the table. "My dear, we've discussed this matter—how many times now? I know how much it grieves you, but you must accept the Vosira's decision. There's nothing more to be done."

"Well, I won't accept it, and you know that." She folded her arms across her chest. "I don't care how many times you tell me it's a done deal. They're my friends. I can't believe you don't understand that."

"I do understand—better than you can imagine."

"So then, why haven't you told the Vosira not to go through with it? You haven't even brought it up in the Council meetings. You could have advised him to do something different. He listens to you."

He smiled. "Aye, my dear, he does—usually." He tentatively stretched out a hand to her. His eyebrows went up in surprise as she grasped it. "Where his father's murder is concerned, however, he listens to no one."

Kate clung to his fingers, gripping hard with her left hand, the one he had healed. She hoped the significance of the gesture would not be lost on him. "Can I at least visit Nyvas one last time? Surely that isn't so much to ask?"

Just as she precariously clung to this last hope, he knocked it away again, and her hand as well. "Nay, that is impossible. If I were to take you down to his cell, I might as well leave you there—and possibly be forced to stay, myself. Vosira Bedoric was very clear. The boy is not to see anyone, and anyone who defies that order will pay dearly. Even me." Then he looked at her with a softer expression, apparently realizing how abruptly he had broken contact. He reached over to touch her cheek.

"That fhaoli killed the Vosira's father. Trust me on this. He will not change his mind. Do yourself a favor and forget about the boy."

"How can I?" She remembered all too clearly how Nyvas had befriended her, convincing the others, particularly Arric, to trust her. "He saved my life."

"Indeed? How so?"

She swallowed hard, not intending to divulge that information until it tumbled from her lips. "The others thought I was a spy. They were on the verge of abandoning me in the swamp until he convinced them otherwise. Rynar, don't you understand? He trusted me when none of the others did, not even the Dosedra. I owe him."

"Really? That boy?" He stood up and walked over to the window himself, and stared at the moon for a moment. Then he returned to the table, and picked up the quill again.

"That's all you're going to say?" It seemed for a split second that she had gained a foothold, and she didn't want to give up now. "Look, I know how difficult it might be, but you have to find a way to let me see him. Just once. No one needs to know."

"Nay, Kate, I cannot." There was an air of finality in his voice. "It's over. Do not ask it of me again." With his fingertips, he dragged the documents close again. "Now, I beg of you—I must get to work. I must be prepared before the next Council meeting."

"Damn you!" Unable to hold back her frustration, she shoved herself back from the table, and angrily stepped into the inner chamber, alternately crossing and uncrossing her arms. "You're as heartless as the Vosira himself."

Hearing no response, she pushed the door shut, and spent some time sitting at the window, staring at the sky. There had to be something she could do, but trapped as she was, she had run out of options. All she could do was hope for a miracle. Did these gods grant this kind of wish, she wondered, and how might one ask for such a thing?

After what must have been hours of her softly pouring her heart out to any deity who might listen, both those of this world and her own, she decided to go to bed. There was nothing else to do. She climbed into his large bed like she did every night, as Rynar always made himself a pallet on the floor by the door. Tonight, she lay there with her eyes closed, but remaining wide awake. Her mind wandered, still trying to devise a plan, but finding no workable options.

She dozed off at one point, and had an odd dream.

In her dream, she found herself in a dark room without windows or light of any kind. She felt like she was swimming in the darkness, as if the darkness itself had form and could be touched.

"Kate? Is that you?"

"Nyvas!" She was overjoyed to hear his voice. "You're here?"

"Aye. How do you fare?"

"I'm fine, but I'm worried about you."

He dismissed her fears. "There is no need to worry."

"Are you kidding me? It must be terrible for you. The soldiers hurt you so badly. How are you managing?"

"Bedoric cannot break me."

She smiled. It was exactly what she expected from him. "I know. Still, I wish I could save you."

"Aye. You have a good heart, Kate, and I appreciate your friendship more than you could ever know."

"It's not enough though. I haven't been able to convince Rynar to help you. And I'm afraid…"

"Don't worry. It will work out. Have faith in the goddess, and be brave, for me."

She wished she had his confidence. Suddenly self-aware, she said, "I wish this wasn't a dream."

And with that, Kate woke up.

Cracking open her eyes, she spied Rynar blowing out the candles in the other room. Realizing he was about to spread out his blankets to sleep, she remained on her side, her face partly hidden by a pillow, and watched him carefully in the light of the fire that burned in the hearth. He removed the heavy glysar medallion and chain from his neck, the pendant depicting the oak leaves and crossed swords that formed the insignia of the Aldrish. He pulled all the rings from his fingers, save the one glysar band on his right hand that he never removed, and which, although quite simple, he valued above all others. All of this jewelry he laid carefully on top of his wooden chest, and then he paused for a moment to stare at the remaining ring, rubbing it with the thumb and forefinger of his left hand. Then he unbuckled his belt, laying it beside the jewelry. He always removed his sword upon returning to his quarters for the night, and so it already rested there beside the belt, snug in its richly tooled and dyed scabbard.

He glanced at her, but seemed satisfied that she slept. Then he moved to the window and sat on the bench underneath, staring outside. He seemed unusually pensive, and she wondered what the reason might be. Was it something he saw in the documents that he had been so focused on for the past few days, and had spent so long reading this evening? If so, she'd likely never know, as he would not disclose their contents and kept them locked up in a second chest. Or could it be that he was also troubled by Nyvas's impending death? It seemed unlikely, but she remembered how he had not been told of her friend's arrest ahead of time. That was odd, and she wondered if this fact could be somehow turned to her advantage. Someone else was playing a game here, and in this round, Rynar was at a disadvantage for once. It had to irk him to not be calling the shots.

The fire had died down, and quietly he added another log, and stirred the coals long enough to inspire a few new flames to jump forth. Then he pulled off his tunic, leaving him in his shirt and woolen tights. She had to quickly pretend to be rolling over in her sleep, for he had paused to look at her and she thought he might have seen her awake. She kept her eyes closed and tried to keep her breathing steady as he sat beside her and stroked her hair. "If you only knew," he whispered. Then he stood up quickly, as if caught in a compromising position. With little further effort, he unrolled a blanket near the fire, as he did every night, and, still dressed, curled up on it and went to sleep.

She lay there for a while longer, wondering what he had meant by his comment, but eventually, she fell back asleep.

CHAPTER 35

The message had been equally uncompromising in its precision and its urgency. One of the Aldrish's men—spies, she reminded herself—had sent it, demanding the Aldrish meet him in the city immediately.

The message came early in the morning, even before Erdal, Rynar's main attendant, brought in their breakfast.

She had awakened earlier than usual, having barely slept all night. The moment dawn had pulled away the cover of night, she had climbed out of bed. To fight back the chill in the air, she coaxed a new fire in the hearth, and as the bark of fresh logs crackled into flames, she splashed water from the basin onto her face.

"Mmmph," Rynar mumbled as he rolled over at the sound of the water. "Kate, is that you?" he mumbled, still groggy.

"Yeah." She felt waves of nausea as she reached for the towel. "I'm just getting ready." It wasn't going to be an easy day.

He pushed himself up slowly, running his hands through his hair to get it out of his eyes. Early mornings was when he seemed most vulnerable. Once he had fully awakened, he would be back in control, his calculating, commanding presence in place. "Did it rain last night?" he asked as he turned his head to one side to pop his neck. "I feel dampness in the air."

"I don't know." She pushed aside the curtain and swung the shutters open. Fog hung over the city, thick like cotton. As she gazed out, she realized the phenomenon made everything seem unfamiliar, even a little sinister. Not that it seemed all that inappropriate for this place—or on this day.

"A rather misty day, is it?" he commented as some of the fog swirled into the room, only to be sizzled into non-existence by the hungry fire. He turned his head to the other side, and his neck made an audible crack. "Fog such as that is downright lethal."

She shrugged and dropped the curtain over the open window. "I suppose."

He pushed himself up to stand beside her, and placed his hand gently on her arm. "It will not be a good day, and I wish I could make it easier for you."

She turned away, fighting back tears.

That was when the messenger knocked urgently on the door.

***

With the strip of parchment still clutched in one hand, Rynar led her and a trio of Senvosra guards through the city streets.

Initially, the soldiers at the gate objected to her joining him in the city, but Rynar reminded them that she was unarmed and between the four men, she was not going to be able to escape. Now, they moved at a rapid pace through the same market square she remembered from her last trip through the city, though this morning it was deserted.

"I do not understand this weather," Rynar admitted as he carefully made his way down a set of uneven steps. "The fog is thicker than ever."

As they began their descent into a new neighborhood, her nose was pummeled by two equally unpleasant odors: the tang of fresh blood and the acrid stench of something much worse. Just as she gagged on the smell, Rynar explained, "this is where the city butchers animals, and where the hides are tanned as well. I know it is unpleasant, but we will pass through quickly."

"Are you sure this is the right direction?" she asked as she covered her nose and mouth against the unbearable smell. The fumes from the tanning made her eyes water, and she tried not to watch the men who were dragging goats onto their platforms. The fog helped hide the worst of the sight, but nothing could disguise the squeals of terrified animals. "Oh god, please hurry."

"Aye, we just have to pass the pens, and go up the alley behind— ah, see, there we go." He sent one of the soldiers ahead, as he always did, and followed close behind. The alley was short, and opened onto a much wider street. "Here, this should be the place." He glanced at the slip of parchment, and then whistled once, paused, then whistled three times more in rapid succession.

It was the signal he was told to use, but it did not get the expected response.

Without warning, they were attacked. Clothed in pale garments that hid them in the fog, their assailants had approached without being seen. Chaos erupted as she heard shouts and the clash of weapons, but she was unable to make out any of the battle that waged around her. Before she could escape, a man covered her mouth with his gloved hand wrapped his other arm tightly around her shoulders. Although she struggled, he was remarkably strong and easily pulled her away from Rynar and the soldiers.

Once they were around the corner, and still hidden by the fog, he and a second man tied a heavy rag tightly over her mouth. Methodically, as the first man pulled a length of rope from his belt, the second held her tight so the other could bind her arms and her legs. As she wriggled and fought back the best she could, her initial abductor hefted her over his shoulder and ran down a flight of stairs into another alleyway. After running at least another block, he carried her through a splintered doorway.

Inside, he dropped her onto a bench, and as she hit the wood, the impact was enough to make her exhale sharply. As her eyesight adjusted to the low light, she looked around at what little she could see from her vantage point. It was a run-down house with very little furniture, and the thin wood paneling was riddled with small holes made by vermin over the years and never repaired.

There was a table immediately in front of her, and someone else sitting there. She rocked her body for a few moments until she was able to swing her legs off the bench, allowing her to sit up. To her surprise, Rynar was sitting across from her, similarly trussed and gagged. His captors had been rougher with him—or he had fought back harder than she had—for his tunic was ripped in several places, and on his upper left arm blood seeped through the fabric. His hair was disheveled and his face was ringed with perspiration. As soon as he lifted his head and saw her, his eyes darkened with rage, and he began to fight against the ropes that bound him, and grunted as if cursing their abductors.

The man who had captured her migrated back to the door, while a second man approached them both. "Well, then, let's see what we have here." The new man was heavy-set, with tangled dark hair and a beard to match. His clothing was well-worn, even threadbare in places, and there was a hole in the leather of his boot. He circled the table, rubbing his chin thoughtfully. "If my eyes do not deceive me, this would be the infamous Aldrish Rynar himself. And," he added, as he approached her with a suggestive leer, and cupped his hand under her chin, "a lovely lady as well. Quite a treasure, in fact."

She yanked her head away from his touch.

"Ah, so you're feisty as well. You shall be worth much to my friends." His eyes rolled up towards the ceiling, and then she noticed the stairs behind him. "Hmm. Perhaps I should charge them more." He grinned, and ran a hand suggestively down her arm and indelicately across her chest. She turned her head away in disgust, and heard Rynar's muffled complaints.

Their captor obviously heard him as well. "Do you have a problem with something?" he snapped as he turned to the Aldrish. He must have found something amusing in the silent hostility of Rynar's stare, for he added in a bemused voice, "then again, it seems to me that you're in no position to have an opinion." With that, the man allowed his hand to drop away from her, and he walked over to the Aldrish, patting his head in a condescending manner. Barely able to suffer the intentional disrespect, Rynar struggled forcefully against the ropes and did his best to snarl despite the gag. "Aye, you are quite a prize as well," the man noted with great humor. "You shall be worth a great deal to us all."

"Now, beauty," he said, crossing back over to her, "you shall come with me. My friends don't want to wait any longer to enjoy your company—and," he added, with a sickening grin, "enjoy you they shall." As if she were nothing but a sack of grain, he tossed her over his shoulder, as the other man had done, and headed towards the stairs. Her eyes were wide with fear, and her worries were compounded when Rynar managed to get on his feet with a grunt, only to have the first man shove him down again, forcing him to fall hard against the floor.

CHAPTER 36

"Good work, Plunchek," she heard from within a room on the second floor. The man carried her through the doorway and then put her down on her feet, and as soon as the door closed behind her, someone was already working to cut the ropes from her hands and legs.

"Now, when they take the gag off, you'll want to scream as loud as you can," she was told in a whisper by another stranger, this one standing in the corner behind her.

As her feet and then hands were free, she shook out her limbs, and began to rub the feeling back into her fingers. Just as the knot was released from the gag, she turned around, and instead of screaming, she gasped.

It wasn't a stranger. Despite everything that had just happened, she couldn't help grinning when she saw the familiar red hair and beard. "Oh god, Fantion, is that really you? I'm so glad to see you!" She ran over to hug him tightly.

"Ah, but there's plenty of time for greetings later," he said. "I'm dead serious about what I said. You need to scream as loud as you can."

Her eyes scanned the room. By the door was the stout man he had called Plunchek, the man who carried her upstairs. On a bench at a rough trestle table, much like the one downstairs, sat two men she did not know. Like the others, they were dressed in old clothes, a hodgepodge of wool, linen and leather. One was about her age, with straight, sable hair and an oblong face. His skin was fair but tinged with red from the sun. The other was perhaps in his late 40s, muscular, with short hair once blond but now almost white, and piercing blue eyes. Not at the table, but standing at the small window in the corner, was another man, too preoccupied to offer greetings.

"Sander?" she said, acknowledging the last man, who didn't look up. She turned back to Fantion. "Is he okay?"

She had hardly spoken these words when she heard a cough behind her. "Excuse me, my lady, but you really do need to make some noise." It was Plunchek again, talking in barely more than a whisper. He pointed to the floor, to indicate where Rynar sat downstairs. "He needs to believe you're being attacked." To illustrate, he walked with rapid, heavy footsteps into the center of the room, stopped, stomped his feet, and walked back. "It can't sound like we're having a Council session in here, you know. You need to make it sound as though we're having our way with you."

In her bewildered state she had not grasped the reason for his request before. "No, that's not right," she argued, shaking her head. "I wouldn't want to do that to him. He's upset enough already."

Fantion began to protest but was silenced by Lysander, who spun around from the window and stormed towards her, his tall, lanky frame seeming to fill the room as he approached. "He's upset?" he said, his voice intentionally low, but seething with pent-up anger. "Kate, you have no idea what it means to be upset." His eyes bored into her with a harshness that he had never shown himself capable of before. "Now, scream. Or—" he threatened, his hand on his knife, "I'll give you reason to do so myself."

Shocked by his bitterness, and not entirely sure it was an empty threat, she nodded and immediately complied, letting loose a great shriek.

Lysander did not back down. "That's nothing," he said critically. "You can do better. Try again." His tone harbored no room for defiance. "Call for help. Cry, if you can."

She looked at the men in the room. Plunchek remained at the door, while the others were frozen in position by the exchange between Kate and Lysander. Then she glanced back at the healer, who showed more of the character of a hardened outlaw than she would have ever expected. She caught her breath, and began to tremble as he advanced, coming so close to her that his bearded face was all she could see. Unwilling to learn the cost of defying him, she hollered out again, this time a wail that reflected her newfound fear. In response, she could hear a bit of commotion downstairs. Clearly that one had done the trick.

"Quiet, bitch," Fantion shouted loudly, and slapped his hands together. Then he stepped to the other side of the table, and with his booted foot, kicked over the bench. "You'll do as we say. Keep screaming like that and we'll cut your throat."

As if rehearsed, Plunchek then stomped once with each foot, and Fantion dragged the bench across the rough wooden floor. Some grunts and a bit more walking and dragging, and then Fantion quietly declared, "I think he'll believe it, now, but Plunchek—do me a favor and keep making noise every so often, while we talk?" As his man nodded, Fantion solemnly waved Lysander over. "Why don't you come sit with us?"

Lysander blinked, and with a nod, slid onto the bench. He was still scowling.

Then Fantion looked towards her, and waved to the spot across from Sander. "Go ahead and sit there," he suggested, "between Marcan and Kels." He then stepped to the head of the table and leaned on it, propping his weight up on his knuckles. Remembering to keep his voice down so that they could not be overheard, he began. "Kate, we heard that Nyvas is scheduled to die today." He looked at her carefully. "Is this true?"

She hung her head down and nodded. "Yeah, when the moon rises." As she contemplated it, she found herself feeling a bit dizzy, and caught herself by grabbing the edge of the table. "Is that what this is about? Are you going to try to rescue him?"

Fantion nodded, but before he could answer, Lysander leaned forward, craning his neck towards her. "How is he faring?" The gruffness in his voice was hard to reconcile with the man she thought she knew.

Although she recognized how poorly the news would sit with these men, she had no reason to withhold what little information she had. Holding onto the edge of the table for strength, she replied, "I don't know for sure. I only saw him right after they arrested him, and he was pretty badly beaten up." She licked her lips, which were dry and painful, and stared at the tabletop, trying to avoid eye contact with Lysander. "It looked like he may have broken bones, but I don't know for sure how bad his injuries really are. They said they had done—things—to get him to tell them who he was, and then when I saw him, they punched him in the face. I think they broke his nose."

"Of course they did. Damn them all," Lysander spat, and jumped up from the table again. His body was tense and his fists clenched, though after a deep breath he folded his arms tightly against his chest and returned to the window.

Trembling, she added, "I wanted to help them," she started, re-membering how the Senvosra had smashed her hand. "If I'd been able to, I would have done anything for Nyvas and Arric, but—"

"Arric?" Marcan interjected. She had not previously met this man, the fair-haired one, so she could only guess at his relationship with the Dosedra. "Is he injured as well?"

She shrugged. "Maybe—I don't know. He was moved to the tower inside the Vosira's quarters, but I haven't heard anything new since that night. I think he's safe for now, since I got the sense that the Vosira doesn't want to hurt his brother. But as for Nyvas—well, I won't lie. It's bad. I got the impression from Rynar—" but then she stopped, finding it hard to talk about him while he was sitting downstairs believing she was being raped.

"Aye?" Marcan prompted, just as Plunchek walked with heavy feet across the floor again, and then tossed a sack of grain onto the floor and dragged it back towards the window.

She swallowed hard before she continued. "Well, from what he said, the Vosira is convinced that Nyvas killed his father, and won't back down because of that. And that's why he sentenced him to—" she closed her eyes, unable to say the words, "—you know."

"How did they find out who he was?" Fantion demanded.

The question surprised her. "Is it true, then?" she asked. "Is he real-ly that boy they say killed the Vosira?"

Fantion nodded a single time. "Aye, he was once called Stavan—that much is true, but there is nothing to the rest of it. He had nothing to do with Parmon's murder."

Kate sighed in relief. "I thought so. I knew he couldn't have done it."

"Never mind that now," Lysander said, impatient to hear more about his friend. "Tell us, how do they know who he is? He'd never have told them himself—not even under duress."

"He didn't," she confirmed. "After he was captured, the castellan recognized him, and then he claimed that Nyvas had confessed, though I don't think he actually did. Just like you say, Nyvas wasn't in any mood to cooperate with them. I mean, even after everything they had done to him, he was more focused on trying to make a mess of the Vosira's chamber than answer their questions."

Fantion smiled, and Marcan and Kels nodded, and Plunchek bit back a laugh. Lysander, however, just rubbed his hands together, as if to warm them against a sudden chill. "I feared as much," he remarked with a frown, his eyebrows furrowed as he struggled to maintain his composure. She just now noticed his face was haggard, and new wrinkles had appeared at his eyes and beside his mouth. Had he slept at all, or eaten, since Nyvas had been captured? "That crazy lad. His stubbornness will have made things harder for him. I pray that the gods, at least, have been gentle with him, since Bedoric has not." He slipped from the bench and walked back to the window. Without turning his attention back to the table, he asked, "Fantion, we don't have much time. Do you think this will work?"

The fhaoli leader addressed her in response. "We have an important question for you. Do you think Bedoric will be willing to trade your man down there," he said, pointing with his thumb to the floor, "for our Nyvas?"

"And Arric," she added.

"Ah, well," Fantion hedged. "Not this time around."

It was a shock. "What do you mean? You can't leave him behind!"

"My lady," Marcan spoke up. "If we do nothing, Nyvas will die, today. From what you have told us, Arric is not in any immediate danger."

She nodded slowly. "That's true, as far as I know. But—"

Fantion leaned his elbows against the table. "Listen, Kate, we have just one chance. After talking about it, we decided that Bedoric might trade a 'worthless' fhaoli such as Nyvas—" and with this comment he winked at Lysander, who turned away and therefore missed the gesture, "for his Aldrish. Add the Dosedra into the trade, though, and I just don't feel it will work. Bedoric won't give up his brother to us so easily. Plus, if fhaoli make the demand for both, it will just twist Arric up more in this crazy conspiracy Bedoric has invented. So you see, this is our best chance to save Nyvas. You have my word on it—we will not give up on Arric either. We just cannot save him today."

She listened to what he said, but the dizziness returned. It didn't seem right—but, she realized, with a growing ache in her stomach, they didn't have many options. Nyvas had run out of time—they had to do something, and they had to do it now. After all, it had been her greatest fear that he would die without anyone even trying to save him. "Okay. So what's the plan?"

Fantion quickly explained what they had in mind: she would be taken back to the keep, and would present the fhaoli's proposal for a swap to Vosira Bedoric. Rynar would serve as a hostage until Nyvas's release.

"You are certain you can get an audience with the Vosira?" Kels asked, a bit skeptical.

"I think so," she nodded. "The Vosira seemed to like me at first, but now—" she flexed her left hand, none the worse for wear. "Well, he did. He's not such a fan now. Even so, I'm pretty sure he'd see me if it had to do with Rynar." She nervously rubbed her palms against her skirt. "But what if he doesn't believe me?"

"Then Nyvas will die," Fantion said matter-of-factly. "Though at least we'll be slitting Rynar's throat to even things out."

"No," she exclaimed, shocked by the suggestion. Although a bit worried, she was all in favor of the plan until that. "You're not going to hurt him?"

"My lady, do you mean the Aldrish?" Plunchek asked from his post at the door, and then he dropped the grain sack again. "You know that man down there is as guilty as they come. He might as well be holding Nyvas prisoner personally. Surely you don't care what happens to him?"

"What if I do?" Her gaze fell to each man in turn, and she realized none of them held any sympathy for her position. She knew they were fhaoli, and had no love for the Vosira himself, but they seemed to be honorable men. Why harm Rynar? He might be the right hand of the Vosira, but he had shown her nothing but kindness, and his ability to heal suggested there was more to him than these men would understand. "Please," she gasped, exasperated, "you have to promise that you'll let him go."

"Let him go?" Lysander, whose temper had been smoldering since she had been brought into the room, now marched from the window back to the table. With a thud he slammed his elbow on the surface, and pointed his finger at her. "You must be joking. After everything he has done? Kate, I thought better of you than that. Nay, that man deserves to die—and he shall, either way, I promise you that. He'll not have the privilege of walking out of this house."

"No!" she shouted, suddenly afraid of these men, people she had considered her friends. These men were indeed outlaws, and would do whatever it took to survive. They were fiercely loyal to one another, and it appeared that the fate of someone outside their circle was trivial. She forgot to keep her voice down, but now she didn't care. "You can't do that!"

"I can't?" Lysander shook his head, and his untied hair scattered over his shoulders. "You must understand, I'll stop at nothing to save Nyvas." He said it again for emphasis. "Nothing." He took a deep breath, sucking in the air through his teeth, his sides trembling. "If I can personally cut the throat of the man who made Nyvas suffer all this time, it will scarcely serve as sufficient payment for his misdeeds." The words were toxic. "Then there's Arric. I've known him nearly his entire life. Don't think I wouldn't sacrifice you—and everyone in here as well—to save him, if that's what it took." He made a fist with each hand. "You know I have half a mind to go downstairs and finish off that blasted Aldrish right here and now."

Her eyes were wide. "You're a healer, Sander. You wouldn't do that!"

"Nay, such is no longer true. Thanks to that bastard down there, I am no healer. Not officially—not anymore." He stood up and wrapped his long arms around his chest, grasping his shoulders, as if trying to restrain himself. "Do you not understand what we're telling you?" He swung an arm free, and pointed to the floor. "He is Aldrish," he said, pronouncing the title with great repulsion. "The Vosira's chief advisor. Knowing Bedoric as I do—and Kate, I know him better than anyone else here—that man downstairs has made every single important decision for Sarducia since he was named to the position. So don't you dare think that man is innocent where Nyvas or Arric are concerned. Believe me, the Aldrish deserves to die, and the gods know I would have already slit his throat if Fantion had not held me back when he was brought in."

"No, I swear." Desperate to change his opinion, she added, "it's not true. Rynar would have saved Nyvas if he could have. He told me he didn't want any of that to happen. It's just that the Vosira—"

"Nay, Kate." Still leaning on the table, Fantion swung his head loosely from his shoulders. "I cannot believe what you're suggesting." He closed his eyes and snorted, and raised himself from the table. "Trust me, if it had suited him, he'd have cleared Nyvas's name a long time ago, and it would never have come to this. The fact is, doing that doesn't suit his purposes at all."

She put her head between her hands. How could she have gotten herself into this mess? She might be able to save Nyvas, but in doing so, she would condemn another man in his place? No matter what her personal feelings were towards Rynar, she could not let them kill him.

"You know what I'm saying is true," Fantion added. "I suspect you tried to convince him to save Nyvas as well."

"Kate, after all you've been through, if you still think that man is honorable," Lysander added, his voice shaking, "then there is only one explanation. He has enchanted you."

She lifted her head. "Oh come on, Sander, I'm not enchanted. I know he's not perfect, but I swear he's not the evil man you think he is."

Lysander raised himself up, and threw his hands over his head. "You can't be that naïve. Don't you see what has happened to you?"

"Nothing has happened to me!"

"Blast it all. For reasons I don't pretend to understand, the Aldrish has you so deeply dependent on him that you cannot see past the lies he feeds you. Somehow in this short time he has manipulated things to the point where he has even convinced Bedoric to lock up men you care about—and yet you defend him! Can you not see it?" Lysander placed his hand on her shoulder. "You're free of Rynar now."

"But that isn't what I want!" She caught herself. Being free was, in fact, exactly what she wanted. "I mean, I just don't want you to kill him—or anyone."

Lysander stood up and crossed his arms in front of him again. In a voice that belied his desperation, he pleaded, "oh Kate, please see him for what he is!"

Fantion put his arm over his friend's shoulder, whispering to him. Then Lysander retreated again to his window while Marcan slid from the bench, making room for Fantion to sit beside her. "Listen to me," he began. "Think back to when we traveled together. I may be speaking out of turn here, but it seemed to me that we began to trust one another. Do you feel that way as well?"

"Of course."

"Then let me ask you this. If it came down to choosing between Arric and Rynar, who would you choose?"

She folded her fingers together in a tight ball and leaned her chin against them. "I can't make a choice like that. I won't choose who lives and who dies."

"You do not have that luxury. If you had to decide, who would it be? Arric or the Aldrish?"

That made her shake her head. "Look, I want to help you, and I will. This is all about saving Arric and Nyvas, and I swear I'll do whatever I can to help them both. Can't we just leave it at that?" Why couldn't he understand that things were not so simple, that it wasn't a matter of black and white, of choosing one person over another? That no one needed to die?

Marcan tapped Fantion on the shoulder. "Let her be. We need Nyvas, not Rynar. If she wants to be with Rynar afterwards, it isn't our concern. If we get the boy back, we can just let the Aldrish go."

Fantion shrugged and stood up. "I don't like it. That bastard would just make our lives difficult later."

"What could he do, Fantion?" Marcan challenged. "Send troops into the forest? Burn our families' homes? Attack our women and children and steal our belongings? Those things are already happening as it is. What else can he do?"

"Aye, perhaps you're right, though I still blame him for all of the fhaoli named under Bedoric, and a whole lot of other things." He rubbed his beard. "What do you say, Sander?"

He glared at the rest of them.

"Sander, please?" she begged him. "I'll do whatever you need me to do, gladly. Just don't hurt him."

"Ah, fine, then," Lysander sighed, and gazed at her with red-rimmed eyes. "I just want Nyvas back." He took a deep breath and centered himself. "Kate, I haven't forgotten what you did for me when I was injured, so I will grant you this favor. I'll agree to spare the Al-drish—but only if you succeed. If anything happens to Nyvas, then—" he stopped with that.

"Just convince Bedoric to make the exchange," Fantion said in his place.

"I can do it," she said, though it was false confidence. If Vosira Bedoric suspected she was a part of the plan, everyone would die. These men, however, were counting on her, and although Nyvas and Rynar didn't know it, both of them would have to count on her as well. Oh god, how could she pull this off, knowing two men's lives were hanging in the balance? Then she reminded herself that at least there was a plan, as preposterous as it sounded. Finally there was something she could do. So she would try, and do the very best she could. It was more than she could have hoped for just a day ago, and she felt like she owed them all her best effort, even at some risk to herself.

They had spent too long talking about Rynar, though. Turning to more practical matters, she looked down at her dress. "Well, if you want people to think I'm telling the truth, then I'll have to look the part. You're going to have to rough me up."

"Rough you up, my lady?" Kels asked, horrified. "We do not wish you to be harmed."

"Do you really think it looks like five men just attacked me?" She tugged hard at the neckline of her dress until it stretched out of shape, and pulled at the waistline until some of the seams popped. With her fingers, she made her hair a more disheveled mess than it must have already been. "Now, come on, someone needs to hit me."

"Nay, Kate," Lysander said, more like his usual self. "None of us will do that."

"Come on, you have to. Just once." She bravely held out her chin. "You, Fantion, I trust you. Just imagine I was..." she tried to think of a suitable opponent. "Imagine I'm Vosira Bedoric."

"Ah, no, if I hit you that hard I'd likely kill you," he said, with a hint of a grin. Still, she angled her chin in his direction. "You really mean it, don't you?" He sounded dubious.

"Of course I do. I'm not looking forward to it, of course, but it needs to be done, so just get on with it. If I'm supposed to convince the Vosira, you have to help me now." She turned to look Lysander in the eye. "You can consider it my way of pledging to bring Nyvas back."

"I cannot do it." Fantion backed away. "I won't hit you."

"Come on, we're wasting time. Sander? I can hear the anger in your voice. You've been ready to punch me since I was carried in. You might as well get it over with."

As Lysander held out his hands in protest and shook his head vehemently, Fantion approached her again. "Nay, Kate, I would not ask him to do such a thing. He is far too troubled already, and doesn't need the guilt of this as well. If anyone were to do this, it would have to be me."

"Well, then?" She again lifted her chin. "It needs to be pretty hard, like you mean it."

"You'll forgive me?"

She rolled her eyes. "If you don't do it right now, I'll kick you in the balls."

That was enough for Fantion, and he swung his hand hard, palm open, against her cheek. He didn't hold back either, from what she could tell. She cried out as she fell to the floor, and clasped her own palm against the burn. For a moment she sat there silently, breathing heavily, until the initial pain subsided. "I think you may have left a mark," she said, with a sheepish grin, even as her eyes watered. Her bottom lip stung, and as she tested it with her tongue, she tasted blood. "Remind me never to ask you to hit me again."

"You'd better not ask, because it won't happen a second time," he assured her, a frown on his face.

The healer within Lysander surfaced, and he knelt beside her. "May I see it?" he asked, and removed her hand. "Oh, Kate, it will bruise, and there's a cut under your eye..."

As he mentioned it, she realized it burned fiercely. "Do you think I'll have a black eye?" she asked, a bit more cheerfully than she should have felt. "That'd be great!"

"Are you sure?" Lysander said, his concern for her discomfort obvious in his voice. In seconds he had totally transformed. "I can mend the worst of this, make it a little less painful, if you'd like."

She pulled away from his touch. "No, save it for Nyvas." Her words came out more harshly than she intended, and as he yanked back his hand, she softened her next words. "I just meant that he'll likely need every bit of healing you can offer him."

He put his long healer's hands on top of his thighs, as he continued to kneel. "I hope he isn't as bad as that," he said in a whisper.

"Enough chat," Plunchek announced from the doorway. "The exchange will take some time to arrange. The girl needs to head back to the keep soon."

Fantion helped her stand, and wincing, admired his handiwork. "Ah, Kate, you're stronger than I thought, though I fear you'll never forgive me."

"Of course I will. Just one more thing. I need everyone's word that Rynar will be safe while I'm gone."

"You mean, we can't even remove a few teeth, as souvenirs?" Plunchek seemed sincerely disappointed.

"Look, if you want my help, you have to promise this. I'm putting my life on the line here, you know. I need to know he will be okay when I return."

Begrudgingly, Fantion nodded. In a light tone, he said to the others, "you heard her, men. No harming the merchandise." Then he turned back to her, adding, "understand, we really can't release the Aldrish if things go badly. Nyvas has to be here by sundown, or Rynar will have to die. You understand why, don't you?"

She nodded. "He'll be here."

CHAPTER 37

With Plunchek at her heels, she stumbled down the steps, barely able to keep her balance. She attributed her wobbly steps to nerves. How was she ever going to pull this off? And, as she looked over the banister to Rynar, who turned in her direction as he heard her descent, how could she ever face him again? Keep focused, Kate told herself. This wasn't about his feelings. It was about saving Nyvas's life. If everything worked out, she would be able to save Rynar's life as well. If she failed... well, she couldn't allow that possibility to gain traction in her mind. Success was the only option. Still, tears came easily as she considered the dilemma.

Back in character as her kidnapper, Plunchek led her roughly by the arm to the table where Rynar sat. "Admirable lady you have here," he said as he shoved her to the bench beside the Aldrish. "Stopped crying and fighting us right away, when she realized there wasn't much she could do about the situation. Made it a lot better for everyone," he added, and grinned.

She hung her head down, ashamed, but not for the reasons Rynar would have thought. His eyes burned her flesh, though, and she finally looked up at him, only to see he was in agony. So he really did care about her, then? It wasn't just a game, or political strategy that caused him to pay attention to her?

That just made everything more difficult.

"Havar, then?" Plunchek asked her as he held out a flask. "I suppose you've earned that much."

She flinched, trying to play the role set out for her convincingly enough that Rynar would believe it, and took the flask and drank. Then she held it in Rynar's direction. "Can he have some as well?"

Plunchek shook his head. "Ah, no my lady. That would mean removing the gag."

"He won't shout out, I promise." She was doing her best to sound like she was the victim of a terrible assault, but it was even harder than she expected. "Right, Rynar?" she asked, sounding desperate.

He scrunched up his face in anger, but nodded.

Plunchek stood looking at the Aldrish with his hands on his hips. "I don't know. He doesn't look like the kind of person I'd be likely to trust."

"Please?" she begged. "Just a sip?"

The fhaoli shrugged. "Might as well. If he hollers out, I'll just cut off his fingers. All the same to me." With that, he untied the rag around the Aldrish's mouth.

"The curse of Yoren on you," Rynar spat out as soon as he could speak. Then he tipped his head to her, and softly, he said, "I am so sorry that this had to happen. I had no idea..." He bit his lip, and drew in a breath. "They hurt you?" he asked her, unable to mistake the swelling on her cheek, but obviously meaning more. He struggled against the ropes, as if trying to release his hands to reach out to her.

She shrugged, unwilling to respond, and turned her gaze to the tabletop. It was too difficult to lie to him. Her misery, genuine as it was, would have to suffice. He would put the pieces together on his own, even if the final picture wasn't the right one.

He read her noncommittal response as an affirmative, as she expected. "You bastards!" he shouted, forgetting his promise of a moment ago. "Release us immediately, or I'll make sure Vosira Bedoric roasts every last one of you! Do you have any idea who I am?"

Plunchek sat down across from at the table. "Aye, we know who you are, Aldrish." He stabbed the table with his knife, as if to reiterate his earlier threat. "But release you?" he added with a smile. "Ah, no, not as of yet. You see, your lady friend here still has some work to do for us."

Rynar looked from him to Kate, and back. "Haven't you done enough to her already?"

***

Her hands were tied again, and Plunchek lifted her up to the saddle of the same horse Nyvas had ridden when she and the others had traveled from Bhoren. Oddly enough, the fog had cleared, and now the day was bright and warm, without a cloud in the sky.

"Remember," he advised her as he climbed into the saddle behind her. "You tell them that you are to bring Nyvas back yourself. Don't agree if you have to stay behind, as that will be a sign of bad faith."

"What if they send Senvosra with me?"

"Oh, we fully expect them to do so, but don't worry, Fantion already has that figured out. Nay, don't worry about us. We'll be in no danger."

"And Nyvas? How are you going to get him out of the city?"

He chuckled. "Don't worry about him either. I expect he'll be able to handle himself."

"You know he's injured—"

"Ah, but it's Nyvas. You'll not meet a man more capable of disappearing when he doesn't want to be seen."

When they reached the gates of the keep, Plunchek squeezed her shoulder. "You'll remember your way back?" he asked.

She nodded. "I noted landmarks, like you told me. I'll find it."

"Good." Then he raised his voice to the guards on the wall. "Hey you! I think you've let a bird escape. I've brought her back for ya, free of charge!" Then he whispered, "this will hurt..."

"Just do it." She braced herself as best as she could as her feet flew over her head and she tumbled to the ground, hitting the grassy field with a thud. The fall knocked the wind out of her, and she was gasping for breath even as Plunchek threw Rynar's insignia and ring at her. When she looked up, he tugged on the horse's reigns and sped off down the main road back into the city.

The guards at the gate rushed down to her, and quickly cut the rope. She gathered up Rynar's belongings and, with as much grace as she could muster, she followed the guards through the gate.

***

It was mid-day, and the Bhagali were gathered in the Council chamber, in the midst of a heated argument, when the guard ushered her inside, unannounced.

"What is the meaning of this interruption?" Vosira Bedoric began to protest, until he saw who it was. Then he bellowed at her, his words like a thunderbolt. "You? What are you doing here?" He looked behind her. "And where is the blasted Aldrish? We've been waiting for ages for him." He narrowed his eyes. "You do know what today is?"

She was standing at the far side of the table, mere feet from where the guard had held Nyvas. Words caught in her throat. Trying to summon her courage, her eyes fell to Tashin, and then quickly she looked elsewhere, and knowing everyone stared at her, she found herself focusing on the flame of the nearest candle.

"Well?" Bedoric stood up and walked around the table, as if to personally throttle her with his own hands. "Where is Aldrish Rynar?" he shouted at her.

She didn't have to pretend to be frightened now, with the Vosira screaming at her. "He received a message to go into the city. It was—I think it had something to do with the fhaoli. We were at the meeting place when—when we were attacked." She hung her head down, trying to look as remorseful as possible. "It all happened so fast—in the fog, we never saw them coming." Even though it was an act, she was still overcome by the situation.

Her words set off a buzz of discussion around the room. "Attacked?" Bedoric repeated, as if trying to decipher what it meant. "Who did it? And why are you alone now?"

"Bandits, my lord Vosira," she spit out the words as fast as she could. "It was a trap. Even with the Senvosra, they outnumbered us..." she swallowed, and did her best to shudder. "They tied us up, and brought us to an old house." Feeling lightheaded, she closed her eyes. "And they forced themselves on me," she added in a whisper.

He leaned against the table, and squinted at her as he shook his head. Apparently now he saw her black eye and split lip, though his concern wasn't for her. "Bandits, you say? Fhaoli?" He frowned, and made a fist. "Your friends, I bet." Scowling, he asked, "what about my Aldrish? What happened to him?"

"They tied him up, and he's still alive—at least for now." For effect, she tossed Rynar's medallion and ring on the table. "They gave these to me and told me to show them to you, so you'd know I was telling the truth." She didn't have to fake tears, as they suddenly flooded her face. "They told me that they're going to kill him at sundown. Tonight."

Bedoric turned and grabbed the ring, and for a moment stared at it, his mouth hanging open. "He would die before he would allow someone to take this from him." He glowered at her, and his voice was grating. He raised the ring over his head, and snatched up the chain and medallion in the other, displaying them to the other men in the room. "This proves nothing, Bhara. How do I know he's not already dead?"

A genuine sob escaped her lips. "Because they need Rynar alive, for a trade. Rynar for Ny—" she stopped, correcting herself, "I mean, St-st-stavan... the f-f-fhaoli boy." Once the words were out, she held her hand over her mouth.

"What?" Bhagal Abranir bolted from his chair. "That fhaoli murderer is as good as dead now. This is intolerable!" He turned to the Vosira. "Surely you do not mean to comply with this blackmail!"

The Vosira slammed both glysar objects on the table. "Bhara, you and my brother both admitted to knowing this fhaoli. Already you have both proven untrustworthy. Why should I believe you now? How do I know it's not just a trick?" Then he caught the ring with his fingertip, dragging it closer to him, and then collapsed into an empty chair. "Oh, how I have been cursed today" She wondered what was running through his head as he sat there, staring at the jewelry taken by force. The medallion shone in the fire of the torches, and its ornate beauty was hard to ignore, but the ring, sitting on the table, even choked her up. The Vosira was right—it must have been hell to get Rynar to part with it. It seemed ordinary enough to her, but he never removed it.

The air was full of tension, and no one spoke. Finally Vosira Bedoric stood up and returned to his seat at the head of the table. He spoke again, though to no one in particular. "Why did it have to be my Aldrish?" He sat silently for a moment, rubbing his palms in front of his face, and no one else interrupted his thoughts. He glanced once to the empty chair to his right, where Rynar would have sat, and she realized it probably pained him to not have the Aldrish's counsel at a moment like this. If the situation had not been so grave, the irony of it would have made her laugh. As it was, she felt sick to her stomach.

Castellan Solerav looked at her, his facial muscles tensing up as if he was clenching his teeth. "You're involved in this, girl," he said as he pointed at her, discarding the 'Bhara' title. "I see it all too clearly. You somehow convinced the Aldrish to leave the keep so that your friends could capture him. He would never have done so today, of all days, unless you had somehow seduced him into it."

She shook her head rapidly. "You're wrong—there was a message. Erdal, the man who works for Rynar, will confirm it."

Solerav turned to the others. "Does anyone believe the girl's lies?" Pointing to Tashin, he asked, "you?" Waving his arms, he added, "this story is preposterous. Vosira, surely you can see this is just a trick?"

Abranir nodded. "Aye, it's a trick. They're all in it together."

A couple of the others whispered to each other. Tashin, though, was shaking his head. "Look at the girl. She's injured, and from the look of it, she's about to collapse. Clearly something has happened to her. Vosira, what do you wish to do?"

Bedoric had been watching the others with a scowl on his face. Then he lifted the medallion and then threw it back down on the table, with a dejected shake of his head. "Ah, Rynar, what would you have me do?" He stared at it as he chewed on his lip, and then suddenly slammed his fist on the table. "Fhaoli would never allow my Aldrish to live, that is certain," he decided, the realization obviously painful. "It matters not who they are. He is dead already." He pointed to her. "You dare come here and lie to me, bringing me this story. It's merely a trick to save your friend." He seemed on the verge of a breakdown, but he managed to keep the majority of his emotions in check. His lips trembled as he again looked at her and announced, "There's nothing else to be said," he concluded, his face red with anger, "and I'll have nothing more to do with you." He nodded to the guards at the door. "Throw her in with the boy. Let them have a while to share the fruits of their crimes and then burn them both at moonrise."

"No!" She cried out in desperation. He had to believe her, or they were all doomed. "Vosira, Rynar's still alive, I swear. Oh god, please, you have to listen to me. Bhagal Tashin?" she appealed to the only man in the room who had shown inclination to believe her. "They haven't killed him. It's supposed to be a trade, don't you understand? He dies only if I don't bring Nyvas back. They promised me that he would be spared—I wouldn't have agreed to this otherwise!" The guards had already begun to drag her from the room. "Vosira, you have to listen to me!" She sought anyone's eyes who would look at her. "It's the truth! You've got to save him!"

Yet it was pointless. Without another word from anyone in the room, the guards hauled her out of the chamber, backwards, her heels dragging the floor. "Please, someone, listen to me," she continued to cry out as they carried her down the hallway. "It's not too late. You can still save him...."

No one listened. Ignoring her shouts, the guards continued on their journey, deaf to her pleas. After another soldier unlocked a door in one of the towers, the two men plunged down the dark, narrow spiral stairs, hauling her between them, into what appeared to be the deepest part of the keep. Several times her head hit the wall, and her elbow connected painfully with an iron ring used to hold a rope. At the bottom of the steps, a single torch on the wall cast dismal shadows. Without ceremony, as one held her roughly, the other unlocked a second door. Then, working together, the two men literally threw her into the cell, and slammed the door behind her.

CHAPTER 38

"No!" She shouted as she scrambled back to her feet. "Listen to me! You've got to believe me!" She felt for a latch or handle in the darkness, but there was none. "Please, it's the truth," she pleaded to anyone on the outside, as she slid down against the heavy wooden door. "I swear, he's still alive, do you hear me?"

If the Senvosra heard her, they did not respond.

There was no light in this dungeon cell, but she smelled the rank, dead air, as if this part of the keep hadn't had fresh air in a century. There was an occasional scratching sound, and she jumped as something ran across her leg—something that moved too fast for her to identify, but that was larger than an insect. She frantically shook her legs to get it off of her, panicking because she couldn't see what it was, or where it had gone.

"Is that you, Kate?" a weak voice called out from across the cell.

"Nyvas?"

"Aye," he croaked. "Over here."

Still breathing hard, she crawled across the dirt floor until she felt a hand brush across her shoulder.

"So you came to visit me, did you?" he asked, his voice cracking from the effort of talking.

"Nyvas? Is it really you?" It was a hopeful question, full of anxiety and relief at the same time.

He must have sensed the contradictory emotions in her voice because he tried to laugh, but it turned into a cough. "Aye, who else would it be?" As she sat cross-legged beside him, he stroked her forehead. "Are you hurt?"

"No... yes... I mean—" she said in a terrified voice. "Oh god, Nyvas, I'm so sorry."

He smoothed her hair. "Hush. What's happened?"

"I tried. I really did. I really thought it would work, but they didn't believe me, no matter what I said. Now it's hopeless." She squeezed her eyes shut and contorted her face as she tried to stifle a sob, but the intensity of her emotions made it impossible not to cry, and she covered her face.

"Shh. Just tell me what's happened." He coughed again—a deep, hacking cough—and once he finished, he moaned a bit, as if the effort had pained him, but he didn't call attention to it otherwise. "How is it that you're here with me?"

"I can't believe any of this is happening." She hung her head down. "It wasn't supposed to end like this."

"What, Kate?" He felt down her arm for her hand, and grasped it tightly. "Tell me."

She took a couple of deep breaths, and in short, halting phrases she tried to explain the past few hours, her words tinged with the new-found despair that came from hearing her own voice describe what had happened. During her tale, she had to pause several times, waiting through his coughing fits.

"Sander is well, then?" he asked when the coughing subsided.

"Yeah," she said, finding strength in his presence. Her panic would accomplish nothing. "He's fine, but he's worried sick about you. He's so upset that for a moment I thought he'd rip me apart with his bare hands." She omitted the reasons for Lysander's anger, figuring it wouldn't matter anymore.

"Sander?" he said with a half-cough, half-laugh. "I don't believe it. That's not like him at all."

"Yeah, well, I don't blame him. He's really scared that—" she hesitated, and then continued more tentatively, "something will happen to you." She pictured Lysander's face in her mind. "He cares deeply for you, you know."

He didn't respond right away, but sighed, his exhaled breath rattling in his chest.

When more time had passed than she thought reasonable, she asked, "Nyvas? Are you okay?"

"Aye," he said softly. "I guess I hadn't counted on this hurting him as much as it has."

This would break her heart. "I'm so sorry, Nyvas. It was supposed to just be a simple trade. You for the Aldrish. Knowing how much the Vosira depends on him, it really should have worked."

He laughed once, very lightly. "Those crazy fools." After a pause for a thick, rattling breath, he added, "they should have known Bedoric's pride would never allow him to agree to a trade."

"That's exactly what happened. He refused to even consider it." She couldn't avoid replaying the scene in her head, wondering what she could have done differently. "If only I had just—"

"Shh." He squeezed her hand. "You did your best. It was a good plan." His speech, short as it was, sparked a round of hacking coughs. "I'm proud to have a friend like you. I wish you weren't here now— though to be honest, it's been terribly lonely in here." Again, a cough. To Kate's ear it sounded as if he was gravely ill but didn't want to admit it. His voice was hoarse and weak, and his breathing was shallow, but he kept talking. "I suppose you know what they plan to do with us?"

"Oh no... I can't—"

He put his arm around her, in a gesture that likely brought him as much comfort as it brought her. "Tell me. I know it's not good news, but I'd prefer not to be surprised when it happens."

"They plan to... to..." she swallowed, and gasped for air. She felt her heart pounding. So she spit it out all at once. "Oh god, Nyvas, they're going to b-b-burn us tonight." When she said it aloud, it sounded surreal, and even more terrifying. The horrifying images from history books, of people tied to a pyre, with smoke and flames surrounding them, flittered through her mind. Never had she expected that one day, it would happen to her. Never had she ever known the fear she tasted now.

Oddly, Nyvas seemed more amused than frightened. "Fire, eh? I didn't think he meant it, but it seems he's really going to go through with it after all." He coughed again, and sputtered, as if his mouth had filled with liquid. Then he continued. "It's an old, but fitting, punishment for traitors," he commented sarcastically. "Not that either of us could ever be guilty of such a thing."

"How can you be so calm?" she asked, tears falling freely. This was not supposed to happen. They were all going to die tonight, Nyvas, Rynar and herself—while Arric was locked in a tower and unable to do anything about it. She had hoped to be their savior, but she had failed them all, and herself, miserably. While she wanted to be brave, she couldn't stop crying, knowing it wasn't fair, that none of them were guilty of anything. Was this why she had been dragged from her home, to Sarducia? Just so she and her new friends could be killed in some of the worse ways imaginable? It just wasn't right.

"Hush now. You must have faith in the Goddess. Surely you know by now that Kerthal will protect you. You shall not die tonight."

"Oh, Nyvas." She was touched by his strong belief in higher powers, and wanted to be able to share it. "I wish you were right, but I think we're beyond faith now."

"You still do not believe?"

"What do you mean?"

He coughed again, and then tried to clear his throat before continuing. "From the moment I met you, I sensed that you had a connection with the Goddess, though I knew not what it was. But it meant that I could trust you." A cough, and then, in choked words, he added, "I'm glad I was able to get the others to trust you too."

"I don't really think..." she began to protest, and realized there was no point in arguing with him. Let him believe what he would, if it would give him comfort.

Meanwhile, he rested his head on her shoulder. With one hand she reached for his cheek, intending to stroke it. As she did so, she could feel the wiry hairs on his chin, and a substance on his jaw that felt like dried paint. His blood, she realized. "Oh, I'm sorry." She pulled her hand away. "I didn't mean to—"

"Don't worry, it doesn't hurt much now." Mimicking her, he reached up and traced out her chin, and ran a finger across her forehead, and followed the line of her eyebrows. Then he touched one eyelid, and then the other, and stopped. "It's swollen here," he said, startled, as he felt along the base of the orbit of her left eye. "What happened?" he sputtered, trying hard not to cough again. "Did the Senvosra do this?"

"No, it wasn't them. Actually, you wouldn't believe what really happened." In a weird way, she almost wanted to laugh.

"Would I not?"

"I doubt it." She chuckled lightly in spite of her situation, and then, not wanting to keep him in suspense, she blurted out, "Fantion hit me."

"What?" he flinched, as much out of concern as surprise.

"No, it's okay. I made him do it. When they proposed that I come here to offer the trade, I wanted the Vosira to believe I had really been abducted." She inhaled, trying not to cry again, but failing in the effort. "Obviously it didn't work."

He sighed. "Oh, Kate, you did this all for me, even though you barely know me. First you saved Arric, and then Sander, and now me." Again he coughed, and this time the hacking came from deeper down in his chest, and the spasm lasted for quite a while. Then, finally, it passed, and he rocked back and forth for a while, calming himself, and catching his breath. "You know, you were very brave coming here for me," he said, wheezing with each breath, "though you should've tried to free Arric instead. He's a lot more important than fhaoli, especially one as sick as I am." Once the words were out of his mouth, as if to prove himself right, again he coughed. She held him, as if she could keep him from falling apart. He responded by wrapping his arms around her, and he put his head on her shoulder, facing away.

Despite her tears, at his statement she smiled. "I don't know about that," she said, trying to wipe perspiration from his face with her sleeve. "I think you're about equal."

He made a small sound that might have been a bit of a laugh, but couldn't say anything more, because then he began to cough once more, the effort of it hard enough that she feared he'd kill himself from the physical force of it.

***

Once his coughing had finally subsided, Nyvas must have exhaust-ed himself, for he drifted into a light slumber. She cradled his head in her lap, offering a bit of warmth and comfort to the dying man as he lay in the moldy cell. He did his best to sound strong and sure of himself, but she guessed that between the unhealthy conditions of the cell and his injuries, he had developed a serious infection. It was a wonder he had lived this long.

They sat this way for what felt like hours. She clung to him, offer-ing her warmth and strength and drawing the same from him, as if they could transfuse the other with the power to survive. It was unreal to consider that she had been condemned to die, and that this was her last evening alive. Despite his assurances, it was impossible not to feel like her guts had been turned inside out. As she stroked his hair, she tried to come to terms with her life and make some sort of peace with herself.

He was still asleep when unexpected light blinded her. As her eyes adjusted, she realized that there were four men standing at the door, all with torches in their hands. So this was it.

Time was up.

"Get up, the both of you. Don't make us come in after you."

Nyvas raised his head slowly, and buried it again, unprepared for so much light after days of total darkness. As she worked to rouse him, she finally could see some of the visible signs of injury. Blood matted his hair and covered his shirt and face, and as he sat up, he moved with great difficulty. Broken ribs, healing badly, she thought to herself with significant anger. Even though he had been sentenced to die, he should not have been left to suffer like this.

He struggled to stand on his own, and she quickly bent down to as-sist him. From his breathing it was obvious that his pain was considera-ble, but he held his head up and refused to exhibit any discomfort to the soldiers outside.

As they shuffled slowly out of the cell, she discovered that the men outside the door were not Senvosra, as she had expected. "Bhagal Tash-in? Why are *you* here?" It seemed coming down to the depths of hell, as this dungeon seemed to replicate, would be beneath a man of such importance. With him were three other men she recognized from the Council: Bhagali Abranir and Koldren, and Castellan Solerav. Some of her favorite people, she thought snidely. So they would have an escort such as this as they went to their deaths?

Tashin was not inclined to offer her an explanation. Instead, he gruffly barked as he led them to a set of stairs, "hush, girl, and come with us."

Two of the men, Tashin and Abranir, climbed ahead of the condemned pair, and the stronger two, Koldren and Solerav, behind. She urged Nyvas to go first, so she could assist him. Although she knew he was trying desperately to hide his pain from the men, more than once he groaned as he climbed the stairs, and she suspected every single step that he took was sending a rib deeper into an internal organ. Once, he was doubled over from his coughing and they had to stop. Then when they began again to climb the steps, he fell against her arms, and both of them would have toppled backwards if not for Solerav's arm that caught her and held them both upright.

In an automatic reflex, she was about to thank the castellan for his help, but the words caught in her throat. This was the man who was to blame for all of this, for it was Solerav that had named Nyvas as the murderer of Vosira Parmon, and the man who had convinced the Vosira not to believe her earlier today. He certainly deserved no thanks for ushering them to their deaths.

"Are you all right?" she whispered to Nyvas. All of a sudden she was supporting his entire weight. In fact, as she spoke, she saw that his eyes had closed, and she feared he had fainted—or worse. Even this simple exertion might be more than he could manage now. "Nyvas?" she repeated, and as he heard his name, his head bounced up from her chest.

"Hunh... oh aye," he murmured. "Keep pushing me," he pleaded weakly. "Don't let me fall in front of them."

"You got it." As they continued to climb, the same thing happened a second time, but by now she was half-carrying him already, so she was able to hide it from the others. It was fortunate for them both that he wasn't particularly heavy. If he had been Fantion's size, they would all have tumbled down the steps like dominoes.

Finally they made it to the top of the stairs, exiting into the armory. On one wall hung a few dozen bows, with quivers of arrows arranged in rows of pegs beside them. On the opposite wall were several knives and swords. In a moment of fantasy, she imagined reaching for a weapon and using it to escape, and she knew that Nyvas would have done so if he had even half of his strength left.

Remarkably, they didn't leave this room with all its temptations as quickly as she would have expected. Instead, as she stood with Nyvas's arm over her shoulders and her own arm supporting him from the waist, Tashin turned to face them, a scowl on his face.

"You are aware that you and the boy are supposed to die tonight, on the pyre in the city square?" he said to her.

She nodded, and with defiance in her voice, replied, "I believe that was made clear by Vosira Bedoric." There was no point in pretending she wasn't angry, or disguising her hatred for all of them.

"I believe you are also aware how much our Vosira depended on his Aldrish."

His words held out a tantalizing strand of hope. "You say that like it's history. You know, Rynar might still be alive, if the sun hasn't set, that is." The room had no windows, so it was impossible to tell whether it was already too late.

"My lady, do not anger me," he warned her, a finger wagging in her face. "As I was saying. I don't understand it myself, but Vosira Bedoric seems incapable of leading Sarducia without that damned Aldrish at his side. Already things are not going well, and it has just been the one day." He bent down slightly so he could stare her in the eyes. "We were able to convince him that he had acted in haste, turning down the trade you offered—this worthless half-dead boy for his Aldrish. We told him that if there was even a slim chance that Aldrish Rynar still lived, he should take it." He glared at her with naked loathing. "If you have lied, Bhara, and the Aldrish is already dead, you have my personal guarantee that you shall return to suffer the most painful tortures you could ever imagine. Unlike your friend here, you shall be easy to catch, and easier to break."

His threat bounced off her as if it had never been made. A possibility of torture in the future, versus the certainty of being burned alive immediately? She'd take her chances. "I understand."

Tashin waved to men at the doorway. "Very well. Be sure you do not fail, Bhara, for I do not break my promises."

The Bhagali led the pair out to the courtyard, where a horse awaited them, along with six well-armed Senvosra, already mounted. To Kate's relief, it was only late afternoon, but even so, they had little time. Sunset, Fantion had told her. And sunset was not that far off.

"Escort them to their meeting point," Tashin ordered the guards. "I assume that the lady knows the way?" He glanced at her, and she nodded again, barely able to hide her elation at the sudden reprieve.

Then, staring at the horses, she shook her head. "No, this won't work. Nyvas is in no condition to ride."

Solerav grabbed her by the waist and practically threw her into the saddle. "It would be a shame, then, if he were to die on the way to freedom, eh?" He hoisted Nyvas up and dumped him across the saddle in front of her. "I'd suggest you hold on to him."

Nyvas did not complain at his rough treatment. Instead, as his chest slapped the saddle, he moaned once, and then passed out, falling against her and nearly dragging them both off the horse again.

Inexperienced at riding, other than the days spent in the saddle with Arric, she could not fathom how to make the horse move, much less how to do so while holding on to Nyvas at the same time. Finally, she told the nearest of the Senvosra that he would have to lead her horse.

She called out directions to the soldiers, and thanks to Plunchek's landmarks, reached the house without difficulty. However, as planned, she intentionally led the soldiers past it, to ensure their arrival would be noticed, and the men warned of their approach. Then she slid from the saddle, and helped Nyvas, who had been drifting in and out of consciousness, to the ground. It wasn't a graceful descent for him, and he crumpled as he fell to the road, but it was the best she could do. The Senvosra made no effort to assist her.

"They said if they saw soldiers they'd cut the Aldrish's throat," she told the men. "So I'll bring him out."

"Aye, and make it quick, or we'll come in and drag everyone out. Your choice."

She would have flipped them off if it would have meant anything to them. Instead, she focused on her friend. "It will be better soon," she cajoled Nyvas.

He nodded, and again began to cough.

"Can you walk? I'll go slow. If not, I'll have to get the Senvosra to help me."

"Not them. I'll make it," he croaked, his words a terrible lie that he was determined to prove true anyway.

Slowly, they limped together to the door, Kate bearing most of his weight. Fortunately the door was ajar, and she kicked it open.

CHAPTER 39

As Fantion had promised, Rynar was still alive. He was hunched over the table, in the same place she had seen him last, and for the moment he appeared to be alone. Not that he was an escape risk, bound hand foot as he was. Still, she breathed a sigh of relief when she saw him. When he heard her enter, he lifted his head slowly, squinting, and then frowned. From the patterns embossed in his cheek, it appeared that he had tried to sleep by resting his head against the ropes on his wrists, lacking anything better to do to pass the time.

"So Bedoric actually fell for it, did he?" he spat, seeing the fhaoli stumble beside her. "Kate, you could have led the Senvosra back here without that boy. After everything they did—why would you help them now?"

Clinging to Nyvas, lest he collapse on the ground, she half-dragged him to a bench, and as she helped him lay down, she snapped at Rynar. "If you want to know the truth, they never did a thing to me, except when I asked them to do so to fool the Vosira." Overwhelmed by the stress of the day, she wasn't in the mood to put up with anything more. "Right now I think maybe you were better off with the gag on."

Nyvas begged her to pull him to a sitting position, but still slumped against her. Remarkably now he began to laugh lightly despite his pain. "Aldrish," he announced, in a very weak voice, "you don't know how close we all came to dying tonight. If not for her bravery, Kate and I would be fueling a bonfire now, and then you would have had the exquisite experience of having your innards carved out by Fantion himself." After this speech, rather long for him in his frail condition, he again succumbed to his coughing, and she rubbed his back.

"Kate!" Rynar shouted, as if he wanted to pretend he hadn't heard a word the boy said, despite clearly being affected by the idea of being disemboweled. "Aren't you going to cut my ropes, so we can get out of here?"

Disregarding him momentarily, she helped Nyvas lay back on the bench. Then she stood up to face the Aldrish. "No." As he stared her in disbelief, she added, "Don't you realize that I blame you for everything that's happened to him?" she asked, pointing to Nyvas, who again had drifted into unconsciousness.

"Kate, don't be ridiculous. As I told you a dozen times, that was the Vosira's doing, not mine. Now come here, and cut me free!"

She didn't move. "You know as well as I do that you could have convinced the Vosira to spare him, and helped clear Arric's name as well. Instead, it was your idea to keep them both locked up."

"That's all nonsense."

"Is it?" She walked to within a handspan of his shoulder and straddled the bench beside him. "Do you swear it to your gods, then? Do you swear that the Vosira came up with everything involving Nyvas and Arric by himself?"

"Ah, Kate, I shall not swear anything here." He nodded once to Nyvas. "It matters little anyway. He will be dead before morning."

"No, he won't." Her words were firm.

"He will. His chest is filling with blood. You can hear it in his breathing."

"No." She grabbed his chin in her hand. "I am tired of your lies. Look at me and swear that you will work to heal him, here and now, or I will let my friends rip you apart."

He began to sweat. "My dear, I have never lied to you. Not about this, or anything else."

"Then you will not lie to me now. Swear it, Rynar. I trusted you, and I made sure no one hurt you today, which wasn't easy to do. You should know—these men would have killed you immediately if it hadn't been for me. So don't make me regret what I've done."

With remarkable confidence, he replied, "They would not have killed me, my dear. I am Aldrish. They do not dare harm me."

"Want to place a bet on that, Aldrish?" Fantion stood in the doorway. "It is sunset. If that boy dies, according to the promise I made to her earlier today, your life is forfeit to me. And I would take great pleasure in bringing about your demise."

"Fantion, the Senvosra—" she whispered.

"They have been suitably distracted." Just then he noticed his friend sputtering and gasping for air, and he ran to the table. "Ah, sweet Kerthal. Nyvas is dying, and Sander isn't back yet." He looked to the door. "We thought we'd have more time."

"It's okay. He's going to heal him." She nodded towards Rynar.

"The Aldrish? Kate, don't be daft. He can't heal anyone."

She pointed at Fantion's belt. "Give me your knife."

He raised an eyebrow, but did as she asked. "Good plan, Kate. Cut his throat, though not too deeply just yet—I wish to see him die slowly."

"No," she replied, annoyed at his eagerness. "It's for the ropes." She knelt down and cut the rope around Rynar's legs. "Okay. Now swear you'll do this for me, Rynar. I really don't want them to kill you, but I'll stand back and watch if you don't agree to heal Nyvas right now."

Rynar swallowed hard once, and then nodded. "Aye, very well. I'll do what I can to help him."

"Swear it."

He closed his eyes, and licked his lips. "Fine. I swear, under the watchful eye of the Hidden God, that I will try to heal the fhaoli Nyvas." He looked at her with an odd combination of anger and admiration. "Will that do?"

She was surprised that he chose to make such an affirmation, knowing that he didn't personally believe in the Prophet's preachings, and was about to challenge it when Fantion answered in her place. "Bah, that Hidden God nonsense again." He circled around and bent down to stare Rynar in the eye. "Swear to Kerthal as well."

Rynar scowled.

"Just do it."

"Fine." He paused, and closed his eyes. "I swear in the name of the blessed goddess Kerthal that I shall do everything in my power to heal the fhaoli Nyvas." He glared up at Fantion. "Happy now?"

"Aye, that's enough for me."

At that cue, she sliced the remaining ropes. After a very brief moment spent rubbing the feeling back into his hands, and wriggling his blood-deprived toes, Rynar stumbled on still-numb feet over to Nyvas. As she and Fantion watched, he lifted the dying young man into his arms, and gently placed him on the floor. Then he took a series of deep breaths, and kneeling beside the fhaoli man, began to feel for injuries. Fantion knelt at Nyvas's feet, his mouth wide open in disbelief at the care the Aldrish was providing to his friend.

Kate, meanwhile, sat cross-legged opposite Rynar, and took one of Nyvas's hands in her own. "What can I do to help?"

Rynar's eyes fluttered open for a moment. Rather than dismiss her offer, he flashed her a grin, and then instructed her, "imagine him alive, and whole. Don't wish it; fix it as a real, definite thing in your mind. As strong as you can imagine him being, make him so, putting aside your knowledge of how he is now. And don't let go of his hand."

She nodded. Even though it wouldn't actually do anything tangible, she was willing to at least offer her efforts as moral support.

As Rynar touched Nyvas's wounds, and his hands lingered on his face, on the broken nose, and then traveled to the belly, he frowned. She saw the Aldrish's face just before she closed her eyes, and wondered if Nyvas was actually too battered to be saved. She had seen him take a couple good punches in the Vosira's chamber, but she didn't know what might have been done to him before that meeting, or afterwards. She did know how internal injuries would turn out if untreated. In fact, it was incomprehensible how Nyvas had lived this long, or survived the ride out of the keep.

What it did remind her was that he was strong, and he had clung to life despite all odds. She fixed that concept in her head. Hadn't he stood up to the Vosira, despite the pain? He also had walked up those steps from the dungeon. Anyone else would have needed to be carried. A smile twitched on her lips as she remembered meeting him, and how kind he had been, and how confident. She recalled his smile, his gentleness, his long eyelashes blinking over bright blue eyes. He could be like that again, she imagined: smiling, confident, strong. No, she told herself, he would be—he was, even now. She felt his presence strongly, and clung to the sensation, trying to collect her own energy to share with him, to reinforce his strength.

Time passed slowly, but she remained still, holding her friend's hand within her own. All of her energy, all of her thoughts, were focused on him being well and whole again. She replayed memories in her head: meeting him in the inn back in Bhoren; his standing up for her to Arric; his fear for Lysander when his friend rode out to Ryvenor, and then again when he was injured; his assistance when her shoe came off; his amazed expression when he heard Arric play the flute. It was all real in her mind. From memories, she visualized him sitting up, then standing, then mounting a horse outside the house and riding back to the forest, as if nothing had ever injured him.

"Kate," she heard her name called out from a far distance. When she didn't reply, she felt a hand shaking her shoulder.

"Yeah?"

"I think he's gone."

Her eyes snapped open at Fantion's announcement.

She still held Nyvas's hand. Then she looked at his face, half-twisted into a smile. He was completely still—not moving, not even breathing. "No!" she insisted to Fantion, who now crouched beside her. She then looked at Rynar, whose head was buried in his hands. "No." She repeated. "I can still feel—"

A commotion at the door stirred both her and Fantion, although Rynar did not move. Fantion was on his feet instantly, his sword drawn. Then the door slammed open, and Lysander ran into the room, immediately collapsing to his knees beside Nyvas, at Rynar's left shoulder. Remarkably, he didn't seem to notice the Aldrish at all, and ignored everyone other than Nyvas himself.

"Oh, you dear boy," he moaned, his face suddenly drained of all color. Without hesitation he cupped Nyvas's head between his hands as he closed his own eyes.

"I'm sorry," Rynar whispered, first to Lysander, and then to Kate, sitting across from him. His eyes were bloodshot, and his words seemed genuine. "I did everything I knew how to do. His injuries are just too much for any healer."

Lysander shook his head in defiance of Rynar's conclusions, and then he opened his eyes and focused on the Aldrish. Viciously, he snapped, "what are you doing here? You're no healer." For a second his fiery gaze contemplated Kate, but then he lifted his head towards Fantion. "What is this? Why is this man anywhere near Nyvas?"

"There was no one else," Fantion said softly as he knelt across from Lysander. "And to his credit, he did try. She ensured his cooperation."

"But—Nyvas?" He leaned over his companion's chest, listening for a breath or a heartbeat. Hearing none, he grabbed handfuls of Nyvas's bloody shirt in both hands and buried his face in his chest, sobbing lightly. She realized she had never truly understood what it meant for someone's heart to break... until this moment.

Everyone else in the room was silent, bearing witness to Lysander's despair. The fhaoli named Kels had been pacing beside the small fire burning in the hearth, his long strides fast and noisy, all betraying an underlying anxiety. With Lysander's appearance, however he had abruptly stopped walking to and fro. Now, seated at the table, he had buried his head in his arms. Rynar remained next to Nyvas, as he had been from the start. Now, however, his arms were crossed and his head bowed so low his hair hung over his eyes and his chin rested on his chest. Even though Fantion had hovered over Rynar the entire time, watching the Aldrish for any hint of duplicity and keeping a hand on the hilt of his knife, now, with nothing more to be done, he had relaxed his guard slightly, and stood with his eyes cast to the floor and his lips pressed tightly together.

Her eyes spun back down to Nyvas. It was all too unreal to consider that, after everything that had happened, he still had died. At the same time, however, she discovered that she was unable to descend into grief, or anger, or any other intense emotion that the death of such a friend might inspire. There were no tears, no sighs. Had she already shed all her tears back in the dungeon? Was there no more grief and despair left? Usually so demonstrative and emotional, her lack of any suitable response to the events actually unsettled her.

Even though it was dirty and crusted with dried blood, she reached out to touch his black hair—to make one last connection with him. "I'm sorry," she said silently, forming unspoken words on her chapped lips. "This should never have happened to you." She visualized the broken body of her friend being hoisted onto the horse, and all kinds of questions flooded her mind, things she wished she could ask Nyvas now. *Why did you think your Goddess would protect me? She let you die. Why am I still here?*

Her thoughts suddenly shifted back to him physically restored, as if the healing had worked. She wasn't sure why, but somehow his survival mattered, beyond the friendship she had made with him, beyond his relationship with any of the others. Perhaps it was because of all he had endured, but suddenly she realized how he symbolized everything that Arric was trying to accomplish. By being at the very heart of things, his demise marked failure—but his survival would restore hope. She barely understood any of the political machinations of this land its people, but she had no doubts of the sincere goodness of this young man, of his true heart. Never had anything felt more wrong to her than his death under these circumstances. This was a man who deserved to die a hero, in pursuit of something greater than himself—not as a victim of a senseless beating by a soldier.

«Damn it!» she cried out in her mind, her heart near to breaking. She wanted to scream words of anger to the gods of this land or anyone who would listen. «This is not right!» Fury consumed her, and she would fight anyone who would try to take him away from them now. With only the vaguest of awareness that she was doing so, even as Lysander released him, she scooped Nyvas up in her arms and pulled him close, as if daring someone to take him from her. Defiantly, she shouted in her mind: «You can't have him yet. This isn't over. You will not let him die, not here, not today.»

She felt hot winds whip around her, causing her to perspire, but she held on to her friend.

«This is not your battle to fight,» someone replied.

«If not me, then who else is there? If I am to have a purpose, then let this be it. His story is not yet over. If I am to play a part in this, then so shall he.»

«You are bold, to demand this.»

«Perhaps. But it's the right thing to do.»

She felt like she was floating out of her body, adrift on a sea without water, floating in a void. She was alone, and could hear nothing, feel nothing. The sensation seemed to last hours, as if she herself had died and passed into another realm. Was this all there was to it, she wondered? Had her rescue just been a dream, and now she and her friend were dead?

***

A large hand came to rest on her shoulder, abruptly concluding the dream state into which she had so quickly fallen. "Don't blame yourself," the voice said, but again, it sounded far away. "You did more than anyone to save him."

She cracked open one eye, and saw the lifeless face of her friend at her cheek. It was darker in the room, as the sun had set and no one had moved to light candles. Realizing she still embraced Nyvas within her arms, with extraordinary gentleness, she eased him back to the floor, leaving her palm resting protectively on his chest, as if she feared he might disappear if she broke all physical contact. Then she tipped her head to look up at the man speaking. She squinted as she brought Fantion's face into focus. She didn't want to reply, lacking any words that could suffice at that moment.

Her dilemma was quickly resolved with an exclamation from Lysander. "What was that?" he cried out, desperately motioning towards Nyvas. "Look!" His pupils were wide, and he waved his arms wildly. "Fantion, did you see?"

Although everyone leaned over to see what Lysander was talking about, none shared the same excitable demeanor.

"Calm yourself, man. I'm sorry for it, but he's already passed on to Yoren," Rynar said, exhaustion buffering the harsh tone reserved for the many people he disliked. It was a rare unguarded moment, and he slipped by making a reference to a god he had publicly forsaken, but no one seemed to notice. His bloodshot eyes, tousled hair and facial pallor made him look like he had gone without sleep for a week. "There is nothing else to be done."

Lysander was undeterred. "Just look. Kate?" he begged, and then he began to rub Nyvas's cheeks rapidly. "Do you see it?" He leaned over and put his ear to his companion's chest. "I swear, I didn't even try—" he began, new tears filling his eyes. "I couldn't—healers don't dare, once someone is dead—but now, look!"

"Nay, he has already left us," Rynar said softly. "I could even sense it at the end." He placed a hand—a kind hand, a healer's hand—on Lysander's arm. "I am so sorry."

Disregarding Rynar's comment, Fantion circled around to crouch down beside Lysander. "What is it?"

"Just look, will you, please?" Lysander pleaded.

A moment of utter silence stretched out for a lifetime as they all watched Nyvas, uncertain what Lysander had seen.

Then—a breath. It was impossible, but there it was all the same.

"Blessed Kerthal, he's still with us!" Fantion confirmed.

One moment he was still, with no signs of life, and then... Nyvas was suddenly breathing again. Not only breathing—what came next were strong breaths, without any of the earlier rattling in his chest that set off his coughing. In fact, every physical ailment seemed to have been reversed, leaving him in a deep, comfortable sleep.

CHAPTER 40

"If you'll just return my personal items and sword, we'll be on our way," Rynar announced.

With the crisis inexplicably averted, he had quickly gotten to his feet, as if to escape before anyone had second thoughts. His confident swagger was neatly back in place. He could not hide the fact that he was physically exhausted from the day's events, for his posture was sagging and his eyes were red, but even so, he acted as though nothing unusual had happened. He stood beside the door, and with a sharp jerk of his chin gestured for her to join him.

She was still sitting beside Nyvas, and found it difficult to release his hand, even know she sensed he was going to be okay.

Something had happened a short time ago, and although she struggled to put words to it, to explain it to herself, comprehension defied her efforts. Her friend had almost died, but somehow he hadn't—and it wasn't simply a matter of injuries or healing. There was something much more profound about the event, and although she did not comprehend the role she had played, she recognized that she had done something.

"I hate to rush you, my dear, but if you're strong enough, we need to return before the entire force of the Senvosra descends on this neighborhood."

"Oh." It hadn't occurred to her that she might return to the keep. She didn't move from her spot beside Nyvas. "Are you sure that's a good idea?"

"Aye, of course. They'll be waiting on us. If we don't return, the Vosira will send every man he has to find us."

Fantion watched their interaction from a seat on the stairs. At Rynar's comment, he snorted loudly in amusement, and the sound caught the Aldrish's attention. Angry looks were exchanged between the men, and then Rynar turned his eyes back to her. "Come, Kate. Let's go."

"Begging your pardon, Aldrish," Fantion said sarcastically as he walked down the steps, "but I don't think you're in any position to give orders here."

Rynar rolled his eyes. "Fhaoli, you are fortunate I haven't already called the Senvosra on you all," he reminded the outlaw. "One word from me and this house will be up in flames."

"Ah, think that if you'd like, but you know full well there hasn't been any sign of the Vosira's men since sundown." Fantion grinned as he stepped around the banister. In one hand he held Rynar's sword, still sheathed, and casually swung it back and forth, as if it held little value. "Why should she go back with you? Your Vosira ordered her execution, and she was spared only because Bedoric sees some value in your filthy hide." He unsheathed the sword, and he lowered the tip until it hovered a few inches from the floor. "You know she'll be implicated in your abduction and Nyvas's release. Why in Kerthal's name would she want to return to face all of that?"

"Her safety is not your concern," Rynar said, his eyes narrowing, but he could not ignore the sight of the naked blade.

"Aye, it is indeed my concern," Fantion countered. "Whether you like it or not, she's one of us now."

Puffing out his chest, Rynar's anger was reaching the surface, and he barely held it in check. "She's no fhaoli," he spat, his words as caustic as lye. "Kate?" he called out. "Will you come?"

"Leave her alone," Lysander said, his own rage simmering as he stood to face down the Aldrish. "After everything she's done today, you have no right to tell her what to do. None of the rest of us would even dare. She willingly put her life on the line to save both you and Nyvas, and in the end she saved you both, and condemned herself in the process. So you can posture all you want, but you have no authority here, no power whatsoever. Back in your world—back in the nice warm keep, with your soft beds and food and music—you may command others to do your bidding, but here, you're nobody."

To underscore his friend's words, Fantion stepped forward and boldly raised the sword until the tip rested on the Aldrish's shoulder.

To his credit, Rynar did not flinch when the sword's fine edge came within inches of his face. Instead, he stood his ground with a confidence few men could have displayed under such circumstances. "Fhaoli, if your plan is to kill me, then do it quickly. Otherwise return my sword to me and let me go."

Fantion raised an eyebrow. "Calling my bluff, Aldrish?" he said sternly, the blade moving ever closer towards Rynar's neck.

"Fantion, don't." The old animosities were back in place now that Nyvas was out of danger. She pushed herself up from the floor and stood in front of them.

"Aye, perhaps not." Fantion lowered the blade and slid it into the scabbard, and in a gesture she had not predicted, presented it with both hands to the Aldrish. Smiling, he added, "Kate bargained for your life, and since she met her end of the deal, I shall meet mine. However, I promise that if our paths cross again, I may not be so generous."

The corner of Rynar's mouth jerked in annoyance as he grabbed his sword. After fingering the hilt for a few seconds, likely trying to decide whether or not to use the weapon himself, he belted it around his waist. "Nor will I."

Still grinning, Fantion put his hands on his hips. "Your glysar chain and ring we gave to Kate, to use in her negotiations. We assume the Vosira has kept them safe in your absence."

With stiff shoulders, narrowed eyes and lips pressed tightly together, Rynar had a distinctly murderous appearance. He had been used and humiliated, and his exhaustion made him short-tempered. Rather than respond to the flippant remark, he turned his head back towards her, though not quite enough to look at her again. "Please come with me, Kate," he tried again, this time phrasing it as a request rather than a command. "I will protect you from harm, which is more than the likes of this one can promise."

She had listened to the men battling over her like she was a commodity. No one had asked what she wanted to do, and although ostensibly both had her interests in heart, it had almost become a game, to see who had the stronger argument, whose force of will would prevail.

She didn't want to go back with Rynar. Here she was with friends, with men she believed she could trust, despite their status—while the Aldrish had unclear motives. There was also the distinct possibility that she would be held accountable for the day's events, and not entirely without cause. But in the end, there was only one decision she could make, for there was a bigger picture to consider, and things still to do.

She turned to Fantion. "I'm sorry, but I have to go back. You understand why."

He nodded, and Lysander stepped forward. "Do what you can for him, Kate."

"I will."

After rapid farewells, she was the first one out of the house. As Fantion had described, the Senvosra—and the horses—were nowhere to be found.

That left Rynar and Kate no choice but to walk back to the keep.

CHAPTER 41

She was jarred awake by a door slamming shut.

"What's going on?" she asked as she sat up, a bit groggy and disoriented. She had dropped onto Rynar's bed and passed out almost as soon as they had returned to the keep. She looked over to the floor but the blankets he always slept on were nowhere to be found.

First there was an exasperated sigh, and then she turned to see Rynar in the doorway, shaking his head. "It was unbelievable." He crumpled into the closest chair and dropped his medallion on the table beside him. "I've been up all night trying to convince the Vosira not to execute us both at midday." He was completely worn out and defeated, his eyes once again red and puffy, and his hair completely disheveled. It was a look he did not wear well. "Although he finally relented, I'm not convinced that he won't change his mind."

"What?" His words set her heart racing. As he poured himself a mug of wine, she stepped over to the window and peeked beyond the curtain. "It's nearly dawn."

"Aye, it is," he said, his weariness evident in his words.

She took a seat beside him. "So what happened? Are things really that bad?" She expected to be safe in his company, and hadn't considered that Bedoric would threaten the Aldrish himself. "Surely he won't do it?"

With a sigh, he continued. "The Vosira and nearly everyone on the Council were absolutely convinced that you had masterminded everything that happened yesterday. Even worse, because your friends didn't kill me, someone, Solerav maybe, suggested it was some conspiracy we came up with together, although to what end, I have no idea." He drained his cup. Then he narrowed his eyes as he glared at her. "I don't suppose I need to tell you how humiliating it was for me to have to argue my own innocence in this affair."

It was the wrong thing to say, and anger flushed her cheeks. "Did you succeed?" she asked, sarcasm heavy in her words.

He seemed not to notice her tone. "Aye, they finally realized it was complete foolishness, but it still took all blasted night." His careful facade had fallen, and he was being overly emotional. Stress and exhaustion had taken their toll on him. "You have no idea what it was like."

"Oh. Well, I'm so sorry to have inconvenienced you like that. Next time I'll arrange for a more convenient kidnapping."

He had just pulled off one of his boots. When she said that, he froze with his hands on his ankle. "What are you talking about, Kate? I just saved your life."

"Then we're even."

From the blank look on his face, she could tell her words shocked him. "Blast it all, Kate," he exclaimed, and threw his boot across the room. "So you would have preferred that I let him burn you in the square?"

"Oh stop it already! You wouldn't have let him do that. You're just saying that now because you want me to be grateful to you. I really wish you'd stop trying so hard to impress me."

He shook his head violently, and in the back of his throat, made a sound of disgust. "What are you talking about? It's not about impressing you. Didn't you hear me a moment ago? I spent this whole night trying to save your life!"

"Save me? From what you said a minute ago, it sounds like you were trying to save yourself." She flung her arms into the air, as if ready to fight him physically as much as verbally. "At any rate, I never asked you to be my personal savior. Who the hell do you think you are, anyway?"

"I—" he began, and then his mouth moved without speaking, as he choked back a comment he thought better of saying. Then he threw his head back and breathed in a long, deep breath, releasing it slowly.

"Why don't you just admit it, Rynar? You've been lying to me since day one, trying to win me over to your 'side', though for the life of me, I can't figure out which side that is."

"That isn't true, my dear," he said in a low voice. "I haven't lied to you."

"So you keep telling me. And yet, you still deny that it was your idea to imprison both Nyvas and Dosedra Arric in the first place?"

"Aye!" He sucked in a breath. "Why won't you believe me? Their arrests were as much a surprise to me as they were to you. I had no part to play in that."

"Do you still think they're guilty of murder?"

"Kate, do we need to discuss this now? I'm exhausted."

No better time than the present, she thought. She hadn't forgotten how he had tried to pump her for information right after she had returned from Bhoren, and there might never be another chance to discuss this when his guard was down. "Yes, we do. You always try to avoid this conversation, and I want to know where you stand. The honest truth of it all."

"I don't want to avoid it, I just—"

"Then tell me the truth, right here and now."

He leaned back in the chair, and swung his head back. "Nay. I do not believe they're guilty."

"Seriously? Then you need to help Arric now."

He rolled his head upright again. "My dear, be reasonable. I'm not going to betray Vosira Bedoric."

"You already have."

He stared at her suspiciously. "What do you mean?"

"Well, I doubt he'd want to hear what happened last night, and how you helped save Nyvas's life."

"You wouldn't dare say anything." He scowled at her. "I just convinced him that we're innocent. Why would you try to undo all of that?"

"I'm not. I'm just trying to make a point. Sometimes there are things more important than politics and blind loyalty. Don't you see? I'm just trying to do what's right. And if you care about that, you'll help me."

He sighed again, and his chin bobbed up a bit. "My dear, I can barely keep my eyes open. Allow me to sleep on it, and I promise, we shall discuss this later."

CHAPTER 42

Shortly after Rynar fell asleep, Lillia appeared with a tray of food.

"My lady, where is the Aldrish? Erdal said that he would not need breakfast." She set the tray on the table by the window. "I told him I'd bring yours."

Kate gestured to the closed door. "He was up all night with Vosira Bedoric and just now fell asleep."

"Indeed? I have never heard of him sleeping past sunrise. May I?" Lillia asked.

"Be my guest." She opened the door to the inner chamber herself. Inside, the Aldrish was passed out, face-down, on his bed, still fully-clothed and laying on top of the blankets. He snored lightly and rolled over even as the two women spied on him.

Lillia smiled, and turned her attention to the tray on the table, where she worked to slice a small loaf of bread. "It must have been quite a meeting." She shook her head as she stacked the slices neatly, and then dusted the crumbs from her hands onto her apron. "I heard what happened yesterday. We were all quite worried for you and the Aldrish. Word is that you both returned unharmed, but—" her eyes traveled from Kate's face to the gown, which was torn and filthy. "Oh, my lady, I had no idea." She stepped closer and examined the bruises on her face. "That must hurt quite a bit."

"No, I'm fine," she lied. In truth, not only her face hurt. Even though the kidnapping had been by friends, twice she had been tied up, and she had been thrown from a horse, dragged down dungeon stairs, and faced the possibility of her own death and quite nearly the death of a friend. Without question, it was the most frightening day of her life. When she had fallen asleep, she hadn't given herself any time to process any of it, and this morning she had awakened so abruptly that her thoughts hadn't sorted themselves out. She had been standing at the window, but now found a chair and fell into it, feeling her body starting to quiver.

"You're anything but fine," Lillia remarked, shaking her head. "You've been through a terrible ordeal, and I cannot imagine how you must be feeling." She poured a mug full of wine, and handed it to Kate. "Drink this first, it will calm you. Then I'll help you clean yourself up."

True to her word, once she had drained the mug, Lillia took her to the baths, and for the first time in days, soldiers didn't trail her every move. While she soaked in a tub of warm water, Lillia brought the more formal gown she usually only wore in the evenings.

As she inspected Kate's face and arms, she shook her head. "My lady, these bruises..." She made a tsk-tsk sound with her tongue. "After this, I'm going to take you to Torv for some salves."

"Torv?"

"Aye, he's the apothecary, and should have something to fix you right up." She poured water over Kate's hair.

"Thanks." The combination of the wine and the bath was calming her down again. "That would help, I guess."

"Do you wish to talk about what happened?" Lillia asked while they remained within the privacy of the bath. "I heard you were able to negotiate for the Aldrish's release. That was quite brave."

"Really? You know about that?"

"Aye, of course. The whole keep is abuzz with the story. You're quite a hero to go such lengths to save your friend." She winked.

"It wasn't quite like that..."

Lillia smiled. "You don't need to say anything more, my lady. I knew Stavan as a boy, and I never believed he was involved in the Vosira's murder. It's not in his nature to harm another. I also know that you and the Dosedra traveled with him and their friends."

"Wow, I had no idea that was all common knowledge..."

She winked at Kate. "It's not."

"Well, that's good to know. But now that it's over, I'm even more worried about Dosedra Arric. If Bedoric believes he was involved in a conspiracy..."

The maid stared at her for a moment, as if surprised that she would confide such a fact in her. Then she glanced to the closed door to the baths. "I am concerned about him as well." She tapped her lips. "I really shouldn't say this—no one is supposed to speak with the Dosedra, but..." she looked over her shoulder, as if to confirm again that the door was shut. In a low voice, she continued. "A boy, Haras, takes him his meals and cares for his personal needs. And Haras' mother is a good friend of mine." She frowned. "From what the boy has said, the Dosedra was initially quite agitated and active in the tower, demanding to be released, but the past few days he's become quite sullen and hasn't even chatted with Haras at all. He just sits at the window and stares out. I don't believe he's eaten anything for days."

Kate realized that Arric would not have heard about yesterday's events, and Nyvas's rescue. He probably believed his friend had died. "Lillia, I wish we could help him."

The maid met her eyes. "Ah, my lady, I've had the same desire myself. He has many enemies in Loraden, but none among the servants. We all remember him fondly, for he treated us with respect, something his brother never has. I only wish he knew it himself, because I think it would help him to know his people care about him."

"His people?" The phrase surprised her. "You say that as though he was Vosira, not his brother."

"He's a royal son. Even if he's not Vosira, people still look up to him, even after all that's happened." She reached for a towel and handed it to Kate. "Let's get you dressed so I can take you to Torv."

CHAPTER 43

The kitchens were hot and smoky, thick with the smells of yeast, animal blood and grease. On long wooden tables stretching under the stone archways, women were busy kneading dough that would rise through the day and be ready for the ovens before nightfall. At wide hearths, boys turned newly-butchered lambs and goats on spits, the fat sizzling and sputtering on the fire. Such labors would continue through the day, she realized, so that the Bhagali would have a luxurious evening meal.

Lillia had instructed her to wait there, but as she watched the workers, she couldn't fathom why the maid had left her here.

Suddenly a voice greeted her from behind. "I've been looking forward to meeting you."

Kate spun around, only to come face to face with a tall man, perhaps in his sixties, wearing a simple lightweight tunic and trousers. His hair was shaggy and ill-cut, and entirely gray, and under a thick beard his face was pale, and heavily creased with wrinkles, like a freshly-plowed field. He was also barefoot. All in all he reminded Kate of hermits depicted in comic strips.

She squeaked in surprise, not expecting this at all. "Who are you?"

"I am Torv. Did Lillia not tell you she was bringing you to see me?"

"Yeah, but—" she looked around the kitchen.

Offering no further explanation, he began walking and waved her to follow. "Come with me, my child, come along. I promise not to keep you long."

Without pausing to see if she was behind him, Torv nimbly headed towards the far wall of the kitchen, stopping at a narrow wooden door in the tower. Hoisting a torch from a bracket on the wall, he waved her forward. "Follow me."

It was a staircase almost identical to the one that led to the dungeons, and she stopped cold. "No, I'm not doing this again," she said in a panic, backing away from the stairwell that stretched downward.

"Bhara, it simply leads to my workshop. Ask anyone here," he offered, waving to the many cooks. "I heard what happened to you, so I understand your hesitation, but I promise there is nothing down here that will harm you. Please join me, as I believe I have something that can help you."

"It's just bruises." She took another step backwards, feeling her heart racing.

"Child, there are more than bruises that ail you. Come along."

There was something intriguing about how he said that, and she wondered what he referred to. Surely Lillia hadn't led her to a trap, and if Vosira Bedoric wanted her in prison, there were much simpler ways to make that happen. So with trepidation, she allowed Torv to lead her down the narrow, winding steps, and she tried to reassure herself that she was safe.

After yesterday, it wasn't an easy descent, however, and more than once she had to catch her breath and will herself past the terror that she felt welling up inside her. But even knowing the potential danger, she kept going. At the base of the steps, she followed him down a hallway that was close and damp, with walls of dirty stone, unpainted and unwashed. It continued to be so much like the dungeon that she had to struggle to maintain her composure and fight against the urge to run back upstairs.

There was one difference; there was a single light shining from a room halfway down the hall. Torv shuffled towards the doorway.

She held her breath, and braced herself for an attack. However, when she stepped inside, instead of a small, somber room, she was astonished to find a spacious chamber with whitewashed walls, lined with shelves loaded with hundreds of jars, bottles, boxes, and bowls. Along the back wall there were several rows of large books stacked neatly. A fire was crackling in a small hearth, and a pair of large work tables filled much of the space.

So it really was the apothecary?

"There is much to discuss, child, and no safer place to do so," he explained, and over his shoulder waved for her to sit on a stool by the fire. He reached into a closed cabinet and pulled out several items, and then spun around with a tall bottle and a pair of narrow glasses on a glysar tray, which he brought to a small table beside her. He poured a fair measure of liquid into each of the glasses, and as he handed her one, he allowed his fingers to brush against hers. As they touched, immediately her initial fear dissipated, but from the physical contact she also somehow realized he was not as decrepit as she first thought.

She sat quietly for a moment, allowing the firelight to sparkle within the crystal. It was the first use of glass she had seen in the keep, and that alone piqued her curiosity. And the wine was a beautiful rose color.

He gestured for her to take a sip, as he did so himself.

She tasted a little on her tongue, and realized what it was. "Arbishi."

"You've had it before?"

She nodded. "Sarnoc Vaj served it at Altopon," she explained, and only after she spoke the words did she realize this was the first she had mentioned her trip there since returning to the keep.

"Indeed. Perhaps this will be an equally special occasion."

Eyeing him warily, she lowered her glass. "How so?"

"I had hoped to meet you for a while, but never had there been an opportunity to do so unobserved and in private before now. However, it seems that the timing has worked to our benefit." He was gazing at her with an intensity that she didn't expect. "I believe we have much to discuss."

"I'm sorry, but I don't understand. Why would you want to meet me?"

"Child, ever since your arrival, my colleagues have spoken incessantly about the event, and pondered its significance for all of Sarducia.

We believe that it is a sign that we are again in the gods' favor, and you are here to help us restore a balance that has been missing for quite some time."

"We?" She glanced around the room. "Who are these 'colleagues'?" She half expected him to tell her he spoke to mice.

He didn't answer right away, but instead watched her closely, in a way that was oddly familiar. Finally he said, in a low, confident voice, "child, would it surprise you to learn that I am Sarnoc?"

She stared at the disheveled man as he took another sip of the liqueur. The Sarnoc were banned from the city—so how could he be here, in the keep, right out in the open? She thought about Sarnoc Vaj, and realized how different he was from Torv. It seemed highly improbable that this man was anything like what he suggested. "What? That's impossible…"

"You expected me to be wearing a white tunic, a long braid, and a glysar ring?"

"Well, no—yes—well, to be honest, I don't really know." Her time at Altopon was too brief to understand what the Sarnoc were all about, but still, it didn't seem to fit.

He nodded, and walked to one of the shelves where dozens of items had been crammed together. He reached for a soot-smeared wooden jar and carried it back to the fire. A quick twist revealed a small compartment under the main one. And from inside, he produced a glysar band engraved with unfamiliar designs.

"You are new to our lands, but this may help convince you all the same." He reached out for her right hand placed the ring within her palm. "You feel it, do you not? The energy within the ring?"

She allowed her fingers to curl over the band, and closed her eyes. There was an ever-so-slight vibration to the ring itself, but even more, she had a sudden rush of images, memories, faces, so intense that she dropped the ring in surprise.

"Aye, so you do." He bent down to retrieve the ring from the floor and placed it back in its hiding place.

Even with the ring, she wasn't convinced. "I'm still not sure I understand. Why are you down here, then, if you're Sarnoc? From what I understand, the Sarnoc were banned from the city years ago."

"Aye, that is true enough. Bedoric thought if he forced us all to leave, no one would be left to challenge his reign. Loraden has been my home for a long time, though, and it was not so easy to run me off. You see, child, many years ago, likely before you were even born, I was appointed to the Council, and served Vosira Parmon for a long time. When Bedoric became Vosira and then forced the Sarnoc to leave Loraden, I refused to give up my post, forcing them to accuse me of a terrible crime so I'd have to flee." His eyes sparkled, the memories appearing to be more amusing than painful. "Perhaps it was me acting out of spite, but I was determined to stay here and keep an eye on things."

She noticed how he had referred to the Vosira without his title, which was odd enough as it was, but it was his reference to his former position that made her gasp. She remembered how Fantion had been outlawed after standing up for a Sarnoc, and if Rynar could be believed, this was the same person Arric had sought in Bhoren. "Are you telling me that you're Sarnoc Sofinar?" It hardly seemed possible.

His eyes blinked at her pronouncement of his name. "Aye, so you've heard of me, then. That saves us some time. Indeed, that was once my name, but I had to abandon it, and all of the trappings of a Sarnoc, out of self-preservation. Now I am known as Torv. Contrary to Bedoric's demands, I have survived, and do my best to serve the goddess. Indeed, with each passing season, my faith in Kerthal grows stronger."

This man's revelation did not bring her comfort, however, if that had been his intention. "Arric—I mean, the Dosedra—went to Bhoren to find you, but was told you had died."

His gnarled hand rubbed the back of his neck, and then he looked back at her with his grey eyes, clear and focused. "Aye, none of that has escaped my notice. Child, I was born in Bhoren. My father's younger brother runs the town's inn, and after my banishment from Loraden and Altopon, I did my best to make my enemies believe I had returned home. As Arric's mentor and friend for many years, I'm touched that he went looking for me. Had I known he had intended such a journey, I would have saved him all that trouble." Her frustration must have been obvious, for he continued. "Do not fret, child. Arric's journey was not in vain."

"You say that, but he's a prisoner now because of it."

"Aye, that much is true. For the moment, let's set aside talk of Arric, and instead, would you do me the honor of telling me what happened yesterday? The whole story, not what Bedoric was convinced to believe."

Her eyes widened. "You know about it?"

He nodded once. "I know that the Aldrish received a mysterious message that sent him deep into Loraden city, and that the Pasadhi arranged for a fog to settle over the city, so that you could be captured by those who wished to help their friend. After that, I do not know anything other than that you succeeded, as the boy is no longer a prisoner, and you have returned to the keep safely."

"Oh my god, was it a Sarnoc plan?"

"It was mine," he said simply. "I knew the boy many years ago, and I know he is not guilty of the crime he was accused of committing. I did not wish to see an injustice carried through to its conclusion. Now, tell me what I don't already know, if you don't mind."

Slowly, she recounted the events of the day from the moment Rynar received the note, describing the attack, her argument with Fantion and the others, and her return to the keep. She had kept her composure throughout, until she got to the part where she failed to convince the Vosira to accept the trade and he threw her into the dungeon cell with Nyvas.

"I really thought I was about to die. And while I was freaking out, Nyvas bravely faced it as if it wasn't a big deal."

"Have you ever faced death before, my child?"

"No, not like that, not really believing it was going to happen, and waiting for it. I was so scared. In some ways, I still am."

He nodded. "That is entirely normal, and I'm afraid to tell you that you will be haunted by it for some time to come. There's nothing I can offer you to soothe that wound, other than to encourage you to draw strength from the experience."

Leaning forward, he refilled her glass. When she shook her head, realizing it was rather early for alcohol, he placed his hand on hers. "Please, indulge me."

With a smile, she took another sip, and he continued. "As for the boy, as you may have heard, he nearly died eight years ago, when he was first captured, and who knows how many times he's faced danger again since that day. He's had plenty of time to come to terms with his mortality. You, on the other hand, have lived a much different life. It is nothing to be ashamed of, it is simply what it is."

"But—"

"Do not hold yourself as less worthy just because you knew the fear of death. Now, tell me what happened after that."

She licked a drop of arbishi from her bottom lip and then explained how they had returned to the house, with Nyvas near death.

He seemed unimpressed by her description of Rynar's attempt to heal Nyvas, but then he asked, "you did something too, at the end?"

"How did you know?"

"When energies are expended in the lines between the worlds, and between life and death itself, there is a ripple effect. Anyone trained to sense them would have known."

"I don't know what I did, but it seemed to help."

He nodded. "It's your calling, my child. You are finally discovering the power within your Mosumi heritage."

"What are you talking about?" She said it as a protest, but even as the words came out of her mouth, she knew it was true.

"You didn't know?"

"No." Her mind raced. Her mother, the ring. "I had no idea, but to hear you say it… it makes sense."

"Aye. You are very intuitive, and you've long known you were different. As time goes on, you'll learn more about what it means. For now, though, would you finish your tale? After you aided in Nyvas's healing, you returned to the keep rather than remain with him, and your other friends?"

She interpreted that as a criticism. "I had to. Arric's still here, and someone has to help him. I figured if I could return, maybe I could find a way to get him released. I hoped Rynar would help me, since he keeps telling me it's not his idea to keep Arric locked up, but I know he's lying."

"Indeed? How so?"

She repeated what Fantion and Lysander had told her. "I had hoped I could change his mind, so he could convince the Vosira to release Arric, but after everything that happened yesterday, he's worried about his own standing with the Vosira, so I don't think he's going to do anything. He was my last hope, too, so I'm not sure what else to do."

As she dropped her gaze, he reached for her hand. "Do not despair. There's always something you haven't tried yet."

His words triggered a memory. "Wait, I do have an idea." She pulled out the ring that hung on a chain around her neck. "Arric asked me to hold this for him, and told me to give this to the Sarnoc if anything happened to him." She pulled the chain over her head to remove it, and then extended it out to him.

He reached out for the ring, and whistled as he examined it. "Arric gave this to you?"

"Yes. Do you know what it is?"

"Oh, aye. Do you?"

She shook her head. "He didn't tell me anything about it, other than to keep it hidden. What's so special about it?"

He folded his lips tightly as he considered her question. "Nay, it cannot be as easy as that, I'm afraid. If he gave this to you, but told you nothing about it, then it is not my place to do so. What I can tell you is that it's very important."

"That's all? It can't help him?"

"Not in the way you wish, I'm afraid."

Kate sunk back into her chair, disappointed.

"Again, do not despair." As she looked up, his eyes sparkled with bright energy. He smiled, and allowed the ring to drop, the chain dangling from his finger. "You did not cause any of this to happen, because it has been in the works for many years. However, you will help to reverse all of the wrongdoings that have taken place."

"But how? I don't understand." Then she imagined herself back at Nyvas's side last night. Somehow, she had saved him when no one else could. "Maybe I do."

"Aye, my child. It's a journey, and you're well on your way. Give it time. You barely know the person you'll become."

That was a strange thing to say. "Won't you at least take the ring?"

"Nay, you must take it yourself to Altopon. No matter what else happens, if you do that, you will not have failed your friends."

"Altopon might as well be a million miles away," she sighed. "I could try to escape, but with all of the Senvosra around, it wouldn't be easy, and I honestly don't want to leave as long as Arric is still here."

"Patience, my child. It may well be the gods have a plan, and we simply haven't witnessed its outcome yet." He reached to a cabinet, and retrieved a small wooden container. "Take this, for your bruises." He handed it to her, and then dusted his hands on his trousers.

"Now, my child, you need to return to the Aldrish's quarters, before he wonders where you've wandered off. Lillia will be waiting for you at the top of the stairs." He caught hold her of her wrist. "And please, do not share any of what we discussed with anyone. Our secret?"

She nodded, and headed back to Lillia.

CHAPTER 44

"What is this?" Rynar asked, as he picked up the wooden container on the table and examined it closely in front of the window. He had awakened after she had returned, and walked in as she was finishing breakfast.

"Torv, the apothecary, gave it to me."

He coughed abruptly, and set the jar back on the table. "Torv? You spoke to him?"

"Yeah. Lillia thought he could help me with my bruises." Delicately she rubbed at her swollen face. "It's a salve."

"Indeed?" He removed the lid and made a face, as if it smelled bad. "Interesting." He waved her over. "There's no need for the salve. Let me take care of your injuries for you."

"You must still be worn out from yesterday. You've barely even slept."

"It's midday, I've slept enough. Any more and it would raise suspicion."

"But surely you don't want to do another healing..."

He stared at her. "Better I heal your face than you walk around the keep like you've been brawling in the stables. Come now, it will just take a moment."

She waved him away. "So what happens now?"

He was standing over her. "Hmm? Hold still," he admonished her as he held her head between his hands. "Let me do this first."

She squirmed under his touch. "Really, I'm okay. I don't need..." Even as the words left her mouth she felt calmer, and she sank into the cushions of the chair. She didn't want to trust him, but even as his fingers brushed against her cheek, her anxiety melted away under his touch. It was as if he wasn't healing her at all, but forcing her into a deep relaxation, and rather than fight him, she allowed herself to sink into it. Freed of all immediate concerns and fears, she almost felt like she was floating.

As she sat there in silence, as Rynar continued to work on healing her, she began to hallucinate, to dream, to wander into another place.

First she was swimming in a sea of silver water, the sun warm on her face as she floated and dove down under the shiny waves.

The feeling of being in the ocean faded, and now she imagined herself laying in the sun on a blanket, feeling the cool breezes tangling her hair and tickling her feet. It was another memory of her mother, a trip back to the picnic they had, and she recalled her mother's voice as she softly sang pop songs they heard on the radio. Cat Stevens, Simon and Garfunkel, America... it was one of her favorite memories, that quintessential moment where she felt safe and loved and knew nothing could ever happen to her to change any of that.

Then the memory dissipated, as all daydreaming does, and she allowed her thoughts to bob along the river of her imagination, shifting without warning back to Sarducia. Once again she found herself at Altopon, walking among the gardens, but this time she wasn't alone. Arric was with her, holding her hand as they wandered along a path lined with small blue flowers. He was safe, and beyond the reach of his brother.

Kate couldn't help rejoicing at the sight, at the idea he was free, and at that moment she abruptly stepped back into the present, out of her peaceful reverie, only to stare in the face of the Aldrish, who had dropped his hand broken contact.

"My dear, what is it?"

She scrambled out of the chair and onto her feet. "I don't want to stay here any longer. Can I go back to my room?"

***

Rynar had acquiesced and permitted her to return to her old quarters, and as she had noticed before, her house arrest seemed to be over. She was no longer guarded at the door, and Lillia told her that she was once again allowed to go wherever she wished, provided she stayed within the keep itself and didn't try going into the city.

Oddly, as a few days passed, the Aldrish was nowhere to be seen. He didn't visit her, he was absent from meals in the great hall, and when, finally out of curiosity she asked Lillia what was happening, it appeared there had been no sign of him within the keep for days. "Isn't that unusual?" Kate asked.

"My lady, the Aldrish is an odd man, and does many things that defy explanation." Lillia had been making Kate's bed, as usual with Kate's assistance, and now plumped the pillow. "Around here, we don't question it."

"But isn't the Vosira upset that he's not around?"

"Didn't you want to get away from him?" Lillia asked, in a playful challenge. "Seems like you should be happy he's not here."

"Well, that's true enough. I find it strange that after everything that happened, he's just vanished."

"I'd accept it as a blessing. You've been increasingly annoyed by his attention, so be glad it's over, at least for the time being." She opened the wardrobe and pulled out a new gown, again blue, but this time a deeper shade, much like the livery and banners. Sarducian blue. "Shall we see if this new dress fits, my lady? You should look nice for your meeting with the Council."

Kate reached out and rubbed the fabric of the dress between her fingers. This one was a bit heavier. "I go through a lot of clothing don't I?"

Lillia laughed. "You do, indeed, but then again, most women don't seem to have all the adventures you do. Come, let's get you dressed."

"I'm really worried about this meeting. I don't know what they want to discuss. After the whole kidnapping incident, I'm not sure if—"

"If they wanted to punish you further, they would have done so already, don't you think?"

"I don't know. I can't help remembering what Rynar told me the day we got back, that the Council was convinced it was a conspiracy, and wanted to execute both of us. I mean, that's a hard thing to live with, you know?"

Lillia helped her slip the gown over her head, and now stood facing her, tugging the dress down so it would settle into place. "My lady, if the Vosira was still upset with you, he would not have asked you to attend the meeting." She stepped behind Kate and worked to lace up the back. "You would have been arrested and dragged in there. And hasn't he been polite at meals again?"

"I guess so. I still don't understand..."

"It's best not to worry too much about it. If you're in trouble, you can't do much about it anyway. You'll know soon enough."

CHAPTER 45

She was back in the Council chamber. Memories of her friends being arrested, and her own attempts to convince the Vosira to save them, tainted her experience here, and she could feel her heart racing as she was shown a seat near the Vosira. Already most of the men were in their own seats; Tashin looked a bit surprised to see her, and Abranir glared as usual. Beyond that, she didn't even try to make eye contact with anyone, and instead kept her eyes directed down at the wooden tabletop, and to her goblet of wine, which reassured her that she wasn't about to be arrested.

"Bhara, it is good to see you again," Vosira Bedoric announced, quite graciously given their recent interactions.

Kate swallowed hard, and as she took a deep breath, she turned in his direction and smiled as best she could. "Thank you, Vosira." She immediately took a drink of wine to try to hide her discomfort.

"I am glad we were able to clear up the business of your abduction some time ago," he continued. "The Aldrish convinced us of your innocence, that you were not involved in what happened, other than as a pawn to secure his release."

She nodded. "He told me, and I'm glad, because everything that happened was all as much a surprise to me as it was to him."

"Aye, that is what he told us all. And yet, the boy was an acquaintance of yours?"

Setting her goblet down, she again turned towards him, and this time did catch his eye. "I did meet him when I traveled with the Dosedra, but I did not instigate his escape, if that's what you're implying."

"Calm yourself, Bhara," Bedoric said, clearly finding the conversation amusing. "I did not ask you here to interrogate you about that incident, as I consider it closed. Furthermore, the fact that you have behaved yourself in the Aldrish's absence speaks highly of you."

He was complimenting her? "Thank you, Vosira."

He waved a boy to fill her goblet. "No hard feelings, my dear?"

She lowered her eyes and shook her head. "No sir," she replied, but her mind was racing. If this wasn't to talk about that incident, why was she here now?

"Aha! And here's the Aldrish now. Come, man, take your seat. We have an important discussion ahead of us."

Seeing him for the first time in several days was a bit of a shock. He took the empty seat beside her, his customary spot to the Vosira's right, and then turned to her. "Are you well?" he whispered.

Before she could reply, the Vosira greeted him. "Aldrish, it is good to have you back with us. I take it your aunt is well?"

"Aye, she is feeling much better now. Thank you for allowing me leave to visit her. I apologize for my tardiness, but I just arrived by river a short time ago. "

Bedoric nodded. "I am glad you made it a quick visit, as we do have things to discuss." He stood up. "Men, as you are all aware, my brother has been accused of conspiring against me, and against us all."

These words raised a bit of muttered comments, and Bhagal Avir spoke up. "Aye, we are all quite concerned to hear he consorted with your father's murderer. What might they have done, I wonder, had they not been stopped?"

Kate was about to speak up, but Rynar nudged her with his elbow, and when she glanced at him, he signaled her to stay silent with a slight shake of his head.

"Aye, Avir, I share your concerns." Bedoric leaned forward on his palms. "As everyone knows, my brother currently resides in the tower above the royal apartments, but that is not a solution, nor does it address the severity of his crimes. Today I called you all together for one purpose: I wish for the entire council to discuss his fate."

"Vosira, do you intend to execute him for treason?" Bhagal Jamra said, his voice not disguising his outrage at the idea.

"Ah, Jamra, it is good to hear from you. Aye, it is one possibility. I would like to hear everyone's thoughts on the matter."

"Executing your own brother would appear rather drastic to your subjects," Tashin pointed out. "Most people do not understand the crime he has committed, and may not support such a decision."

"Does it matter what the people think?" Solerav countered. "We have sufficient troops to quell any discontent that may arise afterwards."

"How about the Sarnoc? Would we face any repercussions from them?" Ulvicar asked. "They have been known to oppose political executions in the past."

"Aye, men, these are all good points to consider. Aldrish, what is your opinion in this matter?"

Rynar adjusted himself in the seat slightly so that he sat straight up. "I do not believe execution is warranted, as the Dosedra's crime was caught in the early stages, before he could do anything against the Vosira. Instead, I would recommend immediate banishment from Sarducia, with an armed escort taking him to the coast."

Kate looked at him. "What are you saying? He hasn't done anything wrong!"

Rynar looked at her from the corner of his eye, but did not turn towards her. Ignoring her protest, he continued. "In fact, I would recommend we take action immediately, before any more time has passed for his friends to plan another escape. The penalty he would face for returning would, of course, be death."

Tashin smiled, and nodded to the Aldrish. "A very interesting idea. Perhaps we could even convince people he left on his own again, as he already has a history of disappearing without notice."

The Vosira stood up straight again, and rubbed his beard. "Aye, I agree that this could be a good solution. It solves many of our concerns."

"Thank you, Vosira. However, before we pass a final judgment on him, I believe he should be brought here, to address us all, and to be held accountable to the Council as a whole. His arrest was quite sudden, and most were not there to witness him implicating himself in the crime. Perhaps after we all hear his story, we will be better able to make a decision."

"Indeed, Aldrish, that is an excellent idea. Solerav, could you please fetch my brother, and bring him here? Perhaps this time he should have his hands tied, so he doesn't have the opportunity to cause mischief."

The castellan stood. "It would be my pleasure, Vosira. I shall return shortly."

As Solerav and a couple of guards disappeared from the council chamber, servants walked around and filled everyone's goblet, as if preparing for a grand theatrical performance. She sat there, stunned. Just as her friends had told her, it was the Aldrish who called the shots, and made all the decisions where the Dosedra was concerned. And now, he proposed to send Arric away forever. As the Vosira took his seat and leaned back with his wine, she tugged at Rynar's sleeve.

"How could you?" She mouthed the words to him, angry that he would work so openly against Arric. It was just as the others had said.

He glanced down at her, and then looked away, as if her comment had no meaning to him. Seeing there was nothing to be done but sit and wait for the drama to unfold, she lowered her eyes, fuming. She held her right hand against her chest, where Arric's ring secretly lay under her gown. Had she failed him so utterly, by not getting it to the Sarnoc in time? Exile, or death. None of the men had even suggested...

"What if he's innocent?" she asked everyone at the table. "What if this is all just a huge misunderstanding, and everything the Dosedra did was taken out of context? Perhaps he could be given another chance to prove his loyalty?"

The Vosira leaned forward, his eyes wide. "Bhara, you would presume to suggest he was not working against me?"

"Yeah, if no one else will. You asked me to attend this meeting, so surely you want to hear what I have to say." She squared her shoulders and looked around the table. "You're all automatically assuming he's guilty of some terrible crime. Where's the evidence of that? I know he spent time with fhaoli, but think about it. They were his friends from a long time ago. Two weren't even outlawed when he left for Froida, and the third—how was he supposed to know who Nyvas really was? So when you think about it, he just returned from the battlefield, and decided to spend time with two of his oldest friends. From the way things happened at the quantrill, none of you were willing to welcome him back, so why wouldn't he look elsewhere? I know there's a law about consorting with outlaws, but—Vosira, he's your only brother. Surely it's worth giving him another chance?"

"The Bhara is brave to say such things," Ulvicar said, and beside him, Gevinsin nodded. "I am not happy to hear Dosedra Arric might be a traitor, and if he is willing to submit to your authority, Vosira, I think—"

"He is *not* innocent," Vosira Bedoric countered. "He has been trying for eight years to—" he began, but was cut off by the door of the chamber swinging open quickly, and banging against the wall.

"Vosira, come quickly. Something is wrong." Solerav waved to Bedoric, and dashed back out of the room.

"What is this?" Bedoric snapped, and pushed himself away from the table. "Everyone, stay here." He turned, and paused. "Rynar, you come along."

The Aldrish stood up, not appearing to be as alarmed as the Vosira. As he pushed in his chair, he touched Kate's arm, and when she looked up, she saw something in his eyes that suggested she should join him.

***

Kate followed closely behind Rynar as they made their way down the hall and around the corner, heading towards the Vosira's quarters. When she realized where the small party was headed, she had an uneasy feeling. "Oh no," she mumbled to herself a couple of times. "I don't like this."

Rynar rushed into the Vosira's chambers. Just inside the door, in the corner, was a wooden door that led to the tower room. The door was wide open. He sprinted up the stairs, Kate at his heels. Before they reached the door at the top, she heard the Vosira cry out. "Rynar, what's happening?"

When they pushed their way into the tiny room, already crowded with Solerav, the two soldiers and Bedoric, they found Arric, heavily bearded, laying cross-wise on his thin mattress, his skin tinged yellow. He wasn't moving.

"Oh my god, Arric?" She fell down on her knees beside him and felt for a pulse. In her panic she couldn't find one, and instead leaned over him to see if he was breathing. "Rynar?" Now she was terrified, not able to ask the question everyone in the room had on their lips as well.

"Vosira, what is this?" Rynar demanded, even as he knelt beside her. One hand lay on the Dosedra's chest, ostensibly also to see if he was breathing, though she realized he was hiding a stronger healing presence. "How did this happen?"

Bedoric towered over them both. "Aldrish, is he alive?" he asked, his face damp with perspiration.

Rynar leaned back on his heels. "Aye, just barely. He breathes, but his body is shutting down. It looks like poison."

"Poison?" Bedoric repeated, as if in a daze. "How..."

"You did this to him!" Kate shouted, pointing at the Vosira, unconcerned with the consequences. Then she turned to the Aldrish. "Rynar, can you save him?"

"I don't know, Kate." He looked back to Bedoric. "Vosira, what do you want to do?"

Bedoric stared at his motionless brother with his mouth hanging open. Kate's hostility didn't even seem to register. In fact, he looked as lost as a child. "I—I don't know."

"Somebody, do something!" She grabbed Rynar's sleeve. "Help him!"

He shook his head. "No, my dear. The Dosedra needs healers. We can't do anything here."

Even with the Dosedra on the verge of dying, Rynar wasn't going to divulge his secret. Furious, she looked to the Vosira. "You need to do something!"

Bedoric was now leaning against the wall, looking as if he was going to be ill. "Aye. Rynar, do whatever you need to do." He turned and quickly ran down the stairs.

Rynar looked up at her. "I will take care of this. Wait for me in my quarters." He was entirely calm, as if the Dosedra's condition was of little concern to him.

"No, I don't want to leave him!"

He made a face, and then nodded to a soldier in the doorway. At his signal, the guard took her arm and pulled her down the stairs after him.

***

"It is intolerable! We will do no such thing. No Sarnoc have been allowed in this keep since Parmon's murder!"

It had been an hour and the Aldrish had not returned with an update. At the sound of raised voices in the hall, she ran to the door, but the guard would not allow her to open it.

"The Vosira gave me leave to do whatever's necessary." That was Rynar, his voice much calmer than the man with whom he argued. "With such a poison, there's no one else who can help him."

"If it's poison, why not just get a healer? Why drag the Sarnoc back?"

There was a pause in the argument. She figured Rynar had again said something, but could not hear his response.

"Nay, Aldrish. It's too dangerous."

"The danger is in letting him die." Rynar said, his voice betraying his impatience. His voice seemed louder, as if they had moved closer to the open door. "If we don't allow the Sarnoc to help him, they may dissolve the truce with the Vosira."

"And what if that was their plan all along? What if this is just a ploy to help him escape?"

"Since when do Sarnoc poison people? Tashin, use your head. The man has more enemies than anyone else on this land. Someone wants him dead."

"Aye, that's true enough. But we need another solution, not Sarnoc."

"Do you want to deal with the Vosira if he dies? I promise you, the Dosedra will not survive without Sarnoc here."

"Bah," Tashin growled. "This is wrong and you know it. You say you follow the Prophet but now—ah, blast it, you are as bad as the rest. I will be speaking to the Vosira about this."

"As you wish."

A few moments later, Rynar opened the door to his chamber. His dark eyebrows arched in surprise as he saw her standing just beyond the sweep of the door. "My dear Kate, were you listening to that?"

She nodded.

"Ah, very well." He seemed oddly pleased. "Come, sit with me for a moment."

"How is he? Was it really poison?"

Rynar nodded. "Aye." He walked past her and poured wine into two goblets.

"Oh god." She sat at the edge of a chair by the fire. "Is he going to make it?" Seeing him offering her a drink, she threw her hands out in front of her. "No, I don't need that, not at a time like this. Tell me how he is!"

"My dear, calm yourself." He set her goblet on the table beside her, and reached out and placed his palm on her shoulder. "He will be fine."

She jerked her arm away, as if an ember from the fire had landed on her sleeve, and then jumped to her feet. "How can you say that? You already said he's dying—"

He allowed his hand to hover for a moment, and then dropped it to his lap. "He's not dying. The Sarnoc will know what to do. You need to—"

"But there aren't any Sarnoc here. *You* need to help him."

He shook his head, and took a sip of his wine. "I cannot, Kate. No one else knows of my healing talent. I can't possibly use it on the Dosedra."

"Even if it means he dies?"

"He won't die, my dear. Trust me."

"Are you kidding? How can I ever trust you again?"

CHAPTER 46

I t was difficult to keep up with Rynar's long strides, and Kate's shins burned with each step. Often she had to run several yards to regain his side, but inevitably she remained at least two paces behind. It was not a short walk to the torrapon, the large stone pavilion outside Loraden, and at this pace, she would never keep up.

She hadn't wanted to be with him at all.

The Sarnoc had arrived over a week before, as Rynar had promised, but even with their attention, Arric remained gravely ill and unable to have visitors, and she alone knew the Aldrish was to blame for that. With Arric still fighting for his life, the last thing she wanted to do was leave the keep now, but Rynar had been adamant. This was a festival to mark the end of the summer, and prepare for the long winter ahead.

"Doesn't the Prophet preach against the old traditions?" she taunted him.

"Aye, but this is Jiona. Everyone participates."

Now, she was racing behind him, each step making her dislike him a little more. "Come on, Rynar, you've got to slow down," she said after she jogged up to him again. "I can't keep up with you."

"Nay, we must hurry. I am expected to be there early so I can monitor the event." As he spoke, he slowed long enough to add, "you'll also want to be close enough to watch everything, I suspect." Then he increased his pace once again.

By the time they arrived at the torrapon, she was out of breath and her calves burned. All she wanted to do was collapse; instead they joined a line of people that was forming up to wind around the stone structure, forming a human spiral.

As they took their place, she watched as dozens and dozens of people queued up behind them, with the line growing longer by the minute. After the rush to get there, the line now crept along, as each person went individually to their place on the hillside. When they reached their final position on the incline overlooking the torrapon, Rynar noted how lucky they were to be aligned with one of the openings between the circle of stones, since their ultimate position was essentially random, depending on how the spiral fell. She was happy to take her seat on the grass.

They sat in silence for a while, watching hundreds of people spin around the torrapon and take their seats in ever-growing concentric circles. It was fascinating to watch people from the city mingling with those from the surrounding villages. Members of the Bhagali sat shoulder to shoulder with peasants, servants next to traders, all huddled together on the grass as if equals. In a land with such rigid hierarchy and separation of classes, it was peculiar to see such distinctions appear meaningless as they did today.

Meanwhile, inside the torrapon itself she could see glimpses of a few Sarnoc, with their white tunics and long braids, preparing for the impending ceremony. She thought she recognized Vaj, though she couldn't really be sure. In the center, seated quietly on the ground, was another Sarnoc, this one robed in folds of rust-colored cloth, with his head buried in a cowl and bowed deeply as if in contemplation.

If the Sarnoc were here, she wondered who was with Arric. Senvosra? Servants? She was increasingly worried that Rynar had dragged her out so she wouldn't know what was happening back at the keep.

"Arric's going to recover, isn't he?" she asked without any preamble.

Rynar nodded. "The Sarnoc have taken good care of him. My dear, can you please put him out of your mind, just for the afternoon?"

"Are all of the Sarnoc here?"

He shook his head. "Just a few. There are ceremonies elsewhere that also require their attention—and," he added, as if knowing her next question, "someone must keep an eye on the Dosedra."

That put her a little more at ease. "So what's going on in there?"

Rynar merely held up his hand. "Shh. The ceremony will begin soon." He added, a bit more gently, "watch, you will see."

At about that same moment, someone struck a drum sharply three times, and at that signal the crowd fell silent, all conversation ending abruptly and completely. Across the entire field there was only the sound of the breeze rustling in the trees, and distant birds, and the faint crash of the ocean surf. Initially everything within the torrapon was also still, and no one moved or made a sound inside. Then Sarnoc Vaj emerged. With his head bowed and his hands folded in front of him, he began to slowly walk in a circle around the structure.

Hundreds of people sitting cross-legged in the grass now bent forward, lowering their heads towards the ground and cupping their hands in front of them. Bewildered, she looked at Rynar, and mimicked what he was doing. Every minute or so she turned her head slightly to the side, glancing at him to see if he did something new. As she sat in this awkward posture, she considered whether it was intended to be a form of supplication, or if it was more symbolic of submission.

Soon the sound of jespar pipes echoed from behind them. A piper had performed at one of the long dinners she had attended with Rynar but they had left soon after the music started. He explained that he found the sound, which to her resembled bagpipes but in a lower register, unsettling.

Everyone began to hum in unison to the pipes, and the combined sound vibrated in her chest. She stole a glance at Rynar, wondering if he felt the same way out here that he did in the great hall, but he remained perfectly still, with his eyes closed. Others seemed to have fallen into similar states, though some had taken to rocking back and forth. With a slight upturning of her head she looked towards the torrapon, and noticed that four Sarnoc had located themselves at equidistant points beyond the stone walls. They too appeared to be humming, their heads hanging to their chests and their bodies slowly swinging back and forth, as if swaying in a light breeze.

With so much hostility towards the Sarnoc, it seemed odd that so many people were participating. Maybe it was like Christmas, where the religious meaning over time had been overshadowed by a general sense of tradition.

Without warning, the jespar pipes ceased their music, and everyone's humming likewise stopped.

There were two drumbeats.

All the people in the crowd sat up again, other than Kate, whose response was a step behind.

She felt a little light-headed, but as that sensation quickly wore off, she realized she was more alert, as if her senses were heightened by the ritual meditation. Or maybe it was that she could take deep breaths again, now that she wasn't bent over towards the ground.

From inside the torrapon, the Sarnoc began speaking in unison, a long and complex chant in the ancient language of the island. Not even a child cried out during the extended prayer, which she wondered if most of the people understood. From Rynar she had learned that some of the land's ancient customs had long ago been adopted by the Sardic conquerors, but even so, could the people today really comprehend the meaning behind such a lengthy and complicated invocation? She ached to ask Rynar about it, but his eyes were transfixed on the torrapon, and she did not dare make a sound.

The prayer ended, and there was a pause. Rynar leaned over. "The one in the dark robe is the caliaga, the lord of the festival," he described, in a whisper. "He represents the god Yoren, who rules over winter, and serves as witness to our prayers for a mild winter and early spring."

Kate watched as the Sarnoc returned inside the torrapon, and adorned their brown-robed colleague with a crown of tree boughs and golden autumn leaves. When this was complete, the four Sarnoc bowed to their caliaga, and then raised their arms to the sky with a shout.

There was another lengthy prayer, and this time the people within the crowd reached out to their neighbors, joining hands to make a single unbroken chain of bodies. Kate grasped the hand of a young girl with her left hand, and held Rynar's hand with her right. It was the first time they had had physical contact since the morning of the Council meeting that had ended with the discovery of Arric's poisoning, and she wished she wasn't obligated to touch him now. For someone else, it might not have mattered, but he was a healer and could influence her well-being with the quickest touch. There seemed to be no way around it, however, so she suffered the hand-holding, while remaining on her guard.

When the prayer was over, there were three drumbeats and more humming, but this time Kate thought she could feel the energy of the crowd flowing through them. It was as if they were tangled up in an immense skein of power wrapped around the hillside. Then there were two additional drumbeats, and everyone dropped their hands, and although there was no evidence of this, she sensed that the energy had flowed downhill to be caught within the torrapon by the Sarnoc.

"They are about to present the caliaga to the people," Rynar explained softly. "He will hear our prayers, bringing them all to Yoren so that the god might spare us a harsh winter." Just then, as if on cue, Sarnoc Vaj led the caliaga out from the stones and presented him to the crowd on the side of the torrapon opposite where they sat. She could hear the crowd roaring in a great cheer as the caliaga emerged, but then several shouts marred the general response, though the reason wasn't clear. Although the outer rings of people still shouted ritual greetings, there seemed to be confusion among those closest to the stones.

"That is not a proper response," he murmured, as if it was an academic matter.

The Sarnoc walked a quarter of the way around the torrapon, and again presented the caliaga. More cheers, these also tempered by shouts of something other than exaltation.

"I still can't see anything."

"Patience, Kate."

Finally it was their quadrant's turn to receive the caliaga. The Sarnoc made an announcement in the foreign tongue, and then the man in the robe stepped forth.

He was tall, with wavy dark hair crowned by a wreath of leaves and vines, and a face that was gaunt and pale under a scruffy beard.

It was Dosedra Arric.

Kate cupped her hand over her mouth. Her first response was elation, and she pressed her lips together to prevent from crying out to him. It was more than she could have hoped for. Not only had the

Sarnoc been able to reverse the poison—but here he was, outside, and under the Sarnoc's protection.

She turned to Rynar, whose attention was split between the activity at the torrapon and the Vosira, who sat with his soldiers at the top of the hill.

What would the Vosira do if he thought he had been double-crossed by the Sarnoc?

Mirroring her own agitation, the festival itself was no longer a se-rene occasion, as conversation and gossip erupted among the people, and a few even shouted support for the Hidden God. She had to admit, it made a twisted sort of sense. From their perspective, if the Sarnoc chose Arric as caliaga, wouldn't it mean the Sarnoc were traitors? Why would they have taken such a risk? She glanced around, sensing the crowd's growing restlessness. "What's going to happen?"

He turned around, and now was resting on the balls of his feet, ready to spring up at the first sign of trouble. "For what it's worth, the Dosedra's safe for now, but he'll be hunted after the ceremony has concluded. I'm sure Bedoric will offer a reward to whoever brings him back."

"You mean, you'll tell him to do so." She recognized the now-familiar pattern. "Oh, no, what am I thinking? You're probably trying to figure out how you can arrest him right now yourself."

"Nay, I will do my best to ensure that the ceremony is not under-mined. No matter what else he may be, and whether or not the Vosira determines he is guilty of treason, tonight he is caliaga, and that is sacred to all Sarducians. As such, he must be allowed to leave the torrapon safely, or the ceremony will fail, and the gods will punish the people. Afterwards, though… all I can say is, if you want your friend to survive, you'd better hope he can run."

Arric, meanwhile, had not allowed the crowd's consternation to disrupt his solemn duties as caliaga. In fact, as he calmly made the circuit around the torrapon, he didn't seem to notice anything was amiss at all. He continued to walk slowly until he finished, and then stepped back within the torrapon.

A few moments later, Arric reemerged, this time closely followed by two Sarnoc. Sarnoc Vaj carried thick folds of light green fabric, and another Sarnoc she hadn't met held a silver tray heaped with late-blooming flowers and a small basket.

Absently, Rynar mumbled an explanation, without his eyes leaving the torrapon. "This is when the riliaga is chosen."

Kate shielded her eyes to block the glare of the sun as she tried to see any activity within the torrapon. "What's that?"

He sat back on his heels, but kept his back straight, providing a better vantage point for himself. "The riliaga shall rule over the summer Laveli festival, and offers herself to the goddess Kerthal as a prayer for healthy crops and a plentiful harvest." He actually managed to smile slightly.

Meanwhile, Arric took slow, deliberate steps past each stone, facing the crowd in front of him. He kept his eyes low to the ground, never looking up as townspeople alternately cheered or shouted abusive comments.

It was as he faced the crowd that she noticed something odd about him. "Is he in some sort of trance—or drugged? He acts like he doesn't know what's going on."

"Aye, a bit of both. He probably has only a vague sense of where he is or what he's doing," Rynar whispered back. "At sunrise the Sarnoc administered herbs to focus his mind and remove all distractions. The humming would have put him under, with the prayer we offered designed to trigger certain thoughts for when he awoke." He flicked a small insect from his nose. "He has to walk the circle four more times, once to honor each of the gods. Then he will choose the riliaga."

Just as he had done the first time, Arric twice more passed without looking directly at them. She noticed that on his third pass he tipped his head up to scan the crowd. Even in the trance his attention seemed to be attracted to something, or someone, beyond them and to the left.

"Is that Bhara Merel?" she asked aloud as she turned to watch, though she needed no confirmation of her identity. The petite woman with thick curls was unmistakable, even in this crowd. Today she was quite stunning in a gown of autumn colors of crimson and gold, with her curls caught up at her neck with cords of scarlet. Given her bright adornment, she wondered if Merel had been given advance notice of the identity of the caliaga.

"Hmm? Oh, I believe it is. You may not know, but he courted her before he was sent away to Froida. I must give him credit, for Gevinsin is in good stead with the Vosira. Perhaps this is how he hopes to be spared. While his choice is supposed to reflect the will of the Goddess, it looks like he's hoping to save his skin."

Arric made his fourth pass, and again looked to Merel, who seemed to raise herself up slightly, crouching on her toes. He would choose her when next he appeared.

On his final circuit, Kate bit her lip and watched Arric approach. The intensity of the crowd's alternating excitement and restrained hostility took her breath away. With such a volatile situation, her concerns for his safety outpaced any joy she might have otherwise felt at seeing him alive and healthy.

With painstaking slowness, he began to step amid a mob of Sarducians, a patchwork of smiles and scowls, followed closely behind by the two Sarnoc, their feet following the same path through the crowd. Not a single person tried to hinder him. Maybe it was the intimidating power of the Sarnoc that held people at bay.

A dozen yards away, the three men passed by where Kate and Rynar sat, too far away for Arric to see her. She craned her neck to watch as he continued up the hill, searching, she supposed, for the most direct course towards Merel. Then he stopped, appearing confused. At that moment he reversed his route by taking a few steps backwards.

Of course, she realized, he must have lost track of his former fiancée in the crowd. Struck with an overwhelming need to look away, she instead turned her attention to the Sarnoc behind him, and remarkably, Vaj caught her gaze.

«You worry too much,» he said to her in the way only Sarnoc could communicate, with the words touching her mind. «We have everything under control. The Dosedra will be fine.»

So the Sarnoc had a plan? She relaxed, secretly pleased to have information Rynar did not know, and turned back to the torrapon to await the next stage of the ceremony.

Just then a hand fell to her shoulder. Startled, she turned to Rynar, but it wasn't him. When she looked up, Dosedra Arric held out his hand.

To her?

"*Y sav talieven na riliaga.*"

She hesitated, and looked to Rynar. What was going on? Where had he come from?

The Aldrish paled significantly, as if he had suddenly taken ill. Although it appeared he wished to lodge a protest, the sea of people around him must have made him think twice about it. Instead, he explained through clenched teeth, "the Dosedra has chosen you as riliaga." His voice wavered. "You must follow him. It is Goddess Kerthal's wish." His speech was bitter, and she knew inside he was seething, but he did not let anyone see it.

She stared up at Arric, whose eyes seemed unfocused, the gaze of a stranger.

"Go with him, Kate," Rynar directed her, and nudged her shoulder. "You have no choice. Everyone is watching."

As if she was a puppet, Kate took his hand, allowing him to pull her to her feet. Feeling dizzy from the intensity of the ritual that had just completed, she stumbled as they stepped past the people in the makeshift aisle. Although she recognized the solemnity of the ritual, she could not hold back a smile. He was here, alive and well. For just that moment, she wanted to be happy, and forget the danger he faced.

When the pair reached the clearing in front of the stones, a startled Sarnoc unfolded the green cloth he carried, a robe exactly like Arric's other than the color. Allowing the wind to capture the thin fabric in his hands, it fluttered dramatically over Kate's head like a banner, and the crowd cheered. Then he pulled it down over her shoulders. Turning her to face the crowd, Sarnoc Vaj crowned her with flowers and handed her the small basket, which was filled with seeds.

Then the Sarnoc led the pair inside the torrapon.

Once inside the stone pavilion, none of the Sarnoc spoke at first, though Vaj stared at them with a solemn expression. Then he held out a glysar goblet and indicated with a nod that both Arric and Kate were to sip from it.

She noticed that the liquid had little flavor, though it numbed her tongue. It also cleared the fog in her head almost immediately, and she saw it had a similar effect on Arric, whose vision refocused as he shook his head.

"Kate?" he asked, surprised as he stared at her, as if he had been unaware of everything he had done up to this point. "I chose *you?*" He seemed sincerely dumbfounded and, to her ear, maybe a bit disappointed.

How could he not have known? "Hi," she murmured with a nervous smile. "Yeah, I guess so."

He nodded slowly, as if trying to remember. "Aye, so I did. I didn't expect that." He took her hand and held it high. In a low voice he explained as he led her between the stones, "we must walk around four times before we can leave." As they stepped forth, he added, "is it me, or do the people seem reluctant to cheer us?"

They completed three of the four circles around the torrapon in silence. Then she whispered to him, "what happens when we finish this?"

Arric mumbled, "Sarnoc Vaj will give us his blessings for the rest of the ceremony, and then..."

"And then what?"

"Ah—well, it would be best if he explains the rest to you."

At the end of their four circuits, the pair returned inside the torrapon. The ceremony now complete, the four Sarnoc converged upon them. Those who were not acquainted with Kate began to offer their congratulations when Vaj cut them off.

"Dosedra Arric, I must point out that Bhara Kate was not the best choice. You were told to choose someone who you could complete the ceremony with, and given—"

Arric shook his head. Adamantly he stated, "I had nothing to do with choosing her."

"Come, Dosedra, we all know..."

He again shook his head. "Sarnoc Vaj, when I was a boy, I was taught that Goddess Kerthal tells the caliaga who shall be the riliaga. The riliaga must please Kerthal, aye?" He raised an eyebrow towards the Sarnoc. "Or are you questioning your own teachings?"

"Sofinar taught you that?" one of the Sarnoc said, smiling despite himself. He had a ruddy complexion and light brown hair so fine that wisps flew free of his braid. "That was all meant symbolically, of course," he explained. "We all know that the caliaga picks his sweetheart."

"Aye, Sarnoc Hissil, that may be. However, while I do care about her well-being, I do not consider Kate my 'sweetheart'." His voice had an edge to it that she hadn't heard before. "Plus, with everything at stake, I certainly would not have wished to anger the Aldrish." He wrinkled his forehead as if willing himself to remember what had happened, and then turned to her. "Truly, I mean no offense. I had intended to choose Bhara Merel, who would have been much safer for me—for both of us," he amended. "But when I tried, I found that I could not do it."

This Sarnoc looked at Kate. "What are your feelings on this matter? Will serving as riliaga jeopardize your relationship with the Aldrish?"

Did everyone really think there was something going on between her and Rynar? It took a great deal of self-control not to laugh at that suggestion. All five men were staring at her, and she could not for a second forget that there were hundreds of people sitting yards from where they now stood, one of whom was Rynar himself, not to mention the Vosira and at least a dozen Senvosra. She opened her mouth to speak, wanting to disabuse them all of the notion that she and the Aldrish were an item, that in fact she had grown to despise him, but she stumbled for words. "Honestly, I'm not sure what to think. It's a lot to take in, you know?" She swallowed, and tried to get a glimpse of the crowd. Where was Rynar? He might even now be rousing the Senvosra.

Before she could elaborate on her comment, the fourth Sarnoc stepped closer. "Bhara, you must tell us truthfully what your feelings are in this matter," he said, his manner quite direct. This Sarnoc had a shorter braid than the others, and seemed younger, perhaps only as old as she was. The discussion had made him impatient, and he asked briskly, "are you willing to serve as riliaga?"

She wavered, and turned back to Arric. He still looked puzzled, but he lifted his eyes to her, and reached for her hand. "Kate, if you'll agree to come with me now, you shall do Sarducia—and me—a great favor."

In that moment she knew she couldn't let him down, regardless of the danger they might face.

"Let's do it," she agreed. As the answer flowed off her lips, she smiled, to prove her own bravery. "So what happens next?"

Vaj cleared his throat. He had been watching them both carefully. "Yvan," he said to the Sarnoc who had asked the question, "the Dosedra followed the Goddess' bidding out there, and it must not be questioned by us, or by anyone. Indeed, it may work to our advantage. Bhara Kate, it seems best that you travel to Altopon with the Dosedra after you have completed the ceremony."

"Altopon?" Were the Sarnoc going to offer Arric sanctuary, then?

Arric nodded. "Aye, that is a good idea, Sarnoc. Kate, are you willing?"

Before she could respond, Sarnoc Hissil interrupted them. "Dosedra, the people are growing restless. We must complete Jiona. Do you know the rest of the ceremony?"

"I do. Though I had hoped you could explain—"

Hissil cut him off in mid-sentence. "Then you should continue with all haste, before someone in the crowd does something foolish."

With no further delay, Sarnoc Vaj raised his arms. "Gods' blessings to the caliaga and riliaga!" he shouted, loud enough for the entire crowd to hear. This raised a cheer, weaker than one would expect from so many people, but heartening all the same.

«Good luck, Kate.» Vaj offered in mind-speak. «Our prayers are with you both. We will meet again soon.»

Arric took her left hand, as her right still held the basket the Sarnoc had given her. "Take care that you do not lose that," he cautioned her. With that, he took his first steps towards the crowd.

As they emerged from between the stones, everyone stood, and the concentric circles of men and women split along the path he chose. She held her breath as they passed dozens of Sarducians, many with disagreeable expressions, and she struggled to maintain her poise. Staring out into the crowd, she sought out Rynar, but could not find him.

"If the people respect tradition, no one will dare touch us until the moon rises tonight," he said as they cleared the last of the people and walked across the field towards a line of trees. "By then, we should be far from Loraden."

"And if they don't?"

He didn't look at her as he replied. "Let's not think about that right now."

CHAPTER 47

Within the sheltering arms of the Arsdala forest, their progress was regularly hampered by thorns and branches that raked their skin and snagged on their clothing.

It was difficult for Kate to maneuver with the robe over her dress and the silly basket in her hand, but when she asked, Arric was adamant that she keep both. The wreath of flowers she wore on her head, however, quickly caught on a branch and tumbled from her hair, and she did not go back to get it. Both snuck regular glances over their shoulders, in case they were followed, but there was neither sound nor sight of pursuit.

Eventually, after a good half-hour of crashing through the thick brush, Arric felt safe enough to stop in a small clearing. He fell against a tree trunk, breathing hard, and listened carefully for sounds of pursuit. Then he bent over, his hands on his thighs, trying to draw a full breath. "That was quite a race," he said. "I apologize for what I put you through, but we could not chance discovery too near the edge of the forest." He panted for a moment, and then pulled at the crown of leaves and branches, which had become tangled in his hair. "Nor did I wish to indicate that I was not taking the ceremony seriously by removing these too soon."

Kate was also tired from the struggle through the thicket, but even hampered as she had been by her dress, she realized she was not as winded as he was. Without a word she reached up and helped unwind his hair from the wreath. Then Arric shed the rust-colored robe, exposing a simple shirt and trousers that he had chosen as the best for flight from the city. He tossed both the robe and the wreath to the ground and kicked a pile of newly-fallen leaves over them.

Watching Arric remove his ceremonial garb, she did the same. "I can't believe you're here." She was nervous, as if she was unsure how to speak to him. It was difficult to accept the fact that, after everything that had happened, he was now right in front of her. She found herself unintentionally staring at him, astonished at how much a thick beard and the loss of at least fifteen pounds had changed his appearance. He also seemed pale, as if his skin had faded from amber to honey.

"Aye, to be honest, I'm a little surprised myself. I never thought I would leave that wretched tower alive. You didn't worry too much on my account, I hope?"

There was so much to tell him, but this wasn't the time or place. She shrugged, and replied, "I'm just glad to see you again. I wasn't really sure what would happen."

He wiped his forehead with his sleeve. "I'm also very happy to see you," he replied, sounding equally awkward. "You seem well?" He gazed down at her hand. "Your injuries were healed?"

"Yeah, I'm fine." She waved her hand to demonstrate it, though she didn't *feel* fine. He likely would know little of what had happened in the days since his arrest, but her memories remained in the forefront of her mind. She didn't feel like the same woman who had traveled through the Muras swamp with him. "How are you? When I saw you laying there in the tower I thought—I mean, I didn't know what to think. I was afraid you were dead."

He had been leaning against a tree, and now he flexed a thin branch between his fingers. "Aye, well, I've been better," he replied, a sarcastic, half-hearted chuckle in his voice. "At least the adoli has mostly left my system, though to be honest I would not wish that on my worst enemy."

"I can imagine." She inspected their surroundings, wondering if it was safe to linger here so casually and chat. The clearing was tiny and unremarkable, a small space walled in with tall oaks, brush and vines.

They had no vantage point beyond the trees, and could be attacked from any direction. "Will we be able to find Fantion now?"

"Fantion?" he looked at her quizzically. "Why would we do that?"

"I just assumed—I mean, we're in Lockleaf, without any weapons or supplies. I figured the best thing to do would be to go to his camp."

"Ah, well, it would be nice to see him, but that's not possible." He shook his head and bent down to tuck his trousers into his boots. "We'll be followed, and I cannot risk leading Senvosra to them. We'll make it, aye, you and me?" he asked with an encouraging smile, though it sounded as if he himself was unconvinced.

"We can try." When she first saw him in the torrapon, she was so happy to see him alive, but now, her relief was tempered by their current situation. She was troubled both by the danger they faced and the fact that she had become a key participant in an important ceremony she knew nothing about. "You shouldn't have chosen me back there, you know. I'm not Sarducian. How can I be the queen of the summer, or whatever?" Even as she said that, she realized it would be a long time until summer came around again. "I'm not even sure I'll still be here by then."

"Really?" he asked. He had been smiling, but the expression promptly faded, and his eyes were wide with surprise. "You were planning on leaving?"

She scrambled to explain. "Well, I mean, I don't know. I might be, but—" She always suspected her tenure in Sarducia wasn't up to her to decide, although, with the ceremony, maybe she had been given an extension. However, she couldn't explain any of this this to Arric, since he knew nothing of how she had come to be in this land in the first place. "I meant, this isn't my home, you know? I might end up leaving at any time."

"Maybe the Goddess knows something we don't," he replied with a chuckle. "I mean, it's not likely she'd make a mistake like that."

She rolled her eyes. "So choosing me really wasn't part of your plan?"

He seemed confused by her words. "Nay, I had no plan other than to leave the city, nor did the Sarnoc suggest anything of the sort. Their concern over my choice was genuine, as far as I know." He rubbed at a pair of fresh scratches on his palm. "To be honest, even I knew nothing of being named caliaga until this morning. The Sarnoc said it was my only way out of Loraden, so despite my reservations over using the ceremony for personal gain, I agreed. After they told me, they immediately had me drink several potions, so I was scarcely myself. I certainly had no chance to consider the implications or make a more detailed plan for how to proceed." He leaned back his head and took a deep breath. "After all you've done, I'm very sorry that I involved you, and put you in danger again. Truly, I had no idea what had happened until after it was done."

It seemed so ludicrous, but she knew he wouldn't lie about something like this. "Don't worry about it. We'll make it work." She smiled bravely. Then she took the opportunity to observe him more closely. "You don't look fully recovered, though. Are you sure you can go through with this?"

"Aye, there's no going back." He gave her a concerned look. "Still, if you must know, I worry more about you."

His words surprised her. "What do you mean? Surely you know by now that I'm willing to help you, and if you can make it, so can I."

"Aye, from all you've done so far, that's true enough." He curled up one side of his mouth. "It's just that—well, the ceremony has a few specific requirements, and I never—" He kicked at a rock under his heel. "I know you won't believe me, but I'll swear on the name of the Goddess Kerthal herself that I did not plan to choose you."

"Well, thanks a lot."

"Nay, you misunderstand me. I meant no insult. When I was out there, I had intended something else—"

"You were going to choose Merel."

"Aye—but suddenly I felt compelled to turn around, and the next thing I knew, I chose you. It was as if there was no one else in the crowd. It must have been the Goddess guiding me—what else could it have been? Like I said, Kerthal is not known for her mistakes." Again he smiled, though it was a troubled grin. "It's funny how the Sarnoc didn't believe it either."

"Yeah, so there's that. Why did they make such an issue about it? Why was it such a big deal who you chose?"

He scratched at his beard. "Ah, well. I'm sure that's because of the final step of the ceremony. Even though the Sarnoc do not expect me to be able to complete it, I think they had hoped for at least a public pretense to the contrary."

"What does that mean?"

Again he toed at a rock stuck in the ground, making a point not to look at her. "There are four torrapons that host identical ceremonies. Afterwards, all the couples go out into the woods, or onto the beach or into the hills, depending where they are."

"And?" She stared down at the basket of seeds, suddenly apprehensive. "What are we expected to do?"

He tipped his head back, gazing into the tops of the trees above. "The idea is that one child must be conceived as a result of Jiona."

For a moment there was silence. Her jaw had fallen open, but nothing else on her body moved, save an involuntary twitch of her right eye. It took her a moment to summon up the courage to ask for clarification. "What do you mean? You're trying to say that we're supposed to..." As her face flushed, all she could do was laugh. She suddenly understood at least one reason why Rynar seemed so aggrieved when she had been chosen. "That's ridiculous!"

He popped his head up and looked at her with surprise. "Aye, well." He grinned. "I thought you might be angry, after that time in Bhoren."

"Hey, at least you thought of my feelings this time," she said, still shaking her head at the absurdity of this news. "So what happens if we don't complete the ceremony?"

Arric shrugged, and crumpled a leaf in his hand. "Given what we have ahead of us today, I don't think it will be an issue, and I'm sure the Sarnoc understand that. To be honest, I had no intention of pushing you into completing the ceremony."

"I appreciate that."

"Aye." He nodded once, as if to suggest a pact had been sealed. His forehead was thick with sweat, and he wiped it with his sleeve. "We will continue on to Altopon after we have rested, and that's that."

She turned her head from side to side, as if a road or landmark might manifest itself, even though she was firmly lost in the grasp of the forest, and couldn't have even pointed out the direction of Loraden now. 'Lockleaf,' indeed. "How far is it from here, anyway?"

He gazed up at the sun. "It is nearly directly east of here, maybe five days' journey on the roads? Most people take the Amberia River, which is much faster. To be honest, I've never made the journey on foot, nor know anyone who has, and certainly no one who was trying to avoid being captured by Senvosra."

"Five days?" She considered what he had said, and shook her head. "You know Arric, this is crazy. You're the Dosedra, and you're outlawed, with your brother surely after you. You've been held prisoner for weeks, and poisoned, and are obviously still weak as hell. Yet we're expected to walk all the way to Altopon without any supplies or weapons? Did Sarnoc Vaj really think you'd make it?"

"I don't know," he admitted. "He warned me that it wouldn't be easy, but I agreed to try. It's my only chance. Though I'd likely have agreed to anything—the adoli was making me crazy. I still feel it now, a bit, and it's been what, four or five days now?"

"Actually, it was nine."

"Really? I guess I was in and out of consciousness for longer than I thought." He sighed, and pushed his hair from his eyes. "As for supplies, I could not carry anything from the torrapon, or people would have argued I was improperly chosen. After all, the couples do not have need of such things on the night of Jiona." He tried to smile. "We do have one advantage. This way there are no horses or campfires to give us away. I've already decided that we should not follow the roads, and as Bedoric will discover, it will be difficult to track us through the Arsdala. The Sarnoc said they would have provisions hidden in a few different locations, so if we can reach one of those points, that will help." He examined her expression, one of distrust and vexation. "Aye, Kate, it's going to be hard, but I think we have a chance."

She nodded, reminded that in many respects things could have been much worse. At least he was alive, and they were both free from imprisonment—and in the end, those things were paramount. She leaned against a tree to stretch the muscles in her exhausted legs. "We'll do the best we can."

"Aye. We should probably get moving." He pointed to his left. "The Amberia is that way, to the south. Bedoric likely expects us to head that way so we can hire a riversmith. He surprised me once; I do not intend for it to happen a second time. We continue east on foot."

CHAPTER 48

The sun had been at its highest point when the festival began; now, evening was descending fast upon them, with sunset likely no more than a couple of hours away.

"Will he send dogs after us?" she asked, after trudging along for a few miles in silence. Her feet were sore and she had been suffering a stitch in her side for a while, but most of all she wished she had some water to drink.

"Dogs?" Arric asked, surprised. He seemed worn out, and she wondered how much further he could go.

"To track our scent."

"Ah. You mean, will my brother hunt us?" He wiped his forehead on the back of his sleeve. "Nay, I expect not, at least not on the night of Jiona. Certainly he will send soldiers along the roads, to mark our route, and some may slip into the forest. He will deny that they are after us, of course. Likely there's some fhaoli camp or something needing to be monitored, or so he will tell anyone who asks." They came upon a fallen limb, and Arric held out his hand to help her climb over it.

"But one way or another he'll try to capture us?" She hiked up her skirt and stepped over the obstacle.

There was no hesitation. "He will. I cannot see him allowing me to gain sanctuary with the Sarnoc."

"And if he does? He's not likely to just lock you back in the tower, not after what happened today."

"True. He will be extremely angry that I escaped, particularly because the Sarnoc helped me. If we are caught, it will likely be bad for us both. I do not intend for him to find us, though. I just wish I..." he stopped, and dropped to his knees. Quickly he yanked the hem of her skirt, and she toppled beside him. To her unasked question, he replied, with a word that was barely more than a breath on the wind, "horses."

"Where?" she mouthed.

Arric pointed to a grove of trees behind them. "They may not know we're here, but be ready to run."

The possibility that they would be captured brought new clarity to fears that had been growing throughout the afternoon. The danger facing them now was no abstract concept. She had seen the dungeons, and she knew what Senvosra had done to Nyvas. She had even faced the possibility of being burned alive as a traitor. Most of all, she remembered Tashin threatening her with torture that day when she went to rescue Rynar. They could not be arrested now.

Arric must have seen the terror in her eyes. As softly as he could, he tried to sound optimistic as he encouraged her. "We can outrun them—the trees are too thick for horses to maneuver. There's a branch of the Amberia just ahead, and that's where I hope to find shelter."

There was no time to discuss plans further. Shouts behind them indicated that the soldiers had spotted them, and Arric leapt up and bolted through the trees, hauling her to her feet so she could scramble behind. Fortunately, since they were heading into a river valley, the run was downhill.

"We can make it—come!" Arric jumped into a dry creek bed, scattering rocks as his boots slipped in the gravel, and she nearly fell from the loose footing. Despite the uneven surface, neither one slowed down.

Soon the narrow confines of the forest burst open as a wide canyon stretched out in front of them. It had not rained often the past few weeks, and the level of the river was low enough that the riverbed was partly exposed. In rainy weather, when the river would swell, Kate could imagine the entire channel becoming dangerous rapids. Now, however, the river weaved past slabs of gray stone jutting up from the riverbed like giant fossilized teeth. As it was now, it was impassible for any water traffic, but part of the riverbed was dry and could be followed on foot.

Arric went first, and scampered over the rocks, forced to literally climb around the tilted boulders in order to make his way downstream. She tried to follow, jumping from one slab to the next, careful to avoid slick wet stones and swirling pools of water. They had to pick their routes carefully, skirting around the largest rocks when possible, sliding down them when it wasn't. Their progress was slow and maddening, for it was like climbing steps of irregular height and width. Since he was ahead of her, she relied on his judgment to find the easiest route through the obstacles. More than once they passed snakes sunning themselves besides deep pools of stagnant water, and on the assumption they could be venomous, they gave them wide berth.

They were able to go perhaps a half-mile downstream, but then there was nowhere further they could go. The river flowed into a single stream at the edge of a cliff, the water cascading over the edge into a deep pool below. Making matters worse, they couldn't leave the riverbed, as the banks were now steep walls of sand and mud, meaning they were trapped.

Approaching the edge of the waterfall, they carefully stood to one side where the rocks were still dry and stared at the churning white foam at the base of the falls. "Can you swim?" Arric shouted over the roar of the water.

"Yeah but—you've got to be crazy!" She looked over the edge into the pool below. "There's no way we can jump—we'd kill ourselves on the rocks!"

He looked behind them, and nodded to one side. "They're close. It's the Senvosra or the river. Personally, right now I'd prefer to take my chances with the river. The pool at the bottom looks deep enough that we might make it." Again he looked over his shoulder. "They'll be here any moment, Kate. I can hear the horses behind us, on the banks. And the cave I want to reach is just ahead. Once we find it, we'll be safe. Come on—we have no choice."

She wasn't afraid of heights, or the river, for that matter. She had always been a strong swimmer. Faced with a waterfall like this, however, all bets were off. It was a long way down, and there was no way to know what would greet them under the water's surface. There was a good chance they'd break their necks—literally. "I can't!" She tried pleading with him. "There's got to be another way!"

He again glanced over his shoulder. "Nay, it's our only chance." He didn't seem any happier about this idea than she was, but she knew he was driven by the knowledge of his fate if he were to be captured again. "I have no choice but to jump, but surely the Aldrish will protect you if you go back."

Kate stared at the crash of foam below.

Until now it hadn't occurred to her that she did have options. She could choose to follow him, or she could choose to end her journey now. Why was she risking her life? He was free, and that was more than she had hoped for. Her continued presence would likely only slow him down.

While she didn't share Arric's confidence in Rynar's response, so far he had protected her, and he might do so again. It offered better odds than jumping over a waterfall, at any rate. Stepping back from the edge, she waved him on. "I'm sorry, Arric, but I just can't do it."

He nodded sharply, and looked away, obviously disappointed. Then he turned back and said, "You're certain?"

Before either could say another word, an arrow flew past them, and clattered against the rocks on the opposite bank. It was their only warning of the troops that even now emerged from the trees and ran towards them—as well as the realization that, Jiona or not, the soldiers planned to capture the fugitives. Over the roar of the waterfall, neither Arric nor she had heard their approach.

"Sweet goddess, they've found us!" He stepped closer to the edge, as if about to jump, but looked back at her. "Come with me," he implored, and took her hand.

The next thing she knew she was falling.

At the last moment, she had agreed, and now her feet pointed for the white foam below. She had just enough time to grab hold of her nose before crashing under the water's churning surface. She sank deeply, and her feet touched bottom, but it was a clean fall, and then the current whisked her away. The river dragged her under water for quite a distance, and she lost all sense of direction. When she sensed she couldn't last much longer, she surfaced, gasping desperately for air. Yet there was no reprieve. Even as she tried to catch a couple of breaths, rapids whipped her around curves like a demonic waterslide.

What was that sound? In a heartbreaking moment, as she raised her head, she heard a second waterfall. She started kicking as hard as she could, trying to swim for the bank, but there wasn't enough time to reach shore, nor did she have enough strength to fight the current.

There was just enough time to panic. Unable to save herself, she tumbled over the second waterfall.

For an eternity water pounded her from every direction as she sank to the bottom of the pool. There was no air, no chance to get a breath. She prayed to any gods who might be listening as she clawed at the water, feeling the terror that came on the verge of drowning. Her feet hit a large rock, and she kicked off from it, hoping the effort would be enough to propel her to the surface. At her lungs' threshold, when she knew she could not go another moment without air, her eyes found the sun, and she popped up from the surface, gulping and gasping at the air, trying to bring oxygen into her desperate lungs.

Sputtering, she was able to catch her breath; this pool was deeper than the first, and wider, and there wasn't much of a current. Slowly, she paddled slowly to the edge of the pool. Grappling at the rocks at the water's edge, she coughed and tried to breathe. Then she pulled herself halfway out of the water, collapsing in the gravel, unable to move further, and scarcely able to remain conscious.

One thing she noted before she passed out. There was no sign of Arric.

CHAPTER 49

"**K**ate!"

Lifting her head painfully, she spied Arric kneeling behind a rock in the side of the cliff. Unable to move, she dropped her head again.

He jogged down to her side, scattering gravel under his boots. Before she could argue, he was already helping her to stand, and then with his arm wrapped around her, he helped support her weight as he led her from the narrow gravel beach to a crevice in the rocks above the water.

She bent over to get past a low overhang, but once she had cleared the edge of the rock she entered a cavern with a ceiling high enough to stand up. A little sunlight sliced past the rocks at one side of the cave, but her eyes still needed to adjust to the dimmer light. Soaking wet, she was at least grateful that it was warmer here than outside.

Exhausted, they sat beside each other for a short time, resting and catching their breath. As she struggled to get her wits about her, she noticed that her gown, which was heavy with water, was frayed but intact, though it was twisted all wrong on her torso. Her hair was matted against her face, and she pushed it out of her eyes. As for Arric, his dark hair was peppered with sand, and his shirt and trousers were both torn in several places. On his left arm, where the fabric had ripped wide open, there was a trickle of blood.

Their silence was broken when she pointed to the blood on his arm. "You're hurt."

He waved his hand over his injuries, dismissing them. "It's nothing. I've been injured worse than this a hundred times or more. But you—" he said, pointing to her chin. "That doesn't look good."

As he called attention to it, she felt a new throbbing along her jaw, and probed it with her fingers. The chill of the river must have numbed it temporarily. "Oh I think you're right." She pulled her hand away and it was covered with blood. "I didn't even feel it happen. Is it deep?"

He directed her to turn towards the sunlight, so he could better see her face. He held his sleeve to her chin to soak up the blood, but even with his light touch she winced. "Nay, I think it looks worse than it is," he said, though she wondered if he was just saying that so she wouldn't be frightened further. "Still, we need to stop the bleeding."

He clumsily attempted to put pressure on it with his sleeve, but then she held up her skirt. "Let me just use this instead." Arric released his grip and helped her press a handful of fabric to her chin. It was starting to hurt, but she tried to push the pain to the back of her mind. A cut on her chin seemed the least of her worries right now. "Is this the cave you were looking for?" she asked, keeping her voice low.

"Aye, it is. Because of the cliffs on either side, no one can reach the cave from above—the river is the only way. It's possible someone will see the cave across the river it as they search for us, but it will be all but impossible for them to get here unless they come the way we did, or travel quite far downstream. Nay, with nightfall so close, I'm confident we'll be safe."

"So what do we do now?"

"We rest, and pray that our luck holds."

She didn't figure they had great odds, but she was so tired from the race through the forest and their river escapade that she wasn't going to argue. Instead, she visually inspected the cave from where she sat. It wasn't a large space, but there was more than enough room for both of them to sleep. "Does that go anywhere?" She pointed to a dark gap behind them. It was wide enough for a person to climb into, though she wasn't about to find out what lay beyond it.

"It opens into a larger cave, carved out by an underground river." He turned his head towards the opening and looked inside. "Tomorrow we shall follow that river, and eventually it should take us close to Altopon. It should also confuse the Senvosra."

She locked her eyes on the tunnel opening. "Wait—you're joking, right? We're not really going in there, are we?"

"Aye. It doesn't appeal to me much either, but it really is the safest route. To leave here the way we came would be to march right into the hands of the soldiers." He glanced into the dark tunnel again and grimaced. "Trust me, the Sarnoc offered me nothing better to avoid pursuit." Crouching low, Arric crawled forward and peered around the edge of the rock that concealed their current hiding spot, and once he was satisfied that no one approached, he moved back to Kate, whose chin was now cradled in an armful of cloth. "Is it very painful?"

She shook her head lightly, downplaying the discomfort. "Not too much."

"That is good to hear. It will be a few days before a healer can attend to it."

His mention of healers brought her mind back to Rynar. She could picture clearly how his cheeks had flushed with anger when Arric chose her as riliaga. There wasn't any doubt in her mind that he was out there even now searching for her. "I'm sure I'll be okay." She shifted her weight a little and propped her elbow against a rock ledge.

Meanwhile, he leaned against the wall opposite her and pulled off a waterlogged boot. He poured out its contents, a slurry of sand and dirt, and dropped it onto the dusty floor of the cave, its thud punctuated by a spray of mud. The other boot fell with similar results, followed by the slap of wet woolen socks. As he wiggled his wrinkled toes to dry them, she decided to do the same. Longing to remove her cold and itchy stockings underneath her dress, she pulled one of her feet onto her lap. She dropped the skirt from her chin and started to unlace her slipper, finding it difficult to force loose the water-swollen leather laces.

"Let me do that," he offered, and knelt before her. Nimble fingers untied the laces and quickly removed her shoes. When she started to pull off her hose, he retreated to the other side of the cave and averted his eyes to give her privacy. "The Sarnoc told me you saved Nyvas's life," he said, making conversation as he stared in the direction of the river.

"Yeah, that was quite a day." She untied the garters above her knees and slipped the soggy wool from her legs with a contented sigh. "You know, it wasn't all my doing."

"Not as they told the story. Others were involved, to be sure, but you took all the risks. I'm terribly impressed, and grateful, of course, that you were willing to do all that for someone you barely know. I hear you confronted my brother, and you even bargained with Fantion for the Aldrish's life, neither of which could have been easy to do. Indeed, it was quite a brave thing you did all around."

"You can turn back around now." She wasn't sure what else to say. It was difficult to think about all of that now.

He didn't seem to notice her reticence, and instead crawled to sit beside her again. "Is it still bleeding?" he asked about her chin, leaning close.

She could feel his breath on her cheek, and his proximity unnerved her. "I can't tell." She dropped her hand.

Arric whistled as he saw the bright stains on her skirt. "It may be worse than I thought. May I?" he asked, and pulled a clean portion of fabric from her lap. She held her head steady as he probed the wound lightly. "The worst has past," he decided, although he sought out another clean fold of her dress. Once he had taken over applying the pressure, he came back around to his previous topic. "The Sarnoc also told me that you spent your nights in the Aldrish's chambers."

Defensively, she explained, "It was a bargain he struck with the Vosira to keep me out of the dungeon. I had to either be with him or the Senvosra, so I chose him."

"So I heard." Bitterly, he added, "I should have known the Aldrish would suggest something like that."

She wasn't sure if he was being serious or sarcastic. Nudging his hand from her face so she could apply the pressure again, she tipped her head to look at him. "Really, it's not what you think. He treated me well, in his own way, and kept me out of danger."

"Of course he did." Released from assisting with her injury, he leaned back against the wall. "That was the whole point, I'm sure," he added, his comment loaded with sarcasm.

Why was he making such a big deal out of it? "Honestly, it wasn't like that. I think he was just trying to help me."

"Help you? Hmmm... I can imagine what 'help' he offered you." He made a few quick nods of his head.

"Can we change the subject?" Even thinking about Rynar made her nervous. Finding eye contact difficult, she pretended to be fascinated with the interior of their hiding place, and with her free hand, scattered a few pebbles across the ground. "It's a good thing you found this cave."

"Aye. Sarnoc Vaj suggested it to me." His response was more genial than a moment before. "It's ironic that we're here, because this one of the escape routes the Mosumi used in the time of the Sard conquests, when the Sarnoc's ancestors tried to avoid persecution from my own." His words were solemn. "In fact, I may be the first Sard to know of the cave's existence. Kerthal has done us a great favor by concealing us here."

The name of the goddess reminded her of the circumstances that brought them there in the first place. Aware that the light was fading, she asked, "how long do you think we have until it gets dark?"

He looked to the opening of the cave again. "Sunset is nearly upon us, and tonight the moon will be a late riser..." He let the words hang there suspended, without forming a complete thought. To finish his comment would be to revisit the point of the festival, and remind them that they would not be completing it. Shamed into silence, he shrugged the linen shirt from his back and began to wring out the water from his sleeves.

It occurred to her that she had not seen him without his shirt before. He had a good physique, but it was marred by a number of pale scars, some rather broad, that chipped away at the curves of his arms and chest. The dark whorls of hair at his breastbone were unable to hide one particularly wide, jagged scar across his torso that in the twilight gave his body the appearance of cracked pottery, inexpertly repaired. He had lived a very different life from hers, a life so different that it was almost impossible to imagine.

Unaware of her scrutiny, he worked to twist the fabric of his shirt as hard as he could, forcing out thin streams of water onto the stone floor. Then, without saying anything, he threw the shirt against the wall.

The sudden movement startled Kate. "What's wrong?"

He fell back against the stones, leaning his head against the back wall and staring at the ceiling of the cave. "This is not right. Tonight is the night when Jorell's and Kerthal's combined power reaches its peak before fading at dawn, to be relinquished to Yoren and Cira. These are our gods, you understand? This is the night of Kerthal's greatest power." Without waiting for a response, he continued, "for eight years I have missed this night, wishing I could be home in Loraden, honoring the gods and enjoying the festivities with friends. Now that I've returned, everything is different, and instead of celebrating it properly, I'm hiding in a cave, avoiding arrest by my own brother's troops."

"That's not what makes you angry, though, is it?"

"Nay, it is not." He crossed his arms, and a frown grew on his face. "All I wanted to do—all I've ever wanted to do—was honor my gods and do good by my people, but at my first opportunity I used my people's most sacred traditions for my own benefit. I was not chosen as caliaga because I was the most worthy, it was because I was the most needy." He balled up his hand into a fist and punched his thigh. "It bothers me greatly to think that the Sarnoc used such a special, holy ritual to help me escape. After all I've done, they should have just let me die." He let his head fall hard against the stone wall of the cave behind him. "Worst of all, Bhara," he said, using the formal title even as he tipped his head back to her, "is that you must be here, to suffer needlessly on my account, when you could have been safe in Loraden enjoying the celebration yourself. It will be such a beautiful night, with the entire city participating, and you're here with me instead." He shook his head, and then stood up and grabbed his shirt. He twisted the linen once more, wringing it so tightly that the threads threatened to snap between his fists.

"It's fine, Dosedra," she replied in kind. "I agreed to come with you, so don't worry on my account." Watching him, it occurred to her that wringing out the water in her dress would be a very good idea. No longer concerned with modesty, she untied the lacing in front and then pulled her dress over her head, remaining in her damp, long-sleeved linen shift. With all of the wet woolen fabric, the gown was quite heavy, and she immediately felt better without its sodden weight against her skin. As tightly as she could, she twisted a handful of the skirt fabric to squeeze it dry, making a face as the wool burned her skin.

"Here, let me have that," Arric mumbled as he reached out for her dress. While she had struggled with the extensive yardage, he had already slipped his shirt back on, and had wrung out his socks, which now dangled on a root nearby beside her stockings, which he had also hung up for her.

"No, I can manage..." she tried to argue, but then she saw his expression, a twist of pain camouflaged by rigid determination, and she allowed her gown to slip from her grasp. Then other words tumbled from her lips. "I missed you, you know."

"Hmm?" He began to wring out her dress, throwing the bulk of it over his lap so it would not drag the ground as he twisted handfuls of water from the wool. Even this mundane task received his full effort.

"When they locked you in the tower. It wasn't the same without you." She folded her arms at her waist and rubbed them, trying to warm herself. "I tried to visit, but no matter how many times I asked, Rynar wouldn't let me see you."

He stopped his work for a moment, and looked at her. "While I appreciate the effort, that was foolish. It would have been safer to disassociate yourself from the matter as best you could. You should have just forgotten about me."

"I couldn't do that."

He shook out her dress and then folded over a new section. "Well, I thank you for that, then. I doubt many others shared your sentiments." He twisted the fabric until his knuckles were white from the effort. "When he arrested me, I didn't care what Bedoric planned to do with me. But you and Nyvas? Ah, the Goddess knows how scared I was for you both. I was relieved, but not by much, when the Aldrish spoke up for you. Though now I think maybe you would have been safer in the dungeons."

"I wouldn't go that far." She thought back to her half-day in the darkness, and shivered, but didn't want to tell him about that. "To be honest, it was strange being in the keep without you around. The dances I attended just weren't the same," she admitted truthfully, trying to lighten the subject, and now she was smiling.

He raised an eyebrow. "Really? I hear the Aldrish is quite a skilled dancer. Surely he kept you entertained?"

Why would he not drop that subject? Rather than respond, she shrugged, and feeling a dribble of blood, dabbed at her chin again.

Little light was left from the day, and as it departed it was replaced by a bone-chilling darkness, with a breeze that forced its way past the overhang to embrace them in its frosty grip. They had no blankets or dry clothes, no food or fire, and to warm herself, she pulled up her knees to her chest and wrapped her arms around them.

As if in answer to her unspoken complaint, Arric said, "the Sarnoc expected the season's first icewind tonight. Great timing, eh?" He stretched to hook the sleeves of her dress around a rock above his head, so it could hang to dry. "I fear this is too wet for you to wear tonight, but it should be somewhat drier by morning. Anyway, it is the best that I can do."

Restless in the cold, she crawled to the side of the cave where the tunnel began. "It's a little warmer here." She huddled near the opening.

"Aye, the cave will not be so cold, though having said that, I'm not quite ready to go into the tunnel." He sat down beside her, on the other side of the opening, his hands folded under his arms. "I know it will be difficult, but I think we should try to sleep, despite the cold." With no further comment, he leaned his head against the stone wall and took several calming breaths, eventually closing his eyes.

Damn him, how does he make it seem so easy? She tried to make herself comfortable. She was exhausted, but between the frost-filled air and the stone walls and floors, which might as well have been carved from a block of ice, it would be impossible to sleep. Already she shivered, and as the night progressed it would get worse. The clammy dampness of her shift seemed to coax the cold air even closer. As she struggled to find a position slightly warmer than another, her legs brushed against his. He did not flinch at her touch, instead rearranging his position slightly so he would not bump into her.

As she sat there in the cold, she considered the expectations that the Sarnoc had for both of them. The Jiona festival brought joy and celebration, as something everyone, even the poorest inhabitants of the city and villages, could share. Its significance was still not fully clear to her, but apparently Arric considered it a sacred time and regretted that he had used it in such a base manner. "I'm sorry about how things turned out tonight." She spoke softly, almost hoping he was already asleep.

Arric did not open his eyes. "You must not be. For my part I regret that you continue to be dragged into my problems. Every time, you've been insulted, abused, or injured as a result. Kate, I should never have pulled you into the river."

She felt her chin, now encrusted with dried blood. "You didn't." She wasn't sure where she found the courage, but she had jumped at the last minute. "As far as the Jiona festival goes, though, I wish I could understand—"

"Ah, don't worry about it. I'm just glad you're safe."

She could barely see his outline in the darkness. "What were the seeds in the basket for?"

"As part of the ceremony, the riliaga scatters the fruits of nature to give thanks to Kerthal for all life."

"Oh." How many people, over how many centuries, had come before them and had been able to successfully complete the entire ritual? "I'm sorry I lost them, then."

"Like I said, don't worry about it. The ceremony is over for us, anyway. Please, try to sleep. It will be a difficult journey in the morning."

Silence again fell between them. She tried to fall asleep seated upright, but she couldn't get comfortable. Frustrated that she could be so physically exhausted, yet not sleepy, she noted that Arric's breathing had become deep and regular, meaning he had drifted off. Unable to do much else, she listened to him breathe, realizing just how thankful she was that he had escaped.

Maybe, with time, he could clear his name and return home. She couldn't imagine him living as fhaoli for long.

A strong wind gusted through the cave, and she began to shiver anew. To fight the chill, she kicked her legs out in front of her, hoping to shake out the numbness.

Stirring at the sound, Arric asked, "Is something wrong?"

"No, I'm just really cold. I'm sorry if I woke you."

"Ah, don't worry about it. I wasn't asleep anyway. I've been praying."

His statement caught her off-guard. "Praying? All this time?"

"Aye. I have this feeling that the gods have protected me more often than I deserve, and I must ask their forgiveness for having failed them."

"Failed them?" She sucked in a breath so hard she had to cough. "You mean, because of today?"

"Aye, perhaps in part, but only among other things." Although in the darkness she couldn't see anything, she heard him shift his weight.

She folded her legs against her body, and began to rub her arms in what she knew would be a futile attempt to warm them. "At least you didn't try to force the issue. That should count for something."

His voice seemed much farther away when he replied. "If you expected anything different, then you have the wrong idea about me. I promised you back in Bhoren that I would never again disrespect you in such a manner." He sighed, and leaned his head against the wall. Softly, he asked, "what do you want from me, Kate?"

"What do you mean?"

"Ah, don't you know? You torment me, my lady, acting as if you were one of my comrades—my male comrades—not as the woman that you are." He sighed again. "You never defer to my position, and you always question what I do. When I'm with you, I scarcely know how to act. I constantly feel like I should do something different, but I never know what that should be."

He wasn't making any sense at all. "Why should you act any differently around me?"

"Kate, like it or not, you are different," he said, his voice dropping in pitch, "though I'm glad that you are." He hesitated, as if something had occurred to him in that moment. "Back in Loraden, you never betrayed me." It was a question, but one without inflection, spoken as though he knew the answer.

She felt small, like a speck of dust. Her face burned, and her hands shook. "No."

"Surely you knew that lying to the Vosira was a dangerous thing to do?"

It seemed like such a stupid question. "I'm your friend, Arric, and friends look out for one another."

"Friends?" he repeated. "You and me? Hmm." He considered this. "You've said that before. It's odd to think of you that way, since I've never had female friends." He leaned forward. "Is that why you came with me today, then? As a friend?"

"Of course. I wanted to help you."

"Truly?" he chuckled, though he sounded a bit nervous as he did so. "You know how odd that sounds to me?"

"Why?"

"After everything you've endured in my company, I should expect you to run the other way where I'm involved." He moved closer, and his touch startled her. "Hush. You're shivering—I can hear it in your voice," he explained, and placed his arm over her shoulder. "I cannot allow a friend of mine to freeze to death. You do not mind, do you?"

She welcomed his warmth and snuggled close to him. "I think I can live with it." After struggling so long to find her personal independence, she was glad at that moment that someone was there to look after her.

As she folded an arm around his chest, he cleared his throat. "I have a request, if you don't mind," he said.

"Sure, what is it?"

"Would you tell me of your relationship with the Aldrish? It seems like something I should try to understand."

This made her sit up. "What do you mean?" What was his obsession with Rynar? "I've already told you."

"Shh, I did not intend to upset you," he said, and pulled her close again. "Sitting here with you made me curious, that's all. He is special to you, is he not?"

"Why do you keep asking me about him?"

"He is my brother's chief advisor, and therefore as things stand, he's my enemy. Regardless of Bedoric's orders, by all accounts you have become very close to him, much more so than if he was simply a guardian. I do not wish to pry into your private affairs, but I would like to know where things stand."

She stiffened. "So you don't trust me?"

Arric sighed, but continued to hold her. "I trust you, Kate. It's the Aldrish I cannot trust. He's either in love, or he's up to something. Or am I wrong?"

"It's not like that..." How could she explain? "Everything got really complicated after you were arrested." She swallowed hard.

Arric made a rough sound in his throat, one of either derision or anger. "You mean, spending the night with him made it complicated."

She heard him inhale sharply, as if he was angry. "Nothing ever happened, Arric."

"Hmm."

"You've got to believe me. He slept on the floor every night. He never wanted more than that."

"Really? I doubt that. The Aldrish is one of the most calculating, scheming bastards I have ever met." Now she was glad she couldn't see his face. "This is all part of some grand plan, although I cannot guess its nature. I just hope he will not tire of you before he gets what he wants."

As he said that, she fought to retain her composure. With quivering lips and stinging eyes, she pulled away from him. He really didn't understand that Rynar meant nothing to her—that he had begun to frighten her—and that she was as confused as Arric was about his intentions where she was concerned.

Rather than allow her to escape, he crawled after her, until he brushed against her shoulder, and then he knelt beside her. "I'm sorry. I had no right to say those things."

She did not answer, and a shiver ran through her, but she dismissed it, blaming it on the cold.

"Kate, I will not hide my dislike for the Aldrish—no more than he hides his for me—but I will not let that affect the way I feel about you." He reached again for her shoulder and rested his palm on it. "You say we are friends, but I must admit, I have given little thought to your feelings or your needs since I met you. In fact, I have been so absorbed with my own problems that I've thought of little else. For that, I must apologize."

"It's all right. You had more important things to worry about."

"Nay, nothing was ever so important that I could not give a moment to listen, or to help." He made a little noise in his throat. "Perhaps that is the difference between the Aldrish and me. I think perhaps he did listen." He traced the line of her arm up to her neck, and then, careful not to rub her injury, down her chin. "I hope you will accept my apology, though." He leaned over and kissed her cheek, his lips surely tasting the tears that had secretly fallen moments before.

His lips stung where they touched her skin, and she felt her face flush. "Are you trying to seduce me?" Uncertainty and nerves, rather than malice, had prompted the comment, which she had spoken without thinking.

To Arric, however, her words had the effect of a slap, and he fell against the wall of the cave with an explosive sigh, as if she had punched him. "Nay," he said, hurt by the accusation. "I had no such intentions."

They sat that way, without further conversation, for a long time. She could hear his breathing, but she did not speak. With what had just occurred, she was so distracted that she didn't feel the cold. Unlike Arric, she was not religious, and had no use for prayer. So she stared into the black night, wrestling with her emotions. Never had she needed clarity in her life more than now, but instead everything was hopelessly muddied. Then, another sigh from him. He was angry now, she decided. Her lapse in judgment had ruined her one chance to reach a common understanding, and maybe something more. As she had discovered, he didn't easily admit weakness, but he had nevertheless started to open up to her, and even more remarkably, to accept her, but she dismissed his efforts with a stupid comment that she hadn't really meant the way it came out.

Time seemed to stand on one end as they sat in the cave, each second measurable and agonizingly long.

Her emotions, the entire confusing web of them, were building up inside. She couldn't untangle them long enough to label them, much less try to figure out how to deal with them. Finally she exploded. "Damn it, Arric, why do you have to be who you are?"

He coughed. Then, after a pause, he asked, "what do you mean?"

She crawled to the cave opening. The sky was dark, and she could not see the river, although she could hear it crashing against the banks. There were a few birds whistling, but little sound other than that. Then she spun around on her knees, facing back into the cave. "I don't know what I mean. I don't know anything. I've been sitting here for however long now trying to figure out how I feel about you, and whether or not it's okay to feel that way, and I just come up empty."

He didn't respond. She could make out nothing in the darkness, not even his outline against the black walls, but she heard him exhale heavily. Carefully, she crawled towards him, one hand held in front of her so she would not overstep her goal. A finger grazed his arm, and traced the line to his hand. A wave of her other hand guessed where his face would be, and she found the ruffle of his hair, still damp from the river. He didn't move. Without a pause, she dropped to sit beside him.

"I never intended to force you to choose between the Aldrish and myself," he said softly. "Hopefully he'll take you back when this is all over."

She laughed, but it sounded more like a whimper. Had Fantion not told her she might have to choose between them one day? "You say that as if it's what I want."

"Nay?" he asked, sounding genuinely surprised. "Is it not, then?"

She drew herself closer, almost into his lap, and kissed him.

At first he didn't move, as if her forwardness shocked him. That hesitation lasted for only the briefest moment, however. Then his hands, broad and strong, grasped her shoulders and pulled her closer.

There was no need for second-guesses. When he kissed her, this time passionately, she returned it with equal intensity. Her own hands roughly grabbed the back of his head, and then slid down his shoulders.

Before she could accept what she was doing, she had tangled her fingers in his shirt laces, pulling the collar away from his neck, and she explored the curves of his shoulders. With one hand under his shirt, her fingertips explored the cold skin of his shoulders, and down the expanse of his back. She touched his scars, the raised lines that offered a sharp reminder of his past. Instead of revulsion, these battle souvenirs helped her delve deeper into who he was, leading to understanding rather than fear or pity.

Arric, meanwhile, continued to use his tongue in an exploration of her mouth, her teeth, her lips. Gently he nipped at her earlobe. Then he moved his hands down to her arms, and lifted her up. She couldn't figure out why he wanted her to stand until she realized he had already undone the laces in the back of her shift and now was working feverishly to pull it off. As a cold hand cupped her breast, she jumped, and giggled, and then returned the favor, pulling off his shirt and then slipping a set of icy fingers into his trousers. He gasped, and then moaned once, before pulling her hand free so he could lead her to the opening of the tunnel, where the air was much warmer. Then he tugged slightly at her fingers and both collapsed to their knees.

He bent his head down and kissed one of her breasts, while his fingers lightly rubbed her back. She nuzzled her face in his hair, which despite the river still held the slightest scent of rosemary and lavender, scents she had come to associate with him.

He traced out the roundness of her breasts, and the curve of her waist and hips. He untangled the fabric of her shift from her legs and tossed it aside, affording him a more thorough examination of her thighs and the warm space between them. Then she bent down to kiss him again, and he grabbed her shoulders to pull her down on top of him as he fell to the floor, so he would take the brunt of the ice-cold stone.

She untied the lacing at his waist, exposing the last of his flesh to the bite of the winter air. He quickly grabbed his trousers before she could fling them away, and she worried she had gone too far, until she discovered he only meant to lay them on the floor of the cave beside her shift. It was a crude bed, and when he rolled her over onto it she gritted her teeth against the new shock of the dampness, but instantly the heat of his body melted into her and she completely forgot about the cold.

For a string of heartbeats they forgot their personal torments and the physical discomfort of the cold cave, instead finding solace with each other. And then, once they found their release together, dreams were but a breath away. He nudged her further into the relative warmth of the tunnel, and then she snuggled close to him, nestled in the protective crook of his arm. It was in this way that they lay together until sunrise, wrapped in a confident bond of shared slumber.

CHAPTER 50

Actually, sunrise snuck past them.

"Kate," Arric whispered, "it's morning." As she stirred, mumbling something unintelligible, he added, "we've no time to spare. I heard soldiers on the hill above us, so we need to move into the cave. I definitely don't wish to be caught now." Standing in the outer cave, he had already laced up his trousers, and buckled his belt over his shirt. Now he was working pull his stiff but dry stockings onto his feet, and then he shook out the rest of the sand from his boots.

Alarmed by his words, she sat up quickly and wiped her eyes. Her shift still lay underneath her on the floor, and self-conscious about her undressed state in the daylight, she quickly pulled it free and slipped it over her head. Only then did she stretch out the stiffness from her arms and shoulders, and crawl out of the tunnel.

Arric tossed her dress to her. Thanks to the breezes that slipped past the cave opening, it was dry save a few spots that had folded over on themselves, and the blue wool was now spotted with the rust of old blood. Still, she pulled it over her head without comment, grateful for its warmth in the crisp dawn air.

Now in daylight, she was scared to look directly at Arric, unsure how to interpret what had happened between them. Patiently she waited instead to see how he responded to her.

She was relieved that he behaved exactly as he had before. "The Sarnoc had this waiting for us," he whispered as he held out a leather satchel. "I found it a little ways further inside the cave."

Opening the bag, she saw a healthy supply of jerky and small parcels wrapped in leaves that turned out to be tiny loaves of a moist, sweet bread. She broke one in half and handed it to him, and he took it gratefully.

"They also left a flask with water," he added, his mouth lined with crumbs, "and we should be able to refill it from the underground river." He handed it to her. "Just a few sips. We should save the rest in case we need it later."

"Did they provide us with torches or candles?"

"Nay, no such luck. Perhaps they feared fire would lead troops to us, or maybe it was to lighten the burden?" He must have seen panic on her face, for he quickly added, "don't worry, we should be able to manage with my land-instinct to guide us." He slung the satchel over his shoulder, and swiveled on his heels. "Are you ready?"

She nodded, almost imperceptibly. With every fiber of her being she wished that she would not have to enter the blackness beyond. Only her faith in Arric's innate ability enabled her to agree to this folly. Even as she hesitated, he bowed his head and slipped between the rocks, one hand extended to her.

They plunged into absolute darkness that folded itself around them more securely than the hug of the musty stone walls. Compared to the chill of the morning outside, the cavern's warm air was welcome. Small comfort, she thought, as she slid forward on her hands and knees after him, holding her breath as the light from the cave mouth rapidly vanished.

"I don't think I can do this." She spoke after they stood up in the room that had opened up after only about fifteen feet of tunnel. Never before had she faced a place as sinister and foreboding as this cave. One candle, one torch, and the cavern would seem manageable, for she would have dispelled the unknown with fire. As it was, the dark was overwhelming, and she struggled against panic.

"Kate, I can guide us," he said, his voice confident. "We shall be in no danger."

"That's easy for you to say." The drip of water, the scuttle of blind cave critters, the squeal of bats high overhead—all were magnified in her mind. Nothing could harm her here, but she was unable to fully rationalize her safety in the dark.

"It's difficult, but you must stop thinking of whatever it is that frightens you about this place," he advised. "There is likely nowhere safer than this cave, even in the best of times. It's a pity that we have no light to appreciate this space."

She shrugged, a gesture he couldn't see. He also couldn't see her tears, coming unbidden. She was terrified, and hated feeling that way, particularly around him. As a result, she couldn't speak.

He turned, felt for her, and then folded her in his arms. "You'll be fine, I promise."

His tenderness immediately eased her fears, though nothing would erase them entirely. At least now she could breathe, and when he released her, he took her hand. "We must stay together, and keep hold of one another, whenever we are in a wide-open area such as this. I will sense the best path to follow, just as if I could see it in front of me, but you will not. Without being able to see you, this is the easiest way for me to know where you are."

"Don't worry about me. I'll be like glue. Please, keep talking."

"Aye, that's easy enough. So what would you like to talk about?"

She thought about it for a moment. "Well, I was wondering. Have you and your brother—I mean, Vosira Bedoric—always..." she hunted for the right word.

"Disagreed? Fought?" He guessed, and then laughed. "Ah, that's an innocent enough topic to start off." He led her into a fissure in the limestone. "Careful—it seems like it will be a tight fit. Just hang on to me."

Once they cleared the passage, the next room opened up and their footsteps echoed in the wide space. "I expect this would be a beautiful cavern if we could see it."

"You've been in caves before?" In her world, with electricity and flashlights anyone could be an amateur spelunker, and once at summer camp she had even rappelled down into a sinkhole, the walls of which were filled with miniature stalactites. She loved caves, usually, but this time, in the dark, it was different.

"Aye, in Froida, we slept in caves in the winter. Naturally, dozens of men idle for months on end could not possibly leave their surroundings unexplored." He turned to the left and she followed dutifully, if also slowly. "That is a good story, perhaps for another time. For now, you asked me about Bedoric." He took a deep breath. "You know he's older than me, by about five years. You might be surprised to learn that he was the serious, studious one, not me—at least for a while. I was always so much better with the sword, and on horseback, and honestly I never thought too much about studying history, learning languages, that sort of thing. So we led very different lives, really. I looked up to him as any younger brother might, but as I think on it, perhaps he resented me."

She wasn't too surprised by this comment. "Really? Why, do you think?"

"Oh, I suspect I know the reason. You see, in Sarducia book-learning is all well and good, and expected of all charnok, especially those who are the sons of the Vosira. Leaders, however, are born in the exercise yard. Even though Sarducia has not been at war in many life-times, it was important that the Vosira was someone who could fight if it became necessary. Bedoric was always clumsy and big. Not like he is now, mind you, but even as a boy he was awkward."

"I know what that's like." She had always been a bit on the heavy side, and tall. She never felt graceful, and now, in a place where she was expected to wear long, fitted gowns, her own awkwardness was intensified.

Her words caught him by surprise. "You, Kate? Nay, you're not like that at all. True, you're not a delicate, fragile girl. That's not a bad thing, though, don't get me wrong. You have strength about you, and confidence. That makes you so much more beautiful than the other women in Loraden."

It was Kate's turn to be surprised. He thought she was beautiful? "Thanks."

In response, he squeezed her hand. "Now, you've made me lose track of what I was saying."

"You were saying your brother resented you."

"Aye, that's right. Well, there really wasn't much to be done about it." Again, they turned, this time following a narrowing corridor to the right. "We had our own talents and interests," he continued, "and that was that. And for a while it did not present a problem."

She tried to imagine Vosira Bedoric as a studious child, and it was difficult. "Something happened, didn't it? I mean, between you and your brother?"

"Aye. You would not believe it, but I once was rather prideful."

"Really, you?" she said lightly, amused. "You're right, I don't believe it."

"Oh indeed. I was all of twelve in years, but I thought I was quite the horseman. I was so sure of myself that I believed I could beat the best riders among the Senvosra. So, to teach me a lesson, a couple of the soldiers challenged me to a race."

"This isn't going to end well, is it?" She laughed. It was entertaining to imagine him as a young boy.

He whistled. "Nay, you are quite right. It was a sunny summer day, and we all went out to the paddocks just below the city gates. I had chosen this one young stallion, quite a spirited horse. He was one of the fastest horses I had ridden. The race was to be the first to make it around the field three times, and on that horse I was sure to win. A lot of people followed us down, and I assumed everyone was cheering me on. In hindsight I heard they had all wagered on me—not that I would win the race, but on how long it would take before I fell off that horse." He laughed, and the sound echoed in the cave. "Of course I knew nothing about that at the time. I felt so confident, like nothing could go wrong." He paused, remembering the moment. "Ah, in all ways it was a perfect day."

Kate was enjoying the mental vision of the bright sun, and imagining Arric as a boy being so cocky and stubborn. "What happened?"

"Ah well, I hadn't counted on my horse getting spooked after the first circuit. I think it was a dog that ran into the field, but I'm not sure—it all happened so fast. The horse reared up, and I fell off and hit the ground wrong. The bone in my calf snapped in two, and as I lay there screaming in pain, the fool horse's hooves nearly cracked my head open."

"You broke your leg?" She seemed surprised. "Which one?"

"It was my right leg, just below the knee. It was a serious break, too, because I could see the bone sticking out of the skin. It was awful." He chuckled at the memory. "You know, as I think about it, I'm pretty sure I passed out from the pain. I didn't have a healer at first, because Sander was helping in a difficult birth elsewhere."

"Sander? You mean, Lysander was there then?"

He laughed again. "Of course. He used to be the royal healer. Didn't he tell you that?"

"Yeah, I knew that, but I guess I didn't realize he was around when you were growing up." So he hadn't exaggerated when he said he had known Arric for a long time.

"Aye, he wasn't outlawed until much later. Anyway, the Senvosra carried me back to the keep, but because Sander wasn't able to help me right away, the bone splintered further."

"That sounds terrible."

"Oh, aye. I screamed like a baby the whole way back. Every step they took when they were carrying me felt like they were driving a horseshoe nail into my leg. After all that, because of the way the bone broke and the delay in healing it, even with all of Sander's skill, he couldn't fully mend it. I was unable to put any weight on it for many days, and then could not walk without pain for a full season. There was an ache, you see, that didn't go away even when the bone was healed." He lowered his voice slightly, out of habit, as he continued. "Even now, sometimes when it's cold and damp, the pain will come back, and it's all I can do not to limp on it. I do not share this fact with many people, though."

"I bet it hurt last night, then." Kate marveled that he had said nothing about it. "And in the Muras?"

"Aye, back in the swamp it did bother me, that's the truth. Anyway, for the rest of that summer I rarely left my quarters, though it was due as much to my shame as it was the pain. While I was indoors, I was forced to take my studies more seriously, and Bedoric was forced out into the exercise yards twice a day rather than once every other day." He laughed. "I do not believe he ever forgave me for breaking my leg."

"Still, he's Vosira now, rather than you."

"Aye." He took a few steps and stopped. "I hear water dripping. There must be a pool just ahead."

It wasn't much, just a shallow puddle collecting one drop at a time in a depression in the rock floor. Regardless, it was the first water they had encountered, and they both scooped out what they could to drink, saving the remainder of the flask for later. The water was pleasantly cool, but it was salty-tasting from the dissolved minerals of the rocks around them.

When they resumed their journey, the ceiling rapidly sloped downwards, and Arric stopped after walking only a few feet. "From here it appears that we'll have to crawl for a while," he announced, and released her hand.

Between the discomfort of crawling and the presence of a very low ceiling, it was difficult to continue their conversation. With the silence came a flood of thoughts and emotions that she had not yet had a chance to process.

When she had first met Arric, she thought him self-important and intimidating. As time had passed, she began to see past the facade, only to realize that it was his sense of duty, as well as compassion and a commitment to his friends, which fed the intensity that she had mistaken for arrogance. She couldn't help but be influenced by the loyalty that Fantion, Sander and Nyvas had shown for him. Most of all, despite the accumulation of sorrow and guilt, he still allowed humor and joy to be part of his life. She had developed a fondness for him, a friendship built on a few days' close association, and that had fueled the first spark of attraction, but there had been no chance to see where it might go.

When they returned to Loraden, he had been harassed, imprisoned, and poisoned, all in the span of a few weeks. Then, inexplicably, they participated in Jiona together. When he described the expectations for Jiona participants, the idea of sleeping with him to satisfy those demands had been absurd. Yet the intimacy had happened, and not because of the festival—at least, not on her part.

She wanted desperately to deny that she had feelings for him, because to admit it would make her life exponentially more difficult. She wasn't inclined to start a relationship with anyone in Sarducia, guessing that her time here was limited, and sooner or later she would return to her own home. She couldn't explain why that was, but she imagined that her time here was likely close to an end. Pragmatically, he was of royal blood, and when—or if—he cleared his name, she understood enough of Sarducian customs to know that she would not be considered a suitable partner.

Despite all her rational arguments, she could not deny one obvious fact. What had happened last night meant something to her, and perhaps to him as well. There did not seem to be any sense of duty in their intimacy. What was she supposed to think—how should she feel?

The funny thing was, everyone here would say it was the goddess Kerthal's handiwork.

She pondered it all in silence, and kept returning to what seemed to be the most obvious conclusion. Last night was a one-time thing. They were scared, it was cold, they were lonely—and beyond all that, he was compelled by religious duty that she respected, even if she couldn't share it. Crazier things happened to people all the time for lesser reasons. It didn't mean that they had to have feelings for one another, and it didn't mean that they were going to start a relationship. It just happened. She knew that it was best that she push away her feelings before things got any more difficult.

While she was distracted by her thoughts, she had been paying little attention to the sounds ahead of her. Since Arric did not have to contend with the difficulties of crawling in a long skirt, his pace had substantially increased over hers, though she hadn't noticed. When she paused for a moment to brush away a bit of debris on her palm, absolute silence surrounded her. "Arric?" she called out, but her voice was weak, and he did not respond. With a deep breath, she repeated his name, louder this time.

After a heart-stopping pause, he responded. "I'm here, just ahead." His voice echoed against the constricting walls of the tunnel. She resumed crawling forward until she finally emerged into the cavern ahead, her head colliding with the hand he held out to catch her.

"You can stand up now," he announced. She felt his hand travel from her shoulder to her wrist, and he took hold of her hand to help her up. "I just entered this large chamber, and I was waiting for you. The good news is, from here we should be safe from pursuit, should any soldiers be so foolish as to follow us this far. Even in the darkness I can sense many passages leading from this spot. They could never track us from this point. And—listen!"

She turned her head and strained to hear what he did. "Water? Is it the river?"

He laughed. "Aye, and it's not too far from here. Come. Let's see if we can find it!"

With impossibly confident steps he led her across the smooth and slightly inclined cavern floor and into a narrower passageway. Unlike the tunnel they had previously exited, however, this one had a high ceiling and they could stand, although they still had to walk single-file. Frequently drops of water fell from above and pelted their heads and arms. Damp rocks made traction difficult, but when she held out her free hand to keep from falling, her fingers discovered the wall was actually a slick latticework of stalactites rather than solid stone—just as she had remembered from the sinkhole. The memory cheered her, since climbing down into that hole had been one of the most terrifying things she had ever attempted, and yet at the bottom she had reveled in the beauty of the space.

She kept walking, knowing the river was nearer with every step, and soon she could feel the spray of a waterfall crashing into an invisible pool.

"Careful now, the floor is very wet here," Arric warned her as he skirted around the spray. "It is too narrow here to stop and rest, but it shouldn't be long now before the cave widens."

Licking her cracked lips, she said nothing but squeezed his hand in agreement. The last taste of water had not left her, and only made her crave another drink.

"Blast," he cursed a moment later. Quickly he added, "Kate, stop where you are, and stand perfectly still." He released her hand.

"Okay. I won't move a muscle." Her heart pounded.

"Stay exactly where you are," he barked to her, his tone brooking no argument.

"I heard you. I'm not going anywhere," she replied. "But what's wrong?"

Rather than respond to her question, he continued to give her instructions. "Don't move your feet. Hold out your left hand, and see if you can you feel the wall."

She tentatively held out her arm, expecting to hit solid rock, but felt nothing. "No. Is that a problem?"

Calmly, he said, "Do exactly as I say."

She held her breath. "Why? What's going on?"

"Just do what I tell you. Very carefully, lower yourself until you can touch the floor, feeling your way as you go, but do not sit, and do not move your feet. Use your hands if you need to maintain your balance. Then, very slowly, drop to your knees and move to your left, but feel the floor to the side before you move."

Panic began to set in, and she resisted the urge to run to his voice. "Arric, what's happening?"

"I'm going to try to find you, so keep talking."

"Okay, what should I talk about? You didn't tell me what's going on."

"Aye, that's perfect. Are you moving?"

She was having problems with her clothing getting in the way. "No, I'm afraid that I might trip on this stupid dress. I need your help."

"Then stay where you are." She could hear him sliding his feet along the stone, and then his palm brushed her elbow, startling her slightly, but with his help she was able to keep from falling. "Good. Now get on your hands and knees, but stay there just a moment longer." He paused, feeling his way around, and then instructed her, "get down on your hands and knees, carefully. Follow my voice, and crawl to me. I'm over to your left, not in front of you."

She knelt down and began to slide her legs to the side. Her hands picked up a bit of sludge from the rocks. "I wish I could see where I'm going."

"Just keep scooting to your left. Carefully, now."

She continued slowly until she bumped into him. "Okay."

Arric sighed. "Blessed Kerthal, you're safe." He fell to a sitting position beside her. "You have no idea how close we were to the edge. I was afraid one of us would fall."

"Uhh, edge?"

"The pool was right at our feet. The floor just dropped off, right at the edge of the water, and there's no way to know how deep the water is. I put my foot into it but was able to pull back just in time. I wasn't sure what was to the left, if the river circled around, so I had to check before you could move away."

Shaky, she sat beside him, and caught her breath. "I thought you could sense these things."

"Nay, not that. I can sense the proper directions, so we don't get lost, but in terms of something like that drop-off, I am as blind in here as you."

"So you don't know if there's something like a rock ledge or something ahead?"

Again he sighed. "Only if I run into it," he said, and from the way he said it, she could tell it had already happened several times. "I just hope I can help you avoid the same fate."

With this new revelation, she appreciated anew the sacrifices he was making for her, but she also felt a bit less confident about their progress. Still, he had gotten them this far, and it couldn't be that much longer. "Will we be able to continue this way?"

"Aye, but we'll need to move more slowly." He cleared his throat, scratchy from thirst. "I hope we can get a drink soon, but I fear leaning over that edge."

"I'm okay, really. We can save what we have for later." Although she too was thirsty, she was in no mood to take unnecessary risks. "I'll trust your judgment."

"Then I suggest we keep going." He found her hand locked his fingers over it. "Ready?"

"Sure."

He led her along the wall, their progress painfully slow. Twice he left her standing alone, with strict instructions to keep her hand on the wall and her feet planted on the rock beneath her, so he could investigate the possibility of access to the water. She couldn't see him, but she knew he was crawling away from the security of the wall, and each time she prayed she wouldn't hear a loud splash as he tumbled into the river. On the second try, however, she heard him laugh in relief. Apparently this time he was successful.

"It's rough, so you won't slip," he explained, and sure enough, the floor was pocked with places where the ancient ones must have broken stalagmites off at the base. The sudden realization that they were not the first ones to find this space comforted her, and with the evidence of other people having been here before them, a bit of the hopelessness of their situation faded. If others had done this, and survived, they could do it too.

He led her to the water's edge, this time a handspan above the water itself, and situated on a bit of a backward slope. As she reached down, she quickly scooped up several handfuls to quench her thirst. The river was cold, and it was clear of the sediments of their previous stop. She splashed handfuls of water over her head, and on her face, taking care to cleanse the wound from her mishap the day before as well as she could without being able to see it. From the sound of it, Arric was doing much the same thing, washing off dirt and cleaning his own wounds.

When she was done, she wiped her face on her sleeves. "How long do you think we've been in here?"

"It must be close to midday, do you think?"

She considered the time more closely. His guess would mean they had been in the cave about four hours. The blindness was maddening, and she was ravenously hungry. "It has to be later than that. We've been crawling forever."

"I hope you're right," he said as he shook excess water from his hair, and a few drops fell on her. This didn't bother her, for it just meant he was very close. "It's been a difficult journey already, and I'd rather not be in here a moment longer than absolutely necessary." A moment later she heard him rustling around in the satchel and then one of his hands found hers, and he placed a piece of jerky in her palm. "This is a shortcut to Altopon, but even so it will not be quick. Did I tell you that Vaj expected it would take us at least four days to clear the cave?"

Her heart sank. "Oh no. Four days? You've got to be kidding." She hoped to be out before nightfall. All of a sudden the dismal reality of being lost in the belly of this cave seemed insurmountable. "How can we possibly keep going for another three and a half days?"

He laughed, and the hearty sound reverberated through the room. "Feel free to leave whenever you'd like."

If she could have seen him, Kate might have punched him.

CHAPTER 51

"**D**o you need a break?"

They had been crawling on their hands and knees for a while, and Kate noticed he had been slowing down, and his breathing sounded labored, as if he was struggling to keep moving.

"Aye, that's a good idea."

She heard the bag of provisions hit the floor, and the scrape of boot heels. It didn't take long for her to reach him, and she sat next to him, their backs against the wall and their knees touching. "Are you okay?"

He uncorked the flask and took a sip. "It's the adoli. I keep thinking it's cleared out of my system and then its effects hit me again, and it's all I can do to keep going."

"That's the poison? I had no idea it was still bothering you."

He reached out for her hand, and offered her the flask as he continued. "Aye. As much as it's bothering me now, I really don't want to complain. It may have saved my life."

"What does it feel like?"

"Hmm, well, it's difficult to explain. I'll be feeling fine one moment and then my muscles tighten up and feel like they're on fire. When that happens, walking—or really moving at all—is really painful. Then it passes and everything's fine. The problem is that it happens without warning, and I have to fight to keep going."

"Really? I had no idea it would still be bothering you."

"Aye. The effects of adoli only last a few days, but my last dose was the day before Jiona. The Sarnoc wanted to convince Bedoric that I was still unwell so he wouldn't send me back to the tower, so they kept making me drink the stuff. Now that it's clearing my system, I feel better, but I still have those moments."

"Wait—they weren't afraid of it killing you?"

"Nay, adoli cannot kill a man, though in large enough doses it can have the appearance of doing so. When I was a boy, Sarnoc Sofinar taught me about different potions. He said that adoli was his favorite because of its varied uses. A few sips, and it can relax someone in extreme pain, and with more, a person will fall into a deep sleep. Because of that, it is most often used for assisting people with serious injuries when no healer is available. Yet for all that, it is impossible to consume enough to die. It has uncomfortable effects, though, especially after the amount I consumed."

"Oh, Arric, I'm sorry you had to go through all that."

"Ah, you have nothing to be sorry about. You had nothing to do with it. I am curious, though, to discover how it could have made it into my wine. The Sarnoc claimed not to know the source of it."

She had wondered the same thing. "Oh. Well..."

He sensed her hesitation. "Kate, do you know something about it?" The question was asked gently, without accusation.

She sat in silence for a moment, unsure how to proceed. Finally, she flattened her back against the stone wall, feeling the uneven texture between her shoulder blades, and said simply, "I don't know how it got into your wine, but I'm pretty sure Rynar knew what it was."

"The Aldrish?" he replied, surprise evident in his voice. He was quiet for a moment. Then he repeated the name a couple more times, more softly, as if saying it aloud would help him understand. "Are you certain?"

"No, but it makes sense. He seemed surprised when it happened, but then he didn't act like you were in any real danger, except when he talked to Vosira Bedoric, and Tashin. It was as if he wanted them to think you were in more danger than you really were."

"The Aldrish," he said yet again, as if he was trying to accustom himself with the concept. "It's curious then." He cleared his throat, and then took another sip of water. "Since it didn't come from the Sarnoc, I wonder if someone thought it really was poison."

"I hate to ask, but—do you think it was your brother?"

"Hmm, it's possible, I suppose, though if he wanted to kill me, why use poison? He could have had me executed, after all. Since it was poison, it makes more sense that it came from someone else, maybe one of the Bhagali. I certainly have my fair share of enemies."

"That's true. Well, whoever it was, I'm glad they used adoli and not a real poison."

"Aye, on that point we are agreed."

***

Like burrowing insects, they continued through the cave, blindly crawling forward, only marking the passage of time and distance by the increasing soreness of their knees and backs. The cave stretched on endlessly, and the oppressive darkness and silence was maddening.

In the silence of another narrow tunnel, Kate was able to entertain herself with creative uses of memories, imagining herself in various places and situations that she found comforting. As time slipped by, certain visions kept returning, nagging her with their insistent demands on her attention. She re-lived childhood moments spent with her mother, as well as the last hours she spent with her. She remembered how excited she was to get her job, beating out fifty other applicants. Then there was the trip to Hawaii with her ex-fiancé Alex, although those memories were quickly overshadowed by her recollection of the night she had found him with her best friend. Then the swirl of images, good and bad, stopped, her mind as blank as the reality before her sightless eyes.

In a terrifying moment, it was as if she had been born blind, and could recall no memories of a time when she could see. It became difficult to breathe. As anxiety took over, she tried to stand up, but in her desperation she crashed hard against the rock ceiling, and then collapsed face down. Irrationally, she tried again, with the same results. "Get me out of here," she cried, and began to kick at the stone.

"Kate?" Hearing her thrashing around, he reached out for her arms, and pulled her to him. "What's wrong?" She didn't stop kicking, so he pulled her into his lap, wrapping his arms tightly around her. "Shh. I'm here."

"I've got to get out of here," she pleaded, her voice a medley of fragmented pitches punctuated with scattered breaths. "I can't deal with it any more. I have to get out, somehow, now. I just have to. It's too dark. You have to get me out of here. Please," she cried, desperate with claustrophobia and panic, "get me out of this place."

He cradled her shoulders in one arm, as if she was a child, and smoothed her hair. "Kate, hush, it's all right. You're safe. I know you can get past this. Just try to think about something else."

"No, you don't understand." In between gasping breaths she said, "I can't breathe. All I can think about is the rock coming down on us. Oh, god, Arric, get me out of here. There's got to be a way out. I'll do anything, just don't let me die here."

"Nay, you're not going to die. You're safe with me. I will not allow anything to happen to you." He stroked her hair, and then rubbed her arms, as if willing life back into her. "Now, listen to me. You need to take a slow, deep breath."

"I can't do this, Arric, I just can't."

"Breathe."

"But—"

"Breathe!" He was insistent, and waited until she complied. "Good. And another." She followed his commands, inhaling as deeply as she could. "You can do this. I know you can. You're a brave woman, and this is just a cave. It has been here as long as the ancients walked this land, and will be here long after we're gone." He buried his face in her hair, close to her ear, and whispered light endearments, gently willing her to relax. Then he began to hum to her, a gentle melody that sounded like the music he had played on the flute. It took some time, but eventually he helped her bring her haphazard breathing under control.

Then he asked her, "what's behind your fears? Is it the darkness?"

She opened her eyes, but everything was still black. The warmth of his palm on her cheek served as an anchor. Closing her eyes again, she inhaled sharply and focused on his touch. "Your brother. I feel like he's here with us. He's still hunting us."

"Bedoric?" he said, surprised by her comment. "You think so?"

"Arric, you know he's looking for me—for both of us. I know he's going to find us both, and I don't know what he'll do when he does. He was so angry at me the day I went to him, offering to trade Rynar for Nyvas, and even after Rynar returned, he was ready to execute us both." She allowed herself to cry, now, the fear being named at last. "I don't want him to catch us now. Not after everything we've gone through to get this far. I don't want to die."

"Shh, Minara, he cannot find us. You are safe with me," he affirmed, in a voice that carried confidence. "Even if he came with a thousand troops, you would still be safe. He cannot fight us in the cave. You know that." He nudged her shoulder and tried to get her to sit up. "To prove it, I will get you out of here. You have my solemn promise—I will not allow you to die in this place."

***

Eventually she overcame her panic, and they continued as before, crawling or, when they were lucky, walking through the cave. When exhaustion called a halt to their progress a few hours later, they curled up together and slept fitfully against the damp rock walls, huddled together both for warmth and security. Their slumber was short-lived, however, as much due to discomfort as to their shared desperation to escape the underground passage. Once awake, they resumed their trek immediately, having no reason to delay.

When they took their next break, they dug into their diminishing provisions, and then took turns massaging each other's muscle cramps and soreness. Arric insisted she be first. He kneaded her shoulders, and then her lower back just above her hips. His hands were strong, and he knew how to find the soreness and work it out. "That feels really good," she said, her words slurred a little as she sat there enjoying the way he worked out the knots. When he was done, he encouraged her to rest, and she dozed off for a little while. When she awoke, she insisted on returning the favor, though she didn't think her skill matched his. He seemed to appreciate it, though, moaning lightly as she dug fingertips, and then knuckles, into his sore muscles.

"I should have had the Sarnoc do this for me. It really helps loosen everything up," he muttered.

"Somehow, I can't really see that happening," she said with a smirk. "They seem too dignified to give massages, somehow."

"Aye, they leave it up to healers, who know exactly where to work out the pain." As she moved back to his neck, he caught her hands in his. "That's enough. I don't want you to wear yourself out on my account."

She nodded, though he couldn't see the gesture, and silently wrapped her arms around him and rested her head on his shoulders.

"Take heart, Kate. I think we are nearly halfway now. It should be no more than a couple more days if my reckoning is correct."

"Really? I hope you're right. I've never hated the dark as much as I do now." At her comment she heard him laugh, and she wished she could see his face at least for a moment. She was tired of talking into the darkness, and his smile would have cheered her. "Can I ask you something?"

"Aye."

"What was it you called me yesterday when I was so upset?"

"Hmm. What was it?" he thought for a moment. "You know, I don't recall." Then he added, suddenly, "oh of course. I do remember. I called you 'Minara'."

"Minara?" She liked the sound on her tongue. "What's that?"

"The minara are small blue flowers that grow at the base of Monmora, the hill across the river from Loraden. From a distance you might not even see them, but when you approach and look closely, you discover how complex the flowers' petals are." She imagined his smile. "It is a rare flower, but an exquisite one. They say the Mosumi planted it to mark special places."

She smiled in return. "I like that."

He reached behind him and caught her hair in his fingers. "I do not know why I thought of it, but for some reason it just seems like you. To me, you are like minara blossoms: uncommon and complicated, but quite beautiful."

She scooted around, finding his face with her fingers. Quickly, before she lost track of him, she leaned close and kissed him.

"Mmm." He reached out and wrapped his hand around her head, pulling her close so he could return the kiss. Then his fingers traveled to her neck, and he fingered the chain that hung there. "I've been meaning to mention this. I'm very relieved to know that you still have my ring."

Kate felt at her collarbone and found the thin chain under her shift. "You know, I probably should give it back to you now."

She felt his hand on hers. "Nay, you must keep it. It is much safer with you than with me."

"Are you sure?"

"Oh, aye. You know, I first noticed it on you the other night, and though I was pleased you still had it, I was in no position to tell you so at the time." He laughed lightly with those words. "I would be honored if you will bring it to Altopon for me."

"What's special about it? You still haven't told me."

"I dare not." Hearing her grunt, he added, "it's not that I cannot trust you—it's just that you are better off not knowing."

"Okay."

He laughed again. "That was too easy. Are you agreeing to drop it because you trust my judgment, or because you know you can't talk me into telling you?"

She liked hearing his laughter. He had a nice voice, and his laughs were solid, and came from his chest rather than his nose. "I don't know, maybe both?"

"That sounds about right, then."

"Do you really think the Sarnoc can help you?"

"Oh, aye." He offered no explanation as to the kind of assistance he hoped for, and instead kicked out his legs in front of him and shook them out. "Speaking of secrets—you've never told me how you came to be in Sarducia."

She started to gnaw at a jagged fingernail. "No, it's too complicated." She felt as little inclined to tell this story as he was to explain the significance of the ring.

"We have plenty of time, do we not?" He reached out and grasped her hand, instinctively preventing her from the nervous habit.

For the first time in three days she began to sweat, and she pulled her hand back. "If I told you what I know about it, you might have a different opinion of me afterwards, and I don't want that to happen."

"Really? Have you not been honest about something, then?" he asked, sounding dubious.

"Well, it's just..." she bit her lip. On one hand she desperately wanted to tell him everything, but here, in the darkness, she feared he would abandon her if he knew the truth. How could she explain her heritage, and that she traveled using magic?

"Surely it can't be that controversial. What is it, Kate?"

She swallowed, and her eyes sought any vision, anything to focus on other than perpetual unyielding blackness, but there was nothing. "It all started when I inherited this ring—" she guided his hand to touch the ring on her hand, "after my mother died. Something about it allowed me to travel here. That's how I ended up in the torrapon where you found me." More softly, a little less confidently, she added, "she was Mosumi. I don't know how that's possible, though, since she never told me about it."

This time he laughed, but she was certain there was a note of derision in the response. "Mosumi, eh?"

"Arric, it doesn't mean anything. I never—" She stopped, trying to catch her breath, and find the right words. "Whatever's happening here, whatever game people are playing, please understand—I'm not part of it. I'm not your enemy. I'm really just like you—I'm just trying to survive, to figure out what the hell is going on, and as I go along I'm trying to do what I think is right. This is all new to me. But at the same time, I promise you, I have never betrayed you, and I never will."

She heard him suck in a breath, as if at the brink of releasing a tempest in the small space, but then he expelled the breath in a deep exhale. When he was done the cave returned to its usual deathly silence. All she could hear was his labored breathing, and her own racing heartbeat.

"Something else you should know. The land I'm from is an entirely different world. No one has heard of Sarducia—as far as anyone there knows, it doesn't even exist. Where I live, people can't heal someone else just by touching them. We don't have quinsa and we don't have glysar.

My world is nothing like this one, and people don't know how to travel from one world to the other. But we have technology you could never imagine, ways of traveling in machines, and ways to communicate with anyone in an instant." With that she stopped, because even keeping it vague made it sound fantastic, almost unbelievable, given all she had experienced. Would it be as strange to him as this land had been to her? "Anyway, I don't know how I came here, or why. This is all at least as bizarre to me as it is to you."

There. She finally told him the truth, and no matter what happened, she was glad the truth was finally out. Surely he would understand. And if not, maybe it was best that they were headed to Altopon. Maybe the Sarnoc could find a way to send her back home.

"Hmm. I need a moment."

While she sat against the cave wall swimming in fear and regret, she heard the shuffle of his boot soles on the stone. His breathing seemed to get quieter, until she could no longer hear it.

Was he trying to slip away, and leave her behind? The paranoia of the darkness again crept into her, and with it came another wave of crushing panic. Without him, she would certainly die in here. "Arric?" she called out as she stood up, grateful that she didn't collide against the ceiling. "Where are you?" She jumped when a hand patted her right arm, and then followed it down to her own hand.

"I'm right here," he announced, his tone quite genial. "I simply needed to relieve myself. You were so quiet that it was hard to find you."

"Oh, god, Arric, I thought you were gone—"

He lifted his right hand, the one hand not already linked with hers, until he found her face. Then a finger brushed the fleshy apple of her cheek. "Did you think telling me you were Mosumi would change anything? I'll admit, it's a bit of a shock, and complicates matters somewhat. But it doesn't change how I feel about you."

She practically collapsed into his arms, and he wrapped them snugly around her. "I didn't know what to think. Oh, Arric, I'm so sorry for everything. I know how it must all sound."

"Minara, I'm the one who needs to apologize." He chuckled lightly, in a self-deprecating way. "Being in this cave, half-starved, is bringing out the worst in me." Even as he said it, his stomach growled in agreement, and they both laughed.

They stood where they were for a while, holding each other in defiance of the dark. Finally, he loosened his grip, and tipped his head down, catching her unaware as he kissed her.

"I am glad you're here, no matter how it happened, or why." His hands found her wrists, and with a light tug he encouraged her to sit down. "The other night was Jiona, and what happened was the work of the gods." Hearing her begin to protest, he put his fingers over her lips. "Nay, I know you do not believe such things, but I do. Ever since that time I've been wondering... no, that is not what I mean to say. I was hoping that maybe you would be willing to try it again, to see if it might work out between us, when it's just us, without the gods interfering."

Astonished that he would make such an offer—but enormously happy that he had—she laughed, and pulled him closer.

CHAPTER 52

When they woke up, whether it was the next morning or late afternoon, it was all the same to them. She raised a hand to his head, and used her fingers to comb through his wavy hair. He lay quite still, and groaned slightly.

"I cannot wait until we get out of here, and I can lay my eyes on you again, you Mosumi witch," he said.

Kate countered, "you'd just better hope I don't take one look at you, all filthy and bruised up, and run back to Loraden!"

"You wouldn't dare," he taunted.

"Well, if you want me to stay, you'd better make it worth my while."

"Oh really?" he twisted around, and grasped one of her wrists, not hard, but enough that she gasped. "Maybe I just need to make you my prisoner, then."

She pushed him with her shoulder so that he released her and fell back onto the floor, and then she pounced and slid her cold hand into his yet-unlaced trousers. "Maybe we should reconsider who is the prisoner here?"

He laughed. "I surrender!" he croaked. Then he sat up in a hurry. "Kate—over there. What is that?"

"Do you think I'm going to fall for that trick?" she giggled in return. "You know I can't see anything!"

"Nay, I'm serious. Look!"

She turned her head, not sure which way he meant. Not that it would matter, because she knew she wouldn't actually see anything. The odd thing was, she did.

"Is that sunlight?" she asked, spellbound. In the distance was the tiniest stream of light, sneaking in overhead through a fissure in the ceiling.

"I think it is!" he replied, thoroughly excited. "Come, we must be close!"

They jumped up, both with visions of a sun-bleached hillside and mounds of food ahead.

At first they jogged along the cave passages, moving as rapidly as Arric could navigate. Eventually, as no opening presented itself, and they had traveled for at least a half-hour by Kate's reckoning, they slowed to a more normal pace.

"I really thought we were going to get out of here." Her voice was heavy with defeat, and she could scarcely find the energy to keep walking. "I was so sure."

He squeezed her hand. "Come on, we can do this. It cannot be long. I do not know where the exit is, precisely, but I can sense it."

"It's okay," she said, defeat apparent in her voice. "I bet you don't really know how far it is."

He was adamant. "I do. The end of the tunnel is not far ahead."

When a short time later she again spied a sliver of daylight, she thought she was hallucinating.

As they turned the final corner, they stumbled into a full blaze of light, as if every combustible item in the whole world had been set on fire in front of them. Both gasped, and fell to their knees, clutching their arms over their eyes. The shock of the sudden light was exquisite, a wonderful, miraculous thing. Squinting, she dropped her arm eventually, so she could seek out the source of the light: a small opening just an arm's length over her head. It looked like it opened into a small rock outcropping, and the hole itself was the size of a manhole in her world, small, but just wide enough that they should be able to climb through.

"Arric, this is it!" She tugged at his arm, and he dropped it from his face, where he had raised it to shade his eyes from the light.

He considered the distance, and looked appraisingly at her. "One of us needs to give the other a boost and climb out first, and then help pull out the other. What do you think?"

She measured the distance. "I think you should go first. If there's any danger, you'd know it before I would. Anyway, I don't think I could pull you out."

He nodded. "Fair enough." He put one of his booted feet on the improvised step provided by her interlinked fingers, and she heaved him up about a foot, just enough for him to grasp the sides of the hole. With little effort he pulled himself out, and crouched at its edge.

"See anything?"

"Aye!" he said joyously. "I see lots of rocks, and trees, and grass, and the Amberia River, and sheep, and..." he looked back down the hole. "And best of all, I see you." He smiled. "Come here, Minara." He knelt down, and leaned into the hole, reaching for her.

She had never had someone lift her by the arms eight feet off the ground, and never before had she felt so much like a sack of grain—an oversized, lumpy sack at that. As he pulled, her feet dangled uselessly beneath her, and she scrambled to hook her toes on the edge of the hole so she could push herself out the rest of the way. Despite her own self-consciousness, he seemed not to mind at all, and once they were both out of the cave, he rolled beside her and kissed her.

"So, Minara, we did it!" He fell back onto his shoulders, and she lay beside him, soaking in the warmth and light overhead.

"Did I ever tell you how much I like your new look?" she asked.

"My what?"

She rolled over onto her stomach, and curled his hair around her finger. "I understand the beard, but why did you cut your hair?"

"Ah." He smiled, his teeth seemingly whiter than she remembered, in contrast to the dark hair of his beard. "I wasn't able to wash or shave when I was in the tower. I also apparently thrashed around quite a bit under the influence of the blasted drug, and my hair got quite tangled and knotted. When they cleaned me up, the Sarnoc said I should keep the beard for appearances' sake, but they decided the easiest solution for my hair was to cut it short. You know, whatever they may say, the adoli may not have killed me, but having it in my system that long isn't my idea of fun, either."

"Well, all the same, I like the way you look. You look like a hippie."

He raised his eyes. "Dare I ask what that is?"

She shook her head. "It would take forever to explain." Then she sat up and looked around. They were on a hillside above the river, and in the distance, a wide plain swept before them, a deep green carpet under the autumn sun. From here, the river turned sharply to the west, in the direction of the afternoon sun. Turning in the opposite direction, she exclaimed, "Arric, look! I can see the towers from here!"

He sat up. "Aye." He shielded his eyes, still a bit sensitive to the sunlight, and scanned the horizon. "It is hard to believe we came so far on foot."

They climbed up the escarpment and followed it in the direction of the Sarnoc city. Suddenly the ridge shifted to the south, forcing them to climb down a steep hillside. As they passed out of a small copse of trees, heading towards the Amberia, she saw something that instantly chilled her blood. Near the river, perhaps a quarter-mile from where they stood, and waiting to greet anyone who attempted to enter Altopon, were several tents and a dozen well-armed soldiers.

Arric fell to his knees. "Blast that brother of mine. He guessed our plans. He has men waiting for us."

"Oh no," she replied, the dread suddenly returning. They were so close. "Are you sure that's who they are? Maybe they are Sarnoc soldiers?"

Watching the activity below, Arric explained, "the Sarnoc do not maintain armed troops. Those are royal men in their blue and gold livery, and they're clearly expecting us." He pressed his lips together to fight back a curse, clearly disappointed, and stepped back towards the trees. "We won't be able to reach the city without being seen."

She gazed out at the soldiers, the agony of failure swelling inside. They had worked so hard to get here, and seeing that the Vosira's troops had beaten them to Altopon represented a crushing defeat.

"Ah, do not fear, Minara, it appears my brother is not among them."

Hope swelled in her chest. "Are you sure? How can you tell?"

"I am. If Bedoric were among them, they'd have a large tent for him, and many more soldiers. Nay, this is just a small party meant to ensure we don't reach our goal."

She noted a solitary figure emerge from the largest tent and approach a pair of men. His slight build indicated that he was not a soldier like the rest of them, but his short dark hair and glysar chain shining against the deep blue of his tunic confirmed his identity. "Oh god, Rynar's there."

Arric leapt to her side and pulled her back into the trees. "Shh... They might hear you. They are not so far from here."

"Why did he come alone? Maybe he'll help us?"

"The Aldrish?" he laughed at the absurdity of her comment. "Regardless of how he feels about you, that man despises me, and after what we did at Jiona, I can't imagine he will show me mercy. Why else do you think he's here with so many soldiers?"

She watched as Rynar pointed towards the road, and a soldier mounted his horse and rode off in the direction indicated. Despite what Arric said, the Aldrish was a healer, not a murderer. "No, I don't think so."

"Ah, Kate, remember, I am fhaoli now, and as such my life is forfeit to him."

"But—I hate to say this, but what if he's here for me, not for you?"

Arric weighed the possibility. "Aye, that could be, though again, if his purpose was benign, why travel with such a large contingent of Senvosra?" He grimly shook his head. "We dare not chance it. I will try to find a riversmith. That way we can at least go to a village for food and shelter, and come up with a plan once we're rested."

Her mind was racing, putting together possible scenarios and outcomes. Regardless of what happened, and how she felt about the man now, she had a gut feeling that Rynar would be happy to see her unharmed. He must have received reports about how they had gone over the waterfall, and surely he wondered if either of them had survived. At the same time, she understood that Arric rightfully would argue against any plan that required them to trust Rynar, a sentiment she shared.

Was there a way to benefit from Rynar's presence, though, without needing to trust his motives? For once, maybe she could use Rynar's constant fussing over her to her advantage. If she could distract Rynar sufficiently, it might be enough to get her and Arric through those stone, and into the Sarnocs' protection. She knew Arric would never agree to her plan, so she couldn't tell him what she intended to do.

Even as Arric turned to hike towards the river, she left the safety of the trees and walked with silent deliberation towards the soldiers. Arric spun around and called out to her in a sharp whisper, but she was already too far to turn back, for at that moment a soldier spotted her and raised a cry. Two more men raced towards her, and the figure in the blue tunic stopped to see what had happened. She continued walking very slowly towards the main tent, and as the figure in blue raised his arm, she began to run.

"Kate!" Rynar shouted joyfully, and rushed out to meet her, wrapping her within his arms. Quickly, he guided her into the shade of his tent. "My dear, I am so glad you're alive—and safe!" He noted the pallor of her skin, then touched her cheek, tracing around the long scab on her chin. "You have been sorely abused these past few days."

"You have no idea what I've been through." She sniffled a bit and willed tears to fall. "Oh Rynar, I'm so glad to see you. I can't believe you and the Vosira came all the way out here."

"Nay, the Vosira is not here," he said, confirming what Arric suspected. "He sent me ahead by river."

"How did you know to come here?"

"Ah, Kate, was it so hard to guess? Where else would Arric go?" He looked around. "Is he not with you?"

"He's close, but when we saw the soldiers, he wouldn't come with me." Lowering her voice, she continued, doing her best to sound conspiratorial. "I don't know what I was thinking. It was very difficult getting here, and he turned out to not be all that I expected." It was the truth, although she hoped he would take it differently than she meant it. To reinforce that misunderstanding, she buried her face against his shoulder. "I'm so sorry. You don't resent me for going, do you?"

"Of course not, my dear Kate." He was practically cooing as he caressed her hair and held her close. "Tell me, where is the Dosedra now?"

She leaned back, and just then her eyes strayed. Rynar had no furniture, but on a tray on the tent floor were the remains of his midday meal. Without realizing it, she licked her lips.

Rynar noted the gesture. "You're hungry? Have you not eaten today?"

"No, we haven't had anything to eat since the festival," she lied. It would not be a good idea for him to know the Sarnoc had left them supplies.

"Nothing?" he replied, shocked by the news. "All these days?" He guided her to a pile of pillows. "Oh my poor dear. Please, help yourself. There's still plenty, as I have not had much of an appetite myself since you left."

Without further hesitation she flopped down on the floor. She grabbed a slab of cheese and began to furiously gnaw at it.

"Be careful," he warned her with a smile, "after such a fast you must not eat too quickly. You might start with the fruit, and take it slowly."

As she ate, he stood behind her, and with his fingers began to comb out tangles in her unwashed hair.

"If I tell you where Arric is, will you promise not to hurt him? We've been so hungry. He needs to eat." Seeing his skepticism, she adopted the appearance of a lost child who had finally found her way home. "He's not well, you know. The poison never really cleared his system."

"Truly? Hmm, well, my dear, I shall do what I can," he nodded in agreement. "Where is he?"

She pointed in the general direction from which she had come. "He's waiting for me by the river. I think he's waiting for me to come back."

"He is?" he said, apparently surprised that she had acknowledged it so easily. "Shall I send men to find him?"

"If you must. I don't want him harmed, Rynar. He needs help." She had doubted whether she could seem sincere, but hopefully this clinched it.

"Aye." He smiled, convinced he had scored a victory. "You have a good heart, my dear."

His greedy, self-satisfied grin made her anxious. What would Arric think of her? Instantly she regretted not sharing her plan with him, even though it had barely jelled in her own head. He needed to be caught by surprise, so his reaction would reinforce her story and give her just enough room to maneuver around the Aldrish. It was all a gamble, that Rynar's dislike of Arric would not get the better of him, and that she had enough courage to follow through to the end.

Meanwhile, Rynar brought her clean clothing from his own chest. "I regret that I have nothing better," he said as he handed her one of his own shirts, one with delicate blue embroidery at the neck and along the shoulders, and a pair of soft woolen trousers. "Feel free to wash up in the basin there," he added just before he excused himself to speak to the Senvosra.

She washed her hair and face quickly, and was just lacing up the shirt when she heard shouts nearby. Soldiers were dragging Arric from the river's edge. She fought back tears, not wanting him harmed, but also fearing that any emotional response would betray her true feelings on the matter. Rynar returned and wrapped his arms around her from behind as they watched the soldiers bind the Dosedra's arms and legs tightly with rope, trussing him like a vicious animal. Then they carried Arric down the hill and threw him to the ground at Rynar and Kate's feet, just as if the men had killed a stag and were presenting it to them.

Rynar lowered his arms from her shoulders and took a step forward, intentionally kicking dirt in Arric's face. "Dosedra, by now you should realize that you took a foolish gamble by participating in the Jiona festival. A gamble, I might add, that you have lost. Your brother will be greatly pleased at your capture, particularly as it comes just outside the enemy's city."

"The Sarnoc are not your enemy," Arric said as he spit the dirt from his mouth. "And neither am I."

"Tell me, fhaoli, did you force yourself on the lady?"

He blinked in surprise. "No, of course not. I would never..."

"Yet you ensured the ceremony was complete?"

Arric hesitated, his eyes wild. "What did she tell you?"

In response, she stepped forward and reached for the Aldrish's hand. "He tried, Rynar, but I wouldn't let him anywhere near me.

That's when I realized what kind of person he really was." She smiled, doing her best to appear disdainful. "I guess I misjudged him."

"Ah, my dear, that's good to hear. It may not please the Goddess, but it certainly pleases me." Rynar bent his head down, affectionately addressing her. "Dearest Kate, you should go back to my tent and have something else to eat, and allow me to deal with this one." Then he knelt down, a triumphant expression on his face. "You did not truly believe she would betray me?"

Arric looked up at her, his anguished expression honest. "Kate, after everything that happened, why would you do this?"

He really believed she had sold him out, and it felt like she had just swallowed broken glass. "I'm sorry, Arric, but you really made a bad choice at the festival." She turned to Rynar. "What are you going to do with him? You won't kill him, will you?"

Rynar raised an eyebrow. "So you still care, a little, for him?" He dusted his hands on his tunic. Sensing her awkwardness, he added, "Don't worry, my dear. I appreciate your compassion. To set your mind at ease, though, you need not worry. I shall not harm him. Such is not my way." He gently pushed her hair from her eyes and allowed his touch to linger a moment longer than necessary. "In truth, his fate lies in the hands of Vosira Bedoric. It is possible that his brother shall have him executed, but we shall see. He may even show mercy, particularly since, on your word, he did not harm you."

She was relieved that she had judged this correctly. As far as she could tell, the Aldrish didn't want to harm Arric, but he also recognized his duty to the Vosira. Thinking she had chosen him over the Dosedra had to seal the deal. "Are we going back to Loraden, then?"

She stole a glance at Arric, but he would not look at her.

"Nay, we have other plans." He held his arms up to the torrapon, perhaps a couple of hundred feet away. "Vosira Bedoric plans to hold the Sarnoc accountable for their treachery. He travels even now with more Senvosra. He will take their city."

Arric had watched their exchange with sourness. He coughed when he heard the words. "A siege, Aldrish? Here? Bedoric would never dare."

Rynar turned his back to the Dosedra, with a sniff in the air, and waved to the solders to take him. "Throw him into the supply tent for now." He tapped his finger to his lips. "Give him something to eat, but nothing fancy. I wouldn't want the Vosira to think we had spoiled him too much." As they dragged Arric away, Rynar stepped closer to Kate, and hugged her. "You have done the kingdom a great service today, my lady." He cradled her head in his hands and kissed her forehead. "Come, we have much to discuss."

CHAPTER 53

As the evening came upon them, Rynar jumped up repeatedly to check on the progress of the Vosira's troops, and to inquire if any messengers had arrived.

"I'd think they'd tell you if there was any news," she reminded him after he leapt up for the third time in the midst of their picnic-style meal together on the tent floor.

"Ah, they should, but these are not men I know." He tipped his head towards the doorway of the tent. "Are you sure you didn't hear horses?"

"No, Rynar." She rubbed at a bruise on her palm. "You know, it almost seems like you're afraid to be alone with me."

He snapped his head back towards her, and took a moment to look upon her face, softened by the light of candles burning on iron stands in the corners of the tent and the brazier near the center. "You know that is not true. Surely you know that could never be true."

"I wasn't sure." Kate blushed. "Do you have wine? I'd like to share some with you."

"Aye." Crouching down, he reached for the ceramic bottle and filled their goblets. Then he lifted one and offered it to her, while he grasped his with his other hand. Casually leaning on one knee, he regarded her carefully. After he had taken a few sips, he returned his goblet to the tray, and then reached to her chin. "this is a wicked injury. I should take care of it for you, don't you think?"

She had nearly forgotten the gash along her jawbone. "If you'd like."

With one hand he cupped her chin, while the other rubbed the back of her neck. Quickly the jagged wound on her face was erased entirely, and she rubbed it in amazement. She turned towards him, her head now cradled against the back of her own hand.

"There, now that's better." He leaned back on his hands, cocking his head to one side. "I could not bear to see such an ugly mark on your face, my dear. Are you hurt anywhere else?"

She shook her head, and stared at him. His hair was glowing with the light of the candles behind his head, and when he turned his head, his profile, with his high forehead, the long, angular nose, full lips, and strong, well-defined chin, was enough to take her breath away. He was extraordinarily handsome. He had been kind, and devoted, but she knew there was more to him. People told her that the Aldrish was not a cruel or violent man, but she knew many people had their secret demons, and she feared him for his potential. What might he do if he knew what she planned, even now?

"You have been very quiet this evening." His words made her jump, and the wine sloshed in the goblet, though she was able to prevent a spill. "Are you certain the Dosedra did not hurt you in some way?" he asked gently. "There are more forms of injury than just the physical ones."

"No, I'm okay." She drank more wine. Not too much, she warned herself, or she might never complete her mission. And a mission it was, she reminded herself, nothing more. She was only here to help Arric, and to gain entry into Altopon.

He leaned close in order to pour more wine into her goblet, and his breath filled the hollow at the base of her throat. "It is so good to have you here again. I missed you."

"Thanks." She smiled as she sipped at her wine.

He put the bottle down, never taking his eyes off her. "When you left me at the Jiona ceremony, I was unsure what to do." He reached out and touched her arm, lightly tracing abstract patterns with his fingertips.

"May I share a secret with you?" Without pausing to hear her assent, he continued, "my dear, when you disappeared into the forest, I worried that you truly wished to be with him..."

Unexpectedly, she pressed a finger against his lips. "Please, let's not talk about him right now."

"You must understand my concerns, though? Of all men, he is Dosedra, considered a traitor to Sarducia. To openly align yourself with him would be dangerous enough for you, but to become intimate—"

"He means nothing to me." It was, without question, the biggest lie of her life.

Her words brought a broad smile to his lips. When it came to showing emotion, he was usually quite restrained, but tonight he seemed freer than she had known him to be. "You are quite a treasure, my dear."

Even as he reached out to her, a loud bang outside the tent made them both jump, and with a curse, Rynar stepped outside to investigate.

"A horse knocked over a crate of supplies," he announced when he returned almost immediately. She was sitting peacefully in the same posture as before, and although her eyes were closed, she wore a easy smile. Kneeling down beside her, he observed, "you are exhausted, my dear girl. Come, you should try to sleep."

Rynar offered her several cushions for her to lie down upon, but she refused to take them. "I can manage without them."

"My dear one, you do not need to be so brave. You have endured a great deal. Allow me to spoil you a little."

"Well," she considered, as he unfolded a blanket. "At least let me help you."

She knelt down to straighten one of his blankets and he crouched beside her. "You really do not need to assist me with this," he began, and then reached out like a kitten, toying at the lacings of the shirt that he had loaned her. "My dear, I think I like this new style for you. It is less formal, of course, but I believe it brings out more of your natural beauty. Looking like this, you remind me of someone else I used to know." He reached out to her and pulled a lock of her hair forward, but as he did so, his finger grazed the glysar chain around her neck. "What is this, my dear?" he asked. "I don't recall seeing you wearing it before." Before she could stop him, he had hooked the chain and pulled out the ring, allowing it to drop against her chest.

Now his eyes were huge as he stared at it. His words were sharp with accusation. "Gods, Kate, why do you have this?"

Her heart might have stopped at that moment. "It's nothing, really." Quickly, her hand went to her chest, to the space below her throat, trying to conceal the ring. "It's just..."

He grabbed it and twisted it hard enough that the abnormally strong chain choked her. "Where did you get this?" he demanded in a snarl.

Given that she had just popped out of nowhere after having spent four days, give or take, with Arric, the intensity of his response made sense. If she could have rationally characterized the moment, however, the ring seemed to frighten him more than anger him. Such rationalizations would come later, though. For now, she could barely breathe. Already he had pulled her up to her knees and was half-hanging her with the chain. If he twisted the chain any harder, he would kill her, right there. With the panic one experiences in the first stages of asphyxiation, she struggled to get her fingers underneath the chain, to force enough slack into his grip that she could breathe. "Please, Rynar," she croaked, "let go."

In all one motion he dropped the chain and pushed her away, causing her to fall backwards. "So your lover gave you a token of his affection, then," he said bitterly. He circled around to get a better look into her eyes, like an animal hunting its prey. Never had he gazed upon her with such keen suspicion, like she was a poisonous viper prepared to strike.

What was it about this damn ring? "No, it's not like that. He asked me to hold it for him, as a favor. It doesn't mean anything to me." It was the truth, pure and simple as it was. She suddenly was grateful she knew nothing more about it. There was something about Rynar at this moment that suggested he'd know if she lied to him about this.

He advanced on her again, and again grabbed it between his long fingers. "This is more than a simple favor. Do you truly not know what it is?"

She was forced to rise up to her knees as he again tugged on the chain. "No. He wouldn't tell me. Please Rynar, you're hurting me."

Rynar yanked the chain once, very hard, causing her torso to collide with his. She flailed her arms on either side, but he would not release the ring. Instead, she was forced to stare into his dark pupils, which were only inches from her own. "You owe that man no favors." He pulled it again, as if to break the chain, but it did not snap. "Ah, it's glysar." He flung her back to the cushions. "Take it off," he commanded.

Breathing heavily, she looked down at the ring, and then at him. She had never seen him like this, and wasn't sure what to do.

Noticing she had made no move to comply, he pointed at it. "Well? Come now, you have no business wearing that. Take it off!"

Fearing what he would do if she refused, she unhooked the clasp. As soon as the chain came loose, he snatched the ring from her hands and threw it against the wall of the tent.

His eyes, already dark in color, were absolutely black now. "I never want to see you as much as touch that ring again, do you hear me, Kate? Never!"

The blood was rushing into her ears, filling her head with a roar. She didn't feel like she could remain upright on her own power, and she collapsed back onto the cushions. "Why are you being like this, Rynar? What is it?"

"It is the ring of a fhaoli. If Vosira Bedoric saw you wearing that, he'd have you executed on the spot." Then he squared his shoulders, and shook his head slightly, as if already his anger was dissipating. "You need not worry about it now." His mouth jerked, as if he was about to say something else. Then another loud noise outside brought him back to attention. "Gods," he snapped. "I will be right back."

When the tent was empty, she shook her head. Had he really almost choked her with the chain? Rynar? Never had he done anything but look after her, fawn over her. It seemed to confirm her worst suspicions of him, yet it also struck her as wholly uncharacteristic of him to lash out at her in such a manner.

It was the ring. For the same reasons Arric was so insistent that she take it to Altopon, Rynar seemed determined that it never see the light of day. It was just a ring, a simple unadorned band. Why was it so significant? How could anyone care so much about it?

She wanted—needed—a moment to compose herself after what had just happened, but she did not have a chance. She heard him batting at the tent flaps with his hands. "The Dosedra is hollering for more food," he explained. "I decided that he should be given what he wants, if just to keep the peace for the evening. I do not wish any additional interruptions, at least not from that man." His lips curved into a smile, but it had no warmth to it. "There are more important things that require my attention."

Kate was now afraid of him, and didn't want to stay in the tent. Could he have killed her? Would he have done so, if he had known the truth about what had happened in the cave? She rubbed her hands together. They seemed so cold. It was as if she had been made out of ice. Was it possible to feel colder here, now, than she did in the cave that first night after almost drowning in the river? There was no warmth in this tent, not from the candles, nor from the brazier that burned red hot, nor from her companion. She had planned to be charming, to catch him off-guard, but she was at a loss, unable to do what was needed. With regret, she realized she had lost her nerve. All she wanted now was to find her shoes, which were somewhere by the flap of the tent, and run away. The only thing that kept her in the tent now was knowing she still had to save Arric.

"I frightened you." He didn't ask, and it wasn't a question.

She could do little other than field a blank stare.

"Oh, my dear, that ring. You must understand, I believed it lost, and I expected never to see it again. It is a thing of great evil, Kate. If anyone knew you carried it, it would unravel everything I've worked for, and it would put you in grave danger. I wasn't angry at you, you understand, but the fhaoli who dared make you responsible for it." As she continued to stare at him, he added, "ah, but it must not have seemed like that, eh?"

Kate wanted to disembowel him right about then, but instead, she did her best to appear contrite, as if she accepted the blame for what had happened. "I'm sorry for angering you. I didn't know anything about the ring, I swear."

He gazed down his nose at her. "Truly, my dear?"

She nodded.

"Ah, then, we shall put it behind us, shall we?" He folded his legs underneath him as he sat beside her. "I can see that you're still upset. My dear, that is all over with now. You must forgive me for losing my temper." He placed his index finger and thumb on her neck, just under her jaw.

As he touched her, she felt pinpricks of heat come from his fingertips. For a moment, she allowed his touch, but then she forced a cough, breaking the contact. It was as if there had been an electrical current running through his fingers. What was he doing? Was it a form of healing, or was it something else?

"My dear, are you ill?"

She shook her head, and pretended to cough again. "I think I just need something to drink." She reached for her goblet and took a sip.

Rynar stared at her, as if finding her sudden movement odd, but said nothing.

She set the goblet down beside her. If she was going to act, it had to be now. As much as she loathed Rynar at this moment, for Arric she would be brave. Taking a breath to steady herself, she reached up and wrapped her finger around a tuft of hair by his ear. Before he could register what was happening, she leaned forward to kiss him.

As she did so, he pulled her close, and kissed her back with passion that had been building all these weeks. Then without warning, he gasped and pushed her away.

"What's wrong?" His reaction shocked her. "Haven't you wanted to do that since you met me?" She knew how he looked at her, and had seen him watching her when he thought she was asleep. Surely she had read his desires correctly after all this time.

He blinked as he looked at her, and then stood up. If she had simply intended to make him lose his composure, she could have counted this as a win. He had paled considerably and looked very nervous. "That is not a good idea." Drumming his fingers against his thighs, he looked around the tent, and his eyes alighted on the wine. "Perhaps more wine? The last few days really took a lot out of you, and I think you should regain your strength."

She took a step forward, and reached for his hands. This was too important, and she needed to win him over. She ran the tip of one finger down his nose. "Rynar, can you honestly tell me you aren't interested in me?" She reached for his hands.

He shook his arms to prevent her from touching him. "Let me find your goblet." Retrieving it, he dashed wine into the bowl of the goblet as quickly as he could, and handed it to her.

"Why are you acting like this?" He had to break eventually. Rather than take the goblet, she ran her fingers down his arm. "You have no reason to feel guilty about this."

"Nay, my dear." He held out the wine. "Please, take it."

She smiled sweetly, and blinked her eyes. Could she make it look like she was just a bit tipsy, a tiny bit reckless? "Come on, we must celebrate the fact that we're finally together." She took the wine, and tipping her head back, drank deeply.

He now was refilling his own goblet, seemingly as much to occupy himself as out of any desire to drink more, though he did not set it down as he usually would. "My dear, what has come over you this evening?" He nervously took a sip. "This doesn't seem like you at all."

She let her head fall back, and she shook it lightly, laughing. "Oh Rynar, don't you see? The whole time I was gone, all I could think about was you..." With that, she closed her eyes, as if imagining a night of passion, and making sure there was a smile on her face. Little did he know she was actually imagining her time with Arric, trying to draw strength from the memory.

"Ah, indeed?" He continued to stand a few feet away.

She opened her eyes and sipped again from her goblet, and set it aside. Then she knelt down and patted the pillows. "Come over here."

"Nay, I—"

She sat, crossing her legs in front of her. "Fine, if you can honestly say you're not interested...." She could not figure out why she was failing so badly. He seemed so afraid of her, as if now that he had her, he didn't know what to do with her. "Why don't you just come sit with me, we'll drink more wine, and I'll tell you about my journey."

That made him sigh in relief. "Aye, that is a good idea." He took a seat where he stood, two arm spans away from her. Shaking her head, she shuffled on her knees to reach his goblet and then handed it to him

"I do not need any more wine," he protested.

She thought fast. Unlike everyone else she had met in Sarducia, the Aldrish did not consume much alcohol. He had told her once that remaining sober gave him an edge over others; what he didn't say was that he hated to feel out of control. If her plan were to have any chance of succeeding, however, he had to drink tonight. Holding the goblet in one hand, she reached out to him with the other hand. "Come on, now, Rynar, sit with me."

He shrugged and agreed, "just this one goblet." Then he crawled over to where the pillows were piled and accepted the wine from her.

In return, she began recounting her tale, focusing solely on the race through the forest but stretching it out to sound as though that was all they did all night. After perhaps twenty minutes, she faked a yawn.

"My dear, you must be exhausted."

She nodded, and reclined on the pillows, tugging at his sleeve.

Rather than resist, he curled up beside her. "I should be careful. I might fall asleep myself. It has been a very trying few days."

CHAPTER 54

I t seemed to take forever, but finally she heard a half snore coming from his lips. She had not fueled passion with him, but she had sensed something else—exhaustion. He probably had slept as poorly these past few days as she had. And probably for the better, as any glimmer of hope he had for a relationship with her had vanished, as if it had been sunlight within the cave.

Before anything else could happen, she slipped from under his arm and stepped over to the stool by the tent entrance, where he had placed his sword and dagger. Without taking a second to admire the sleek scabbard or the jewels set into the pommel, she unsheathed the dagger. Standing behind the tent flaps, she listened for the footsteps of the guards on duty. One paced close to the tent, but apparently in one of his forays outside, Rynar had given the soldiers orders not to intrude, so this guard kept a respectable distance. As he turned away, she snuck outside and around to the rear of Rynar's tent unseen. Barefoot on the cold ground, she moved as quickly as she could, knowing she had not a second to spare. If Rynar were to awaken, he and the Senvosra would descend upon her like the hounds of hell.

Fortunately the sun had set in the time she had spent with Rynar, and clouds poured in from the west, leaving no stars and only a pale wash from the moon to illuminate the sky. The light of a few anemic torches left wide swaths of shadow for her to cross the small encampment without being seen.

Most of the dozen or so soldiers must have gone inside their own tent, for she could hear their voices clustered together. Drinking, perhaps? Or gaming? It mattered little to her if it kept them occupied. Of the three soldiers that patrolled the camp, they appeared to be concerned more for the activities inside Altopon's giant torrapon ring rather than beyond it. With the Dosedra now in their custody, it seemed Rynar had expected no threat to come from beyond the camp, and the guard on duty was kept to a minimum. They were not traveling merchants or Bhagali, after all, and the ratio of items worth stealing versus the armaments carried by the soldiers made this an unattractive target for bandits.

As for their prisoner, the soldiers had pushed Arric into the supply tent, which had been placed perhaps a dozen yards away from the others. As she approached it from the side, she noted with relief that Rynar had stationed only a single soldier to guard Arric. Since the Dosedra was weak from his journey, and now firmly tied with ropes, perhaps no one considered him an escape risk.

She hung back, watching Arric's guard carefully. He should have been standing alertly, but instead he was seated on a stool and appeared to be dozing. She noticed that the tent flaps had been tied shut. She felt the walls of the tent, only to discover that crates lined the sides. To reach Arric, she would need to confront the guard, but as soon as he saw her, his cry would alert the entire camp.

Time was now her enemy. The longer she delayed, the better the chance that Rynar would awaken, or the guard would hear her. As she was about to advance, she heard a rustling within the tent. Was that Arric? She longed to call to him, to solicit his assistance, but again, she feared discovery. The noise, however, disturbed the soldier, and as she peered around the side of the tent to watch, he untied the flaps and stuck his head inside to check on the Dosedra.

It was now or never, she told herself. She had no chance to give her plan any rational thought, and if she had, she certainly would have abandoned it. The dagger was heavy in her hand, and awkward. There was a chance she wouldn't even be able to effectively wield the blade, but she had to make the best of the opportunity. She had seen this in the movies so many times. All she had to do was approach from behind, hold the sharp blade at the guard's throat, and he would do her bidding.

With a deep breath, she took two silent steps forward. Even with the care she had taken, the soldier, still leaning into the tent, heard her, and turned. As he reached for his own weapon, she knew she had to do something, and without a second's hesitation she lunged towards him, aiming for his abdomen.

He was surprised by the source of the attack. "Girl, what are you doing?" he asked, and raised his arm, causing her only to nick his hand with the knife. He reached for his sword, and opened his mouth to call out to the others, and in that split second she attacked a second time, this time sending the dagger into his throat.

It all happened in an instant. She had never used a weapon against someone before, but she had not hesitated, and instinct had guided her hand true. The blow was quickly fatal, and blood poured from the wound, and his legs collapsed under his weight.

She could not take the time to process what had happened, to consider that she had just killed a man. Instead, she took another deep breath and pushed into the tent, her arms and legs shaking from the adrenaline.

At first she could see nothing, for there was no light. "Arric?" she whispered. A couple pounding heartbeats later she saw just enough of a shadow on the ground to guess what it was. "Are you here?"

"Kate?" he responded, his voice hoarse. "What are you doing?"

"Shh." She helped him stand, and led him, hobbling, to the opening. He stared at the dead soldier lying in the dark pool of blood flowing by his feet. Astounded by the sight, he had enough presence of mind to notice the weapon that she gripped tightly, the blade and her shirt soaked in blood. "You did this?"

She nodded, a grim expression on her face. She wasn't pleased to admit what she had done, and even as she looked upon the dead man, she felt queasy.

Having assessed the situation, he now whispered back, "use the blade to cut these ropes. Hurry!"

Doing her best to force herself to focus on the task at hand, and not think about the man she had killed, she sawed through the ropes on his feet first. In comparison to dealing the deathblow to an armed soldier, this was maddeningly slow and difficult. Daggers apparently were not designed to cut hemp. Eventually she cut through the rope around his feet, and then she held the dagger with both hands as he pressed against it, sawing the ropes from his wrists himself. Once free, he grabbed the knife and led her behind the tent, as far from the center of the encampment as possible.

Arric pointed with Rynar's knife to the dark shadows of the torrapon, and the Sarnoc towers beyond them. "We just need to pass through the stones," he told her. "They won't dare follow us any further."

She looked back, to make sure they weren't going to be followed—and then she panicked.

"Oh god, I can't." The ring remained in Rynar's tent. She had made a promise to Arric, and she had to go back to retrieve it.

He hadn't heard her. Instead, he nudged her shoulder. "Come on. They will find us any moment."

She shook her head furiously, her feet rooted in place. "No, you go. I have to go back."

He was already prepared to run, and held out his hand. When he heard her, though, his jaw dropped. "What do you mean, you have to go back? Come on, Kate, we must go now, or we're dead."

She feared that she had run out of time. The ropes took far too long to cut. "Arric, trust me. I wouldn't do this if I didn't have to. You go, get the Sarnoc. I'll be right behind you."

He grabbed her arms. "Are you sure? What could possibly be so important?"

"Don't worry about me, please. Just go." There were tears in her eyes. "Go, or they'll kill you."

He took a step towards the torrapon. "Kate?"

"Don't make this all for nothing." She looked at the dead man yards away. "Please, just go."

CHAPTER 55

She ran back to Rynar's tent. In some sort of miracle, he was still snoring on the pillows. "Thank god," she mumbled to herself, and then looked around the tent. There were pillows and blankets piled everywhere. She went to the corner where he had thrown the ring, and began pawing through the blankets to find it.

"Looking for this?"

She whirled around. Rather than being sound asleep on the pillow, he now was standing behind her, with the ring in his hand.

"So you thought to deceive me, did you? You and your fhaoli lover? Ah, Kate, I should have known better. Or perhaps I did?" He smiled cruelly. "So you helped him escape, but you couldn't go to the Sarnoc without this, could you?"

She whirled around to face him. After all that she had done to get to this point, she wasn't going to give up now. "Hand it over, Rynar."

He clucked his tongue at her, and shook his head. He was smiling, the same calculating smile she knew from watching him interact with the other Bhagali in the keep. There was no passion or devotion behind it. "Nay, Kate. It does not belong to you—or to the fhaoli either." He slipped it onto his index finger, and admired it. "Did you ever try it on, my dear?"

"No. Why would I?"

He pretended to shake his head as if some tragedy had occurred. "Pity. It might have surprised you." With exaggerated motions, he twisted it from his index finger and moved the ring to his thumb. Then he slipped it on his middle finger, his ring finger, and his pinkie finger, pausing each time to appreciate its subtle glow in the candlelight. "You know, it fits every finger. Amazing, is it not?"

"Rynar, come on. Just give it to me."

"Nay, I will not." He advanced on her. "I think we have some unfinished business, you and I," he said suggestively, and grasped both of her wrists.

She found it hard to physically resist him, almost as if she was about to pass out, and she sunk to her knees, prevented from collapsing entirely by the fact that he held her firmly. Was this his healing power, causing her to wilt? Could it really work that way? She realized how easily she had slept under his touch. It had been more than physical comfort he had offered her after all.

She tried to struggle, but she could barely move.

"I apologize for dozing off a short time ago. Now perhaps you will tell me what really happened with the Dosedra, and why you were willing to betray me for him, after everything I've done for you."

"No. Rynar, this isn't right. You can't force me...."

He raised his eyebrow in surprise. "What isn't right?" In voice that suggested newfound resentment, he demanded, "you tried to seduce me, did you not? Just to save that fhaoli."

She blinked away tears. "I'm sorry, Rynar. I never meant to hurt you."

His mouth wrenched into a combination of anguish and loathing. He still held her. "After everything I have done for you, still you betray me for a filthy murderer." He threw her to the ground and toed her side where the soldier's blood had splashed onto the shirt. "Do you not see it? I had so much hope for you. I truly believed you would be the one to transcend all the evils of this land. Yet, look at you now. Even I have never taken a life." He made a sound much like a growl, a sound that came from deep in his throat. "I never lied to you, not about anything. Especially not how much you meant to me. And this is how you thank me." He knelt down beside her, and held her hair so she would see his face without turning away. "You have betrayed me, but worse, I fear that you will betray our people, and you shall do it with the help of one who has already walked down that path. Blood is on your hands now. It is all over you. It's the first time, but I daresay it will not be the last."

From behind Rynar a tall shadow blocked the light from the torches outside. "Leave her alone," a voice commanded.

She tipped her head just enough to see a blade come to rest on Rynar's shoulder.

The Aldrish froze in place, releasing his grip on her hair. Kate, still lying on the ground beside Rynar's knees, didn't breathe.

"Alive or dead, Aldrish? Which shall it be?"

Rynar's face paled as the blade tickled his ear. "You would not use my own dagger to kill me, fhaoli?"

"I am Dosedra," he corrected, his voice unyielding. He stepped to one side, and the blade reached for Rynar's chin. "That is the only title I wish to hear from your mouth."

"What of her?" the Aldrish asked. "Kate has killed a man—a member of the Senvosra, no less. That is cold-blooded murder, and treason. You know the Vosira will condemn her for her actions."

"Nay, I think not. She killed him in self-defense."

"Ah." Rynar nodded. "So I shall tell the Vosira that in the process of trying to seduce me, stealing my dagger, and aiding in the escape of a wanted fhaoli, she killed one of his men—not threatened him, or wounded him, but murdered him outright? And that he should look upon her actions as self-defense? The two of you play a dangerous game, and it is Kate who shall pay the price."

"She shall never be punished for saving my life—not while I live, Aldrish—and you know why." The knife left Rynar's chin, the tip of the blade traveling down his right arm to his hand. "I believe that belongs to me," he said, neatly hooking the point under the glysar ring on Rynar's pinkie. "Remove it now, or I shall remove your finger instead."

Without hesitation, Rynar slid it from his hand dropped it onto Kate's chest, as if willing to comply only so far. Then he stood up, no longer intimidated by the dagger.

"Dosedra," he said softly, "take the ring and go. Leave her. She does not belong with you."

With his free left hand, Arric reached down and grabbed the ring. Then he threw the dagger across the tent and lifted her with his right hand. Once she was on her feet, he released her again.

"Aldrish, the lady shall choose her own fate. You will control her no longer." With those words, he spun on his heels and kicked past the tent flaps.

"Kate?" Rynar looked at her.

She turned to him, and saw the anguish in his face. Why did she matter so much to him, even after what had just happened? "I really am sorry," she said, as if it would mend everything, and then she ran out after Arric.

CHAPTER 56

The room was bright, with freshly whitewashed walls. A fire blazed in the hearth, and the chimney efficiently drew the smoke out of the room. The windows, made of beautiful swirling glass, reached from floor to ceiling, while the floor was tiled with spotless white marble.

Arric was pacing rapidly across the small chamber, taking five strides and then spinning on his toe, the hard leather soles of his boots offering no resistance to the smooth tiles. Sarnoc Vaj, meanwhile, was sitting alone, his elbows propped up on a small round table, his chin resting on interlocked fingers. Both seemed lost in concentration and did not notice that Kate and Sebachin were standing silently in the doorway.

Sebachin nudged her to enter first, and when she stepped across the threshold, Arric caught sight of her and nodded, waving her to the table, where she was greeted with a solemn nod from the Sarnoc.

"You look well, Bhara," Sarnoc Vaj said.

She nodded. Since their arrival last night, she had done little but eat, bathe and sleep. She was now wearing a soft tunic and hose of blue, much like what Arric wore, she realized, and bit back a smile. "I feel much better now, thank you."

Addressing her companion, Arric asked, "I must apologize, but have we met?"

"Nay, Dosedra, we have not. I am Pasadhi Sebachin." He bowed his head politely in recognition of Arric's rank, and then joined her and Sarnoc Vaj at the table.

"Good, I'm glad you're here then." Arric walked over to the table, but did not sit. "You should both know, there's been a new development," he announced with a frown. He was gripping a scroll that he twisted between his clenched fists.

At first Kate was happy to see Arric again. When they had arrived a day and a half earlier, three laliri had hustled her off to a private chamber for bathing, food, and rest, and she hadn't seen him since then. However, as she watched him now, she grew increasingly nervous. What had happened?

"Vosira Bedoric arrived outside the city a short time ago," the Sarnoc explained. Although she had seen him before, she couldn't help noticing that Vaj was almost exactly Arric's height, and his shoulders were just as broad. Despite his grey hair and trace of wrinkles near his eyes and mouth, he would be a formidable foe with a sword if he were ever inclined to fight. "He sent an envoy with a message," he said, indicating the scroll Arric held, "demanding that I release the Dosedra into his custody." He appeared calm, but from the clipped tone of each of his words, it was obvious that underneath his placid exterior, he was quite angry. The Sarnoc was not someone to underestimate, and he wasn't the type who would be easily intimidated. It didn't seem in his nature to acquiesce to the Vosira's demands, and she found it hard to believe that this news was the least bit unsettling to him, since everyone, even Kate, had already seen it coming.

Vaj continued. "He makes this demand based on his claim that we are harboring fhaoli, and accuses Sarnoc of violating ancient agreements. According to the Vosira, we have brought an end to centuries of cooperation and coexistence between the Sarnoc and the Sarducian people. Because of this, he believes that he has the right to force our surrender and usurp our authority." He paused, and Kate noticed his lip twitch. His words seemed to be taken directly from the scroll Arric was now mangling, and as he said them, there was a tinge of sarcasm and anger. "The Vosira further demands that I agree to submit myself and all

Sarnoc to his rule. Otherwise he plans to lay siege to Altopon with the intention of destroying our city."

At that moment he turned his gaze to her, causing her to swallow quickly. "Of course, that's not all," he snapped. "According to the message, he claims that we are holding you, Bhara, against your will, and—as if he had the right—he demands that we turn you over to him as well." He pointed to the parchment with a wave of sorts, bidding Arric to read it.

Arric unrolled the crumpled parchment. He seemed less able to contain his anger than the Sarnoc had been. "Aye. After my brother's demands, there is an added piece at the bottom, from the Aldrish." Squinting to read the text, he continued, "this is what the bastard wrote: 'Kate is an unwilling participant in this quarrel between brothers, and must be freed immediately.' " He cleared his throat with a grimace, as if he had a bad taste in his mouth. He then dropped the scroll to the table and looked helplessly to her. "Those are his words, Kate," he said, "and I would spare you any more of this garbage, but—"

"Just finish the message, Dosedra," Vaj admonished him.

Arric sighed. "Very well, Sarnoc." He grabbed the scroll again, but then lowered it. "I can scarcely believe his audacity. 'She still needs to discover who she is and what her place is here in Sarducia, and I alone can provide that information. I care deeply for her, and promise to provide for her welfare and happiness when she leaves Altopon.' "

Kate leaned back in her chair and folded her arms across her chest. "Wow." She exhaled heavily and shook her head. So he had information about her, and never shared it before now? The idea incensed her, as if he was holding out information he knew she desperately sought as a form of currency, a bribe. She could not determine whether the words were honest or strategic—or perhaps, knowing Rynar, a bit of both.

Arric threw the parchment to the table, and snapped his hand in a dismissive gesture. "Sarnoc, Kate will confirm that I did not force her to come with me," he protested. "As a matter of fact, in the Aldrish's camp, Kate rescued me, not the other way around." He spun towards her, entreating her to confirm what he said.

From what he said, she guessed that this had already been a topic of discussion between the two men. Did the Sarnoc not believe Arric's account? At first she was uncertain how to respond. Through his note, it was as if Rynar had reached into this very room to say those words. Then she gazed up at Arric, who stood now near the hearth. There had been an edge to his voice she had never heard before, as if the act of reading the note had caused him pain.

It was the realization of that sharpness, almost desperation, that shook her from the momentary spell the Aldrish had cast. "It's true. I had to trick Rynar so that we could make it here, though Arric helped at the end. But yes, I came here willingly." The last thing she wanted was for the Sarnoc to turn her over to the Aldrish, who likely would want to rip her limb from limb despite what he wrote. "I don't believe anything he wrote in that note—at least, not after what I did..." she couldn't finish that thought, and instead, suddenly fearful, added, "please don't send me back there."

"I do not intend to do so," the Sarnoc reassured her, though his voice was firm and anything but comforting. "However, it is good to have the Dosedra's story confirmed."

Arric reached over and threw the scroll into the fire. "Tell her the rest, Sarnoc."

"There's more still?" Sebachin had been silent the entire time, but now he spoke without thinking, his face betraying his surprise.

Vaj nodded, but hesitated a moment. He pressed his hands together, and tapped them to his lips, while blinking once. It was as if he was drawing strength from an unseen force. "Vosira Bedoric had one more message for us, and this one is quite serious. He claims he holds Sarnoc Sofinar captive in his camp, and will kill him if we do not comply with his demands." He looked to Sebachin and Kate in turn. "All of them."

The color drained from Kate's cheeks, as Sebachin buried his face in his hands, and Arric had resumed pacing. "That's blackmail!"

For the first time, Vaj appeared unsettled. "Aye."

She curled her arms over her head, as if recoiling from a physical blow. This was truly devastating news. How had the Vosira found Torv out after so many years? This raised the stakes for everyone.

The room was silent for several minutes. Then Sebachin asked, in barely more than a whisper, "will the Vosira really go through with it?"

Arric stopped pacing, and stared out the window. Without looking back at the others, he said, "I believe he will. We sons of Parmon are stubborn." He did not smile at the self-effacing remark. "I know Bedoric. He's not bluffing. He fully intends to use every advantage he has to weaken the Sarnoc and defeat Altopon. With the history between them, I think it's safe to say he would have no problem killing Sofinar if we do not agree to his demands. It's funny, though, because before this morning I believed Sofinar dead and buried in Bhoren. Finding out my old friend still lives, but under these conditions, is rather bittersweet."

"Dosedra," Vaj said, his voice not as firm as before, "you understand that I cannot surrender my authority to your brother, not even in exchange for Sofinar's life."

"But he's Sarnoc!" Kate instinctively grasped what it would mean for the Vosira to kill Sofinar. It wasn't just killing a man. It had political, religious and social significance beyond anything she could comprehend. "Arric, can't we do something? We can't just refuse to cooperate, not if it means—"

Arric walked back to the table. "Aye, my thoughts exactly," he agreed, and pulled up a chair beside her. Speaking directly to her, he explained. "While I agree with Sarnoc Vaj that Altopon cannot be compromised, there are things that you and I can do. That is why I requested that you join us. We need to discuss our options."

"You know that your brother won't forgive us for what we've done." Memories of Nyvas, the adoli, the bold escape, and most recently, the murdered guard, all remained keen in her mind. "If we surrender to him like he wants, he'll kill both of us without a second thought. We won't get another chance."

"Aye, Dosedra, she's right," Sebachin agreed.

"I don't plan to surrender, Pasadhi." In a surprising gesture, he smiled. "I plan to fight."

All three stared at him in astonishment.

"Fight, Dosedra?" Vaj asked in measured tones. He had placed his hands, his fingers still interlaced, on the table's surface. Despite the crisis that was unfolding, it seemed that he had regained his composure. "You understand that while you remain within these walls, your brother cannot harm you. However, if you were to leave, I would be unable to offer the same protection, and I cannot supply any men who can fight at your side against the Senvosra."

"Of course. However, I don't intend to fight him with an army. There are other weapons that are much more powerful."

Arric reached into his tunic and pulled out a small pouch. He yanked open the drawstrings, and with a dramatic flourish, he allowed the single item inside to tumble out.

Everyone again fell silent.

Sparkling in the sunlight, dancing as it fell to the table below, was a glysar ring. The ring Kate had carried for him, the ring that had frightened Rynar so desperately last night.

Before, it was a plain silvery band. Now, it seemed to have caught fire as it spun before them.

Arric grinned. "It's about time I claim what is mine."

When the band came to rest on the white marble, the Sarnoc reached for it. He held it up to the sunlight, and whistled. Then he held it out in front of him, in the direction of the others. To Arric specifically, he stated, "this was Vosira Parmon's ring." He again examined the inside of the band. "The inscription inside is the Oath of Vosidari."

"Aye," Arric replied simply. His confidence was solid, and he seemed slightly amused, if such an emotion was possible with all the grim news.

Vaj placed the ring back on the table, and Kate again stared at it. In all the time she had worn it, looking at it in private as if she could decipher its meaning, she had never seen an inscription inside the ring, but now it was clear as day.

"Dosedra, how can it be that you possess this ring?" Vaj asked him. "As I understand it, the ring was stolen immediately after the Vosira's murder, and never found."

Arric's eyes were level with the Sarnoc. He did not so much as blink as he listened to Vaj's words. "Nay, Sarnoc, it was not stolen. My father planned to formally announce his decision to name me as Charvos, and he gave me the ring to seal it. Unfortunately, he was killed that very day. So the announcement was never made, and I never wore the ring. Until now, as far as I know, the only ones to know about his decision were my father, Sofinar and myself."

"May I?" Sebachin asked, pointing to the ring as if he too wished to hold it. When Arric nodded, the Pasadhi leaned forward. He placed the ring in his left palm, folded his fingers over it, and concentrated for a moment with his eyes closed. "It was freely given to you," he confirmed. He held out the ring, returning it to its rightful owner. "What you say is the truth." Then he leaned back again and frowned. "You were the rightful Charvos," the Pasadhi announced. "Your brother has no right to the position he holds. You, Arric, should be Vosira now."

Kate inhaled quickly and held her breath, as if afraid to exhale and break the spell. She hadn't expected any of this, and was frozen in place as the idea slammed into her consciousness. Now she understood why no one had been willing to tell her about the ring. Its secret was potent, with political ramifications well beyond anything she would have expected. No wonder Sofinar would not take it from her. No wonder Rynar had become apoplectic. It changed everything.

He should have been Vosira.

Arric should have been the king.

"Blast it all!" Arric shouted, shattering the silence. Then he unclenched his fist which held the ring. "I should have claimed this as my right." He stared at the ring and everyone remained still.

Finally, he continued. "Eight years I've had to think on this. Back then, I believed I was making the right decision. When I found out my father was dead, I could barely think straight. I didn't even question the fact that I was sent out on some fool's errand to find his killer, only to discover that in my absence the Council had met and proclaimed Bedoric as Vosira. I was so naïve then, and frightened. I kept my silence, foolishly thinking that if I spoke up at that point, I'd be accused of killing him myself." He exhaled loudly. "Bedoric was older, and I thought he'd be a good ruler. Had I known what kind of Vosira my brother would become, I would have taken the chance." He made a face of utter disgust.

Kate stared between the two men. "You couldn't have predicted this."

"Nay, in truth I knew from the start, but I didn't want to admit it." He stared at his ring. "Bedoric wasn't even Vosira yet when he had Stavan arrested and thrown in that damn cage to rot. The boy was no more guilty than I was, but he was a convenient scapegoat." Again he pounded his thigh. "Now when I think back on it, it was as if my brother knew about the ring, and when whoever killed my father disappeared afterwards, Bedoric found someone to take the blame. And I just played along. Had I said something, countless people wouldn't have had to suffer like they have all these years. Fantion, Sander, people I've never even met. But what weighs on my conscience more than anything is what happened to Stavan after that. He was just a boy, but because of my cowardice he was forced to grow up in Lockleaf rather than follow his calling."

"What do you mean?" Vaj asked. "I thought the boy was killed by a mob in Loraden."

Arric shook his head. "Nay, he is alive and well, and known as Nyvas. He's the one she helped to rescue while I was held in the tower."

"Nyvas?" Sebachin repeated. "That's the Mosumi word for blood."

"Aye, that's right," Arric agreed. "Friends of mine rescued him, with Sofinar's assistance, and arranged for it to look like he was slaughtered in the square, so that no one would go looking for him." He raked his hair with both hands. "All he had intended to do was meet with Sofinar to find out if a charnok could have a calling, and by being in the wrong part of the keep at the wrong time, he managed to get caught up in a plot he had nothing to do with."

"Dosedra, I do not mean to get sidetracked, but would you clarify the last point?" Vaj did not seem amused. "What do you mean by 'calling'?"

"You don't know?" Arric tipped his head, surprised. "Nyvas is Sarnoc."

Vaj's mouth dropped open for a moment, and it took him a moment to compose himself again. He frowned, and then tried to smile, and finally settled on a cold stare as he responded to the casual announcement. "Nay, Dosedra, you are mistaken," he concluded quickly. "One cannot be Sarnoc without training and the pas'hala ritual. The one you call Nyvas, who was Stavan, has never had those things. Although he might be eligible to become laliri, he is not Sarnoc."

Arric shrugged. "If that's the case, you might wish to find out how it is that he can speak to people in their heads. I thought that was something only a Sarnoc could do." He paused, as if waiting for Vaj to interrupt, and when he didn't, Arric continued. "When Bedoric locked me in the tower room, I thought I would go mad listening to the boy. From his cell, Nyvas had nothing better to do than make up horrible poetry and inflict it on me, knowing I could not respond. One of these days I'll have to find a way to repay that favor."

To the sound of Sebachin's and Kate's smirks, Vaj shook out his sleeves, and tried to regain command of the conversation. "Very well. At another time we shall invite Nyvas here so that we can investigate that further. But that's of little concern at the moment." Vaj turned back to Arric, and soberly, he asked, "Dosedra, what do you wish to do now?"

Arric's grin vanished as held the ring in front of him, staring at it as if he had never seen it before. "Sarnoc, this has gone on long enough. Without delay, I must confront my brother about our father's death, and try to reverse some of the wrongs that I caused by my silence over all these years." He turned to Kate. "And as much as I hate to say it, you need to come with me. We all know how much Bedoric relies on his Aldrish, and you are the only one who may be able to get the truth out of that bastard."

CHAPTER 57

"In the name of all those within Altopon, I order you to withdraw!"

In the last glow of daylight, standing on the Altopon side of the giant standing stones, Sarnoc Vaj shouted to the men before them.

Kate stood behind him, flanked by Arric. The wind snapped their tunics fiercely, and she felt like a big flag.

As Vaj called out to the men, some of the soldiers stared at the Sarnoc, while others turned to each other in confusion or fear. It seemed the Vosira had not prepared them for Sarnoc defiance. Dozens of men rushed about, some grabbing weapons or brandishing swords. After a moment of uncertainty, several archers took positions on the edge of the tents. They pulled arrows and nocked them against loose bowstrings, ready to draw if ordered.

Finally Vosira Bedoric stepped from his tent. "Greetings, Sarnoc," he announced, his voice carrying easily on the wind. No one was surprised that the Aldrish stood at his side. "I welcome the chance to discuss the terms of your surrender."

"There shall be no surrender," Sarnoc Vaj called back. "Sarnoc submit to no authority other than the gods themselves." He stood confidently even as the wind tugged at his braid. "There are other matters we wish to discuss."

"What other matters?" Bedoric shouted. "You are traitors and oath-breakers, and as such, you have nothing to discuss other than your immediate surrender."

"Ah, Vosira, but we have much to speak about, and we will," Vaj responded calmly, a smile on his face. "We shall join you to explain."

With that announcement, Sarnoc Vaj led the procession through the stones, Kate and Arric following closely behind. Arric's face was stern, his jaw clenched tightly. His right hand was fidgeting at his waist, and she recognized the twitching fingers. He wanted his sword. They were walking into the middle of an armed camp, a sizable military force that would arrest them both on sight, and they came only with a Sarnoc as protection. Despite his own anxiety, he leaned over to her and grasped her hand. "You will be safe," he promised her. "The Sarnoc have this situation well under control."

"I hope you're right," she replied. "I'm not sure who hates us more at this point: your brother or the Aldrish."

He grunted in response, and squeezed her hand. She took that as a sign that they were equally nervous.

As they approached, a shout rose up among the soldiers, and several gathered just beyond the torrapon stones that rose up like a great fence.

Vaj leaned towards Arric. "Dosedra, it is not too late to turn back."

"Nay, Sarnoc. I am not afraid of him."

***

The trio was rapidly ushered into the Vosira's tent. Despite the rising wind, two sides had been tied back, so it was little more than a canopy over their heads. The Vosira and Aldrish already sat at a low table, a portable contraption with boards that could be pulled apart for easy transportation. There were no chairs, but as in Rynar's tent the night before, they would sit on large cushions.

"Please make yourselves comfortable," Vosira Bedoric began, opening the meeting with trivial pleasantries, "I apologize for the minimal furnishings, but with so little notice, we can only do so much, you know," he added with a smirk.

"We can provide all the furniture you require, Vosira," Sarnoc Vaj replied graciously. "You simply need to ask." He took his seat across the table from the Aldrish, while Arric positioned himself across from his brother. Kate sat between them.

"Thank you Sarnoc, but I believe we shall manage." Vosira Bedoric waved his attendant over. "Please see that they have suitable refreshments."

As wine was poured for the three newcomers, Rynar stared at Kate. Oddly, he displayed none of the animosity that he had shown towards her last night. In fact, he seemed pleased to see her, and she noticed that he had nodded politely to her as she had entered the tent.

"Sarnoc, I appreciate you bringing these fhaoli back to me, so that they may be placed into custody," Bedoric said. "In respect to you and your colleagues, I will delay having them put into restraints until we have concluded this discussion."

Sarnoc Vaj never blinked. Instead, he quickly responded, "there shall be no arrests today. Arric and Bhara Kate are under my personal protection." She realized that Vaj had not referred to Arric by his title, and she wondered if the omission would be noticed. Rynar may have raised his eyebrow in surprise, but she wasn't sure.

"Ah, Sarnoc, this is no game we play," Vosira Bedoric replied. "You are aware, of course, that I traveled all the way to Altopon to retrieve these two fhaoli, seeing as they both recently escaped from my custody. You have no claim on them, nor do you have any right under Sarducian law to provide them sanctuary. As fhaoli, their lives are forfeit to the Vosira, and they must be surrendered to me immediately."

"That is your opinion," Vaj stated. "Mine is somewhat different. This is one of the matters I hope we can clarify this evening."

"Opinion? It is the law, as agreed upon by your predecessors and mine. You are obliged to comply." He turned his head. "Aldrish, what do you say on the matter?"

"Aye, Vosira, you have stated the law correctly." Rynar sat with his hands folded on the table. "Dosedra, I see your relationship with Bhara Kate has blossomed since the Jiona Festival. I assume the ceremony was a great success for you both?"

Arric offered a practiced, polite smile in return. "Alas, Aldrish, against ancient tradition, we were pursued for many days by Senvosra. As you surely would expect, that gave us little opportunity to complete the ceremony."

If ever she needed a poker face, it was now. As Arric replied, she sucked in a deep breath and stared straight ahead, focusing on a spot on the tent wall behind Rynar.

"Indeed?"

She sensed that despite his unblemished facade, Rynar remained unsettled by her decision to seek sanctuary in Altopon with Arric. In response, she tugged a bit at the cushion on which she sat, giving her an excuse to slide just a tiny bit closer to the Dosedra, bringing their shoulders together. From the corner of his eye, and without turning his head, Arric glanced at her, and smiled. Although Rynar tried not to exhibit any response, she noted that his nostrils flared.

"There will be time for such social conversation later," Sarnoc Vaj admonished the Aldrish, working on a tip from Kate that small digs were likely to have a greater effect than outright challenges. "Instead, we have come for Sarnoc Sofinar."

Bedoric shook his head, his cheeks flushed. "Nay, Sarnoc, such a thing is impossible. That man is a traitor and a murderer. He shall never go free."

Vaj's demeanor never wavered, and he kept his poise as he continued in a smooth voice. "My lord Vosira, he is Sarnoc. He is incapable of such crimes. Furthermore, in light of new information, we have rescinded his expulsion from Altopon and welcome him home. I expect that you will grant him safe passage to our city, as required by the ancient agreement between our ancestors."

The Vosira glared at him, a vicious stare that she likened to a wild dog on the verge of attack. All he needed to do was bare his teeth and the analogy would be complete. "He is fhaoli. You have no rights over his fate."

Vaj was not ruffled. "He is Sarnoc," he repeated, in a tone that allowed no debate. "I will not leave without him."

Bedoric continued to observe him with palpable hatred, and did not respond. After such a long ride from Loraden, he was likely quite tired, and in no mood for polite conversation or games. This was why Arric had wanted to have this meeting before the day's end, so that they could take advantage of his brother when he was at his weakest.

Rynar spoke up. "Vosira, perhaps we should consider a trade?"

Before Bedoric could respond, Vaj nodded. "That will be acceptable. In fact, my companions were willing to serve in that capacity if necessary. If that is your decision, they will be released from my protection."

"If necessary?" Bedoric spat the words. "There was never any question that they would be allowed to leave this camp, under your protection or not." His lip twitched. "Captain Joven, bring the Sarnoc to me."

The captain, who had lingered at the doorway, saluted and pivoted, heading out to retrieve the Sarnoc captive. Neither Vaj nor Arric made note of his disappearance, instead fixing their attention on the Vosira.

While they waited for Joven's return, Bedoric continued. "You understand that you must turn the fhaoli over to me immediately, without further conditions, or I will not allow any of you to leave this tent alive."

"Threats, Vosira?" Vaj pursed his lips, shaking his head like a parent disappointed in the action of a misbehaving child. "Do not threaten me."

Before Bedoric could respond, and before Arric could speak in his own defense, Joven and two other soldiers returned, dragging a semiconscious man towards them. They dumped him, teetering on his knees, at Vaj's feet.

Kate's eyes nearly popped out of her head.

The man had been sorely abused. His head had been shaved, and there were many cuts and abrasions on his scalp. He was filthy, with his face purple with bruises. His hands and legs were bound behind his back, not quite hog-tied, but enough that he was unable to move. Remarkably, however, when he was brought into the tent, he made no effort to acknowledge his rescuers or show that he was in any pain.

"Here is your Sarnoc," Bedoric offered casually.

Arric sat motionless, staring in disbelief as Sofinar, his mentor and friend—a man that until a day ago he believed had died—was tossed like rubbish on the grass a few feet away from him.

Meanwhile, Rynar pretended to rub a spot on his forehead, the gesture perhaps intended to hide his own discomfort at the abuse the Sarnoc had received.

Unable to hide his own astonishment at Sofinar's treatment, Vaj stared without speaking, the look in his eyes akin to what might expect to see from someone stabbed through the chest and pinned against a wall with a dagger. From what Kate understood, for centuries people had treated the Sarnoc with deference and respect, and as far as she understood it, not even the Vosira ever dared a hand on any of their number. Yet, unbelievably, Bedoric had broken an ancient agreement.

Unlike her dumbstruck companions, Kate could not remain silent. Sofinar—or as she knew him, Torv—was a kindly older man who deserved none of this. "Why did you do this to him? How could you?"

Bedoric held out his hands as if helpless. "He resisted arrest. My men were under orders to take him into custody, no matter what it took. When he fought, they had to fight back. That is all."

Vaj's face contorted into anger. "This is an outrage," he exclaimed, his eyes moving directly to the silver torc around Bedoric's neck. "You made an oath to work with Sarnoc, and to share the land with us. Such treatment of Sarnoc Sofinar proves that you are the oath-breaker in this tent, Vosira, not the Sarnoc. You have broken faith with us, and such a transgression shall never be forgiven."

Bedoric's hand instinctively moved to his collarbone, and he touched the glysar band, as if expecting something to happen. When nothing did, he smiled. "Sarnoc, you yourself acknowledged Sofinar's fhaoli status years ago. By doing so you granted me the absolute right over this man's life or death."

"Nay, Vosira. We had agreed. His life was to be spared, and he was to leave Loraden and go into exile."

"Then what would you say to the fact that he was captured not only in Loraden, but in the keep itself, where he had been living under my nose for years? Again, it appears he was the one to break a promise, Sarnoc, not me." He measured the response of each of his visitors in turn. "You all appear gravely concerned for the fhaoli here. Shall I ensure his pain comes to a swift end?" He nodded to Joven, who immediately unsheathed his blade.

Seeing the sword, Vaj did not move from his seat, but he glared at the Vosira as if daring him. On the other hand, Kate nearly tumbled from her cushion, and Arric had already gotten his feet underneath him, and crouched beside her.

The Senvosra captain never looked to the visitors. Instead, after two precise steps forward, and without ceremony, Joven quickly sank the blade into the man's heart.

Sofinar made a deep sigh as he collapsed onto the grass, the life pouring from him.

Kate screamed.

Arric jumped up and tackled Joven, knocking him to the tent floor and pinning him down.

And Vaj jumped forward and fell to his knees beside his colleague, cradling his fellow Sarnoc's head in his lap, using his hands to seek the source of the blood, as if he alone could slow the bleeding.

Even Rynar was unhinged by the action. "By the gods, Bedoric, what have you done?" Without waiting for a response, he was on his feet, and he climbed over the table, knocking over one of the goblets, and then pushed a soldier aside.

Bedoric did not offer a response to his Aldrish, nor had he lost his presence of mind. With a wave of each hand, he called soldiers, standing on either side of the doorway of the tent, towards him. "Arrest the girl and my brother. Escort the Sarnoc back to the torrapon. And then, prepare our assault."

Immediately a half-dozen men surrounded Arric and Kate, holding them firmly.

No one moved after that. Instead, they all stared as Rynar bent over Sofinar's bound, bleeding body. All were familiar with healers in general, but none but Kate had seen the Aldrish play this role. While Vaj worked to untie the ropes, Rynar placed his hands over Sofinar's abdomen, and with perspiration beading on his forehead, he struggled to stop the flow of blood. When the Sarnoc had finished with the ropes, the unlikely team laid the Sarnoc flat on his back while Rynar continued to work.

Bedoric oversaw the efforts with his mouth standing open, and his arms crossed. As his Aldrish sunk into deep concentration, his eyes closed and his head slumped forward, it was too much for the Vosira.

"Aldrish—what are you doing?" he shouted. "Do not interfere with this!" It was as if barking commands was his only means to deal with such an unexpected turn of events. "Guards, take the Aldrish back to his tent."

After the other soldier had grabbed Arric, Joven had regained his position next to the Vosira. Intending to remove the Aldrish, he placed his hands on Rynar's shoulders, only to jerk them away and sway backwards. "He's burning up!" he said with a start. "What is he doing? It's like he's on fire!"

Struggling against the grip of the soldier, Kate tried to break free so she could sit beside Rynar. She didn't know what she could do, but she remembered Nyvas, and it seemed that her presence had helped somehow—or at least Rynar thought it had. As she strained against the guards who held her, leaning towards Rynar and Sofinar, she heard a woman's voice in her head. Not a Sarnoc, but a woman.

«This is done.» The voice was firm. «Do not intervene. Everyone dies. Sofinar chose this time and place for a reason. Do not despair, but help him see.»

What? Help whom? She didn't know what was going on, or who was speaking to her. She quickly framed a series of questions in her head, but the voice did not answer.

Meanwhile, she noticed that Rynar began to sway from the effort of healing. She understood that a healer took on a measure of the pain and weakness of the injured person, and suddenly it dawned on her that in doing so, it was possible to cross a line from which it would be impossible to return. This was why Lysander had not tried to heal Nyvas; once someone died, if a healer tried to revive that person, his own life energy might get sucked into the corpse without any means to return.

What was happening in front of her now was a struggle between a dying man, desperate to pass into Yoren's world, and a stubborn healer who was caught up in the idea of saving a murdered Sarnoc.

Despite the tight grip of two soldiers, their leather gloves bruising her skin as they held her, she pulled forward, but with new intent. "Rynar, leave him."

Arric swung his head in her direction. Like her, he could not move, thanks to the consideration of his brother's troops. "Kate? What are you doing?"

She tried to raise her arms against the solders' grip, and struggled to get free of them. "Let me go," she snarled, in a low voice that offered no room for debate. "I'm not going anywhere." Surprised by her tone, the soldier on her left relaxed his hold, and as soon as she sensed that, she pulled forward, breaking free of the second man. Then she knelt down beside the Aldrish. "It's okay, he wanted this to happen," she whispered. "Let him go."

Rynar was too deeply engrossed in the act of healing to respond to her, but Vaj looked up, his steel gray eyes searching as he caught her glance. "Why would you say this, Bhara?"

"Never mind. Sarnoc, help me bring him out."

"Who, the Aldrish?" Vaj looked at the dying Sarnoc and Rynar, and caught her meaning. He seemed disinclined to assist her. "Nay, Kate, he knows what he's doing."

"You would allow him to die, as well?" When the sword had sliced into Sofinar, she was angry. Now, however, she was inflamed with utter outrage at his suggestion. "Do it, Sarnoc."

Vaj looked at her, his eyes narrowed. He was unaccustomed to anyone challenging his authority. "Bhara, you dare to presume this?"

"Yes, I dare it. Bring him out."

"Very well." Vaj brought his hands to Rynar's chin. As he lifted the man's head, she noticed that the Aldrish's face was flushed red, as if he had attempted to soak up Sofinar's blood into his own body. Then he slumped over to the side.

Vaj nodded. "Sofinar's heart has stopped. I told the Aldrish it was over."

Rynar quickly regained consciousness, but for a moment his movements were sluggish. His face was slick with sweat, although the flush had subsided. "Kate, you should not have done that," he said weakly.

It wasn't exactly what she expected him to say, and she made a nervous smile before she stood up again. "I didn't do anything," she suggested to the small audience gathered around the dead Sarnoc, though her words were lost in the larger events around them.

As Sofinar lay on the blood-soaked grass under their feet, Vaj stood up as well, his tunic and trousers stained red. "Vosira," he began, his tone indicating that his emotions would remain tightly leashed, "such an act as this is clearly in violation of the oath you took." He pointed at Bedoric's collarbone. "That torc symbolizes a bond of trust that you have flagrantly discarded."

"Aye, Sarnoc," Bedoric replied, with a grin, "but it is mine all the same. I am Vosira, and you cannot change that."

"Perhaps not, but I can show Sarducia what kind of Vosira you are." His arm shot out to the side. "Release your brother. He has things he wishes to say to you."

"The fhaoli has no rights here, Sarnoc. I shall not release him." He waved his arms at the Senvosra in the tent. "Take the Sarnoc back to the stones. I am finished listening to him." Despite his command, however, the Senvosra avoided contact with Sarnoc Vaj. Bedoric gasped. "Fools!" he cried. "You retreat from one of them?"

"Your men are wise," Vaj said. "They understand who wields the power here. It is the Sarnoc, not you."

"I am Vosira," Bedoric reminded him, his voice raised in anger. Staring at Sofinar's body, he said with confidence, "I think it's clear here that Sarnoc hold no authority within in this tent." He stood up and pulled his own sword from his belt, and gesturing with it, pointed it in Sarnoc Vaj's direction. "The Sarnoc are traitors to the kingdom. By consorting with these fhaoli and providing them shelter, you become fhaoli as well. If you do not leave immediately, I shall have you arrested."

Still, Vaj's voice was firm. "Nay, Vosira. Order your men to stand down."

Kate blinked. Had they come to a stalemate?

Surprised by the Sarnoc's defiance even as a blade hovered before him, Bedoric's eyes widened. In response, he pressed the tip against the Sarnoc's chest. He looked over each shoulder in search of his officers. "Men, I order you to arrest him." He glared at the Sarnoc. "You and your kind have meddled in the affairs of Sarducia for too long."

She held her breath. Arric had promised the Sarnoc would protect them, but so far the promise had been shown to be an empty one. If Vaj could not save Sofinar, and if the Vosira had so little compunction about killing him in front of the Sarnoc leader himself, then she feared they were all doomed. This time, with all the soldiers around, there would be no easy escape back to Altopon.

During the exchange, no one noticed that Rynar had gotten to his feet and stumbled to the rear of the tent. He now returned, moving slowly, his blank expression exhibiting the physical and psychological drain of an intense healing attempt, and his clothing stained with Sofinar's blood. "Vosira," he said, his voice mellow like sweet pudding, "do not allow your anger to cloud your judgment." Even in his state, he had the presence of mind to lift the Vosira's goblet and fill it with wine.

Bedoric turned to him as if to ask a question, but Rynar just handed him the goblet and shrugged. Using this distraction to his advantage, Vaj stepped beside the Vosira and boldly took the hilt of the Vosira's weapon from under his sweaty fingers. Oddly, Bedoric didn't resist. Had he lost his nerve, she wondered? Or was he just confused?

"Before you take us into custody, Vosira," the Sarnoc said, "I would like to remind you that Arric has a few words he would like to say to you." Vaj held the sword, point to the ground, and stepped back three paces.

Bedoric's rage was still etched on his face, but the edges had softened. She wondered if he was affected most by the realization he had killed a Sarnoc, that the Sarnoc leader was threatening him, or that his Aldrish had tried to save Sofinar through healing.

Or perhaps it was that his brother was now standing in front of him with his right hand pressed against his chest, a bright glysar ring sparkling on his middle finger.

Hatred had fueled his courage to face down the Sarnoc leader, but now, a goblet of wine in his left hand, and suddenly grasping at air with his right, belatedly realizing that his hand no longer held his sword, the Vosira glared at his brother. "What could you possibly have to say to me?"

Arric glanced down at the hands gripping his arms, and wrenched himself free. Then he stood alone in the middle of the tent, in front of his brother. Both Kate and Vaj stepped to the side, and even Rynar backed up a few paces. The presence of others wasn't likely a matter of concern to the two brothers, who now stood face to face. Bedoric's eyes would not remain in one place, but shifted between his brother's face, the ground, and to Rynar, while Arric's were locked in an inflexible stare.

Arric raised his hand, palm down and outspread, as if offering it to Bedoric to embrace, or kiss. It was his right hand, with the glysar ring. "Shall you reconsider the names you call me, brother?"

"Where did you get that ring?"

Arric dropped his hand again, and this time, hanging at his side, it had clenched into a fist. "Our father gave it to me, Bedoric, as you have known all along."

CHAPTER 58

Despite the chill in the evening air, Vosira Bedoric was sweating now, but said nothing.

Arric must have taken Bedoric's silence as an admission of guilt. He turned, and in a clear voice, called out, "members of the Senvosra! It is for everyone here to bear witness to what I am about to say!" Several soldiers heard him shout, and out of curiosity began to approach, ducking under the canvas flaps of the canopy. She guessed there were probably fifty soldiers camped outside Altopon tonight, and already a third had stopped what they were doing to witness the confrontation between the two royal brothers.

As men crowded around, Arric turned back to the Vosira, and with his head bowed, spoke very softly. "I once loved you, Bedoric, even idolized you," he whispered, so low even she could barely hear him. "What I must do pains me more than you will ever know."

At these words Bedoric began to sweat in earnest, but he did not respond. Without the strength of his Aldrish, who had retreated to the corner of the tent, he had abandoned his confident swagger. He licked his lips and looked around the tent, but it was futile—no one would join him at his side, to offer reinforcement. He had to face his brother alone.

Arric continued to gaze into his brother's eyes under the shaggy brows. His fists were clenched at his sides, as if it took tremendous courage for him to stand there. But when the next words came from his mouth there was no hesitation or wavering in his voice. "I name you,

Vosira Bedoric é Sarducia, as party to the murders of our father, Vosira Parmon, and of Sarnoc Sofinar, a man that you knew to be innocent of any crime, and whose blood even now stains the ground on which you walk. Because you have aided in the death of both Vosira and Sarnoc, I name you traitor to the Sarducian people and to the Oath Vosidari."

All the soldiers in the camp heard these words. Many drew their weapons and stood ready to defend their monarch. Others, uncertain, remained still.

Bedoric's lips moved, but no sound came. It was as if he was incapable of denying the charges laid against him.

Then Vaj stepped beside Arric. "Heed these words, men of Sarducia," he said, his voice loud enough to be heard in every tent. "You have all been misled by the Vosira." He paused to allow the soldiers to react to his statement. There were several shouts and complaints, but no one approached Arric or the Sarnoc to challenge them. After the initial outburst of surprise and denial, Vaj continued. "The man before you, Vosira Bedoric, allowed Sarnoc Sofinar and an innocent boy, the son of Bhagal Elric, to unjustly bear the blame for a crime that he himself committed." He took a step towards the closest soldiers. "Upon learning that his brother had been named Charvos, Bedoric killed Vosira Parmon, their father, and then manipulated the Council Vosidari to proclaim him as the next Vosira before the truth could be known. He then dared to take an oath to the gods promising to protect the land promote justice among its people. Such was a false oath. Let it be known throughout the isle—as Sarnoc leader I renounce our pledge of peace with all of Sarducia as long as you support this man as your Vosira."

The soldiers stared at him, dumbfounded. Several moved closer to the canvas pavilion, outrage plain upon their faces.

For his part, Bedoric still did not deny any of the charges against him. Instead, he stood in place, perspiring heavily, his head hung low and his shoulders hunched.

Captain Joven stepped forth. "Vosira, are the Sarnoc's words true?" he asked, challenging Bedoric in a manner none would have imagined doing moments before.

Bedoric licked his lips and backed up a few steps, towards the opening behind him. Kate realized there was a second tent behind him that likely served as his personal chambers, while this tent's purpose was more akin to his council or audience chamber.

A commotion from the edges of the camp called their attention away from the Vosira. A soldier on horseback, someone who would not have heard the recent exchange, was galloping up the hill, racing directly towards them under the yellow canopy. "My lord Vosira," he pronounced, his words slurred. Then he fell from the horse, an arrow shaft protruding from between his shoulders.

"Well, that was unexpected," she said under her breath. Had the Senvosra turned on themselves? It seemed unlikely.

"What's happening?" Bedoric murmured, his eyes shifting from Arric to the hillside. He still clutched the goblet of wine, he realized at that moment, and took a deep swallow.

By now everyone was distracted.

She craned her neck to see what was happening. Her answer came almost immediately, as a line of men appeared on the low ridge just beyond the camp, near where she and Arric had been when they spied the encampment yesterday. It was not difficult for her to recognize the new arrivals. "It's Fantion!" She was astounded. What were his men doing here? Even though she was glad to see them, she wondered what would have made them take such a risk.

Meanwhile, Joven would not be put off. "My lord Vosira, please answer me. Are the Dosedra's and Sarnoc's words true?"

Bedoric's eyes were wide. He never looked at his captain, or acknowledged his presence. Finally he found words again. "Don't you dare say any more!" he ordered his brother. "You don't know what you're saying. I am Vosira. It is done." He pointed to Arric's ring with a shaking hand. "That is not yours to wear. It is mine. I am Vosira. You see, I wear the torc, not you. The ring means nothing. I am Vosira."

It was as if he thought the repetition would make everyone forget what he was being accused of now. Faced with the doubt of everyone in the tent, she realized that even the hard, physical evidence of his rank, the glysar torc, seemed ephemeral, and she saw the truth of the situation register in Bedoric's eyes. Did Arric read it the same way? She tried to decipher the look on his face. There was solid, unflinching determination, but little else. Was he afraid? She wondered. Was he sorry? Or had the final accounting of his brother's guilt erased lesser emotions?

Bedoric saw neither sorrow nor fear in his brother's lethal stance. Arric carried no weapon, but he might have killed him right then if he could, and his brother knew it. Finding his options evaporating in the sinking cold, Bedoric turned away and fled into the folds of the tent behind him.

The Vosira's captain, bewildered at the sudden turn of events, looked to the Sarnoc leader, who closed his eyes. Then he glanced to Arric.

In response, Arric held up his hand to silence any questions, and then said in a loud and powerful voice, "justice must be brought to Sarducia tonight. The people must never believe that the Vosira is above his own laws. For the crimes against our father, and our land, I declare Bedoric's life to be forfeit to me."

Vaj handed Bedoric's sword to Arric, who accepted it with a grimace, as if just touching it might bring his own death. For a moment, a long span of time in which she dared not breathe, he held the bejeweled weapon in silence, as if weighing it with his hand. The hilt was elaborate and luxuriously decorated, but the blade was a fine piece of steel.

Then, with determination etched on his face, Arric disappeared into the tent after his brother.

No one moved to stop him.

"Brother, are you here?" she heard him call out, his voice muffled by a layer of canvas.

There was no response.

"By the gods, brother, show yourself!" There was the sound of him kicking aside pillows and the crash of pottery and silver utensils as he knocked over a tray. "Bedoric?"

Silence.

"Damn you, Bedoric!" He turned and stormed out of the tent. "I must have light! It is pitch black in there!"

Vaj nodded and stepped forth. "I can assist you."

"I need a torch, Sarnoc."

In response, Vaj cast a ball of blue light in the direction of the tent.

"What are you... oh, never mind," Arric said, exasperated. "Follow me."

He returned to the tent, this time with the Sarnoc magelight illuminating his way. "Bedoric—where are you?"

She saw the Vosira run into the tent. Everyone had seen him. There was likely just the one entrance. Why was Arric having such a difficult time locating him?

Having nothing else to do, she slowly turned to Rynar, to see his expression. How had he weathered the accusations? She suspected he knew how Vosira Parmon had died, and wondered how Arric would deal with him.

The Aldrish was no longer standing near the corner of the tent, however. At some point during the confrontation, he had disappeared entirely.

"Oh sweet Kerthal," Arric cried out, and Kate's attention returned to the voices inside the tent, now filled with a blue light. "What in the gods' names happened?"

"It was this," Vaj announced. "Poison."

"What? How is that possible? He could not have..."

"I can definitely detect the herbs used here—they are quite potent. For someone who consumed them, death would be almost instantaneous."

"Let me see it." There was a pause, and then the sound of pottery smashing against something hard, such as a chest. Then the tent flap opened, and the two men walked out.

Arric's face was flushed. "Blast it, Sarnoc. Bedoric came here with confidence—he would not have doubted his success. Yet he drank poison? This is an admission of defeat! It makes no sense..."

Rynar.

The thought must have occurred to him at the same time it did to Kate. "Ahh!" Arric cried out, his fist pounding the air. "He shall die for this!" he announced, enraged. He stormed out of the tent looking for the Aldrish.

She ran behind him.

CHAPTER 59

When she found him again inside the Aldrish's tent, Arric already held the sword at Rynar's back. "Filthy coward. You shall answer to me now."

Arric was not one to hide his emotions, and she had seen him angry more than once, but nothing she had witnessed before compared to the naked hostility that possessed him at this moment. He was prepared to lunge and drive the blade right through the Aldrish. Every hair on his head and arms bristled with the intensity of this burst of hatred coming from him; it oozed from his pores. Even when he confronted Bedoric he hadn't been like this. His fury knew no match, his impatience for revenge terrifying.

With the blade between his shoulder blades, she saw the Aldrish stiffen, but then without warning he somersaulted forward, escaping the danger. In a remarkable move, he had located his own weapon and regained his footing by the time Arric had reached him again. Unlike Arric, Rynar was calm, and stared at his opponent with cool calculation. He showed none of the illness from a few moments before, and remarkably, appeared fully recovered from the failed healing attempt.

She didn't want to watch the two men fight. Not these two. It was a terrible match. Arric was taller, and more muscular, and had served as a soldier. Rynar was smaller, and spent most of his time indoors, but she had watched him practice. He was fast, and agile, and in all the times she had seen him engage an opponent, he had never lost.

A vicious dog pitted against a rattlesnake.

"Don't do this, Arric." She saw his shoulder twitch as she addressed him, but he did not lower his sword or turn around towards her. "Let the Sarnoc deal with him." There would be no winners here, not in this tent. "Haven't enough men died tonight?"

"Nay." It was addressed more towards Rynar than herself. "Thanks to him, my brother is dead. Now it's his turn."

"Kate is right, Dosedra. I am not your enemy. We need not fight."

"You afraid, Aldrish?"

"Of you, Dosedra? Never." He took a step to the side, easily avoiding Arric's first maneuver. "My dear, leave us," he suggested to Kate, his eyes never leaving his foe. He held his sword low, but was ready to strike at any moment. "It appears that he and I have a bit of unfinished business."

"Aye, Kate, go find Sarnoc Vaj," Arric said, and took a step away from the tent opening, his own gaze locked on his intended opponent.

She realized he would kill the Aldrish, or die trying. It seemed Arric had no self-control left. Tonight, Rynar represented everything he had learned to hate in this world. Did he really think eight years of frustration, guilt and anger could be assuaged in a single fight? "No, I won't leave you two to chop each other to bits." It was her attempt to impose a tiny bit of reason into the impending conflict. She assessed the posture of each, and their expressions. Whether or not either would die, all the same it would be bloody, she was sure of it. "Arric, let's just walk out of here. You've accomplished what you came for."

He took another step away from the opening, and kicked away a pile of blankets. She could tell he was measuring up his opponent, searching for weaknesses. "Nay. This man must answer to me for all he has done, to you and to my brother. To Nyvas." He stumbled into a tray and knocked it away with a swing of his arm. "And to Sofinar."

"I'm impressed, Dosedra. I never thought you would find a way to blame me for all of those things." He nodded once in appreciation, as he circled a little to the left. From the way his eyes danced over Arric's figure, he also was considering his strategy. "You know, I had nothing to do with any of that."

"Don't try to erase your guilt in all of this. Even with what you tried to do in there," he nodded towards the other tent, where even now Sofinar's corpse lay on the grass, "his death is on your hands." Arric shifted his weight between his legs, looking for an opening. "After everything you have done, you don't deserve to walk on Sarducian soil."

"On the contrary, Dosedra, it is you who should not be here. Who between us has committed the worse crimes, eh?" Boldly he added, "you cannot deny that there is much Mosumi blood on your hands."

Arric's elbow jerked, and she gasped, thinking he was about to impale Rynar right then and there. He withheld the blow, however. "That was your doing as well, Aldrish."

Rynar chuckled. "Nay, not mine. If you weren't driven by such blind hatred, Dosedra, you'd recognize that I have been trying to bring an end to Sarducia's relationship with Hansar, not make it stronger. I never endorsed the killing of Mosumi, just as I didn't want Sarducia to trade any more of its glysar." He took a deep breath, his sword arm remaining steady. "If you wish to hate anyone, you might start with your brother and father. They were the ones to weaken Sarducia by giving up our precious glysar for some bits of cloth and wine. Do you have any idea how much metal ore has been shipped abroad?"

"What? You're trying to tell me that this is all about glysar?" Arric asked, incredulous. "All these deaths have been over some damn metal?"

"Dosedra, do you not understand how important glysar is? Without it, Sarducia itself will collapse."

"Aldrish, that's nothing but a legend." Even as he spoke, he circled around in the tent, seeking an opening, and Rynar matched his steps.

"Nay, it is true, and the Sarnoc will confirm it. Did Sofinar never teach you that it is the source of all that is unique to our land, from the power of the Sarnoc down to your own land-instinct? Already, with what we've lost, those skills are not what they once were."

"That's ridiculous."

Kate realized that Rynar's explanation accounted for the manifests she had seen on his table. He was no glorified accountant; he had been calculating the loss of that silvery metal.

"Very well, Dosedra, believe what you will. I did what was necessary to save this land. If your brother had only listened to me, this all could have been avoided."

"No matter what twisted rationale you might offer now for your actions, for your support of my brother's crimes, had the opportunity presented itself, I would have killed you long before now." Arric narrowed his eyes and issued a verbal challenge. "It ends here, tonight, Aldrish. I shall not spare you."

"Nor I, Dosedra." Rynar did not flinch. From where she stood, she could see into his eyes, the dark pupils like drops of black ink against his paper-white eyes. "I welcome the opportunity to fight you, finally."

So they had expressed their intentions. It was to be a fight to the death.

She held her breath. It had come to this?

Who would strike first?

Her answer came as Rynar leapt over a large pillow and thrust his sword at the Dosedra. His momentum caused his blade to slam hard against Arric's sword, but Arric was able to knock it away with a wide swing of his arms, his hands firm on the leather grip of his weapon. It was then that she realized he had retained his brother's sword, rather than take one from a soldier. Fitting, she thought, that he would avenge his brother with the Vosira's own sword. She watched as he took two broad steps towards Rynar, forcing the Aldrish back against the wall of the tent.

Again their blades crashed together, and again, and again.

Both fought skillfully. Arric was the more passionate, emotional attacker, while Rynar seemed almost detached, as if it was little more than an academic exercise, but that led to his greater precision. When he noticed that he had been backed up against the side of the tent, he swung low, at Arric's knees, and although Arric was able to parry the blow, the two weapons came together with a shuddering clang. They both grimaced, struggling to hold off the other, pushing with their shoulders, and the weight of their chests, against the other. The swords screamed, squealed, the high pitch of steel scraping against steel.

In the press of the moment Rynar managed somehow to shove at Arric with his free hand with enough force to compel him to retreat slightly, breaking them apart.

Another jab by Arric, and Rynar knocked it away, swinging the sword with the strength and accuracy of a batter hitting a home run. She was surprised that Rynar's slight build could hide such power. Apparently Arric was too, for he had a shocked expression, his eyebrows raised and his nose slightly scrunched up. He answered with a low feint and then a high swing of his sword, and Rynar, his foot caught in a blanket, did not respond fast enough. Arric's sword caught him on the shoulder, and tore the fabric of his shirt, cutting the skin below.

"Stop it," she screamed as she saw new blood spilled. "Both of you, stop it!" Without thinking about the repercussions, she advanced on the men locked in combat, as if to throw herself between them.

Rynar did not flinch as she approached, but Arric, seeing her out of the corner of his eye, turned his head for a split second, and in that second, Rynar jabbed his blade and connected with Arric's thigh.

"Ahhh," Arric gasped in pain. Then in a scathing tone, he snapped, "Kate, out. Now." This time there was no room for negotiation or argument, and thus scolded for her transgression, she made her way, backwards, to the tent opening. As soon as her feet touched the ground outside the tent, she stopped, standing there to watch the continuation of the grueling grudge match between the men.

Although Arric had drawn first blood, the wound Rynar had inflicted on his leg was bleeding more than the injury he had caused the Aldrish. Rather than it slowing him down, however, Arric seemed reenergized by the pain. He leapt forward, swinging the sword dangerously. His resurgence of strength caused Rynar to back up again, but then he raised his own sword with a circular sweep and connected with Arric's, the two metal blades again grinding together. After that, the men crossed back and forth in the tent, appearing to be little more than shadow puppets in the dim light of the candles in the corners. Arric's taller silhouette raised his shadow sword high, and swung it down hard, but the shorter silhouette met the trajectory and, as the two heavy steel blades again collided, both men groaned.

So it went, grunts and growls, thuds and clangs. As the sound of the fight echoed in the camp, several Senvosra approached, and a few stood beside Kate at the doorway of the tent. None made an effort to enter, though if they had tried, they would have had to fight her first.

Again Rynar slipped past his defenses, and this time the tip of his blade connected with Arric's cheek. They were close enough to her that she could see the line of dark blood seep down to his chin, and she shrank back from the doorway.

Was it actually possible that Rynar would win this conflict? He was in good health and had been able to keep his skills honed with daily practice. Yet he had engaged in a healing attempt a short time ago that must have tired him. Then there was Arric, who was by far the superior swordsman, but who had been imprisoned for weeks, unable to practice or exercise, followed by their difficult journey to Altopon, and the lingering effects of adoli. Did the Aldrish have the advantage here? A few minutes later, she had new reason to worry. He should have been exhausted, but Rynar's resilience was remarkable, and for him the fight appeared almost amusing, and he continued to parry Arric's offense without significant physical cost. Arric, meanwhile, was rapidly tiring, perspiration soaking his hair and his shirt.

Eight years in Froida fighting in god knows what conditions, only to be defeated back home, in a battle against the Aldrish? The irony that Rynar was likely of Mosumi ancestry himself wasn't lost on Kate. Neither was the rapidly deteriorating situation. As she watched, Arric suddenly had a clear line of attack when Rynar overcompensated on a lunge and lost his balance, and with that opening Arric should have been able to inflict a significant wound to his opponent. Whether it was exhaustion or unwillingness to attack, he allowed the moment to pass him by, instead taking the time to catch his breath and wipe the sweat from his face with the back of his hand.

The lapse was not lost on Rynar. When he recovered, he raised his sword again, holding it so the tip was pointed at Arric's heaving chest, just a foot away.

She gasped. Never before in her life had she felt such dark, intense anger towards another person as she did towards Rynar, who looked like he was on the verge of killing Arric. At that moment, she would have run towards the combatants had a hand not clapped down on her shoulder.

"This is not your fight, Bhara," Sarnoc Vaj commanded. "Stay here."

Every muscle in her body was tensed. Her breathing was shallow and shaky. "But—" The compulsion to run inside was too great to ignore, but Vaj held her firmly.

"Stay here."

Both men were unaware of their audience. "Do you yield?" Rynar demanded of him.

"Nay, Aldrish," Arric responded defiantly. He shook his head and droplets of sweat flew from his hair, sparkling for a second as they caught the light of the candles before vanishing into the shadows of the carpet. "I have fought far better opponents than you, and for far longer than this."

"In such a weakened state, though?" Rynar said, in mock concern. "I somehow doubt that. Really, Arric," he said, using no title, and speaking to him as if chiding one of the charnok, "you should learn to recognize your own limitations. Yield to me, now, and I shall spare your life." He bit back a smile, and tipped his head to see Kate and Vaj standing just beyond the tent. "Or shall she watch me kill you?"

Arric jerked his head to the side, so he could see her. "Kate, you should go."

She did not move.

"Kate, do as I say," he tried to order her, though his words lacked the conviction of a short time ago. "Sarnoc, take her away."

"I'm not leaving," she responded both to him and to the Sarnoc. "Arric, if you're stupid enough to let him kill you, then I'll stay here to witness it."

"Kate," he cried, a note of desperation in his voice now. "Please go."

"No."

Rynar took this opportunity to wave his sword in front of Arric's face. "You cannot fight me any longer, you know." He swayed his hips slightly, as if mocking him. "Even if I spare you now, I shall surely kill you in a half-dozen strokes. Do not challenge me further, for if you do, I shall be forced to seal your fate."

"Then do it. I shall not surrender to you." Then, with energy none of them expected, he raised his sword again and lunged towards him in a fury. As Rynar backed up, Arric shouted something unintelligible and swung the sword as if he would decapitate the Aldrish. With much faster reflexes, Rynar simply ducked, and Arric's sword did not connect with anything, causing him to whirl around unexpectedly.

"Damn you, Aldrish," he hissed, and attacked again. This time, his determination paid off. Although Rynar tried again to avoid him, Arric used a maneuver the Aldrish could never have expected—he bashed Rynar's collarbone with his elbow, the impact stunning the Aldrish and causing him to fall to his knees.

Rynar could only look up, with his mouth open, as Arric raised his sword for the killing stroke, intending to deliver the mate to the blow that had gone wild just a moment before.

His intentions registered with her just in time for her to scream. "No! Don't do it!" She ran to Arric's side. "Don't!"

He stared at her and then at Rynar, who glared back at him with eyes that seemed to still offer a challenge, daring him to finish it.

She understood Rynar's expression, but she raised her hand to Arric's arm. "Please don't do this."

He paused, looking from Rynar to her and back again. "Minara, I must. He killed my brother. I cannot allow him to walk from this tent alive."

"Go ahead, fhaoli. Kill me, if you dare." Rynar's arrogance was astounding, given his position. "You can add me to your list of innocent Mosumi deaths."

"Innocent?" Arric raised the tip of the sword to the height of the Aldrish's chin, and held it level. He stood there for a moment, and as he hesitated, Rynar continued smiling.

"Aye. I had nothing to do with Bedoric's death. He was a coward who drank the very potion he expected both of you to consume."

That caused Arric to freeze. Still holding the sword at his opponent's neck, Arric said, "tell me this Rynar, and perhaps I will spare you.

What did you mean in your note, when you said that Kate needed to discover who she really was?"

That erased Rynar's smile. "This is not the time or place."

Sarnoc Vaj bowed his head, acknowledging the truth of it. "Aye, he is right." He nodded once to Arric. "You may claim victory here, but you must also spare Rynar's life."

Arric bowed his head. With a sigh, he acquiesced. "Very well, Sarnoc."

CHAPTER 60

Arric stood outside the tent, surveying the blood on the ground, and turned his head halfway back in the direction of Bedoric's tent. He noticed that the sword was still in his hand, and tossed it away, as if the touch of it stung his skin.

"My father. Then my mentor and friend. And now, my brother." Arric laughed uneasily, a hiccup of irony. The words were for no one, and everyone.

He had come to deliver justice this evening, and it had been stolen from him. Everyone who stood nearby—and the numbers of Senvosra had grown in the past few minutes—were silent as stone, to a man. Their heads were bowed.

"The deed is done, at any rate. The people must be told."

With no notice paid to his wounds, he walked away from the tents, with the Sarnoc and Kate following him, and a line of soldiers yet again behind them. Already it was as if a funeral had begun. Arric's boots made no sound in the grass as he walked out onto the hillside, beyond the shielding of the tent walls.

"The Vosira is dead," he announced, much too quietly. "Please tell the men."

Captain Joven had been standing nearby throughout the fight with Rynar. He nodded, and repeated the call, "Vosira Bedoric is dead!" to the company assembled.

Then he turned to Arric, and knelt before him, his sword offered on his outstretched palms. "Vosira," Joven said, bowing his head. "Please forgive my past actions against you, and allow me to be the first to pledge myself to you."

Arric stared at Joven, as if he had no idea what to do next. He shook his head as if emerging from a dream. "What is this?"

Sarnoc Vaj stepped beside him. "Your brother has gone to Yoren's kingdom. Now you are Vosira."

Arric shook his head vigorously. "That's not right—what about the boy? I am Dosedra. I do not inherit this title. Ruill is Charvos, and will become Vosira."

"Nay. Bedoric became Vosira through illegitimate means, and thus his actions dishonored his line," Vaj explained somberly. "Your people will not follow the son of a man who stole the position through murder. However, they will follow you." He winked, or at least she thought she saw a wink. "You were—or, should I say, are Charvos. It is your right." He turned his gaze to Arric's hand. "You even wear the ring."

"I have no desire for this," he protested, his eyes wide in what almost seemed to be panic. "Sarnoc—you know that this is not why I came here. I only wore the ring to challenge Bedoric, not to claim his title."

"Then perhaps that means that you are ready." Vaj bowed his head deeply towards him.

"Oh, sweet goddess," Arric murmured, and then stared at Joven, still kneeling. As reality settled on his shoulders, he understood that now was not the time for indecision. Then he nodded. "Very well. Joven, do you swear in the name of our gods to serve me and Sarducia faithfully and with integrity, never using your service as excuse to cause unnecessary harm or injury, or bring disgrace to our land?"

Joven snapped his head up in surprise. "My lord Vosira? That is not the oath—"

"It is now. Do you swear?"

The captain swallowed. "I do swear."

"As Vosira of Sarducia, I accept your pledge. Arise, Captain." As Joven stood, Arric leaned towards him. "Please take charge of my brother's body. He will need to be brought to Loraden immediately for the comrall."

Sarnoc Vaj turned to him, his voice largely dispassionate. "Vosira, we shall conduct the formal Oath of Vosidari ceremonies in Loraden as well. I suggest that you rest here tonight, and tomorrow return home with your men. I shall see to Sofinar." Then he stepped away, returning to the tents.

His men? Kate swallowed hard. Feeling comfortably invisible in this sea of blue tunics, she stepped back, watching Arric as he surveyed the scores of men camped beyond the Altopon stones.

It was a heady moment, she realized, when a man became a king. As Arric turned, she watched the men all fall to their knees. Back in the keep, Rynar had taught her a game called Gai, where the object was to topple your opponent's pieces. To her, it seemed that this field was nothing more than a larger scale version of that game, and the men, bowing as one unit, were the game pieces. It was a breathtaking sight, a moment when theory became reality, when a man was transformed into a monarch.

Arric's gaze then shifted to the ridge. At least a dozen fhaoli positioned themselves there, weapons and torches in hand. They were extremely vulnerable out there, and she considered how their decision to appear represented a combination of loyalty and recklessness. Who had tipped them off, she wondered. Had a Sarnoc spoken to them? Then she turned her head back to the tent. Perhaps Sofinar told Nyvas? She had no idea, but it made sense. Now, Arric lifted his hand to wave to them, signaling that it was safe to approach. At the gesture, Fantion's men fell to their knees instead. Even their red-haired leader knelt and lowered his head to acknowledge Arric as Vosira.

Finally, he turned to her. Of everyone on the field, other than Arric himself, she was now the only person not yet bowing to him. As soon as his eyes fell on her, she dropped into a deep curtsy, as if someone had pushed her. Momentarily surprised by her action, he just nodded and said nothing.

The ritual of transformation was complete. The battle-weary soldier, the dirty fhaoli, even the groomed and polished Dosedra—all were gone, erased forever. Now Arric was Vosira, now and forever unto his death.

The truth of what had occurred fell hard upon his shoulders, for she noticed that, humbled by the sheer scope of the moment, he had begun to tremble. Still, she didn't fear for him. After all, he had spent the better part of his life training for this role. He was Vosira now, and she knew that he would act appropriately.

As she expected, with the bearing of a king he straightened his shoulders and cleared his throat.

"My father named me Charvos, and even now I bear the ring as proof. Now, upon my brother's death, I have been named Vosira," Arric announced, his voice a bit shaky. "This is not a title I coveted, and I do not take the responsibility lightly." He surveyed the people around him. "I am Vosira. It is my pledge to you all that I will endeavor to rule with fairness and mercy. In that way I hope I will be able to earn your loyalty."

She looked up at him. The wound from Rynar's sword still oozed blood down his chin, but it underscored what he had endured to make it to this point. It was difficult to comprehend that he was standing here openly, amidst all these soldiers that just a short time ago would have taken him prisoner; what must he be thinking now? Not only was he standing here without fear of arrest—in sweet irony, he was now their commander!

Again, he cleared his throat, and spoke as loudly as he could. "I desire to make a proclamation this eve, and you shall all serve as my witnesses. I declare that Bhara Kate, as well as all men who have declared allegiance to Bhagal Fantion of Lesheri, and their families, shall no longer be known as fhaoli. Henceforth they are free men and women and shall again enjoy their rights as Sarducians."

At his proclamation, members of the Senvosra nodded approval or at worst, muttered a word of apprehension. Most, in fact, just shrugged, not understanding the significance. The response was different for the men standing on the ridge. Immediately they came rushing down to greet their Vosira, shouting and whooping in joy.

Perhaps Arric had made a hasty decision, she thought humorously as the non-standard force ran through the uniformed Senvosra. Yet no one stopped them; it was a good sign with which to begin his reign.

Fantion and Lysander were first to reach Arric's side, where they both fell to their knees to pledge their loyalty to their new Vosira. Nyvas was behind them, aided down the hill by Plunchek. The others, though, were strangers to her, but Arric seemed to know them all.

"Come now, none of that!" he said to the kneeling men, and he smiled as he motioned for them to stand. To Fantion he said, "Before things go any further, I fear I must ask a great favor of you, my friend. Fantion of Lesheri, would you be willing to serve me as Aldrish?"

Grinning broadly, Fantion nodded. "I would be honored, Vosira," his tongue dancing over the title, to Arric's chagrin. "You realize, however, by making that proclamation you have loosened chaos into your kingdom." To Arric's confused glance, he added quickly, "I meant, how are you going to run a country with the likes of us running through the castle halls and village squares?"

"You are right, Fantion," he laughed, "how will I indeed?" Then he spied Kate again, and beckoned her over, crushing her in his arms. "It's time to go home."

"Not quite yet," Sarnoc Vaj said as he returned to join the merry band of well-wishers. "Bhara Kate, I must request that you return to Altopon. We still have a few matters that must be discussed."

"What—now?" Kate looked to her friends.

Vaj smiled, something he didn't do often. "I understand, Bhara. There is much to celebrate. However, our new Vosira has much he must organize and prepare." He looked at Arric. "Assuming he wants to get all these troops and supplies back to the city in time for his Oath ceremony."

"Aye, Sarnoc," Arric nodded. He pulled her to one side. "He's right. I have a lot of logistics to sort out, not least of which is figuring out how many men are here and the best route to take, and then I'll have a stack of matters to address back in Loraden. While I'd love to have you with me, I won't have much time to talk. Best you go with Sarnoc Vaj and have a nice bed to sleep in, and an easier return to Loraden by river. I'll see you in a couple of days."

"But—"

In front of everyone, he leaned down and kissed her. "Hopefully that will hold you over until I see you again."

CHAPTER 61

"You are not easy to find."

Startled by the sudden interruption, Kate turned towards the voice. She relaxed only a little when she identified the newcomer from his trademark green. It was Pasadhi Sebachin. "Was I supposed to be?" After a long, frustrating night of tossing and turning, she had risen before dawn and left her quarters to wander the halls in the main building at Altopon, seeking respite from the chaos in her heart. Remarkably, no one had challenged her, and she had gone where she pleased. Eventually spotting a bench in a breezeway overlooking the gardens, she stretched out her legs and leaned back, glad for the warmth of a thick wool blanket she had brought along. The sun had just risen when the Pasadhi found her.

"Nay, not really." Sebachin took a seat next to her. "Sarnoc Vaj wanted me to let you know when you awakened that he is convening all of the Sarnoc, and the laliri, later today, and wanted to make sure you would be ready."

She blinked. "Already? To talk about the Dos—Vosira Arric?"

"I suspect so, and I'm certain he'll wish to address the death of Sarnoc Sofinar. He was very insistent that you attend."

She buried her head under her arms. "I can't deal with that now. Can't I just get a little time to think and process everything that's happened?"

Tipping his head sideways, he noted, "you've had a difficult few days."

She dared to look up at him again. He sat easily across from her, his hands resting easy on his lap, his curly hair as unruly and tangled as ever. He smiled, but it was a gentle, easy expression, neither of amusement nor judgment, just the look of someone with nothing to hide, someone at peace with himself.

"Yeah, you could say that." She started to chew on her thumbnail. "I'm not sure I even know who I am any more. The last couple days—I haven't been myself." She sought out his eyes. "Have you ever felt like that? Like someone else had taken over your body, and all you could do was watch helplessly?"

He nodded. "Sometimes, when I feel the goddess Kerthal's presence within me, it seems like I have little control over what I'm doing. It's not a frequent sensation now, or maybe I've just become accustomed to it. All the same, when it happens I welcome it, because only good comes as a result."

"Has the goddess ever had you kill someone?"

"No," he admitted, "but I also haven't helped to heal anyone either." He smiled, and brushed hair from her eyes. Gently, he suggested, "would you like to tell me about it?" When she stiffened, he added, "I don't want to pressure you, Kate. Just know that I'm here, and I want to help. I'm happy to listen." When she hung her head down, he grasped her hand. "I heard about the guard. You must have been terrified."

She shrugged, feeling miserable. "That's the funny thing. I don't know how it even happened. I knew I had to save Arric, but why did I choose that option, of all things? Why did I do that?"

"You did what you had to do."

"That's what I keep telling myself. God knows I've never wanted to hurt anyone, much less..." A tear rolled down her cheek. "But when it happened, it was like I knew exactly how to do it—like I've done it hundreds of times before. How could I have known that? And now, what's weird is that I don't even regret it, and I know I should."

"Now, Kate, you are here, alive and well, and because of your courage, a great many wrongs have been corrected, and the rightful man is now Vosira. Isn't that enough? I cannot be your conscience, but I don't think you need to feel ashamed about it. You've aided someone you love... why should you regret it?" He looked at her from under his thick lashes. "Am I right?"

She blushed. "It isn't that obvious, is it?"

"Hmm." He lifted a finger to her flushed cheek, and then winked at her. "It is now." He grinned, and she covered her face with her hands. "Before you ask, I won't tell anyone." Then he reached up and pulled a hand away. "Don't be embarrassed."

"But he's Vosira now! I can't..."

"He's a man, Kate, just like me or anyone else. He wouldn't want you to think of him in any other way." He caught up her hands within his own. "All the same, I beg you to proceed carefully. You must be aware that some will resent an outsider being a part of his life." When she made an involuntary jerk of her head, he smiled. "At the same time, it doesn't mean it's wrong to feel the way you do. I just wanted to warn you that it may be difficult."

Nodding, she licked her lips. "I don't think Sarnoc Vaj will be as understanding as you are." Reminded that she had been summoned, she added, "I'm sure he's got a ton of questions that I won't want to answer."

Sebachin wrinkled his nose, but it was out of amusement rather than disdain. "Aye, that may be true. In his defense, he's Sarnoc, and the Sarnoc always want information. That's what makes them Sarnoc, I think." He chucked, and she smiled a bit at that as well. "However," he added with a wink, "if it helps any, you don't have to tell him everything."

She looked into his eyes. "Really?"

He shrugged. "That's just my opinion, of course. Sarnoc Vaj is not likely to share it." Again he smiled at her, and then wrapped his arms around her. As she sunk into his embrace, he offered her words of encouragement: "Take heart, Kate. The Sarnoc do not force people to do things against their will, especially here."

CHAPTER 62

Their footsteps echoed within the Sarnoc audience chamber—the beautiful room with the catwalks and blue glass skylight—as Sebachin led her to a short table at which there were three chairs.

Their table faced a second, larger one in the form of a half-circle, and a dozen empty chairs wrapping along the far side. As it was late afternoon, the sun was low, so the tables were lit with candles, and glass-paned oil lamps lined the walls.

"What's going to happen here?"

"It is just an accounting of events, Kate. Sarnoc Vaj and a few of the others will ask you some questions, so they can understand everything that's happened recently." He grasped her hand. "Remember, it's up to you what you want to tell them. Don't be nervous."

"Easy for you to say." She stared at the white marble table.

"You'll do fine," he reassured her, and filled a crystal goblet in front of her with wine from a tall decanter.

Their attention was distracted by the doors opening again, and she smiled to see Nyvas, who had been scrubbed and polished in the short time since they had arrived, step into the room. He was now attired in a grey laliri tunic, his hair remarkably a bright blond color.

Sebachin stood up. "You are Stavan?" he asked as he held out his hands.

"Aye, but I do not use that name now," Nyvas said, and allowed the Pasadhi to take his hands in his own.

Sebachin's eyes widened as the two men made physical contact. "Very well, Nyvas. I daresay you shall make this an interesting afternoon." He glanced to Kate, and then back to the young man. "I sense that what I heard about you is true."

Nyvas shrugged his shoulders. "The Sarnoc say it is impossible that I'd have abilities without their preparations and ritual, but it's been this way since just after Vosira Parmon's murder."

"Aye," the Pasadhi nodded. "Please, take a seat there," he said, indicating that Nyvas should take the chair on the other side of Kate. "When the other Sarnoc arrive, I will offer my own explanation for that."

***

Sarnoc Vaj stood up. "Shall we begin?"

Immediately the laliri standing above stopped their whispering, and the room fell silent. In fact, for so many people, it seemed unnaturally quiet, with no one above as much as fidgeting on the catwalks.

"As you may have heard, several events just transpired beyond our walls that will have significant impact on the Sarnoc and Altopon as a whole."

Sebachin smiled at Kate, and Nyvas grabbed her hand.

"However, before we begin, I'd like to acquaint everyone with our two guests, and then introduce the Sarnoc. This is the first time in a great many years when all of the Sarnoc have been at Altopon at the same time, so it may be that not everyone is familiar with us."

As the Sarnoc spoke, a different voice entered Kate's head.

«What is he doing here?»

Kate turned to her right. "Nyvas?" she whispered. "Was that you?"

Without turning to look at her, he continued. «Why is Aldrish Rynar sitting at the table with the Sarnoc?»

"What?" She scanned the semi-circular row of men. One man at the end of the table did not look like he belonged. Short hair, and blond, the man was focused on a parchment document in front of him and had not looked up since their arrival. His face was hard to make out. "That's impossible."

«Nay, I'm certain of it. I'd never forget any of the faces of the men in the room that day. It's him.»

She knew he referred to the day he was arrested and brutally injured in the Council chamber. Three times her eyes scanned the faces of the men sitting across from her, pretending to be casually taking it all in. Each time her eyes fell to the man with short hair, she paused to stare briefly, but never could she get a good look at him because he seemed to intentionally be looking down. Then Sarnoc Vaj mentioned Bedoric, and the man raised his head for an instant, and she saw his features.

It *was* Rynar. There was no doubt in her mind. The man who had tried to strangle her, the man who had almost killed Arric, the man who had been Vosira Bedoric's right hand man all these years—here he was now, sitting with the Sarnoc, as if he had done nothing wrong.

Everything that had happened in the past day and a half flashed before her eyes. Rynar had been at the center of it all, and even now she could not escape him.

No, that wasn't true.

She had a choice. She always had a choice.

Even as Sarnoc Vaj began to introduce the other Sarnoc, she bolted from her seat. Before anyone could react, she had reached the tall wooden doors, and pushed one open so hard the door slammed against the wall. Without looking back, she sprinted down the marble hallway.

As she turned the corner, heading towards the exit to the gardens, she realized she wasn't alone. "Nyvas?" She slowed just long enough to see if others had pursued them.

He kept running, however, and waved for her to join him outside. Following him as well as she could through the manicured ornamental garden, the two made their way to the fields just past the great hall's perimeter, and it looked like it was his intention to flee into the city beyond.

"Hold up," she called out to him. "We should find a place to hide until we can figure out what's going on."

Nyvas nodded and immediately fell into tall grass, and signaled for her to do the same. She was breathing hard, and despite the chill in the air, wiped perspiration from her eyes after she dropped to the ground beside him. "Wait—do you think we're safe here?"

He rolled onto his stomach, and encouraged her to do the same. "Aye." He drew a couple of deep breaths that sounded a little rough. The healing he had undergone was amazing, but not entirely complete. "Kate, I don't understand. How could the Aldrish be here?"

She was trying to process it, but nothing made sense. "I don't know. He was their enemy..." she trailed off, and covered her head with her arms. "I mean, he's a healer, we know that. But a Sarnoc? There's just no way. This has to be a trick."

Nyvas raised his finger over his mouth, and pointed with his other. «They're looking for us. Over there, do you see them? And they're getting closer.»

Her heart was racing. Laliri and Sarnoc alike were outside, and she could hear her name being called out. Never had she felt unsafe or threatened at Altopon. But now, Rynar was here, and it changed everything. She couldn't even contemplate why they would be working against her now.

«Clear your mind.»

"What?" she whispered.

«Try to remember Arric's music, the tune you liked the most. Keep it playing in your head, now, no matter what happens. And stay low to the ground.»

It was an odd request, but she did as he directed. Moments later a laliri passed within a couple yards of where they lay. Fortunately they were in the shadow of a large oak, and their tunics—his grey, hers blue—helped them to blend in with the shadows, and their improvised hiding place seemed to work.

As two more laliri walked by, she was sure they would hear her heart roaring. They were so close.

«Don't look at them. Keep your face down. Eyes closed. Remember the music.»

She closed her eyes.

Ten minutes passed by. Twenty. She peeked up and thought she saw Sarnoc Vaj once. And more white robes.

"Your hiding places are getting better," she heard a voice whisper behind her.

She jumped. "Seb?" She thought she was about to have a heart attack.

Pasadhi Sebachin crawled into the space between her and Nyvas. "Don't worry, I'll make sure they won't find us now, so you can sit up." He grinned. "I have to admit, the two of you did pretty well without my help."

For the first time in the better part of an hour she thought she could breathe again. "Oh, that's all thanks to Nyvas. I heard that he was good at hiding, but I had no idea until now what that really meant."

Sebachin laughed, and waved for Nyvas to sit up. "I promise, no one will find us here." Then as they huddled together, he asked, "why did you both bolt like that?"

Kate licked her lips. "Rynar was there."

"Ah." He nodded. "So Sarnoc Vaj never told you?"

"Told me what?"

Sebachin actually looked annoyed for once. "I thought you knew, especially after all the time you spent with him."

"What do you mean? What about him?"

He rubbed his face nervously. "Oh, Kate, I'm sorry. It's really not my place to explain, though I wish I could. Vaj would have my hide if he knew I broke that confidence. But now, I understand, and I don't blame you for running out." Nodding towards Nyvas, "especially you. From what I've heard, you have no reason to trust that man."

Nyvas's expression was hard to read, but his words betrayed his feelings. "I was wrong to think this is was the place for me," he said angrily, his eyes constantly scanning the area nearby. "I was better off in the forest. At least there I knew who I could trust."

"Nay, you are right where you should be." Sebachin looked around their hiding place as well. "And I mean right this instant—you both should be here in the garden, unseen. In my opinion, the Sarnoc need some time to consider this development. Sometimes they can be a bit presumptuous where outsiders are concerned." He made a face of disgust. "They really should have explained things to you both before they invited you into that chamber." He turned to each in turn, shared a moment of eye contact, and then explained, "it wasn't a trick, but there's more going on than they have disclosed so far. You're both perfectly safe, believe me."

Nyvas looked to Kate, and the edge on his voice was slightly dulled, as if he was willing to consider it. "Do you trust him?"

"You mean, Sebachin?" When Nyvas nodded, she answered, "absolutely."

In response, he released a deep breath, reassured by her faith in the Pasadhi. "Very well. Pasadhi, you may not wish to harm or mislead us, but I'm not convinced about them." He waved his arm to indicate the Sarnoc still searching for them. "I still sense that this is a trap, and I have to wonder if they've been working with Bedoric the whole time, and now want their revenge."

"Nyvas, you can't be serious?" While she was still suspicious of the recent developments, she wasn't prepared to wrap it all up in a conspiracy theory of that magnitude. She leaned down to catch his eyes, and realized he had the look of a trapped animal. Half his life living as an outlaw, imprisonment, torture, and threat of execution twice had taught him to hate the Vosira and his men, Rynar included, as well as to trust no one other than fhaoli—not even the Sarnoc. No wonder he hadn't ever come here, even after his skills began to manifest. In fact, as she pieced all of this together, she wondered why he had trusted her so rapidly. "Ah, yeah, okay, maybe you *are* serious." And even though she wasn't willing to completely follow Nyvas's train of thought, too many things had happened for her to give her trust blindly either. She was shaking just from the thought that Rynar was so close. "Seb, what can we do? We can't go back there."

Sebachin rubbed his chin. "Aye. Your position is fair, and I don't blame you. Still, we need to resolve this. Nyvas, do you know about the Pasadhi's tower—and would you consider it a safe location for further discussion?"

The boy blinked, but did not hesitate to reply. "Aye."

Sebachin turned to Kate. "If I can guarantee no one sees you, can you find your way back to my quarters?"

"Yeah, but what are you proposing?"

"Just get there quickly. My concealment won't last forever."

CHAPTER 63

It was a long climb, after a day that seemed to stretch on forever. The tower was dark, though this time she didn't care about light, and instead she just focused on taking the steps one at a time. Nyvas struggled a bit as well, the physical injuries he had endured still hampering his movement.

When they reached the top of the tower, the door was already ajar, but the rooms beyond were dark, and no fire burned in the hearth. In the small amount of ambient light provided by the rising moon, Kate waved Nyvas over to the window, where they could look down on the torches marking the encampment of troops beyond the stones of the torrapon. They were Arric's men now, she realized with a smile. Forgetting for a moment what had brought them to the tower, she could only feel a welling up of pride for her friends. "It worked out well for him, didn't it?"

Nyvas shrugged. "He doesn't want to be Vosira, Kate." He glanced out, and added with a frown, "I don't think he ever did."

She weighed his words, and wondered if this wasn't the real reason why Arric had kept the ring a secret after his father's death, and acquiesced when Bedoric took charge. "Well, at least he's free, and can decide what happens to him from this point on. It's something."

"Aye, that's true enough." He walked to the next window and traced his finger along the leaded panes.

"If only things could be resolved for us in the same way."

"Patience, Kate." He turned around, and leaned against the windowsill. The terror in his eyes earlier had faded, and he seemed to have returned to being the Nyvas she had come to know, the boy with wisdom far beyond his years. "I don't know what the Sarnoc are up to, but at least we're safe for now."

She had started pacing, anxiety getting the best of her. "I wish I could believe that."

"We're in the Pasadhi's tower, and the Goddess will protect us here." Apparently he noticed her blank look, as he offered an explanation. "The tower is a sacred place, and no one can harm us, or deceive us, while we are here. It is impossible to act in bad faith within this tower."

"Ah, well that's good to know. And it explains a lot," she added, more to herself than to him, as she considered the meeting she once had with Sarnoc Vaj and Sebachin in this room. So that's why on her first visit they had made her climb all the way up here for what seemed, at the time, to be an innocent enough meeting. She wondered if they had considered her a threat back then. At any rate, it was an interesting perspective now.

Nyvas turned to look out the window again, seemingly intrigued by both the vantage point and the leaded glass windows, both of which were so rare in Sarducia. He kept rubbing his fingers on the glass, tracing out the bubbles and imperfections. Meanwhile, squinting in the dim light, she searched the room for something to drink. Seeing a flagon on a tray, she lifted the lid and smelled inside.

"Wine, Nyvas? It looks like there's a bit left."

"Aye, that sounds good." He didn't turn back around. "You know, it's strange being here now. I feel I've cheated Yoren twice."

"That's because Kerthal isn't ready to give you up yet." The new voice startled them both. Suddenly the room was filled with blue light.

Nyvas spun around. "What are *you* doing here?" he said, his words spoken in a low growl that seemed very uncharacteristic of him.

Kate, meanwhile, had been focused on trying to pour the wine in the dark, and at the announcement, she missed the cup, spilling wine onto the table. "Rynar?" She choked on the name.

"Aye, my dear." He reached past her to the candles on the shelf above the table, which he lit from the small lamp he carried. After doing the same for candles on a smaller table by the window, the blue light faded away. "I am surprised to see you here. I expected only the boy."

"The feeling's mutual," she snapped back, and walked over to where Nyvas stood, for mutual protection and solidarity. "Why are you here?"

"I was asked to speak to Nyvas."

"No, damn it. Why are you *here*?" She waved her arm around. "Why the hell would you be in this city, of all places?" Then she shook her hands in his direction. "And dressed like that? You're not Sarnoc!"

He pulled out a chair for her. "My dear, it's been a long day. Why don't you come sit—"

"Nay, Aldrish. None of your charm," Nyvas blurted out, and raised his palms in front of him, as if to ward himself. "You'll tell us the truth here, with no games. And don't pretend that either of us are your friend."

Rynar hesitated, not accustomed to being challenged like that. "You and I need to talk, and come to some sort of understanding, that is certain. But do not presume to know what kind of relationship Bhara Kate and I share."

"And don't you pretend there's something between us." Her nostrils flared. How dare he come here, to the one place she felt safe from his influence, and try to manipulate her? "You need to be dead honest with us right now and tell us what's going on, and you need to do it without trying to manipulate either of us."

"Aye," Nyvas added, his voice lowered, "or I'll deal with you when we leave the tower."

Rynar laughed. "A threat?" She could tell his tongue wanted to dish out an insult, but he paused. "Ah, dear boy, you should know better than that."

Suddenly her fear was gone, evaporated in an instant, sizzled away by her anger. "Rynar, I'm warning you, don't mess with either of us, or Nyvas and I will finish the fight Arric started last night. I swear to god, I'm sick of these games of yours. You need to start explaining what's going on, here and now."

"Indeed, Kate, I intend to do exactly that," he said.

"Then begin by telling us how you could show up here after your fight with Arric, and act like nothing's happened." Her fury was rising as fast as a thermometer in boiling water. "In Sarnoc robes, no less. How dare you!"

"Ah, Kate, do you not understand? I 'dare' because I can. It's who I am. I am Sarnoc." He rested his hands on the back of the chair, the gesture casual, relaxed. "In fact, I have been Sarnoc for about nine years now."

"That's not possible." Her voice was shaky, and she sucked in a deep breath through her nose. Really, if she thought she could have ripped him apart with her bare hands, she might have tried. "I know the stories. You were the Aldrish, you did whatever Vosira Bedoric wanted. You helped keep the Sarnoc out of the city all those years. There's no way you've been working with them all this time."

He sat down in the chair he had pulled out for her a short time before, and filled a third cup. "Come. Both of you, sit down with me."

"I'm fine where I am," Nyvas spat from his spot at the window.

Kate, however, dropped into a chair across from him, and grabbed two of the cups, reaching behind her to hand one to Nyvas. She could feel her face flushing hot with anger. "If you're telling the truth, then how can you possibly explain all the things you did?"

"Of course I am speaking the truth." He gazed around the room, as if he had never been in the tower, or perhaps testing the power within the stones. "Not that I had any intention of lying to you before. As I have insisted multiple times, my dear, I have never lied to you."

"Bullshit. You've lied to me every second since you met me," she replied, "and don't try to deny it. You made me think you were the exact opposite of who you claim to be now."

"Aye, you bastard," Nyvas agreed, advancing on him. "If you were Sarnoc, how could you have allowed Bedoric to do all those horrible things all these years? You could have saved so many people—but instead, you encouraged his actions, you endorsed them. Some even say you were the one that came up with all those things in the first place."

"Indeed, that was my mission," Rynar replied calmly, as if entirely unconcerned by their open animosity towards him. "My dear Kate," he said, addressing her specifically, "can you not see that? It was my job to make everyone believe I was the most loyal man in Bedoric's service, and along with that, I had to agree with most of his ideas about the Sarnoc. It was the only way I could gain his trust, or that of anyone else in Loraden."

"You could have told me." She propped her elbows on the table, and clenched her hands into fists. It was all she could do to restrain herself. "You lied to me—to my face—about all of this. Even when I asked you to help me save my friends." Her voice was loud and furious, and the words of Lysander and Fantion rang out in her mind, especially when they accused her of being enchanted by this man. "I begged you to help them. But you told me over and over how you couldn't do anything. My friends, especially Nyvas, were suffering, and you wouldn't even let me go see them. If you were really Sarnoc, you would have done something. You would have tried to help. You know as well as I do that you totally had the Vosira within your control. You could have gotten him to release Nyvas, or at least send him a healer. Instead, you did nothing."

Rynar narrowed his eyes. "Nothing, my dear? Nothing?" Now he stood up, and sucked in a breath. His voice was still smooth, like it always was, but there was an edge to it this time. "Do you think it's pure luck that your friend here is still alive?" He leaned forward. "Do you not remember the walk we took into the city, in the fog? Do you think all that happened by accident, that your friends just happened to be ready for us at that exact moment?" And then he snapped his hand to point at Nyvas. "And don't forget—I healed him. I did save him. Or do you not remember that day?"

"Oh what, you're going to take credit for all of that now?" How could he sit here and pretend he had been looking out for her and her friends all this time? "As I recall, we went out that day because you received a message. It wasn't like it was your idea. And you weren't going to do a damned thing for Nyvas until I held a blade to your throat. You were going to let him die, just like that." She snapped her fingers for emphasis.

"My dear, you have it all wrong. Remember, you were never sent to the dungeon while I was in the keep. I saved you from that. And although you wouldn't know it, I saved your friend here from an immediate hanging, and against Bedoric's orders I went to check on him twice, ensuring he didn't die in that cell, though I don't expect he'd remember, as he was in bad shape. I would have done more if I could have, but there were limits, lest anyone discover what I was doing. And even so, I never let you see how much those things cost me. As for Arric, aye, you're correct on his account. I did not speak up for him. I wasn't sure of his motives at the time, and wasn't convinced it was worth the risk of getting in between the brothers. Then again, I truly believed Bedoric would not harm a member of his own family. In fact, until today I was as much in the dark about how their father died as anyone else."

He sipped at his wine, and then lowered his voice when he continued. "Even so, we came up with a plan to help Arric escape. It wasn't an accident that he became gravely ill from adoli, as I suspect you know. Sofinar had none in the apothecary, so I had to travel all the way to Altopon to get some from the apothecary." Not pausing for a response, he continued. "I made sure to remind Bedoric that if Arric died, people would believe he had poisoned his own brother while in captivity. So it offered an opportunity to bring Sarnoc into the keep, and then Jiona provided a chance to get him out of the city."

Kate felt the tears filling her eyes. Tears of anger, tears of confusion. She remembered what Arric told her about his time with the Sarnoc and his subsequent involvement in the Jiona festival, and Rynar's explanation fit perfectly with that. "We?"

"Aye, Sarnoc Vaj and I came up with the plan. With Sofinar's help." He smiled. "Why do you think I wanted to be at Jiona so early? I wanted to make sure I was close enough in case something went wrong. And I was able to hold off most of the soldiers until you had a head start, although some raced off before they could be recalled." He reached out and with one finger on her chin, turned her face towards his. "There were several places we thought he might go, one of which was a cave along the river, which offered his best chances. I hoped if he went that way he could find it using his land-instinct. It would have brought him all the way to Altopon."

She couldn't breathe. Surely he couldn't have known about that detail if he hadn't been involved. Gripping the edge of the table, she spat out, "for someone who claims to have set it up, you didn't seem very happy about how it all turned out."

That surprised him. "My dear, what do you mean?"

"I'm talking about Jiona. When Arric chose me as riliaga, you looked like you wanted to strangle him. Or was that just good acting on your part?"

The question caused Rynar to avert his eyes, and he remained silent.

"Aldrish, answer her."

"I am no longer Aldrish," he snapped in return. Suddenly angry, he kicked his feet forward to push his chair back abruptly, and stepped to the window closest to the door.

"Rynar, answer me. If this is all true, then why were you upset that he chose me?"

He turned around. "I would rather not answer that question."

"What? Why not? It's not a difficult question. Just tell me."

Nyvas stepped over to Kate, and crouched down beside her. "He didn't want you to go with Arric because he has feelings for you." He looked up at Rynar. "Right? You knew what Jiona required, and you wanted her to be with you, not him."

Rynar swallowed. "Nay." He walked back to the table, where he sat down less gracefully than he typically moved, and drank some of the wine. "I didn't know she was going to be chosen as riliaga. Arric was very clear that he planned to choose Bhara Merel. He was going to take her just into the woods, and then find his way to the cave alone. There was no expectation that he would complete his duty as caliaga. At least that way, it wouldn't have seemed suspicious, and would buy him enough time to get out of immediate danger." He drank more wine.

"So I don't understand. Why did it matter that he chose me instead? If your goal was for him to escape, you knew I'd help him, so what was the big deal?"

For the first time since she had met him, Rynar looked like he was at a loss for words, and uncomfortable at the situation unfolding in front of him. He put his hands on the table, and then pulled them back quickly. Then he looked up at the ceiling.

"What aren't you telling me?"

He looked at her, and to Nyvas. "This should be a private conversation between us, Kate."

She shook her head. "I don't think so. You lost that privilege back in your tent, when you screamed at me about the ring, and then when you tried to kill Arric."

He laughed. "Oh Kate, I had no intention of killing him. He challenged me, and I gave him a good fight. After everything that had happened, we both needed that. That's all it was, for me. I never would have issued a deathblow. As for the ring—I am truly sorry for my reaction. I lost my temper, something that surprised me as much as you. It's just that I had no idea where it was, and the sudden sight of it terrified me, and with the way you were acting..." he trailed off, leaving that comment incomplete. "If Bedoric had seen the Charvos ring around your neck, he would have killed you right then and there, to get it back. You know what the ring's significance is, now. Do you not see that?"

"He's right about that, Kate," Nyvas agreed.

"Of course I am."

"So then, what's the deal with Jiona?"

He rolled his head back. "Aye, very well." He leaned forward and pointed a finger at Nyvas. "This is between her and me. You are not to breathe a word of this outside this room, least of all to your friends out there—including the Vosira."

Nyvas blinked rapidly. "You have my word."

"And me?"

"That's up to you, I suppose." He reached across the table for her hand.

She pulled her hands away.

Although the gesture seemed to sting his pride, he still raised his eyes to meet hers. Very softly, he said, "I'm your father."

The words hung in the space between them. "What?" She felt paralyzed. "You're crazy." She wasn't shouting now. As she sat there, she closed her eyes, and the room seemed to spin, until she felt Nyvas's hand on her shoulder.

Meanwhile, Rynar too had closed his eyes, and swallowed a couple of times. "I didn't want you to go with Arric because—I was worried you'd be killed. I was afraid that I'd lose you."

"This can't be happening."

"My dear, I've been wanting to tell you since that first morning when you showed up, but I didn't know you, and I didn't know how you'd respond to a stranger telling you something like this." He took a deep breath. "As the gods are my witness, I loved Melaine, your mother," he said, his words soft and filled with pain. "I loved her more than anything, ever. I still love her. Even so, they sent her away, and only afterwards did they even tell me it was because she was with child." He closed his eyes again. "I never even got to say goodbye to her."

Kate's head was swimming, and now she was clinging to the table. Only Nyvas's touch seemed to keep her from falling over. She was convinced he was lying—that somehow, the master manipulator had found a way around the magic of the tower. "You must have me mixed up with someone else. You're not even old enough to be my father."

He shrugged. "I can't explain that, other than to say that tradition holds that time moves at different paces in other worlds."

"I don't believe you." She was crying in earnest now. "This is just another one of your lies."

His expression was different from anything she had seen before. No longer was he wearing the cocky, self-assured mask she had come to expect from him. "Surely your mother told you something about me?"

"No, of course she didn't, because it's not true. My father's dead." She continued to lean against the table, finding its smooth surface comforting as she felt her heart being cut adrift from her body. There was no reality, no safe place where she could retreat, nothing she could do to center herself. Finally, she found a tiny amount of courage. "How would you even know it was me, anyway? How can you be so sure?"

He reached for her right hand, the one on which she wore her mother's ring. "There were two clues. First, you look so much like Melaine that I thought my heart would break the moment I met you. And second, I would have recognized this anywhere. It was my Sarnoc ring. I gave it to Melaine the morning we spoke the Oath of Alisavi to each other, and in turn, she gave me hers." He held up his glysar ring that was his most prized possession.

"Kate, he is telling the truth," Nyvas said gently.

In response to that, Rynar held up his hands in front of him. "Aye, and I regret now that I couldn't do so before. As Kerthal is my witness, the last thing I'd ever want would be to bring pain or harm to my daughter."

CHAPTER 64

"Is everything sorted out now?" Sebachin asked, as he joined the pair in his quarters, and he peered into the pitcher. "You finished my wine as well, I see," he added playfully.

Rynar had left a few minutes before, but neither Kate nor Nyvas had moved to follow. "Oh Seb, sorry about that."

He laughed. "It's wine, Kate." He pulled up a chair. "Did you sort everything out with him?"

She kicked at the leg of the table with her toes, and didn't look up at him. "Did you know all along that he was Sarnoc?"

Sebachin shook his head. "I did not. He was long gone from Al-topon before I became Pasadhi, and to my knowledge he never set foot in the city after he left, until tonight. I only learned of his identity a few days ago myself, when he set up the camp outside the city, and Sarnoc Vaj called us all together so we wouldn't worry. I assume he told you other things as well?"

She stared at the table. "Like the fact that he's my father?" she said, still resentful about it. "Yeah, he told us."

Sebachin nodded. "Sarnoc Vaj told me that part, in confidence, last night. Kate, I'm really sorry no one told you before now. Things would have been much easier—"

"Nay, it's good she didn't know," Nyvas interjected.

"Why would you say that, Nyvas?" she asked, a bit stung by his words. "He's been hiding it from me all along."

The boy rubbed his hands together, taking the time to collect his thoughts. "You would have acted differently had you known who he really was," he explained. "The distrust you had for him was genuine. Imagine the day you rescued me. You might have made different decisions, and at the very least, you would have felt obligated to tell Fantion and the others. This way, his secret remained safe, as did mine."

"Oh god, I don't know. I guess you're probably right." She swung her head back, and stared at the ceiling for a moment. "I just think back to all the interactions I had with him before, all the things that made me come to hate him, and then I find this out."

"From what I hear, he took great risks to protect you," Sebachin suggested. "And to save Nyvas and Vosira Arric as well."

"When you look back on all of it, you're right, but..." She sighed. "It's all just too much to process."

"Aye, it is indeed." He looked at her and then at Nyvas. "I suspect you're both hungry. From what I gather, neither of you have eaten much all day." He looked to Nyvas in particular. "You look like you need to eat for ten people, truth be told."

The boy shrugged. "I've not been very hungry."

"He's been through a lot, Seb."

The Pasadhi nodded. "Indeed, it takes its toll on a person, having to go through all of what you've both experienced. I don't think either of you have had a quiet, safe day in weeks, am I right?"

Kate traced a random design on the table with her fingertip. "We didn't really have much choice."

"Aye, that may well be, but I don't want either of you falling ill before the Vosira's oath ceremony. You both need some time to relax and recover."

"What do you mean?"

Sebachin held up his hand. "One moment." He walked to the door of the tower and a laliri handed him a tray loaded with food. "Nyvas, would you give me a hand?" He handed the tray to Nyvas as he was given a second one, this time with a pitcher and three stout bottles. As he slid it to the table beside the first one, he announced to the pair, "it's just a start, but the rest of the night is ours to feast."

Kate giggled, just a bit, feeling the mood already lighter. "What's in all of these?" she asked, pointing to the bottles.

"I haven't a clue. Let's find out, shall we?"

The pitcher, it turned out, contained spring water. Each of them opened one of the bottles in turn. "I've got quinsa," Sebachin announced.

"Wine here," Nyvas proclaimed.

Kate had a bit of trouble cracking the wax on hers, but when she uncorked it she sniffed it and appeared puzzled. "Not sure about this." She poured a small bit into a cup and sipped it. "It's havar, but—"

Nyvas tasted it as well. "That doesn't taste like any havar I've had before."

Sebachin followed suit. "Ah, that's because you've never had the Sarnoc version." He poured a measure into two more cups, and refilled the first. "Here, they age it in casks in the cellars for a generation." He looked at markings on a wax seal on the bottle. "This..." he started, and whistled. "They must really think highly of you two. This is older than me!"

After they had all stuffed themselves, and emptied the bottle of quinsa first, Kate leaned back in her chair, her cup now half-full with the aged havar. "So what happens now? Is tomorrow spa day?"

Both men looked at her with curious expressions. "What is that?" Nyvas asked in a solemn tone.

She threw her head back and laughed. "It was a joke. Spas are places where you get facials and pedicures and—" she stopped, realizing neither had any idea what she was talking about. "I was just playing on the idea that we need to relax. So Seb, if there's no spa in my future, what do I have to look forward to?"

"Ah," he nodded in understanding. "Tomorrow, Nyvas will meet with Sarnoc Vaj to determine what he needs to do next. As I understand it, they're not accustomed to anyone just showing up with Sarnoc abilities in place. Usually a boy comes and serves a number of years as laliri, learning the skills and customs of Sarnoc, and serving them. The very few who have proven themselves worthy eventually are initiated and take the oath. With Nyvas everything is upside-down."

"Will they force me to go through that whole process?" Nyvas asked, his apprehension rising.

"To be honest, I doubt even Sarnoc Vaj knows right now what's going to happen. I'm certain of one thing, though." Sebachin made direct eye contact with him. "From here on out, Sarnoc Vaj has given his word to me that you are not to be forced to do anything against your will." He paused, to make sure Nyvas fully grasped what that meant. "The same is true for you, Kate. The Sarnoc are very unhappy at what happened earlier, as they had no intentions of frightening either of you. They wanted me to reiterate that you are both very welcome and honored guests here. In fact, I was instructed to tell you both that you are free to go anywhere within Altopon, other than private quarters and such, and as long as you remain within the torrapon borders, you will be safe from harm. You are also welcome to leave Altopon at any time, though Sarnoc Vaj strongly urges you both to stay until we all head to Loraden in a few days for the ceremony."

"And for now?"

Sebachin smiled. "You both have accommodations in the main wing, where the Sarnoc themselves live, but for tonight I hope you'll both agree to stay here with me. I don't get many opportunities for such excellent company."

***

When she woke, the sun was already high in the sky. Embarrassed to have slept so late, she looked to the other two mattresses, but she was alone in the room, and the blankets had been rolled up. She jumped up and immediately regretted it, as her head was spinning. Groaning, she first found her way to the garderobe, and then wobbled to the table, where she poured herself a cup of water and drained it quickly.

Their evening meal had been cleared away, she noted, and in its place was a selection of dark bread and cheese. She sliced a small chunk of the dry white cheese on the tray and wandered back into the side room, wondering if she had been left alone in the tower.

"Good morning," Sebachin greeted her. He was sitting at a table by the window, taking advantage of the morning sun that spilled across a codex laid out in front of him. "Nyvas is already with Sarnoc Vaj."

"Ah, okay." She leaned over his shoulder to the book. "What's that?"

"Nothing too exciting, I promise you that. It's a protocol manual, I suppose you could call it."

"Protocol?"

"Aye. It explains the steps to becoming Sarnoc and something about how the oath functions. I'm just trying to figure out what happened with Nyvas, so we can better understand how Sarnoc powers work."

"Sarnoc Vaj put you up to that?"

"Ah, no, I suspect he'd rather I not study this very hard."

"Really? That seems strange. Isn't he interested in learning more about it?"

"Of course he is. We all are. Sometimes, though, I think he fears that too much information might be dangerous, lest someone else find out about it as well." He closed the book and turned around to face her. "Along the same lines, we're still puzzling how you activated the ring so you could travel here. Sarnoc Garnell suspected Rynar was involved, but Rynar swears he had nothing to do with it."

"Well if you figure it out, let me know. I'm still wondering myself!"

Sebachin smiled. "We know how the process works, of course, just not how you managed it, untrained and without any knowledge of Sarducia. It's things like that, though, that make the Sarnoc worry. What if others figure it out? What if others from your land started coming here? Or worse, what if our own people stumbled into a torrapon and were sent somewhere unexpectedly? It's dangerous, do you see?"

Kate shrugged. "It sounds like a lot of paranoia to me, especially if it hasn't been happening all along. What's wrong with everyone knowing about the light the Sarnoc use, or the mind-speak? Or what you can do as Pasadhi, for that matter?"

"People respect us, but they do not fear us. If they knew half of what any of us could do, though—well, it's hard to say. You don't know of our history, do you?"

"Just a little."

"Very well. Back in the days of the conquest, the Sards did fear the Mosumi, and all but outlawed magic. They killed many of the Mosumi, and caused the rest to flee to Froida or other lands, or go deeply into hiding here. Some even used the energy lines, traveling to your world, and possibly others. The Sards worked out a deal with the strongest of the mages, those whom they couldn't defeat, to remain apart from the rest of the people. That's why Altopon was built, you know. It was just a village, but the Mosumi mages raised up the defenses against the Sards, and invited as many of their people to live here as possible.

"The mages over time became known by the slang term 'Sarnoc', which means 'wall' in the ancient Sard tongue. After many years of persecutions, these mages agreed to a deal with the conqueror. They promised not to attack Sards and to help protect the land from invasion, and to not practice any of their magic out in the open. In return, the Sards promised to allow the Sarnoc to live in peace here in Altopon, and not to harm any of the remaining Mosumi people in Sarducia. Even after all these centuries the Sarnoc still mostly abide by that. Only healers and riversmiths still regularly employ Mosumi skills out in the open, and that only was allowed again many years after the agreement was reached. And in all the generations since then, nothing has really changed."

"That's so sad. Maybe Arric will change that?"

"It would be nice to imagine, but it's unlikely. There are still too many people who would resist him." He stood up and waved her into the other room, with the food. "Eat up, Kate. I'm going to have to shoo you out of here for a bit so I can study this."

***

She climbed down the million steps from the tower and found herself back in the main hall. Adjacent to this building were a pair of four-story buildings. As she had learned in her previous visit, the wing closest to her was the Sarnoc wing, while the other was for the laliri and serv-ants. Behind, a smaller building was the kitchen area, with its own gardens. It was in that direction that she headed.

She approached a wide, square building, with a tall roof, with win-dows made of vertical wooden slats. The door was open, so she stepped inside.

Immediately she felt intoxicated by the aromas of a hundred differ-ent plants. Encircling the walls were shelves eight feet high and three feet deep, although these were not shelves for books or goods. Each was a wooden frame with a length of muslin stretched across, and many were laden with leaves and flowers placed individually across the expanse of fabric. Above, the ceiling was also a series of wooden louvers, all current-ly set to be open for the sun to filter in, and air to circulate, and hanging from hooks stretching the width of the room were huge bundles of plants.

In the center of the room were two heavy wooden tables, one high-er than the other, presumably to use while standing. A set of knives hung in loops at the end of the table, and at the lower table were three stools, and large mortar and pestles. There was a doorway in the middle of the rear wall, and as she stepped around the tables and passed through the doorway, she entered a second room with tinted glass windows and several rows of shelves crammed with ceramic jars and bottles, along with woven vine baskets hanging from hooks.

It was the Sarnocs' apothecary, she realized.

She also wasn't alone in this second room. A single man worked hunched over, a sheet of parchment to the left of him on the table, and several jars and a bunch of dried herbs in front of him.

He lifted his head when he heard her approach. "Looking for me, my dear?"

It was Rynar, of all people. The last person she wanted to see.

"No, I was just looking around." She tried to take in the grandness of the room. "Seb—I mean, Pasadhi Sebachin—told us we could go wherever we liked."

"Aye. Ah, well, now that you're here—" He pulled up another stool with his foot. "Join me for a little while?"

"I'd rather not." She wasn't prepared to deal with him yet. "Maybe another time."

As she backed into the outer room with the goal of leaving the building without further argument, she heard the stool scrape against the stone floor, and she moved more quickly towards the exit.

"Kate!" he called out. "Wait."

He sounded as if he was just a few steps behind her when her hand touched the latch to the outer door. "Really, I'd rather not do this now."

"Do what? My dear, what has come over you?" He was close, but there was still a table between them.

"Are you serious?" She spun around, her back against the door. "After everything that's happened, you can ask me that?"

"It was my understanding that we had resolved everything when we talked last night."

She snorted at his comment. "Maybe you've resolved it—maybe your conscience is clear. I don't have that luxury right now. My whole life has been turned upside down, and you just expect me to act like nothing's wrong."

"I never suggested that, my dear." He held out his hands as if to show he meant her no harm. "However, I had hoped that once you knew the truth, you would no longer wish to flee every time we met."

"Do you blame me? I mean, seriously. What do you expect from me?"

"You're having a difficult time accepting who I am—am I right?" He plucked at the white fabric at his chest. "If it helps any, it is the same for me, after all this time."

"It's more than that, and you know it." She folded her arms across her chest. "I still don't know what you want from me."

" 'Want,' my dear? I don't want anything from you, other than you accepting me as Sarnoc, and as your fath—"

"Don't!" She snapped, cutting him off. "Don't even say it. It's impossible. My mother would never..." she frowned and shook her head. "And don't think you know me, or her. You don't. None of that's true." Seeing him start to protest, she shook her head. "Don't give me a line about some magic in the tower. Maybe you think you're my father— maybe you believe it to be true. That doesn't mean it is."

"You act like I have a reason to lie to you, as if I had something to gain from it. My dear, I do not—"

"Maybe you do. You've acted all along like you've wanted something from me. I just haven't figured it out yet."

He stared down his nose, in that way of his that suggested disapproval. "And you've never wanted anything from me, or anyone else?" He stepped to one side, as if to go around the table and approach her.

"Rynar, stop it. Stop trying to be Aldrish or whatever." She cast her eyes around the room, as if getting a better sense of her surroundings would help her accept the reality of the moment. "You claim to be Sarnoc, so act like one."

With those words his facial expression changed almost immediately. A moment before he had a smug smile, as if he had gained the upper hand in the conversation, and it was a look she had seen dozens of times before. But with her comment about being a Sarnoc, his smile faded, and he looked almost defeated. "Aye, you may be right." He turned and dropped his hands to the table, his palms smacking against its hard surface. It was like he was deflating right before her eyes. "You're right to call me out for playing my role too well. I'll admit, it's a fair complaint."

Kate had to blink to refocus her eyes. It was as if she was seeing things.

"It's more difficult than you can imagine, coming back here. For nearly eight years I had developed, even perfected, a totally different persona. I had to become the kind of person I hated, this cold, calculating figure who had to take control of every situation, every conversation. It was the only way I could find a place within Loraden, and ultimately, to become Aldrish under someone like Bedoric, who could only respect someone stronger and more confident than himself. My dear, can you not understand? I had to become that other person. In doing so, I may have forgotten who I really am."

She shook her head. "No way. You can't just stand here and tell me that was all an act. You were like that every second we were together. It was always about being in control of everything. Everything," Kate repeated, "down to the smallest detail. Even me. And you know, Sarnoc Vaj can be like that, a little, because he has to lead others. But he never acts like he has to dominate them."

"Aye."

"So I don't know who you are, or what you want, but it just feels like you're trying to control me with these stories of your past now. It's as if you want me to pity you, because you claim to have fallen in love with my mother. Well, I just don't believe it. She never mentioned you, never told me a thing about this place or anyone here. You can tell me you knew her, you can make up all kinds of stories, but that doesn't make any of it true."

With that, she grabbed the latch of the door and flung it open, and ran out into the garden beyond.

In fact, she ran beyond the flowers and the benches that graced the grounds of the main building, and kept running down the hill towards the woods, to where she had found the Isa. In front of her stretched a wide bed of ornamental herbs. Rather than turn to the side so she would avoid it, she ran right through it.

In her haste to get away from the man who caused her so much mental anguish, she tripped on one of the stones that formed the edging, and she fell forward. Landing hard on one knee, she rolled over onto her side and clutched her knee to her chest. Gritting her teeth, she tried not to cry out from the pain, but she groaned all the same.

"Kate!" She heard her name from a ways off, but at this point she didn't care.

She tried to get her feet back under her so she could at least walk away with some dignity, but as she started to rise, her knee shot out stabbing pain under her weight and she collapsed back into the dirt. "Damn it." She steeled herself for what was going to happen next.

"My dear, are you hurt?"

"Just leave me alone."

"I will do no such thing." The man with the blond hair and white robe knelt beside her in a very Sarnoc manner, and gently placed one hand over the arm clutching her knee. "May I?"

Her knee hurt too much for her to get up on her own, so she didn't reply, but she also didn't fight his efforts.

In response, he moved his palm from her arm to the top of the kneecap, and immediately she could feel the warmth flow from his fingertips, taking the edge off the pain. But then he pulled back, removing his hands quickly from her leg.

"What's wrong?" Kate asked, opening her eyes again to look at him, only to notice that he had paled significantly. "What is it?" Again she was on her guard.

"Let's get you out of the dirt," he suggested, and helped her stand up.

She realized he hadn't yet healed her injury, but instead supported her weight as she hobbled over to a bench.

"That was not what I expected."

"What do you mean?" She rubbed her knee. After everything else, this should be simple for him. "Can't you heal it?"

"My dear, of course. But..." he rolled his head up, staring at the sky. "I wish you would trust me again. I wish you could believe me when I say I have never meant you harm."

"It's hard to just forget all the things that happened between us, you know?" It was a little easier with his new appearance, she had to admit. His Sarnoc whites, and newly-bleached hair, helped her pretend he was someone else.

"I sincerely apologize for anything I did that may have hurt you. Perhaps in time, you'll come to understand that I did everything in my power to help you."

"Yeah, maybe." She wasn't one for holding grudges, but there had been too many times when he had frightened or angered her. She couldn't just flip a switch and let bygones be bygones.

"I suppose that will do for now."

"Um, I think I want to go back inside now." She felt bit humiliated by today's interaction with him, particularly now that she needed his help. "Do you think you could..." she rubbed her knee again. "You know..."

"Aye, of course." He placed his hand back on her kneecap, and moments later, as she stretched out her leg, she could tell everything was back to normal.

"Thanks." She felt a little less hostile towards him as she hopped from the bench.

"Before you go, Kate, there's something else."

She turned and looked at him over her shoulder. "Yeah?"

"I hesitate to tell you this, but perhaps it's best coming from me." He waved her back to the bench. "When I touched you a moment ago, I discovered something I hadn't expected." He had a strange look on his face.

She rolled her eyes. "What now?"

"My dear, it appears that you are with child."

She stared at him. "I'm what?" She caught her breath. Had she misunderstood him?

"Didn't the Vosira say the ceremony was incomplete?"

"Well, we thought it was..." This was not a topic of conversation she wanted to have with this man. Because he was Sarnoc, because he was her father, but most of all because he was Rynar. "Are you trying to tell me I'm pregnant?"

Never had he looked so ill in all the time she had known him. "Aye, it appears so." He looked over his shoulder, as if expecting others to be there. "You do understand what this means, my dear?"

Yes, no, goddamn it. She didn't understand a single thing now. It was already difficult enough to have feelings for Arric, who had just become the king of this land. Now, a baby? That was impossible! She wasn't ready to be a mother, with all that entailed.

Apparently the goddess Kerthal had other plans for her.

The story will continue with
The Hidden Moon
Book II of the Chronicles of Sarducia

THANKS FOR READING!

Thank you so very much for reading *By Moonrise*. I hope you enjoyed it! Please share this book with your friends.

I'd also really appreciate it if you'd write an honest review on Amazon.com and Goodreads.com. For indie authors like myself, reviews are our most powerful tool to helping get the word out about our books. If you do write a review, please let me know. I'd love to hear from you!

And join my mailing list at jackiedana.com to be the first to receive updates about my upcoming books, get 'behind the scenes' information, and other freebies.

ACKNOWLEDGMENTS

There are so many people who made this book possible.

First off, I must thank my parents Charles and Mary Dana. They ensured I had an excellent education and they gave me the space to pursue my passions in college and beyond. It was their love that made a book like this possible.

I would also like to thank my friends Marie Shortt, Crawford Shortt, Lisa Bruce, Russell Sherman, Ian Sights, and Chrishaun Keller-Hanna, all of whom were part of my life at some critical juncture and helped me believe in myself. I'd also like to thank Matt Herron and other members of Indie Publishing Austin; the Austin region of NaNoWriMo (go Penguins!); colleagues and friends at UT Austin and Automattic; herbalists I met through Nicole Telkes's Wildflower School of Botanical Medicine; and members of the Texas Freelance Association. Without all of these people, I probably would never have published this book in the first place.

I'd also like to offer a special thanks to those who helped me with various aspects of the book production process: James Egan, David Crews, Laurie Leiker, Kathy Boyd, Vidya Gopalakrishna, Abby Goldsmith, Sue Reading, James Huff, Adrian Hale, Andrea Middleton, and Evin Cooper.

And finally, I'd like to acknowledge the creative minds who inspired me, including writers Katherine Kurtz, Stephen R. Donaldson, Charles De Lint and Diana Gabaldon, and musicians Seamus Egan and Philip Glass.

Live long and prosper!

ABOUT JACKIE DANA

I write speculative fiction novels and short stories.

As an 'outlaw author,' I believe indie publishing gives authors a viable means to escape the confines of the traditional marketplace. Indie publishing brings to life many excellent stories that might once have languished in slush piles, or worse, might never have been read at all. Committed to helping fellow indie authors, I'm currently developing a series of workbooks and other resources to make indie publishing even more accessible.

In my spare time, I'm an herbalist, an amateur photographer, and a homebrewer. I was born in St. Louis, MO, but now I live in Austin, TX, sharing my home with a dog and several cats who constantly strive to revise human-feline power dynamics.

Find me online:

Website: http://jackiedana.com
Facebook: http://www.facebook.com/jackiedanawriter/
Twitter: http://twitter.com/jadana17
Email: jackie@jackiedana.com

www.ingramcontent.com/pod-product-compliance
Lightning Source LLC
Chambersburg PA
CBHW021117260626
47169CB00005B/1321